THE BRATVA'S *Beast*

ROSE CHASE

Copyright

Copyright © 2023 by Rose Chase
All rights reserved.
No part of this publication may be reproduced, distributed, or transmitted in any form or by any means, including photocopying, recording, or other electronic or mechanical methods, without the prior written permission of the publisher, except as permitted by U.S. copyright law. For permission requests, contact rose.chase.author@gmail.com.
The story, all names, characters, and incidents portrayed in this production are fictitious. No identification with actual persons (living or deceased), places, buildings, and products are intended or should be inferred.
Book Cover by Miblart

Content Warning

This book is a contemporary dark romance that contains content that some may find triggering or disturbing.
Contents include: explicit language, explicit violence, sexual violence, abuse, alcohol and drug use, explicit sexual scenes, dub-con/CNC, BDSM elements and tones (pretty heavy in this book), assault, Daddy, primal play, switch play, edge play (knives, guns, breath play).
MENTIONS OF/DISCUSSIONS ABOUT/IMPLICATION OF OFF-SCREEN CHILD ABUSE DEALING WITH A SEXUAL NATURE. NO GRAPHIC DETAILS ARE INCLUDED IN THIS BOOK!!!
If such content triggers you then please do not continue any further or be mindful of skipping areas of trigger!

P.S. There is a glossary at the end of the book for all the foreign terms used within the story.

Dedication

*To all the good (and bad) girls out there who want some switch play with the
Daddy Dom mafia boss, I gotchu!
He whimpers in CH. 36. You're welcome.*

Blurb

HANNA

"The Beast is neither man, nor monster."
Something out there has its eyes on me, I can feel it from the shadows with
every step.
Stepan Volkov seems like prince charming with his enchanting blue eyes
and captivating smile—he is anything but.
The depths he goes for me makes him my own twisted king though.
He provides me with the safety and protection I have sought all my life,
from myself and the demons of my past.
My heart will take a hit, but so will my enemies.
Stepan may be the man behind the rifle.
But I call the shots.
And I've got my targets lined up.

The Bratva's Beast

Volkov Bratva Series Book 2

Rose Chase

Contents

Chapter 1

Stepan

"Would you stop scaring the new recruits off? It is not exactly easy to find decent employees nowadays."

Groaning, I ran my hands down my face. It would be much easier to run the company if Lev wasn't scaring away nearly every new hire during their orientation period. "You're not the one who has to shift through all these applications, nor are you the one sitting through hours of interviews." He should have to suffer with me, considering his position in the company, but he always had a damn good excuse to disappear nearly every time we had an interview.

Okay, it was partially my fault, too, since I stuck the new people with Lev, but I only did so because he's the next big guy in the place below me. Also, as much of a loose cannon as he was, Lev was ironically the best employee around the place. He was just a little rough around the edges and below the surface... and maybe just overall very rough.

"Well, if they can't handle me, then they can't handle the company, simple as that. Besides, I'm doing you a favor by getting rid of them before they become your headache. I mean, you really want to go through all the trouble of paperwork and having them integrated only for them to quit 'cause they don't got the walk to back their talk and shit?" Well, he had a good point there. I would rather deal with all of that sooner than later.

Lev went with the trial-by-fire method and threw people right into the fray while I eased people into things after telling them everything upfront. But hey, if they survived Lev, they'd definitely survive working at the company long-term.

With a sigh, I quickly dug through a stack of paperwork to pull out the file of my next interviewee. But before I could look past the first page, Lev snatched the file from my hands. "Oooh? Mixing it up now, huh? You know I won't take it easy on them just because they're a girl." Lev chuckled deviously with a knowing look at me.

Sighing with a roll of my eyes, I glanced up at him tiredly. "Would it be too much to ask you to dial it back half a notch?" The last thing I wanted was a lawsuit because of Lev's antics.

"Oh come on, she's applying to be a field worker, she needs to know what she's getting into. Not like we'll take it easy on her if we hire her and she decides to stay." Lev remarked as he tossed the file back onto my desk

Before I could get a glance beyond the applicant's name and work history, I was interrupted by a knock at the door. "Come in!" I half shouted, sighing as I set the file down and stood up.

The door quickly opened, revealing one of the assistants who worked the desks on the ground floor. "Mr. Volkov, Hanna is here for her inter-"

Before the assistant could finish her sentence, Lev tersely interrupted her. "You!"

I had to peer around the assistant to see whom Lev's attention was directed at. I had to see who got that reaction out of Lev. Much to my surprise, my eyes met a petite Asian girl who was probably half Lev's size. I thought the assistant was small, being skinny and 5'6, but this woman was probably around 5'0 and equally thin. Although there was this charm to her petite appearance, I couldn't quite put my finger on it.

I had a feeling there was more than met the eye with her, a feeling that made a faint smile curve at my lips when I noticed her flipping Lev the middle finger from behind the assistant. It was a subtle gesture that could've been easily missed if I hadn't paid close attention to her. What amused me more was the innocent smile she kept on her face when she flipped him off.

"Lev, behave," I warned Lev when he started grumbling about payback under his breath in Russian.

"Welcome, please, have a seat, and excuse my brother. He's had a rough day. I Stepan, owner and CEO of Volkov Services Inc." I smiled friendly when I spoke, gesturing at the open seat across the desk with an open hand. "Seems like you have met my brother and co-owner already?"

"I am Hanna. It's nice to meet you both." The woman introduced herself with a polite smile before sitting down across from me. "I have come across your brother on some occasions, but never had the pleasure of personally knowing him." Her taunting eyes drifted over to Lev, her lips curling up a little more to fit her playful eyes.

"That little... I swear to God, Stepan if you hire her..." Well, clearly she got under Lev's skin in a good way, from my point of view.

Lev wanted to pounce on her, but not in his typical 'I'm going to slit your throat' kind of way, more of an 'I'm going teach you a lesson' kind of manner that was playful in nature. Which I found amusing because not many people could bother Lev in such a way, let alone dare to taunt him.

"How do you feel about working with him? You two aren't on bad terms, are you?" I purposely ignored Lev, who was being rather vocal about not hiring Hanna.

I almost wanted to hire her to spite Lev, but that would just be careless because it would reflect poorly on the company if she weren't a good fit.

"We don't necessarily have bad blood, just, our encounters with each other have been... less than ideal." Hanna smirked slightly with a playful and mocking voice as her eyes flicked from me to Lev, "He's just not too happy about me beating him to a few bounties, that's all. It's not like I have anything against him. Besides, I can handle my own against him." Her last statement could have been laughable if it weren't for the daring and determined look in her eyes.

It was the way she held herself that also held my interest. She brought meaning to the saying 'small but mighty,' in my opinion. If I hadn't glanced at her resume, I would be doubtful about hiring her for our field position, especially after seeing her in person.

Shoving my thoughts away, I asked the most important and mundane question in every interview ever. "Why do you want to work here?" I asked while leaning forward and propping my elbows onto my desk.

"Your company has a stellar reputation for providing multiple high-quality services to clients who constantly boast about what they receive. The company's mission statement about providing excellent quality services beyond client satisfaction is something I appreciate and always try to strive for in my own work." Her answer was somewhat typical. At least she got points for mentioning the company's mission statement because it meant she did some research into my place.

"I noticed a hole in your work history. It would seem that you haven't held down a job before, just independent work. Could you please explain and elaborate?" Hiring her with no evidence of her work ethic and habits from past employers could be risky for me.

It would have been one thing for her to have no work history if she were some young teenager, but she was 23. It wasn't impossible for someone her age to never have a job before, but she didn't look like the spoiled rich brat who cried to their parents about everything.

There was another big hole I could spot after looking at her resume again while I waited for her to answer me. I wouldn't touch on this hole, though, not yet, anyway.

"As you can probably see from my resume, I have nothing beyond a high school education, and even that is incomplete. There aren't many places willing to hire someone who didn't even finish high school. I have held odd jobs here and there before, but I funneled all my time and energy into bounty hunting and private investigating because I found myself to be highly proficient and successful with those two careers. I have been working independently for a while, but I applied to your company because I am ready and need a great workplace to commit my time and energy to. A place who is willing to invest their time and energy into helping me grow and better my skills so that I could benefit them." Though confident, I could pick up on her nervousness as she spoke.

Surprisingly, Lev spoke up in a nonthreatening manner. "Why give up independent work to be tied to a company that could hinder your work? How do we know if you can be a team player after all this time working alone?" Given his initial reaction to Hanna, I was afraid he would ask nonsensical questions, so it was good to hear him behaving with his questions.

Once again, she remained relatively confident with her reply. "Even though I pick up contracts independently, I actually have a small crew I often work with. It is somewhat rare for me to go on a completely solo job, so I am used to working in a team. I want to give up my independent work for the stability that a company can provide me and the growth opportunities."

I remained silent, pondering momentarily as I let my eyes bounce back and forth between Hanna and her resume on my desk. If I went by my typical checklist, then she probably wouldn't be hired, given the lack of work history. I had no clue about her credibility and background because she had no past employees I could contact. Her answers so far were solid and typical, so I'd give her some points there.

Logically, based on what we did know and have about her, she should be shown the door. On the other hand, my gut told me otherwise. I couldn't place it, but an energy about her drew me towards her. Was it the way she confidently held herself? Possibly, but there was something else.

Usually, interviewees, no matter how strong and confident, were always anxious to some extent. Their nervousness always spilled over with their words, but Hanna held hers in very well. They usually felt small to me, too, like a criminal on the stand. Yet, it felt as if Hanna controlled the room.

"I am going to be honest, your resume doesn't bode well for you along with what little history you do have on it. Typically, I'd play nice and give you the whole 'we'll call you' spiel, then let you down later, but I am going give you a chance to prove yourself and earn the position." Something very unorthodox of me, but something tells me I wouldn't regret the decision.

I saw Lev open his mouth out of the corner of my eye, but I held my hand out to stop him before he could get a word out. "I will go over the terms and conditions with you, if you agree. Also, this is the only time I will ever offer you something like this, and I expect an answer right now." The offer would go out with her if she walked out the door.

This was the only chance for her to work at my company. Like I told her, I wouldn't hire her based on her resume alone. She would take my offer if she was serious and wanted the position badly enough.

Besides, it's not like I would make her do anything deplorable to earn her position. I wasn't a horrible human being.

Chapter 2
Hanna

PHEW.

I felt myself drop a little when he said he wouldn't have hired me based on my spotty history, which I didn't blame him for. Actually, I was surprised at how far I got. I knew it was a long, colossal shot when I tossed in my application to his company.

My friend Angel had told me her brother-in-law's company had positions open for field workers and to apply. No, she didn't pull any strings to get me this interview either, nor did Stepan know about my connection to Angel. At least, if he did know, then he didn't indicate the knowledge. So, I was shocked when he made the offer about the trial. I have no complaints about it though, because I would take it if he were willing to give me any chance. Honestly, it was better than nothing and a whole lot better than what I had hoped for coming into this interview, given my very shitty resume. Also, seeing Lev react as he did when I walked in did not feel promising.

If I had known Lev would be my potential future boss, then maybe, just maybe, I wouldn't have shoved my wins in his face back then. Well, at least he didn't flat-out throw me out the door, but it looked like he wanted to.

I tried to sound confident and not eager, but my reply came out faster than I could control it. "I'll accept your offer. Whatever you have to throw at me, I'll take it and prove myself." I wasn't worried about him making me do something horrible like spreading my legs for the job; he didn't seem like that kind of man. Stepan carried an aura of confidence, but not overly cocky and rude, not with the proud and sure smile on his face.

The smile on his face didn't give me chills either, so I considered that good as well. Shockingly, his smile was warm and comforting. So, whatever he had in mind for me shouldn't be bad, right?

Stepan wasted no time in laying it out for me. "Perfect, glad to hear the answer I was hoping for. It'll be a simple trial run, a week long. You'll be either with me or Lev, and we're basically going to test you with supervised fieldwork." He paused with a brief smile, "You will be paid for all of it of course, we wouldn't waste your time and energy without compensation for you." Good to hear I wouldn't be working for free. "A formal contract will be drawn up about all of this in more detail while we give you a tour of the place, if you are still in agreement with everything? Do you have any questions?"

"So, basically I'm going to have one week to show you two that I'm worth it." I summarized with a tilt of my head.

"Yes, essentially. Just take it as a week-long test, no pressure." Stepan replied with a soft chuckle. "So, still in?" He asked with an outstretched hand.

Without any hesitation, I reached out and took his hand, shivering a little from the warm contact of his rough hand. "Of course. I never back down." Always forward or nothing, that was my motto in life. One week of working with people watching over my shoulders for a stable job was a walk in the park.

I felt as if his hand lingered more than it should have, not that I minded. "Perfect, I'll have my assistant write up a contract while we show you around." His hand seemed to pull away reluctantly before gesturing for me to stand as he stood.

"Is Lev going to be okay with your decision? He still doesn't seem too content." Lev had silently glared and scowled at me the whole time Stepan questioned me. There was no doubt in my mind that he would make the trial week an absolute nightmare for me.

"Oh if he really wanted you gone then it already would have happened. Either way, he'll have to suck it up. His problem with you is personal, nothing I see that should affect your employment here if we were to hire you." Stepan didn't seem too worried about his brother's attitude toward me, which I won't question for my sake.

"Well, like I said before, I will have no problem working with him. I have nothing against him." I replied with a slight shrug of my shoulders before looking at Lev with a somewhat overly exaggerated, innocent smile. "Why don't we start over?" I offered my hand out to Lev with good intentions.

Yes, I might have stolen some bounties from right under him, but not like he never returned the favor. I held no ill content towards him for the stolen targets as there would always be plenty of bounties out there for me to pick up to make up for any lost ones.

Narrowing his eyes at me, Lev reached out and took my hand roughly. Then, instantly, he jerked my body forward over the desk and hovered his face over mine with a forced smile. "I'm not going to let you off so easily, but I'll play nice with you, for now." He forced through his smiling face. "Good luck with your little trial period, you're going to need it."

His stupid face disappeared from my line of vision in the next instant, with Stepan placing himself between Lev and me, standing protectively in front of me. "Lev!" Stepan scolded him with a stern look.

Lev looked at his brother with a playful grin and replied in Russian with a short chortle before Stepan threw some words back at him. "Sorry about him, I'll make sure he won't give you a harder time than he does others." Stepan assured me while narrowing his eyes and shoving at Lev, who rolled his eyes in response with his arms crossed.

The tour started from the top of the ten-story building because Stepan's office was at the top. I had to admit that the place impressed me greatly. The place had nearly everything: office areas, cafeteria, arsenal area, underground shooting range, gym, locker area. It was a lot to take in, honestly. I felt a little daunted after the whole tour. Everyone seemed professional and well-placed, and I felt like a sore thumb. I didn't try to dwell on the feeling, though. Why should I feel intimidated? Stepan wouldn't have given me a chance if he didn't think I could stack up to his workers. I belonged here, possibly, or at least I had the chance to. Earning my place should be as easy as breathing.

We didn't take long to return to Stepan's office and get situated in our previous positions. "Well, any questions?" Stepan asked as he leaned back in his chair, his fingers lightly tapping against the wooden desk.

"Could I have some insight on what it is you're going to have me do during the trial week?" I had the job posting memorized in my mind, but I wanted to know how much of it was fact and if there were any details that went amiss.

"Since you're applying for a rather general and open field position, we'll try to run you through our typical assignments such as bounties, surveillance work, and protection detail, but it'll probably be heavier on bounty hunting and all that it entails. Of course, you will also have to do the boring office work that comes with it all, such as the research and reports." Stepan replied after some thought. "I'll probably try to see if I can organize something where you have to work as a part of a big team so that we can see how you function as a team player. Even though most of the time you will be paired off in teams of two or three at most, there are times when you might have to partake in larger teams for an assignment." He quickly added with a sweetened smile.

"Alright, sounds fair." So, there was nothing far off from the job posting, which was good. Humming softly, I took a moment to think while tapping my finger against my plush lips. "Any tips on surviving the next week or how to be successful through it?"

Giving me a reassuring and warm smile, he answered my question. "Just do your best, don't be a try-hard, don't get killed, don't let Lev get to you, and don't be afraid to speak your mind. I'm pretty open with my employees and like to hear their thoughts and opinions on everything. I have no doubt that you'll do perfectly fine, and if I had a better insight into your background or it was more solid, then I would probably hire you, so this trial period is just a formality for me to cover my bases."

"Alright, where do I sign?"

Chapter 3
Hanna

"Oh my gosh! I can't believe it! I'm so happy for you!"

My friend squealed and hugged me tightly when she saw me, not bothering to say 'hi' to me.

Chuckling softly, I patted her arms to get her to release me. "Don't be quite that happy yet, it's only a trial period, who knows if it'll go beyond that." I didn't want to keep my expectations high. For all I know, the end of the week will bring an end to everything, and I'd be back to looking for another bounty or another 'official' job. Even if I felt good about all this, I didn't want to give myself too much hope to have it crushed later.

"Oh, come on, you basically got the job already. You're a kick-ass bitch, your skills are top-notch. You've got nothing to worry about. If you didn't then Stepan would have sent you out the door." My friend Angel assured me with a wide grin as she looped her arm around mine to drag me into the club. "The trial really is just a stupid formality, you basically have the job already unless you blow it by being a snob, slob, or a lazy-ass."

Sighing heavily, I shook my head as I let her pull me up to a table in the second-floor VIP area after she nodded at the guard who let us through the moment he saw Angel. "You are way too happy about this. Honestly, he really could just let me go after the trial." I was stuck in limbo for a reason. Stepan didn't show me the door nor welcome me on board fully.

He was skeptical about me, which I didn't fault him for. At least he was willing to give me a chance, one I wouldn't blow.

"Oh please, go back to your cheery self from this afternoon when you texted me about how well the interview went." Angel giggled with a roll of her eyes as she dragged me down into a booth. "You've got this, don't worry, you'll be official by the end of it. You're going to blow him away with the trial week, and there's nothing in your background that would make him say no."

Angel had a good point; nothing in my background would be grounds for making me unhirable. Surprisingly, I've kept out of trouble growing up, at least out of trouble with the law. My school record was nowhere near perfect with how many times I got suspended throughout the years for getting into fights. Other than that smear, and the fact I was a high school dropout, there was nothing terrible.

"Can you like not mention anything about me to him though? I'm pretty sure he doesn't know about my relationship to you, and I doubt knowing would sway his decision, but for my ease of mind and for the sake of keeping things clean for now, can you keep quiet until I'm officially hired or something?" Again, Stepan didn't seem like the type of person to let his relationship with Angel get in the way of his decision regarding my employment, but it felt weird to me if he knew before things would become official.

"If that's what you want. Then don't worry, I won't say a word. Besides, it would feel kind of weird to ask if he hired my friend or not." Angel assured me with a smile before waving down a server and ordering us a round of drinks.

"Is Lev always such an ass?" I asked with a chuckle, picking up the shot glass the moment it was set in front of me.

I'd like to get some insight into the two men I'd be stuck with for the next seven days. Even if Angel hadn't been married to her husband for a long time, surely she would know something about her two brothers-in-law that would help me.

"Dude, he's a male you, so yes, he is. I want to say he's a big teddy bear underneath, but I can't because so far he's been an asshole to me. Granted, I don't blame him, I'm still a stranger to the family, a little blip to his stability. I wouldn't worry about him though, he's just rough around the edges like that." Angel replied with a soft chuckle before downing her shot.

"Oh please, don't compare me to that gorilla. I'm way better." I scoffed playfully with a smile before downing my shot with a scowl. "Vodka? Really?"

"I need to get used to it otherwise Arseny is going to drink me under the table." Angel sighed, chuckling softly at the end before pushing another shot at me.

Shaking my head softly, I chuckled while playing with the shot glass in my hand. "Still can't believe you're married, and to *the* Nikolai Volkov. Honestly, the world is screaming at you at this point to get comfortable with mafia life because there is no escape now."

The mafia life was something no one ever left freely, or left in general unless it was by way of a body bag. I had already long accepted my fate, unlike my friend Angel, who was the daughter of the Qing Triad's head. Even if her presence was almost nonexistent, she was still tied to the triad whether she wanted or not. She had been trying to remove herself from the triad entirely and put the mafia life behind her for a long while, but the world had other plans for her because now she was married to the head of the Volkov Bratva.

Everyone, Angel included, still tried to come to terms with it all because the marriage was very abrupt. Her stepmother kidnapped her after work and forced the arranged marriage on her. The marriage definitely changed the dynamic of everything, but not in a bad way. Thankfully, Angel's husband was more than fine with her continuing her little diabolic plan of tearing down the triad. Still, we had to be more cautious because of the truce between the bratva and the triad until Angel could fully find a way out.

Unlike Angel, I've already long accepted the ill fate the world has dealt me. I was doomed the moment my father was killed, and my mother got her hands on me. While the other kids grew up with friends, I grew up with monsters. My childhood ended the day my father shut his eyes for the last time.

I'd been a part of the triad ever since I could remember, from being their plaything to their weapon. As much as I hated it, at least it gave me Angel and my other friends—all of whom I considered family.

"All jokes aside though, he's treating you good? You know I won't hesitate to put him in his place, whether that be a kick to the balls or six feet underground if he does hurt you." I didn't give a damn if he was the Pahkan of the Volkov Bratva, no one—and I mean no one—lays a hand on any of my friends and gets away scot-free.

I might tease Angel endlessly about her little situation, but I still worried for her deep down. Angel hasn't had it easy when it came to men and love; her last one nearly killed her, literally. I didn't want her to get hurt again because I really might lose her this time if she did.

Nikolai seemed like the perfect man to the world, as did the rest of his four brothers—well, maybe all but one. As crazy as Lev was, he could still put up a good image for the world from what I've seen. Still, images are one thing compared to how people are genuinely underneath. Angel has sworn up and down that Nikolai has been good—almost perfect—to her, which I found to be a good thing. I had my doubts though, just because I was overprotective of her.

"Dude, he's treating me just perfectly, trust me. Besides, I wouldn't need you to get your hands dirty if he ever did truly hurt me." Angel assured me with a confident smile after rolling her eyes.

"I know you're more than capable of killing a man, but I also know how much you hate getting your hands dirty. That's what I'm here for Ange, to make sure your hands stay clean how they should be." Angel hated killing and actively avoided it at all costs. On the other hand, I was more jaded and cold to the fact.

Did I like murdering people? Debatable, depending on my mood. I wouldn't kill someone innocent, but if they deserved it, then I wouldn't mind one bit. I could sleep easy knowing I've killed someone, but Angel could never. That's why I always took the hard part of her job from her to ease her burden.

"You still thinking about dipping out of the marriage?" The idea was put out, and we've come up with plans to run away and stay hidden if she ever did decide to leave Nikolai.

Being married to Nikolai would be the last thing to do if she wanted out of the mafia life. No matter how great he was, he was the head of a big bratva, and it was doubtful he would give up his position anytime soon or ever. Angel would forever be tied to the crime world if she remained chained to him.

Sighing heavily, Angel took another shot before looking at me with a halfhearted smile. "I don't know... I mean, sure an arranged marriage was the last thing I wanted, to a Pahkan nonetheless, but Nikolai he's... I don't know... I mean, he's not *bad* or anything. Minus the bratva head part and he's basically perfect to me, flaws and all."

Uh oh.

She had *that* look on her face. Don't get me wrong, I was ecstatic for her if she finally found her person, but again, I was being protective of her. Angel deserved a good partner in life, one who'd take care of her and undo all the bad that's been done to her. I just hoped Nikolai really was the one, for her sake.

Although, I really shouldn't worry too much about it, especially after seeing how Nikolai looked at her the other night when I finally met him for the first time. The way he looked at her was something else. Even if it had only been days, I could see the devotion, adoration, and pure desire in his eyes when he looked at Angel in his arms—how I wished a blonde-haired man would look at me. That man would treat her right, no doubt about it.

"Whelp." I started with a sigh and smile, holding my shot glass up, "To happier and better futures."

"Cheers to that." Angel giggled with a grin, tapping her glass with mine before downing it. "Don't worry, once this is all over, I'll help you find your perfect psycho lover."

"As long as it's not Lev, I don't care if you match me with a trash can." I scoffed jokingly.

"As alike as you and Lev are, you two together would be hell on earth. You need someone to balance you out, not hype you up past a hundred, girl." Angel responded with a soft laugh. "You need someone more level-headed."

Angel's following words made me choke on my drink. "Like Stepan."

My throat burned as I coughed up the alcohol that went down the wrong tube. "What does he have to do with anything? You could have used any other man as an example." I argued with a soft and playful glare at my friend, who laughed in her seat.

"But no other man would get such a reaction out of you." Angel's joyful tone teased me with her smile.

"Fuck you." I scowled playfully at her while flipping her off.

"Think you'd rather have Stepan do that." She laughed in response, enjoying this a little too much.

"Oh come on, don't deny it, I saw how you looked at him when I pointed him out at the club the other night, and I saw how you looked at him when we were researching his company and there were photos of him." She gave me a knowing look and a warm smile as she tilted her head and raised an eyebrow.

No rebutting her there, not when I couldn't pry my eyes away from those enchanting blue orbs of his. The pictures I saw online did him no justice. Stepan's sharp features, his jawline and tall nose, were dimmed in the photos. His dark stubble didn't show up too well in the pictures I saw, making him look more rugged and homey in person. Did that even make any sense? To look rough but cozy and soft at the same time?

A sharp pump on the brakes threw Stepan into the back of my mind again when I reminded myself about the fact that he was off-limits. "Well, it can't happen, no matter how cute and charming he is, he's gonna be my boss if I get the job." Pretty sure office romance like that was frowned upon, and I didn't want to get stuck with the notion of sleeping with the boss for my position.

"So you do think he's cute." Of course she would only pick up on that part, typical happy-go Angel.

Rolling my eyes, I scoffed softly to myself while shaking my head. "I'm not fucking blind, not going to deny a handsome man when I see one. And I can definitely see what you meant by the Volkov men having drop-dead blue eyes. Those pictures do him no justice." Seeing those sky-blue eyes in person was something else.

I wanted to freeze the moment his mesmerizing eyes snapped to mine the very first time at the office. I could spend forever looking into his eyes like some moth drawn to a flame. Even though he had the same eyes as his brothers, his weren't as stark, which I appreciated. In contrast to his brothers, Stepan was more dirty blonde than honey brown, which made his eyes seem softer. Personally, I preferred his softer look than that of his brothers.

Even though his hair color softened his eyes, he still had an edge that made him look sharp and dangerous—a handsome devil clad in expensive clothes. If I were oblivious to his shady business, I would think nothing of him, but I knew of his bratva connection and standing. According to Angel, Stepan Volkov was no run-of-the-mill businessman; he was the family's somewhat unofficial advisor. So, it would seem like his sharp looks were paired with an equally sharp and witty tongue. Dangerous and intelligent, the kind of man I craved.

As violent of a person as I was, I didn't necessarily want that in a partner. Much like Angel suspected, I wanted someone to balance me out. Unfortunately, my venture into the endeavor has been... Not so good. Not many men want a woman who can kick their ass in a fight or put them down onto the ground, especially the ones I pined for.

The few I have found who were somewhat up my alley didn't pan out because as much as I love being the top occasionally, I didn't want to be anyone's Mommy or Domme more than half the time. It was hard to find a Dom switch who met my needs, let alone a Daddy Dom switch. Well, I also had some commitment issues, but I was being overly cautious because I didn't want to end up hurt.

Also, I just haven't found anyone who lit a certain spark in me. Or if I had, then they were off the market because they either didn't want anything serious, swung the other way, or there was some conflict regarding our views on life. Or, in this case, potentially my future boss. So, at this point, I've resigned myself to late nights at sex clubs if I really need a fix, and my own means at home.

Letting my gaze blur out, I mindlessly traced the rim of my shot glass for a few seconds before downing it with a scrunched-up face. "Did you get into much trouble for hogtying your bodyguard and locking him in the trunk of his own car?" I snickered mischievously with a smirk, glancing up at Angel through my lashes.

"I didn't sit for a day," Angel grumbled with a roll of her eyes, sinking in her seat a little while nursing a glass of water.

"Is he going to come with us on this next raid?" At least the subject was off my nonexistent love life now.

"Yeah, Nikolai made it clear that if I didn't obey then I wouldn't leave the bed next time, so we're going to have to get used to Benjamin." She continued to grumble with a pouting frown.

"Doesn't sound much like a punishment." I teased with a snicker and smirk.

"Uh huh, wait until it happens to you then you can talk." She retorted with a scoffing chuckle. "Either way, hopefully we'll be more successful with this next one. Bao just got back to me with some surveillance photos of the docks and the shipping manifest, so we'll get them this time, hopefully."

Angel gave out a long, heavy sigh before downing another shot. "It'll be a small crew unlike last time too. We'll get there ahead of the shipment and ambush them. Hopefully, we'll avoid a bullet shower."

"Hey, nothing a quick headshot won't fix." The more violence, the better, in my opinion, but if it had to be clean and easy, then so be it.

There were only so many avenues—nearly none—for me to take out my violent tendencies the way I wanted. Beating up criminals and thugs was the only option, so I often looked forward to any raids Angel sent me on or collection runs. No one cared if a gangbanger got banged up and left for dead.

"I swear, you and beating people up," Angel remarked with a roll of her eyes.

"What can I say? I've got too many issues to work out." Was therapy an option? Yeah, but I'm sure they'd send me to the looney bin faster than I could blink if I went to one. So, I settled for beating people up—ones that deserved it.

Probably another big reason why I had trouble finding someone was because of my violent tendencies. I acted out too much and have too much rage at the world to keep bottled up. I've got way too many issues and trauma.

I also didn't want to open up to people about all my shit and make myself vulnerable, only to have them turn away from me. The fewer people I let in, the more protected I am.

"But either way, wait and ambush? Seems simple enough. I'm guessing you'll shoot us the details once Bao gets them to you and you finalize things?" At least I wouldn't have to worry about Angel's plans of taking down the triad getting in the way of work since it was the typical 9-5 almost unless I chose to pull extra hours.

Nodding her head, Angel smiled at me. "I'll probably handle this one from the van with Bao too, for Nikolai's sake."

Although her husband accepted that Angel wouldn't stop with her plans, he still wasn't happy about her coming home injured. So, Angel's been trying to tone it down with being actively involved in the fighting.

"Don't worry, I got it." Angel's lack of presence on the field itself usually meant I was throttled into the leader role, which I didn't mind one bit.

"I hate rushing things, but I want this shit show to be over with before she gets too much of a footing and I lose mine." Angel's heavy sigh, along with the hanging of her, made her stress clear.

Angel and her little crew—including me—have been trying to shut down the Qing Triad for a while now since the current Dragon Head fell into a coma. His sudden turn in health gave his wife—Angel's stepmother—the opening to take temporary leadership along with Angel. Angel's father was a good man and ran things as cleanly as possible; unfortunately, the same couldn't be said for her stepmother.

Even though it wasn't Angel's responsibility to carry out her father's wishes of shutting down the triad completely, she decided to take it on after seeing the horrible things her stepmother had done. No doubt she would continue to do so if she were to remain in charge and have the triad in her hands.

Personally, I was more than happy to help Angel because I've suffered the consequences of her stepmother's actions and my fucked up family who worked closely with her. I wanted to burn everything to the ground, then burn the ashes to nothing so there would be no chance of the triad resurrecting.

They burned me, now it's my turn to burn them.

Chapter 4
Stepan

Hanna Lee.

From a quick look, she seemed like a simple, brown-eyed girl.

But behind that smile were demons waiting to come out to play from how her eyes stormed.

If I didn't know any better, I probably would have fallen for her cute, confident smile, but I did know better. I've talked and interacted with numerous people like her to know all the little nuances to pick up and how to interpret them correctly. It also helped that I grew up with Lev and still have to put up with him nearly every single day. Even though she wasn't as outwardly as Lev, I could still see it behind her mask when she sat across from me, acting all put together.

Drumming my fingers against my desk, I let my eyes drink in every detail of the open file before me.

Like every other employee and applicant, Hanna's life sat prettily printed on some measly sheets of paper after I dug into her. I always did my due diligence on anyone who applied for the company, so this shouldn't be any different.

But why did it feel different?

I've never had any problems reading through these files, nor do I ever put too much thought or effort into them. Yet, I couldn't help but spend time with Hanna's file, even if there wasn't much to it, which could either be a good or bad thing. In her case, I felt it wasn't good for me because it meant I had to figure her out.

There was little on her, and there were holes in her file—ones I wanted filled. Why were the holes there? What happened during those times? There were stretches in her record with nothing for years, and I wanted to know just what the hell happened for those years. There were no indications of her moving; she remained in Nespin, California, for her whole life from the looks of it. It seemed like she fell through the cracks of the system, too, because these reports from the state slowly came to a stop with no conclusion after a while.

Hanna was a mystery, and I wanted to solve her. I wanted to figure her out until I knew her better than she knew herself.

God, what is wrong with me?

I shouldn't be getting this hungover on some girl I just met for less than a few hours, but just something about her has me intrigued like never before. Maybe it was the quick, soft, and mischievous glint in her eyes when we locked gazes yesterday before the wall came up. Or perhaps it was the way she held herself confidently but not arrogantly. No doubt she knew her worth and wasn't afraid to show it. Yet, there was something else. It was brief, very brief, and subtle, but I caught it: her body shivered while her eyes softened and downturned for a millisecond before snapping back up at me challengingly.

Few people could hold my gaze, let alone as strongly as she did.

Ugh, maybe I need to get laid. Getting hung up over some new girl who looked at me, fuck.

That had to be the problem. I was just pent up, and my first female interaction in a while got me too wound up. I just needed to take a trip to one of our many clubs and get it out of my system, simple enough.

I saw no other reason as to why I'd be this intrigued by her from a few micro-expressions that could mean nothing. Well, she definitely didn't look at Lev that way, or anyone else we passed.

No, stop thinking into it.

I needed to clear my head of her before she came in today. I didn't need to figure her out, fill the holes in her file, none of that.

Speak of the devil. "*Bratok*, she's here," Lev announced after knocking on the door and opening it to reveal the little tigress on my mind for the past few hours.

Shutting the file with a smile, I got up behind my desk and rounded it. "Glad to see you back, was afraid you might not show." I teased with a soft chuckle.

"Well, if that's where you've set the bar for me then I've got this in the bag." Her confident and warm smile was more than welcoming and refreshing.

"Someone's a little cocky," Lev grumbled with a roll of his eyes. "Wouldn't get too excited yet missy." He sneered with a soft scoff at Hanna.

"Not cocky, confident." She corrected him with a shit-eating grin.

I couldn't help but smirk a little at her spunk. Again, seeing someone with such a personality who wasn't afraid to dim it for a job was refreshing.

"Alright, well, not too much exciting work today. I will stick you to a case that Lev and I are working on. We're about three weeks into research and just finding some last-minute things before solidifying a plan of attack. You're going to help us with the research, should be simple enough." It would be the simplest of tasks she would have with the job, so if she couldn't pass it, then she had no place in the company.

I had to hold my smirk back when I felt her tiny body shiver under my touch when I settled my hand on the small of her back to lead her around the desk and into my seat. "Since you don't have a desk to work at, this will do for now." I told her while gently pushing the chair in.

Picking up a file, I pulled out a list I had created for her little assignment and set it in front of her. "We already found most of the things on the list, but I wanna see you work. You can use whatever you want to get what the list asks for."

Pulling up a chair from the other desk, I got comfortable beside her while Lev sat on the couch. "Well? Go on." I urged with a smirk, gesturing at the things in front of her.

"Wait, you're going to sit here and watch me?" She didn't sound terrified, more curious than anything.

"Of course, we have to make sure you're not doing anything illegal. We also want to see your workflow and such. Don't worry, just pretend we're not here." It wasn't a complete lie. I did want to see her work a bit and see how she went about getting the information she needed.

She didn't need to know that we didn't need to watch her the whole time; that was more or less for our entertainment to see how she did under pressure and watchful eyes. Also, Lev wanted to see if he could make her sweat a little. On the other hand, I just wanted to watch and admire her.

Maybe if I watched her enough and got my fill, then I'd grow bored of her and move on. Who knows, perhaps I'd see some unsavory habit that would break the deal for me.

Either way, I needed to get over this stupid little schoolboy crush on Hanna sooner rather than later.

Chapter 5

Hanna

THEM SITTING THERE AND watching me was unexpected, but I won't let it throw me off my game.

Picking up the list, I scanned it to get the gist of what they wanted from me. It was basic research on the bounty, nothing new or strange to me. I had this in the bag. "So, anything? Legal that is." Besides what's available to the public through public records, and what I had access to with my credentials with certain sites, I typically had outside help.

"Yes, anything. Like I said, we want to see your workflow and process and to just see how you operate and your means of obtaining information. So, work away." His smile was innocent, unlike his voice, which held an indiscernible edge to it.

"Ooohkay, remember, you gave me the okay." One last chance for him to change his mind before I pulled my strings.

When he showed no sign of backpedaling, I shifted my focus off him and Lev to the computer to type away at the keyboard. Starting from the bottom up, I started generally with a Google search before going to specific records websites and then my own private ones with the law enforcement agencies. Once those avenues were exhausted, I pulled out my phone to get in touch with my contacts, showing my screen to Stepan, who wanted to see exactly what I did and who I talked to.

I'd gotten most of the information I needed from my usual sources and means, but a few required an expertise I wasn't versed in. Of course, I outsourced that to my good friend, Bao, who was our little friend group's techy. I could get the information needed by myself, but that would take longer than I would like. So, more often than not, I turned to Bao to jump through some red rope for me.

Tapping my phone screen a few times, I dialed him and held the phone up to my ear, only to have a hand stop me. Confused, I looked over at Stepan with a tilted head and furrowed brows as the phone rang.

"Speaker." There was a smugness to him with how the corners of his lips curved slightly into a smirk.

Frowning with a soft pout, I let my phone clatter onto the desk after putting it on speaker, showing my clear disdain. I needed to keep this short and to the point; otherwise, I would end up in an endless pit of embarrassment like Angel when her husband made her take our phone call on speaker. Guess Karma's a bitch biting me in the ass now.

After the third ring, a female voice answered. "Hey Hanna, he's not here right now." It wasn't who I expected, but they'd do.

Chuckling softly, I threaded my fingers through my hair. "Nicki, hey, that's fine, you could probably help me with this if you have time." Bao's sister was just as good as him, if not better.

"Sure, who is it this time?" There was no beating around the bush with her.

"Jorge Hart," I replied, tapping my fingers against the desk. "You can just send it to my phone, I'm not at my computer right now."

"Alright, give me a few and you'll know this guy better than his own mother." She laughed softly but heartedly.

Unable to help it, I cracked a smile and laughed. "You're the best."

"Of course, and don't you forget that. I'll catch you later, bye." She replied before hanging up after I uttered a 'goodbye' in response.

Usually, I'd stay on the phone and go over things with the other side, but I wasn't too comfortable with the idea of Stepan and Lev sitting here and watching me like hawks. Also, if I stayed on the phone longer than needed, I'd end up talking nonbusiness things with Nicole, or whom I liked to call Nicki. The last thing I wanted was for these two bozos to hear things about my private life and my little fascination with a certain someone in the room.

The brief awkwardness in the room disappeared when my phone buzzed to life minutes after the call ended as the files flooded through.

Lev looked at my phone wide-eyed after snatching it off the desk. "Holy shit. Who did you call? An FBI hacker?"

"Better." A wide smile spread across my face as I held back the temptation to brag about Nicole's uncanny hacking abilities. The damn woman could find out anything and everything on the net as long as she had a connection and means. If it were ever on the net or in some electronic system, then it would be fair game to our two hackers.

"Well, it might take some of my sources some time to get back to me with the necessary info, but you were just testing my means of obtaining information no? I mean, I have no doubts about the information being good once it actually gets to me, and of course I'd follow up on the leads and such." No way could I do all of that within seven days.

I might be a great hunter, the fact supported by many people always flocking to me with their bounties, but I wasn't some miracle worker. Information took time to shift through; unfortunately, I couldn't control that.

"Well, either I've underestimated you, or you're a cop." Stepan's dry chuckle and slightly narrowed eyes sent a sharp chill down my spine.

My heart shouldn't be racing in my tightening chest that struggled to pull and push my breaths. I wasn't a damn cop or anything near one, so I shouldn't be ready to bolt for the door as if I'd have any chance against two of the bratva's second and third in command if I were caught with my pants down.

Shoving my nerves away, I plastered a smile on my face as I leaned back in the chair to regain my air of comfort. "I can assure you I'm no cop, just a girl with a crap ton of connections because of my upbringing." My voice came out smoothly as the corners of my stretched lips relaxed to a more natural smile.

"I doubt you're a cop, you're too... Unorthodox to be one." The way Stepan's eyes darkened as they swept over me made my stomach tighten with my hitched breath, which I barely hid along with my wondering gaze.

Then, his eyes flickered to a sharper but lighter edge. "Well, if you are one then we'll find out one way or another. But also, a cop wouldn't survive a day with us, let alone a week, not with what we'd make them do." His little half-smirk made my nerves grip my body again before I shook them off.

"Either way." I breathed deeply while sitting back up straight again. "I did what you asked. What next?"

Surprisingly, I managed to drag out the whole thing for nearly three hours. Unfortunately, I had at least five more hours to kill before my 'shift' was technically over.

Rubbing his stubbled chin for a moment, he let his eyes linger on me before replying to me. "Hmm, why don't you take an extended lunch break today and meet us at Cozy Cup at 1? There's some things Lev and I have to do, and it's a little too early for us to go out on surveillance. So, unless you want to sit around the office for the next hour before your scheduled lunchtime, I suggest you take the chance of fresh air I'm giving you."

My words stiffened with my tongue when I bit it to prevent my snark from coming out. I didn't like how he worded the last part. No doubt he did it on purpose because Stepan seemed like the type who spoke after carefully crafting his words before manipulating them with his tongue.

The smug little smirk on his face was all I needed to confirm he worded things purposely. "Well? What's your choice? I wouldn't mind having you sit around the office while I do some work, but for your sake, a little breather is needed." The smug edge to his voice slowly softened with his words. His tone changed to an almost caring one, as if he was doing me some favor by letting me have a long lunch.

"I'll take a longer lunch, I have some things I need to take care of as well." It was a smooth lie that slid off my tongue like butter.

"Enjoy your time then, just don't be late." Stepan almost sounded as if he was disappointed with how his voice dipped a little.

With a small wave, I quickly removed myself from the chair, darted across the room, and slipped through the door after cracking it just enough.

Fucking hell, that was suffocating.

I hadn't realized how heavily his energy weighed on me until I was safely on the other side of the door.

A part of me wanted to challenge him back there.

'I suggest you take the chance I'm giving you.'

I silently mocked him under my breath as I made my way out of the building. I mean, just who in the hell does he think he is? Giving me the chance? Basically giving me permission like some petulant child. Damn asshole.

God, maybe this job would be a mistake.

Well, too late now, because no way in hell was I backing out of this trial. I ain't no fucking quitter, even if my potential boss was a hot asshole.

Chapter 6

Stepan

At least her control seemed impeccable, so I have to give her props there.

Her irritation was clear by how the corner of her lip twitched with her clenching jaw when I pressed her. This wouldn't be the end of it, though. I needed to test her boundaries to see where the break would be. I didn't need some impulsive worker who would cause me more trouble than benefits. Hanna was a wildcard from my research when I called around to her sources. Everyone boasted about her skills and abilities, but they were consistent about how unpredictable she could be with a very sharp tongue.

"What's on your mind?" Lev's voice rumbled in the air, disturbing the silent peace that had filled my office for minutes after Hanna left. "You don't think she's a cop, right?"

"Honestly? No, unless she's a very stupid cop. But, no, I really don't think so. But, there is something we're missing when it comes to her." My chest rose and fell heavily as I ran a hand down my face and rested it on my chin. "Unless she's some damn secret billionaire, there's no way she should have the resources she did, so we're missing something big."

Her sources and access to things amazed me because they were almost as good as our connections, ones we've obtained through our bratva reputation and rather questionable means. Was that what we had missed? Was she mafia? No, it wouldn't make sense for her to work for me if she was. Unless she was sent as a spy, which would be a risky and stupid.

"Look into her sources. I want to know how she made her connection with them." If I couldn't dig up anymore through electronic records, then I'd just have to go at it the old-fashioned way after Lev was done.

Releasing another heavy exhale through my nose, I stood from my chair and ran a hand through my hair. "See what you can dig up until we have to meet back up with her. I am going to see what our little mouse is up to."

"Our little mouse? Nah, you mean rat." Lev corrected me with an amused chuckle before getting up from the couch himself.

"Oh please, give her a little more credit. A rat is disgusting, and she's not." I remarked in a light tone before making my way out of the office.

It didn't take me long to locate and tail her from a distance. I probably wouldn't be catching her doing something nefarious, but any little peek into her life was better than none right now since I knew very little about her.

As much as I expected, nothing exciting. All Hanna did was go to a few stores, specifically a makeup store, a grocery store, and a little sandwich shop.

Hanna did take a quick detour to her place before she made her way to our designated meeting spot, but I already knew where she lived because the address was on file. I knew it was a shady part of town when I saw it on her paperwork, but to walk into the area was a stark reminder for me as to how shitty it really was.

The fact Hanna lived in such a place unsettled me. Even if she seemed more than capable of handling herself, this was no place for anyone to settle for one night—let alone on a daily basis. God, I wish I could whisk her away from this place into a more decent area—like my place. I doubt she would like that very much, if any.

Squaring my shoulders and plastering a friendly smile, I approached Hanna from the side. "Early, I like it." I mused with a faint chuckle. "Do you want to grab something to drink from the cafe?" I offered with a slight nod towards the small, bustling business.

"Hmm I guess something to pep me up wouldn't hurt. Where's Lev?" She replied after tapping her plush lips in thought for a quick moment.

It was hard to hold back the smirk from pulling at the corners of my lips as I replied to her. "Oh, he's busy, so you'll be with just me for the remainder of the time." I quite liked that it would just be me and her, but I couldn't help the tinge of jealousy towards Lev because of her question.

Perhaps it was a mistake to have Lev stay behind because his presence might have eased her walls since the two seemed to be on the same playing field. Honestly, I was a little surprised at how they didn't tear at each other during the interview given how much tension choked at the air. Also, given how similar they were as individuals, I was surprised their impulsiveness didn't take over.

"So, just surveillance?" Hanna asked, looking up at me with a quirked brow as we stood in line.

"Yeah, just simple tailing and mapping out a route and schedule and such. We'll continue into tomorrow as well. Lev has already got everything down because we've been on this case a long while, but again, this is more or less to evaluate you. Just pretend I'm not really here and do what you typically do." Easier said than done, probably, but this could be an excellent opportunity to see how she would do under pressure, too.

Although, judging from earlier, I doubt she'd be too affected by my presence once she got into her flow. She might have hidden it well earlier when I made her do her research out in the open under scrutinizing eyes, but I caught onto how tense her shoulders were with her paced breathing. After the first few successes, though, she fell into her element and worked as if Lev and I weren't there at all.

Once she was done ordering, I quickly stepped in front of her and paid for our drinks. "Wha—hey!" Hanna protested with a soft, glaring pout.

"It would have been rude of me to let you pay." I dismissed her with a soft chuckle, smirking down at her for a moment before settling my hand on the small of her back to lead her off to the side while we waited for our drinks to be made.

"It's not a date, so it wouldn't have been rude." She grumbled while increasing her pout, making her bottom lip stick out more.

Seeing it caused a small wave of temptation to wash over me. It'd be so easy to lean down and capture her lip between my teeth. Perhaps I should give into my temptation and rattle her confidence a little.

I quickly pushed the nagging feeling away to prevent my mind from becoming distracted. I couldn't afford to be distracted by her right now, or ever really.

"Doesn't have to be a date for me to treat you. Besides, I was the one who asked, so it would have been rude of me to let you pay for yourself." I countered smoothly with a charming little smile.

Huffing, she averted her eyes from me and mumbled something under her breath before glancing up at me through her lashes. "Don't make a habit of it, I can handle things myself."

"Too bad you're not the boss between us, so I'll make whatever habit I want." I retorted with a small shrug of my shoulders and a soft chuckle. "Cute that you think you can tell me what to do though." I teased her intentionally with a smirk.

Seems like I might have found her button to push, and I would damn well abuse it if I could get under her skin like this.

"Well, it's going to be a bad habit." Then, the wall was back between us with her stale words. "Thank you for the coffee though." At least she was sincere with her gratefulness, and my observant eyes didn't miss the tiny smile she tried to hide from me when she turned her face.

Reluctantly, I stepped away from her when our drinks were ready by the counter to grab them. "Careful, it's hot." I probably didn't need to state the obvious, but the caring concern slipped my tongue out of habit.

"I know, I know, I'm not stupid." She retorted with a soft scoff and roll of her eyes as she took the cup from me. Taking a sip, she instantly pulled the cup away from herself. "Shit!" She hissed with a pained face.

Sighing knowingly, I rolled my eyes at her. "Told you so princess." I chided playfully with a smirk.

"Shut up." She grumbled in response while glaring up at me. "And don't call me princess." The disdain was apparent in her voice, so I didn't press the matter any because no doubt I would piss her off if I did.

"Whatever you want little tigress." I tested the waters with a slight smirk while glancing down at her, taking in the soft glare she threw at me in response. At least I wasn't met with contempt this time.

Wanting to be free of the sweltering cafe, I quickly led her outside to the tables scattered in front of the business. "You do anything fun on your extended lunch?" Small talk never hurt anyone, even if I knew everything she did.

"Just errands, figured since I'm out already then might as well do them during the day rather than after work when I'll be more tired and less motivated to get them done." She replied simply with a slight shrug of her shoulders before sitting down and sipping at her drink, this time blowing on it first.

"I would ask if you finished what you needed, but I am doubtful since you have a whole company to run. So, business is probably never finished with you." Hanna remarked before her cheeky little tongue momentarily peeked out at me momentarily and slipped back into her smiling lips.

"A fair enough statement that I can't argue with." Unfortunately, business was never done, both legal and illegal.

People were always going to be looking for loans, ones where we had to go collect. Businesses in our territory would always need to pay protection fees, which, again, we had to collect. The bratva life would never be anything close to boring, and I was in it for life... or at least until Death would take me from my brothers.

Clearing my throat, I shifted the subject while sitting across from her. "What do you usually do in your free time?" I asked, genuinely curious about any aspect of her life that didn't include or involve work of any kind.

Hanna's soft features scrunched and twisted in thought as she pressed the lip of her cup to her own. "Nap? Hit the gym? I'm not really that exciting of a person. I mean, I usually would spend all my time on my bounties, so not much free time to myself." Her eyes were downcasted as she chewed on her bottom lip. "And sometimes I'll hang out with my friends, but we've just all gotten too busy recently to do much hanging out."

"Well, you're not going to have all the time in the world to work yourself to death if things work out after this trial period. No point in working yourself into an early grave over stupid criminals who decide to be stupid and run. You're going to have to come up with a new schedule and actually plan to live a life." She seemed way too young to have a boring life just yet.

Hanna looked like she needed to shed a few pounds off her shoulders. I had no doubts she would be hired by the end of the trial period, so hopefully, with her work hours scheduled and capped, she'd get out a little more and lighten up a little. Even if she seemed nice and cheery with her constant smile, I could see the fatigue behind it. Her shoulders would stay overly tense even when she relaxed as if she had weights on them.

I wanted to know what troubles she had to dim her like that. Why was a young lady like her so tired? Granted, everyone in this whole generation lived in a constant zombie state, but still. The typical person unwound enough at the end of the night to look somewhat lively. Even the typical boring person seemed somewhat content, unlike Hanna.

"I'll worry about that when it comes, and what's to stop me from doing research on my off time, hm? Ever stop to think that maybe I like doing that stuff?" Her challenging smile wasn't convincing enough for me.

Chuckling softly with a soft shake of my head, I looked at her with a smirk and raised eyebrow. "So, what you're telling me is that you just *love* to sit in front of a computer screen for hours upon hours and stare at pages after pages of reports, for fun?"

The way her face twisted was a good enough answer for me even if she refused to answer me verbally. "D-don't we have actual work to get to now?" She grumbled with a frowning pout, her eyes firmly locking with mine.

"Whenever you're ready little tigress, it's all on you like I said. I'm just here for the ride, so do what you need and want." I lazily waved my hand in the air almost dismissively as I leaned back in my chair with my legs crossed at my ankles.

Huffing, she narrowed her eyes briefly at me before darting them to the small grocery store across the street from us. "He is still in there."

"Good girl, you caught on." Even though I was hands-off with this, I figured just a slight nudge in the right direction wouldn't hurt.

I purposely chose the cafe at the specific timeframe for a reason. After weeks of observing and tailing him, I had the target's routine down. So, I knew he would be making his weekly grocery trip to a very particular store around this time of day.

"One of my sources got back to me while I was on break. Told me about how there were consistent charges every Monday around 1300 to a small ma 'n pop store. I didn't need the assistance, but thank you." The small smile she quickly flashed at me was unexpected but appreciated.

Although speaking about her sources, Lev still hadn't dug up much, which usually wasn't a good thing. Her sources were well guarded, which only furthered my festering suspicions about her.

Who the hell is Hanna Lee?

Chapter 7
Hanna

"CAN'T BELIEVE YOU GOT a tracker on him. Fucking ballsy."

I couldn't help but grin proudly at Lev's little compliment as he and I, along with Stepan, crowded around a tablet to follow a blinking red dot as it moved through a map.

Scoffing, Stepan looked at me with hard eyes. "It was risky and reckless." He still wasn't happy about my little stunt yesterday with our target, Jorge.

After we had tailed him around town for a bit as he ran his errands, I decided—much against Stepan's wishes—to stick a tracker on Jorge, almost literally. I mean, I could've settled for sticking one on his car, but I didn't want to go get the equipment for it. So, I did the quick little 'oops, sorry' bump into Jorge when he exited the smoke shop and expertly tacked on the small tracking button under the back collar of his jacket.

Well, Stepan wanted to see how I operated, and that's how I went about things. However, I was riskier than usual because, typically, I'd tail him for a few days to a few weeks before attempting to stick something to him like that.

Chuckling, Lev patted my shoulder and grinned widely at me. "But it gets the job done. Well, no wonder her clearance rates are fast." At least Lev could appreciate my work, yet I found myself disappointed and pining for a certain blonde's praises.

A small part of me wanted to hear the words 'good girl' fall from his lips again. He probably didn't mean it *that* way yesterday, but the two words still unintentionally affected me.

"Just be more careful next time, and let me know what you're planning," Stepan said in a low voice before sweeping his hand across the lower half of his face and settling it there.

"Oh careful there *bratok*, you're starting to sound like you care." Lev teased his brother with a hearty laugh, earning a sharp glare from the older Volkov.

A slight shift softened his eyes when they landed on me momentarily, making my chest tighten again with eager wariness. Then, in an instant, the shutters were back in place. "Just shut up and focus on the target."

"So, what's your plan to apprehend him?" Lev asked with a slight tilt of his head as he handed the tablet back to me.

Taking the device, I studied the target's position on the screen for a minute before looking up at the two pairs of beady, blue eyes boring holes into me with the intense curiosity sparking within them.

"Whelp, I'm gonna ask him nicely, and if he decides to not take the easy way then I'll just get a little dirt on me." I said casually with a slight shrug of a shoulder.

Unfortunately, violence wasn't the answer to everything, and not every bounty target will put up a struggle. Some targets were more than happy to go along to avoid a punch to the face, and some were really innocent and had no idea about missing a bail hearing and such. Those were the boring ones, of course, but they were a nice break between the blood-pumping ones.

"Ugh really? You're going to try the diplomatic route like Stepan?" Lev's disappointed eyes rolled with his groan of complaint.

With a quick flip of the bird, I snarked back, "Well, I have to have a good reason for chasing and beating his ass. The law doesn't like it too much when you just beat their asses right out the gate." Still, we had to abide by the law, even to catch a lawbreaker without constraints like how cops had it. Unfortunately, being a bounty hunter didn't mean going completely rogue to the law.

"You seem too excited for someone who's going to talk." Stepan noted, keeping his studious eyes trained on me.

"Because he's going to bolt, so I'm just preparing myself." I just had to do things 'by the book' for the sake of the report later and to show Stepan I could do things mostly correct.

Jorge didn't have a good track record, and from what I gathered from others who have gone after him, he was a runner. Well, he won't get away from me, that's for sure. I was prepared for a chase. My muscles ached from the anxious tension as I sat in the car with the two brothers.

"Can I go get him now?" I didn't mean to sound so eager, like some child asking for their reward, but the adrenaline started to buzz at me for a release.

Chuckling, Stepan's lip twitched into a brief smirk as he unlocked the car's doors. "Go get 'em little tigress."

Grinning like a madwoman, I slid out of the car and slammed the door shut before stalking up to Jorge, who stood from his seat on the porch of the decrepit cabin he'd been hiding in.

"You want to do this the easy way or the hard way bucko!?" I shouted across the way from him as I continued to close the distance between us.

Then, as I anticipated, Jorge took off after vaulting over the porch's railing. At the first movement, I was onto him.

I zipped through the area, letting my adrenaline propel my legs toward my fleeing target, who grew closer and closer with each thump of my heart.

With a grunt, I launched myself at him when he was less than an arm's length away. Tackling him with a grunt, I locked my arms around his waist to keep myself anchored to him as the two of us tumbled to the ground with grunts from the impact of our bodies hitting and rolling against the hard, dirt ground.

Quickly, Jorge rolled onto his side. "Fuck!" I hissed in pain when I felt something hit my face, hard. "You'd hit a girl? How rude!" I seethed sarcastically.

Releasing my arms fully from him, I quickly scrambled on top of him before he could get up fully and gave him two quick jabs to his stomach then landing a solid punch across his face. Before I could give another swing to his face, Jorge threw me off with a buck of his hips and a shove from his hands.

Landing to the side with a soft grunt, I quickly recovered and flipped back onto my feet just as Jorge scrambled upright and ran. Reaching down, I picked up the fallen branch next to me and swung it at his back, knocking him back to the ground. "Don't make me break a leg Jorge." I couldn't help the little maniacal giggle from slipping my lips as I slowly stalked up to his cowering body as he tried to scurry away from me.

"W-wait!" His little Adam's apple bobbed a little with his hard swallow as he looked up at me with terrified eyes. "I-I'll go with you! Just put that stick down, and don't hurt me anymore." He pleaded with his hands in the air protectively over his face.

"Hands out." I demanded, reaching into my pocket and pulling out a pair of handcuffs.

With how he was trembling like a leaf, I thought he would make good on his surrender. Unfortunately, he decided to be stupid and test me.

The moment I was within reach, he kicked my legs out from under me, making me land on my ass with a pained grunt. Jorge jumped to his feet and bolted after he struck me, but I didn't let him get far.

Bouncing right back to my feet, I gripped the branch tightly and pulled my arm back, taking aim before chucking the branch at him. My trained eyes followed the branch as it flew through the air and struck my target right in the head, knocking him out cold upon impact.

The faint *thump* his heavy body made when it fell to the ground brought a victorious smile to my face and a wave of satisfaction to my body as I stalked up to Jorge again.

Sighing softly, I hooked my hands on my hips as I looked down at Jorge's unconscious body. "You just had to make me work out today." It was a playful disappointment, mostly. I wasn't too fond of the fact I had to drag this guy back to the van.

Speaking about the van, I'd forgotten about my little spectators. "Hey, any chance I can get some help lugging this heavy sack of shit back? Pretty please?" I asked over the communications system in a sweet voice, overly saturating it at the end as if I were some child asking for a treat and not some crazy psycho asking for help with moving a body.

"Oh, now she needs our help." I heard Lev scoff in response. No doubt his eyes rolled with his words based on his tone.

Shivers washed over my body at the sound of Stepan's deep chuckle echoing through my ear. "We'll be there in a bit. Good job little tigress." His little praise caused another ripple of shivers to cascade over my warming body as I fought to keep the heat from going to my cheeks.

"Uhh thanks." I replied in a smaller voice than I would have liked.

Why the hell am I getting so worked up over a little pat on the back like that?

Just like yesterday, my body reacted oddly in response to Stepan's words, even if they probably meant nothing or were playful in nature at the most. I wasn't trying to think much about it, but I couldn't help it. I have gotten praises before from people around me, and I've always felt good upon hearing and receiving them. But never have I felt this strongly to anyone in particular. Never have I wanted to hear more from someone.

Never.

Until Stepan.

Which was crazy because I'd barely met him and knew little to nothing about him. So, why the hell did my body react so energetically to him?

"Really? You had to knock him out? He's like three hundred pounds, man." Lev groaned sarcastically as he approached me with Stepan right behind him.

"Oh please, I'm pretty sure you bench that on a daily basis, and he's only two hundred seventy-five." I replied playfully with a snort and smirk.

"Hell of an aim ya got." Lev grinned proudly, patting my shoulder as he passed me.

I expected to feel the warmth of his praise like I did from Stepan, but the feeling never came. Instead, I found my feet rocking back and forth while my eyes softly darted to Stepan from under my lashes in a silent plea.

Looking at me with a proud gleam to his eyes, he gave me a soft smile. "Remind me to never run from you if you have something to throw." Stepan chuckled softly, reaching out and ruffling the top of my head lightly.

Unable to help it, I smiled widely with a soft giggle before going over to Jorge to cuff him in case he woke up and struggled.

One quick workout for the Volkov boys and a car ride later, we were back at the company building after dropping our bounty off at the police station.

Stopping right next to me, Stepan refused to meet me head-on. "Go wash up and take a quick break, then we'll meet in my office to go over some things." Stepan told me with a nod towards the employee locker area before turning his full attention to me once Lev slinked off to do his own thing.

"You did great, good job." His praise and smile was brief, but the warm bloom in my heart was anything but.

"Thanks, I always give my best and nothing else." I replied with a soft smile while gritting my teeth to hold myself back from grinning like a fool.

After a quick rinse, I changed into a fresh pair of black pants with a white, short-sleeve blouse with a black leather jacket thrown over, and a pair of black ankle boots on my feet. Then I made my way to Stepan's office and made myself comfortable on the couch next to Lev after he patted the spot.

Stepan was caught up in a quick meeting, so I was stuck with Lev for the time being. The two of us sat in the suffocating office filled with our tension.

"Still fucking salty, but good job out there." Lev grumbled after a while, averting his eyes from me while running a hand down his face.

"Thanks... But no hard feelings? Ya know I was just doing a job, not like I was purposely upstaging you." God this felt so awkward.

Lev was the asshole for keeping this stupid grudge against me. Honestly, I had no qualms with him because we were both just doing our jobs. Unfortunately, the job put our warring paths together, but I really didn't think anything of it.

Sure, was it annoying to have him take my bounty from me the few times he did? Yes, but nothing a small hissy fit or some drinks couldn't fix. I never hung myself over it at the end of the day.

"Are you going to quit taking my bounties and being a bitch to me?" Lev shot back with a raised brow and straight face.

"I've never been a bitch to you." Okay, maybe I might have flipped him off a few times, but not like I gave him much or any trouble beyond that.

"Maybe not in your book, but you've definitely been one in my eyes." He cracked a slight smirk before reaching up with one hand and flicking my forehead with a chuckle. "We'll get along just fine."

"You two behaving in here?" Stepan asked with a faint chuckle as he entered his office, shutting the door behind him.

"Oh please, if I were to kill her then it wouldn't be in your office and get this nice couch dirty with blood." Lev's tone lightened when he responded to his brother.

"I was more worried about her making a mess with beating your ass, but whatever helps you sleep at night, *bratan*." Stepan retorted with a smirk and glanced at Lev as he passed his brother to the desk.

Settling behind his desk, Stepan leaned back in his chair and got comfortable. "So, how did you think that went?" Stepan settled his sharp eyes trained on me as his fingers tapped at the arm of his chair.

Taking a deep breath, I spend a moment in my head. "Better than I expected, honestly. It was nice and quick, not too much damage to me or the target, no collateral damage either." Granted, the whole thing occurred in a wooded area away from civilization.

"I agree, it did go very well. Now, one experience is hardly enough to judge you on, but if you're consistent with what I witnessed earlier then I should see no problem if I were to employ you. I'm not going to lie, I went in thinking you were going to display yourself to be some liability like Lev." Stepan's eyes quickly glanced at Lev who protested his brother with a glare.

"I've learned to be mindful of my surroundings and actions. I've dealt with my fair share of blowback during my early years of bounty hunting." I replied with a confident smile as I leaned back in my seat, ignoring that he tossed me in the same category as Lev.

Unfortunately, being a bounty hunter didn't mean I was above the law. I could care less about roughing up runaway criminals, though. I got my kicks from my more illegal hunts, so I didn't need to worry about running my energy out with my bounty assignments.

"Good. Well, like I said, I think it went very well from what I saw. Although, your methods are a little straightforward when it comes to surveillance, so maybe just be a little less risky there and everything should be fine." Stepan's short, soft chuckle warmed the room briefly.

"I'm usually not *that* risky, promise. It was just I was on a time constraint and kind of jumped the gun, and I wanted to show you how I did things." I grinned somewhat sheepishly. "Don't worry, I'm usually a lot more patient and careful." Somewhat. I did tend to be a little impatient at times.

The reason why my clearance rates were so high and quick was due to my riskiness. Spending months tracking and locating a target got tedious at times, so I got into a poor habit of tailing close to stick a tracker on them whenever I could. Worse comes to worse, I get made and have to expedite a takedown.

Well, I would dial it back if I got the job.

"Hope you stick to that. Well, either way, excitement is over, now for the boring stuff." Stepan beckoned me over with his fingers.

"Hope you're better than Lev at reports too." He teased with a soft smirk as he got out of his chair.

Chapter 8
Hanna

"Woo! I'm so fucking happy for you!"

"I wouldn't celebrate yet." I chuckled with a light roll of my eyes.

Angel celebrated my successful hunt a little too early, taking it as a sign that the job was secured. She practically showed up at my place to drag me out for celebratory drinks when I told her about my success when I got off work.

"Oh come on, he praised you, which is a very good thing because he never really praises anyone new or anyone in general. Besides, there's no way you won't get the job after today. I mean, if he had any reservations about you then he would have given you the boot as I said before." Angel assured me with a chuckling grin before downing her drink.

"I still have a few more days left of the trial, so don't get too excited for me." I definitely didn't hype myself up about it.

Even if I was confident about getting the job, I didn't want to get my hopes up. Stepan could end up letting me go at the end of it all, even if I did everything by the book nearly perfectly.

Things rarely ever went right in my life, so I always saw the glass as half empty, unlike Angel, who tried to see the glass as half full.

"Quit saying that. You are basically hired, trust me." She assured me with a confident smile. "Now, you gotta drink some more to get that stick out of your ass." She scoffed playfully and pushed a drink towards me after the waitress dropped off another round. "Also, don't be stupid to pass up good-ass booze."

Well, I couldn't argue with her there. Attending any club with Angel often meant getting my drinks covered, but it was all the time now since she married the bratva boss, especially whenever we went to one of the clubs his family owned, like this one.

A smile lifts the corners of my mouth as my eyes twinkled mischievously. I took the shot glass with a mocking sigh and downed it before drumming my fingers on the tabletop.

"What's eating at ya?" Her playful tone died down to a soft, concerned voice as she looked at me quizzically.

Waving a dismissive hand at her, I pulled my best poker smile on. "Nothing, just keeping my hopes down, that's all." It wasn't a total lie; I was trying to keep my hopes from soaring, so if I did crash, then I wouldn't burn.

"Hanna, you can't pull shit past me after all this time. So, what's really on your mind girl?" Leave it to Angel to see right through me after all this time.

"Ange, it's nothing... Just something stupid that will probably pass on its own, I don't want to bother you with it." No point in bringing up something that would never happen or be temporary.

"Hanna." Angel's typical bright voice turned serious when she deadpanned at me.

I could feel my cheeks heat up as I averted my gaze from my best friend. "It's nothing, really, just a stupid little schoolgirl crush that'll go away on its own." I don't know if she heard me through the blaring music of the club, but I got it out and didn't want to repeat myself.

"Lev? Stepan?" I guess she did hear me if she asked for clarification with her teasing smirk.

"God, not Lev, we'd kill each other on our first date." I laughed softly with a shake of my head before grabbing another shot and drinking it.

Lev seemed fun, not going to lie, but I could never see myself with a man like him. As crazy as the relationship would be, I didn't want someone like him as a partner because he was too similar to me.

"Thank God, you have any idea what kind of hell would be brought onto the earth if you two hooked up and ended up together?" She seemed relieved with how her shoulders relaxed with her soft laugh.

"Oh please, I've got more of a leveled head than Lev. Give me more credit." Okay, that might have been a bit of a stretch because I could be just as bad.

"When you are not doing any official businesses and shit, you are on his level bitch." My best friend gave me a knowing look, one I couldn't dispute because of the truth behind it.

"Well, if you've a crush on Stepan then just ask him out." Angel made it sound like it'd be the easiest thing to do in the world.

"Me and him run in two different circles. Besides, if things work out like how we all want it to then he'll be my boss in the end. And like hell am I going to be that office cliché of banging my boss." Hell, as much of a loose cannon Lev was, even he was out of my league.

Unfortunately, life wasn't some stupid fairytale. There was no prince charming, no magical miracles, nothing. I was a peasant while Stepan was the fucking king. There's no way he'd spare a misfit like me a second glance in the game of courting. The second command to the Volkov Bratva had no business with some mercenary like me.

"No you don't. You're both mafia, so that puts you in the same arena already." Angel pointed out with a cheeky smirk.

"Technically I'm not, or won't be once we take down your stepmother and disband the triad. I'm just going to be a freelancing misfit then." Won't be long now until Angel disbands the triad after ripping it to shreds along with her stepmother.

"Then you'll just be a part of the Volkov Bratva like me. Nikolai will have no problems with you in our ranks given your skills and shit. Besides, if he has a problem with it then he can deal with me. I ain't letting my best friend land in limbo after we take down the triad." Angel's perfect little world seemed adorable sometimes, and sometimes I wondered how she could have such a good outlook on life given everything.

Well, never mind, the answer to that was simple: love. Angel used to have a more pessimistic outlook on life until she married Nikolai and fell in love with him. I wasn't jealous or anything because I was happy for her. She might not have had a shitty life like me, but she had her moments. So, she deserved a good man like Nikolai in her life.

Maybe in a happy world, Stepan could be my Nikolai.

How unfortunate.

"Just let things go how they do. Even villains deserve happy endings. So, promise me that whatever happens you won't fight it." She wasn't asking, not with how stern and determined her eyes bore into my own.

Rolling my eyes, I sighed softly before holding up a shot glass and lightly tipping it at her. "Fine, promise."

With a knowing look, she let out a long sigh before jabbing my forehead with her finger. "Or if you're going to be a stubborn ass then screw him, literally, and get him out of your system. Or get him out of your system some other way if you're gonna be a stubborn bitch like you always are."

"We'll see." I chuckled softly before taking a sip of water.

Grinning, Angel giggled before taking another shot and getting up. "Come on, let's dance and have some fun." And that would be all the alcohol hitting her.

Leaning over, she grabbed my arm with another giggle before pulling me up to my feet. "Just a little, I'm a little tired from today." I gave into her with a soft smile, letting her drag me to the dancefloor where all the other sweaty bodies were dancing away.

Much to my word, we only stayed on the floor for a few songs before returning to our little table for more drinks. Then, just as we were about to hit the dancefloor again, we were stopped. Well, more of Angel was stopped.

Nikolai seemingly appeared out of nowhere and trapped her tiny body against his broad one with an arm around her shoulder. "Alright, that's enough for you tonight, *lisichka*." Nikolai's deep chuckle could barely be heard in the place.

"Wha? Noooo, *anh*, just a little more, please." Angel instantly pouted, wrapping her arms around her husband's waist and pressing herself to him.

I watched as Nikolai leaned down and whispered something to Angel, making her loose posture stiffen and eyes widen. Leaning back up with a now blushing Angel in his arms, Nikolai turned his attention to me. "Sorry, I'm going to have to steal her from you. Do you want me to have one of the guards take you home?"

Giving him a polite smile, I shook my head in response. "Thanks, but I'll be fine. I'm gonna stick around for another drink or two maybe and Uber home or something. I don't want to take your guard away from their post, so don't worry."

"Well, I'll have one at the ready just in case you change your mind. Have a good night Hanna." Nikolai gave me a faint smile before dragging his beet-red wife out of the club, leaving me to my lonesome self.

Downing the last of my drink, I left for one more round on the dancefloor. After dancing for a good while, and working up too many hungry men, I left a trail of disappointment in my wake when I went to the bar for one last drink.

A rush of warmth cascaded down my body when I felt an electrifying feeling run across my shoulders.

"I thought that was you I saw."

Chapter 9

Stepan

THE LAST PERSON I expected to see tonight was the person of my interest.

I have yet to find out more about this mysterious woman, which made my clear mind cloud more and more with each dead end.

I thought my eyes were playing tricks on me because I'd been thinking about Hanna so much. Perhaps my mind had manifested her on the dancefloor, and I would have played it off if it weren't for the nasty feeling welling up in my chest at the sight of her and those men.

"Fuck, Stepan, don't sneak up on me like that." Hanna's tense body relaxed with her sigh of relief.

"Were you going to stab me with a straw?" I mused with a chuckle, eyeing the tiny piece of plastic clutched tightly in her hand.

Narrowing her eyes at me playfully, she threw it at me with a huff and took a sip of her drink before replying. "So what if I was? You came out of nowhere, you could have been some handsy creep for all I knew."

"It's a straw." I deadpanned with a slight smirk while nodding at the object that had landed on the table.

"Hey, don't discriminate, anything can be a weapon if enough effort is put into it. I can easily stab that thing into your eye or ear and do some damage." She elaborated proudly with an uptilt of her chin.

Well, I never would've thought about that. "Aren't we creative." I mused with another chuckle.

Reaching over, I plucked the little piece of plastic from her after she grabbed another and watched her pout in response. "I don't want to deal with a report of a straw stabbing from a patron." I half-joked while setting the straw down on the bar top.

"Hey, if they get stabbed then that's their own fault, I don't get violent without a good reason." She clarified with a playful scoff and roll of her eyes.

Making eye contact with the bartender, I held two fingers up and received a nod in return. They already knew what I drank at this point.

"Didn't take you for the clubbing type, let alone a regular." Hanna noted with a quirked brow.

"And you'd be right, I'm not much of a clubber. My older brother owns the place and I just help out more often than not." Besides helping with the books mostly, I stuck around the clubs because they were our main meeting places for our bratva business.

If I could help it, I always tried to partake in business meetings because I was the second in command. My older brother Nikolai, the head of our bratva, could handle himself more than fine, but I wanted to be there with him to have his back.

"What about you? Regular clubber? Or are you here with someone?" Maybe I could get some answers that would let me peek into her life more than the little information I have on her.

"Eh, not really a regular clubber. I was with a friend who just left." Straight to the point, not much I could go on besides that she has at least one friend.

"What do you usually do then if you don't hit the clubs?" I asked, flashing the bartender a quick, grateful smile when she placed our drinks in front of us and then turned my full attention back to Hanna.

"Oh, thanks, you didn't have to." Hanna gave me a grateful smile as she took the drink into her hands. "But to answer your question, I mean, it's basically what I told you the other day. Besides being boring, if I do have a fun night out it's usually just out with my friends or a single date to the movie or Stand Street. What about you?"

Humming softly to myself, I ran my hand across my lower face, holding it there for a moment as I straightened my answer mentally. "If I'm not busy helping my brothers, I like to spend my time at home, either at my pool or in my kitchen." As if I even had that kind of time on my hands nowadays.

I was usually too busy with the company and bratva business to enjoy any downtime like in the past. Especially now since we were starting to run into much more trouble with surrounding mafia crews and the Qing Triad. I was lucky to get a good few hours of sleep and some food in me with how busy I've become with helping Nikolai and his wife keep tabs on Lady Qing, the temporary head of the Qing Triad.

Even though there was a—shaky—truce between the bratva and triad, my sister-in-law advised us against settling because Lady Qing had no intentions of keeping things peaceful. The truce kept the bratva from striking while she pulled her strings with the triad. Hearing all of it pissed me off greatly because we essentially got played; she took us for fools, and we were almost none the wiser to fall for it.

We had gone into the meeting with no intentions of accepting whatever bullshit she put out. At least, that was the plan until she dragged out her offering of a bride, who turned out to be the woman who saved Nikolai from a car crash months ago, and who also happened to be his little obsession. So, the plan went out the window because Nikolai bit the bait, not that I could blame him. After all, I would have done the same in his situation.

Although it went against what we stood for, I was glad he broke his promise of never partaking in an arranged marriage because he was now the happiest he'd ever been in his whole life. Angel didn't seem to mind the impromptu change in relationship status either, even if it was more forced from her end of things. Apparently, she had a little—major—crush on my older brother since the night of the crash. Their marriage wasn't perfect by any means, but the two were smitten with each other beyond comprehension.

Enough about the past, though; what mattered now was the present, which included dealing with the triad as they came, and Hanna.

"Oh? The kitchen? I didn't take you for a cook." Her soft voice had a teasing tone when she spoke, and she looked at me curiously with raised brows.

"Well, don't go telling everyone I like to shut myself in the kitchen, just something I enjoyed doing growing up." I didn't let her in on the real reason why though.

No one, let alone Hanna, needed to know that I enjoyed cooking because it reminded me of happier times with my mother. It was the only time away from my father and brothers back then, the only solace in my life. My father already shoved me aside more than my siblings because of my hair, always insisting that my mother cheated on him and that I was an affair baby—even though half our extended family was blonde. So, my mother always invited me into the kitchen, keeping me safe and happy there.

Hanna's soft smile stiffened briefly. "Bet your girlfriend just loves you." Even though she laughed jokingly, it sounded forced.

It was hard to pick up in the dark club, but I could see the slight sharpening of her usually soft, chocolate-brown eyes and the tensing of her jaw before she brought her drink up to take a sip. Then there was the slight edge to her voice, though it was hidden well.

"If I had one then maybe." As if I had time to dedicate to a relationship, not like any woman would understand either.

"I'm surprised you're not here with your man, or woman." If she wasn't single, then that would be a slight problem.

Wait, why would it be a problem?

The thought of her with anyone caused that nasty feeling from before to claw its way back up to the surface to where it festered right under my sternum.

"If I had someone significant like that then I wouldn't be here alone." She might have replied with a small, joking smile, but it looked forced from my angle.

Okay, so she was single, good. I don't know why, but the fact brought a sense of relief to me.

"But you could fix that." Her shy smile curved suggestively after she downed the last of her drink. "Come on," she said, grabbing my hand after she hopped off the stool, "One dance? Then we can go back to being professional after tonight." The dim of disappointment in her eyes almost went amiss in the dark lighting of the club.

Fuck it. One dance won't hurt... Right?

On a whim, I decided to indulge her in hopes of scratching my itch as well. "How can I say no to lovely you?" I chuckled before finishing my drink and letting her drag us to the dancefloor. Thank God the place wasn't overly crowded, so we had space between us and the other bodies occupying the lighted floor.

My hands locked themselves onto Hanna's hips to prevent her from slipping away as we maneuvered closer to the center of the dance-floor. Then, once we found a good spot, I snapped her body to mine, fitting her backside into me like a puzzle piece. If only I had some more alcohol in my system to loosen me up more.

Hanna's head leaned back onto my shoulder, and she brushed her lips against my ear. "We don't have to if you don't want to, if this is too weird for you." It was almost impossible to hear her soft voice over the music's bass, but I barely caught her words.

"If you're comfortable with it and won't let this turn weird between us afterwards then I'm fine with a dance or two. It's just... It's been a while since I've danced with a beautiful woman." More like a while since I've danced with someone who enamored me, but she definitely didn't need to know that.

"At least make the line believable." Hanna laughed and loosened her body up against mine when I chuckled in response and relaxed a bit.

"Believe what you want, but it's the truth." I merely shrugged her off with a half-smile before letting my body sway with hers to the music.

The more Hanna's hips gyrated against me, the more I started to regret agreeing to the dance because my stupid dick didn't get the memo to stay home. No doubt Hanna would feel it with how her hips swayed across the length of my hips and pressed into me. I only hoped it wouldn't kill the rhythm.

Whatever reason I had in my brain fled the moment I got carried away by Hanna's ministrations. My hands held her hips possessively against me as I ground back at her, matching her movements with my own as I let myself fade a little.

"You're packing tonight aren't you?" Hanna's sultry voice teased at my ear with a giggle as she slowed down her grind to press harder into me. "And I doubt that's your Korth I'm feeling."

"Can you blame me? I got the hottest girl in the club grinding her luscious ass against me." I couldn't tell if Hanna blushed at my words or if it was a reflection of the lights on her fair skin when the redness bloomed on her face.

Leaning my head down, I press my face into the side of her hair to take a quick whiff of her before chuckling into her ear. "Also, if you ever feel my gun anywhere besides its holster or tucked into the back of my pants, take it out and shoot me with it, especially if I'm stupid enough to stuff it down the front of my pants."

"And miss the chance to watch it blow up in your face? Or in that case blow off Stepan junior?" Hanna threw her head back in laughter before looking at me with a relaxed smile as she went back to grinding against me along with the beat of the music.

"You'd want the best part of me to be gone?" I teased back, holding back my cringe at the thought of any bits of me getting shot at—especially anything in my crotch area.

The little gleam in her eyes sparkled under the strobing lights, sending a soft shiver down my spine. "Sweetie, the best part of you isn't between your legs or in your pants, so I'll live." She whispered in my ear with a deep, teasing giggle. "Besides, you'll still have your fingers. Now hush and just dance with me for a little longer."

It didn't take long for us to fall into each other fully as if no one else existed in the place. Our bodies moved in sync like the natural flow of water down the river. If only we could rush over the edge and crash below like a waterfall. Too bad we flowed down into a walled dam.

We only intended to stay for a song or two at most, but time escaped us until Hanna brought reality back by dragging us back to the bar for one last drink. "Well, I probably shouldn't keep you long, it's getting late and I'm sure you need *some* sleep before going into the office tomorrow." She sounded almost disappointed with her words before finishing the rest of her drink with a blank smile.

Finishing the last of my drink, I slid off the stool and placed my hand on the small of her back, helping her off the stool. "Will you be fine to drive? Want me to have one of the people here take you home?" I hope to dear God she doesn't take the latter because I instantly regretted it once I put the idea out there.

Again, the thought of her being in the same space as another person had that icky feeling clutching at my chest. Even if I knew the guards here wouldn't—hopefully—try anything, she was a good-looking woman who could test any man's resolve.

"No, that's okay, I was just going to Uber home." She replied in a small voice after leaning up a bit so she was closer to my ear.

Just when I thought the feeling couldn't get any worse. Fuck it. "I'll drive you home. I won't let you get into some random person's car," I declared firmly as I guided us toward the underground parking garage.

"Yet you just recommended me to get into one of the worker's car, who would be a stranger to me by the way." She remarked with a chuckle and roll of her eyes.

"At least I know them, so I know you'll be safe in the end." And at the very least, I would know who to hunt down if a hair on her head was out of place.

"You don't have to, pretty sure you have—"

I cut her off by stopping and looking at her pointedly. "I'm taking you home, end of discussion little tigress. My business here is done for tonight, I was on my way to leave when I saw you by the bar and decided to make a little detour, so don't worry about me wasting time or anything on you. Now, you can either be a good girl and get in without a fight or I will put you in myself."

"Wow, controlling much?" She retorted with a soft snort and chuckle. "But fine, I'll be a good girl, for now."

I couldn't help but widen my smirk at the feeling of victory when she caved. "Good girl." The way her cheeks were flushed did good to pin the corners of my lips in a smirk, too.

"Holy shit." Not sure if she meant to say it out loud because of how whispery it came out, but her shocked reaction when we stopped at my McLaren was adorable. "I much prefer something more rugged like a Jeep Wrangler, but holy shit that is one sexy car."

Chuckling softly, I opened the passenger door and gestured for her to get in. "Is that why you were practically drooling when I showed you the company's garage and cars the other day?"

Honestly, I much preferred an SUV to a sports car or sedan because of the room and durability. No way could I ram someone with this delicate luxury car, but a nicely modified Range Rover or Land Cruiser was a perfect battering ram if need be. Also, I much preferred the room to store everything needed for my rifles.

"Sweetie, if only you knew. Seriously, I am so going to have so much fun driving half those vehicles around like a giddy girl at a fucking candy shop." She practically bounced on the tip of her toes as she giggled excitedly in her spot for a moment before hesitantly slipping into the seat.

"Man, I feel like I shouldn't be sitting in this sexy thing." Again, with a forced smile and chuckle despite her disappointment.

Leaning against the open door with a raised eyebrow, I looked at her intrigued. "Why would you say that?" Time to try and dig a little into her psyche.

Her smile softened sadly as she stared ahead. "I'm at the bottom rung of society, I don't deserve to be in the same space as anything luxurious."

"Hanna, no. You deserve everything because you're a damn queen in your own right. I don't want to hear any more of that kind of thinking and attitude from you from here on out or else." It disheartened me to see her have self-esteem issues because of how confident she held and displayed herself.

"Or else what?" She challenged with a cocky smirk as her wild eyes sharpened.

"There's my little tigress." I chuckled softly under my breath when I saw the woman I knew come back out. Leaning down close until our faces were mere inches away, I smirked at her knowingly. "Or else you'll find out how uncomfortable it'll be to sit with a burning ass."

"Oh? Don't make empty threats and promises there buddy. Don't you know it's rude to get a girl's hopes up?" Hanna leaned closer to me, narrowing her sharp eyes playfully and daringly.

"I don't make empty promises little tigress."

Fuck, I need to stop this.

Unwillingly, I pulled myself away before I did something the two of us might regret tomorrow. "Buckle up, we need to get you home." I shut the car door on her pouting face with a short chuckle.

Shakily, I took a deep breath and held it briefly before letting it out. I don't know what came over me just now, but I couldn't let it happen again.

As I rounded the front of the car to the driver's side, I recollected and steeled myself. Maybe it was a bad idea to drive her home. After that little exchange, a short car ride alone with her would be suffocating.

Hanna's soft voice and relaxed posture caught me off guard when I sat behind the wheel. "Hey, thanks again for doing this, you really didn't have to." Or maybe not; I guess she let things go faster than I anticipated.

"You gave me some of your time tonight and danced with me when you could have walked away, so it's the least that I can do." I wasn't going to let her know the reason why I didn't want her going off with someone else tonight was because I felt some kind of anger and possessiveness at the thought of it.

"Still, pretty sure you could have used some of the extra time for some sleep or something more productive than driving me home. But, thank you, really." At least she was grateful, and I couldn't help but return her smile with one of my own briefly before turning my attention to the area outside as I pulled the car out of its parking space.

"Trust me, if I didn't want to give you my time then I wouldn't have even glanced in your direction let alone go over to you." Might sound a little harsh, but it was the truth.

As I pulled into the street, I quickly fished my phone out of my pocket and handed it to Hanna after unlocking it. "Put your address into the navigation."

"What? Haven't memorized my address from my file yet?" She joked with a light laugh before I felt my phone slip from my hand.

Keeping my mouth shut, I let out a chuckle in response. I couldn't tell her what I wanted; it would be a little too creepy and forward. I couldn't tell her that her features were what I was too busy committing to my mind than her damn address.

Even when I've tried not to think about Hanna, she still pops up in my mind whenever I'm not fully occupied with work or other business-related things. She was a constant flash at every opening, as if reminding me of the mystery I've yet to solve.

The silent drive to her questionable apartment took little time, a little less than ten minutes with the speeding. One look at the area, and I could feel myself growing uncomfortable at the thought of her sleeping here at night.

"Again, thanks for the ride." She gave me another grateful smile after I threw the car into park.

"It really was no problem, I rather see you home safe myself. I'll walk you up." Like hell was I going to let her head up by herself.

"Stepan, you already drove me home, it's fine, I can still punch a handsy idiot if they try anything." She scoffed with a dismissive wave as she opened the door.

I probably would have been fine with any other woman on any other night, leaving them at that. Then again, any other woman and this treatment wouldn't even be happening.

Well, I'm just looking out for my employee, that's all.

At least, that was the lie I kept telling myself, and it would be the one for now.

Letting out a deep breath, I killed the engine and got out, quickly rounding the car to her side to get the door fully for her and holding my hand out. "Not going to take no for an answer little tigress."

Huffing, Hanna slumped her shoulders as she reached out, letting the rough pads of her fingertips dance across my rough palm before curling those slender, deft fingers of hers around my hand. I could feel her callouses before the softness of her palm pressed against mine as she fully grasped my closing hand.

Stiffly, I tensed my body when I felt her pull herself up and out of the car, letting her use me to steady herself once she was on her feet.

Shutting the car door with my free hand, I quickly reached into my pocket afterward to lock it. Then I let Hanna take the lead up to her place because I sure as hell didn't know where I would be going. Also, with me trailing behind her, at least I could cover her back or pull her back at the first sign of danger.

The dingy place didn't settle my nerves one bit as we made our way up the stairs, which creaked beneath our weight with each step. I could feel the slight give under my feet, and the disgusting, damp smell of mold assaulted my nose. I was surprised the thing didn't collapse and send me into a pile of rotting wood.

I knew not everyone could afford decent living, but seeing Hanna living in a place like this made my stomach churn. Just one look around, and I couldn't help but wonder if the damn locks on these crooked doors even remotely worked. Then, the thought of someone easily breaking into

Hanna's place in the middle of the night made my body heat up to where I could hear my heart pounding in my ears.

"Alright, I'm here, safe and sound, and in one piece." Hanna's crisp and honeyed voice cut through my budding anger.

My attention instantly zoned in on her as the buzzing in my ear dissipated. "Not until I see you go inside." I wouldn't be surprised if she got jumped the moment I turn away in this creepy place.

Rolling her eyes with a mocking pout of a frown, "Fine dad." She turned around and opened her door after fishing her keys out. Taking a step into her place, she pivoted on the heel of her foot and faced me with her arms wide open. "Happy? Still alive."

Well, she seemed laxed enough to keep my worry at bay. I doubt she'd be able to keep her playful eyes on me if someone was hidden in the place if there was even a spot to hide.

With one quick look from the wide open door, I could nearly see the whole studio apartment. The place was practically the size of my walk-in closet if I had to wager a guess. Actually, my closet might be bigger. The cramped place had her bed in the opposite corner of the door, with the kitchen on the other side and a door straight ahead, which led into a tiny ass bathroom. Oh, and her small closet right outside next to the bathroom door.

"Well, unless you're planning on tucking me in and reading my a good night story, you can go." There was that little snarky attitude of hers again, the one that made me want to grab her sometimes to teach her some manners.

Taking in a deep breath, I plastered a smile on my face as I shoved my strange urges away. Did I dare engage with her? It probably would be a bad idea. So, reluctantly, I swallowed my pride and eased back. "Clearly you're still alive and kicking. Well, I'll see you tomorrow in the office bright and early. Have a good night little tigress."

Very reluctantly, I backed up a few steps and watched as she closed the door, only leaving when I heard the faint *click* of the lock.

ROSE CHASE

It's a shame; seeing how far our little game of push and shove could've gone would've been fun.

Chapter 10
Stepan

SOMEONE'S ABOUT TO LOSE a damn hand.

And I'm about to lose a client, permanently.

"Thanks for the offer, but I don't date clients." Hanna was being a little too polite with rejecting the man we were protecting for my liking. I wouldn't mind if she twisted his arm and broke it. I might even turn my head and pretend not to see anything.

Unfortunately, this dumbbell didn't get the message because he continued to press. Even after Hanna threw his arm off from her hip, he reached back out and wrapped it around her curved waist to pull her closer to him again. "I won't be after a few hours, so I see no problems after you're done watching my back."

Hearing him say that made me groan internally because of the reminder. Hanna and I were only two hours into our five-hour protection detail, so we had to put up with this insufferable billionaire asshole for another three whole hours.

The company has done protection details for him before, all going off without any hitches, hence why he kept returning to my company for additional security when needed. I typically paid him no attention because he always paid well for the services, and never once have I gotten a complaint from any of the workers I've sent him. Yet, I started to rethink having him as a future client after he's kept his eyes locked on Hanna this whole time.

My balled fists were hidden from view inside the pockets of my suit jacket, continuing to tighten until my blunt nails dug into my palms. I wanted to reach out and pull the man away from Hanna and possibly shove him into the oncoming traffic.

Hanna looked up at the client with threatening eyes, forcing a smile through her clenched jaw. "Mister Hal, though I appreciate the thought, need I remind you of your own family? I don't think Missus Hal would appreciate your advances on me if she were to ever find out. So, remove your hand from me before I remove it myself again, and this time I won't be as nice."

Atta girl.

I couldn't help the proud little smirk from twitching at my lips as I mentally praised Hanna. Leave it to the crafty little minx to remain polite yet deadly.

The client promptly removed his arm from Hanna, returning it to his side with a forced smile. His response was terse and cold, "Aren't you a witty one." I didn't like the underlying bite to his voice.

Forcing a polite smile on my face, I reached out and settled my hand on his shoulder with a slight grip. "I only hire the best of the best, so don't forget that. I am always very mindful and watchful of them as well as my clients to ensure everyone's safety, so bear that in mind." I could deliver my own threats as well.

"I almost forgot, I have that meeting to go to." He quickly changed the subject as he jerked his shoulder forcefully out of my grip.

"Best we get you there in time then." Hanna chimed with a saccharine smile and slightly sharpened eyes.

"Hanna, why don't you go secure the area ahead and make sure his car isn't bugged." It was more of a command than a suggestion to give her a moment away from the client. I also wanted to get her out of the client's sight for a few minutes.

"Got it boss." At least her cheeky little smile was genuine with me before it disappeared from my view when she turned around and took off towards the parking garage.

The client's face instantly dropped and tightened threateningly as he looked at me with a sunken look. "You better keep your bitch in line Volkov."

"You better watch your tone with me Alfred, or you might find your company going under. These might be my services you are using, but do not forget who I am and what I am capable of. As for Hanna, I saw nothing wrong, just defending herself against a brainless man who can't get a hint. If you keep pushing her then I won't even bother holding her leash." As if I could even control Hanna, not that I wanted to anyway.

No, I didn't want to control her, at least not in some extreme manner. I didn't want to damper or offset her flamboyant personality.

Gripping his shoulder again, I applied more pressure than last time until he shrunk a little under my nearly crushing hold. "And just so you know, she doesn't bite." My eyes darkened, and my lips curled in a devious smirk as I locked my gaze with his paling face. "She mauls."

Not even a split second, and I put on my professional façade. "I believe we have a meeting to attend to." I urged him with a hard pat—shove—of his shoulder, jarring his body forward slightly.

"Didn't know you had favorites Volkov." Alfred sneered lowly with a scowling glare at me.

"I care about all my employees, you can go ahead and test my caring nature if you have a death wish or wish to see why they call me The Silent Volk. Don't forget who you work for at the end of the day Alfred, and we won't have any problems." He may be the company's client, but he worked for us at the end of the day.

His financial business was a good front for laundering and banking, and he owed us too much to pull anything unless he wanted to go to jail or die. I could care less about keeping him as a client for Volkov Inc., though, if it meant getting him away from Hanna. We could always find a new banker. We could handle things just fine ourselves thanks to my brother's wife, mainly her tech friend.

Fortunately for Alfred, he still had some use for the bratva; otherwise, we would've disposed of him. We had to keep him and his company safe in the meantime, hence the part about him being a client for my business and needing my protection details.

I guess my words of advice flew over his head by a mile because he proceeded to slip his arm around Hanna's shoulders after breaking away from me.

Now, I wasn't one for violence out of the gate, but there could be exceptions. I wouldn't hesitate one bit or lose any sleep over putting a bullet into Alfred. No, a bullet would be too easy, too clean. No, he would need to learn a lesson, which meant he would need a reminder. Perhaps lopping his hand off with a dull, rusty saw would be a nice lesson.

My violent fantasies about horrendous and torturous ways to remove Alfred's hand came to a halting screech when Hanna grabbed his arm and twisted it off herself and downwards, making Alfred bend down as his arm became contorted.

"Client or not, it does not give you the right to touch me, especially after I've made it clear that you should keep your hands to yourself." Hanna's overly sweetened smile made her look so hot and twisted.

Alfred whimpered with a grimace when Hanna's grip on his wrist tightened to where I could see the veins on his discolored hand bulge. "Keep this in mind the next time you think about laying a finger on me mister Hal."

God, the way she looked down on him while making him cower was so arousing. I could feel the ache between my legs start to pulse as my member pressed against my pants.

Discreetly, I shifted my legs, fidgeting with my hands in the pockets of my pants to try and adjust my growing erection to hide it against my inner thigh.

Fucking hell, just when I thought I couldn't get more enamored by her. I wouldn't mind her roughing me around one bit.

Swallowing the lump in my throat, I brought a hand up to my face, sweeping it across my lower jaw to hide my amused and excited smirk. My other hand remained in my pocket, holding down my throbbing length to keep it from making a noticeable bulge in my slacks.

My fucked-up mind would have more ammunition to play with late at night now as if the past two nights weren't bad enough.

After dropping her home the other night, I gave my brain too many ideas. Seeing and feeling her body in that little, tight, strapless black dress with her ass barely covered did me in finally. I couldn't get her out of my mind since that night. I never realized how inked up her body was until that night, and seeing the intricate art covering nearly the whole right half of her body from her chest down to her calf made shivers of pleasure trickle down my spine.

If she was some quick lay, then I would have shoved her up against the wall of the alleyway or brought her up to the office and bent her over the desk. The short dress she wore that night barely did anything to hide her round, bubbly ass. It would've been too easy to hike it up to gain access to her.

"Stepan." My name wouldn't sound so pointed like just now. I imagined it to be sweet and whispery when I'd bring her to the brink of pleasure, not like some annoyed person whining my name.

Inhaling a long, shaky breath through my nose, I peered down at Hanna since my 6'2 figure towered over her 5'0 stature. "Hm? Sorry, was thinking about a project back at the office." I lied smoothly through my teeth with a smile.

"Someone needs to get their head in the game." Hanna teased with a cheeky smile and scrunched her face as she stuck her tongue out at me.

Unfortunately, my head was nowhere near the playing area, let alone near the game.

Chapter 11
Stepan

SMACK!

"Fuck!"

My hand slapped against the tile wall of my shower again as I let out another shudder from the aftershock of my release.

My heavy breaths were sharp and ragged as I hung my head against the shower wall, letting the hot water pelt my hunched back. I'd given into my body's demands for a release for the second time this morning in the hope it would settle, hence why I didn't bother with the freezing water today because it would only be a bigger problem later if I didn't try to stroke it out now.

I can't believe I resorted to jacking off in the shower, though. I had my easy pickings of females to curb my needs, yet none of them appealed in the slightest to me. It embarrassed me to admit it, but I couldn't physically sleep with another woman ever since I became hung up on Hanna.

My teeth were already aching from all the tension and gritting, yet I found myself grinding them again as I let out a strained, growling groan. "Fucking hell." I snarled under my breath through my teeth, slamming the shower wall again but with an open palm this time.

The tension still ached at my muscles even though I came twice this morning already, and still not an ounce of relief. My pulsating length remained hard as steel in my tight grasp, and I got more fed up with every passing second. It's barely been a whole week, and somehow, my mind's wrapped around Hanna's tantalizing little body. Of all the women I could be drawn to, it had to be the one I could probably never have.

If I were insane enough, then I'd entertain the thought of kidnapping Hanna and locking her somewhere far away. Besides it being a foolish idea, I'd get no pleasure out of it. I wanted her to want me, to crave me as much as I craved her. I wanted to invade and occupy her mind like she invaded and conquered mine.

Huffing heavily, I reluctantly released myself, slamming both my open palms against the wall and pushing myself up straight. I needed to get out of the damn shower and get on with my day before I let myself become consumed by the little tigress.

At least my erection settled by the time I finished showering and got dressed, and my sexual frustration ebbed enough by the time I got to the office—thank God.

Thankfully, she wasn't physically around my field of vision either because I didn't know if I could keep myself in full check if I saw her feisty face right now. Unfortunately, her melodic voice echoed clearly throughout the place as she conversed with someone, effectively lighting a fire under my already boiling kettle.

Ignore her, just ignore her, go to your office, shut it, ignore-

"Don't you still have that report to do Dave?" I mentally scolded myself for letting my control slip the moment I caught the close distance between Hanna and another worker out of the corner of my eye.

I barely managed to force a fake, friendly smile while doing my best to keep my irritability from slipping through my voice.

"On your desk boss, just like you wanted." The little shit dared turn his goofy, smiling face back to Hanna, who seemed a little too attenuative in response.

"Hanna, I need to talk with you in my office about your assignment today." My legs ached to stride over to Hanna and position myself between her and Dave.

It irked me to see her attention on him or anyone for that matter. The feeling gnawed at my chest again, making me want to scowl to display my disdain.

Smiling innocently, Hanna gave me a small wave of dismissal, making me feel like some annoying fly to be shooed away. "Oh, Lev already gave me my assignment for today, that's what I was talking to Dave about actually. So, don't worry, you don't have to put up with me this morning."

Fucking Lev, the one time he *doesn't* need to do his damn job, he does it.

It was a struggle to maintain the empty smile on my face to seem polite and hide my turbulent emotions. "Oh, then carry on then." No, please don't, because I might end up needing to hide a damn body and fill another open spot if she did.

Hanna instantly turned her attention back to Dave, who seemed more than happy to have it all to himself again.

Did she know what she was doing? Was this on purpose?

It felt like a hammer to my chest when she dismissed me so quickly. Judging from her relaxed body and genuine expressions, she clearly didn't have any ill intentions with her actions and words. Unless she was a damn good actor, it was all in my damn head.

Annoyed, I softly clicked my tongue as I silently slipped into my office, shutting—slamming—the door harder than I intended. Then, one of my irritations sat smugly on the couch to make matters worse.

"What's a matter Stepan? Didn't catch enough sleep?" The lift to Lev's jovial tone, paired with his loosely smug grin and teasing eyes, told me all I needed to know.

The little fucker knew fully well what he did.

"Hanna's fitting in real well I'll say. You know, we should just forgo the rest of her trial period and hire her already. I mean, she's perfect and *everyone* in the office loves her little sparky personality. Always coming in with an excited grin on her face, the little pep and bounce to her step as people like to say, and always dressed in the most—"

THUD!

Lev's heavy body hit the floor with a winded grunt.

Standing above him with a coy smirk, I looked down at him with playful, narrowed eyes. "Sorry, thought I saw something under your foot."

It was too easy to grab Lev by his ankle and throw him onto the ground. Lev had his legs thrown up on the coffee table with his ankles crossed, and his body was stretched out from how he leaned back into the couch with his arms behind his head.

Catching him off guard in such a relaxed state was child's play to me. Even if he was heavier than me, using his legs to twist and pull him off the seating area made his size mean nothing to me.

"*Blyat'*." Lev strained out while glaring up at me. "Okay, but I kind of deserve that." He groaned softly in pain, slowly sitting up by using the edge of the table as support.

Dropping my smirk, I glared deeply at him as my lips dropped into a small scowl. "Ya think?" My leg twitched with an itch to shoot out and kick Lev, playfully, of course.

Just some brotherly love, no actual hostility. I knew Lev was being a teasing little shithead with his words, being the troublesome little brother, but it still twisted my gut the wrong way. So, the temptation to bully him a little to put him back in his place itched at my limbs.

Out of the five of us, Lev was probably the biggest nuisance, in a good way. He was always the troublemaker, stirring up trouble *whenever* he could, no matter how small or big the mess would be. In hindsight, it was all a vie for attention, then pretty sure it was to rebel against our bastard of a father, and at this point in his life, it was a habit, surely.

I should have known better now than to turn my back on Lev in moments like these, but that would be a lesson I'd never learn because I found myself on the ground with the wind knocked out of me and Lev laughing in the background.

The fact he'd grabbed my ankles and tripped me didn't register in my dazed mind until I recovered a minute later. "*Ty, razdrazhayushch-eye malen'koye der'mo.*" I grumbled playfully with a curled upper lip.

Using my arms, I pushed myself backward and kicked my leg out to catch Lev in the chest, knocking him backward onto the floor again.

"*Bratok* has a little crush, how cute." Lev teased with a cheeky little snicker from his position on the floor. "Not that I can blame you, she is quite—"

"Finish that sentence and I'll really lay your ass out." There wasn't a hint of playfulness with how low my voice dropped with my threatening gaze.

At least Lev knew when to back off after all these years of being on the receiving end of many fulfilled threats.

Softly grunting, Lev leaps back up to his feet before straightening himself out with a quick pat down of his hands. "In all seriousness though, we should just hire her. She can kick ass, follow rules like you want, isn't a hot head like me but is as efficient and hardworking like me. Honestly, unless she's a druggie after hours or partakes in very unsavory business, I say we take her on board already. I mean, you haven't found any kind of dirt on her. Sure, her record has some holes in it, but could they be any worse than the men we have employed?"

Unfortunately, I couldn't argue much with Lev because he made valid points, but there was one I could still dig at. "The fact she has so many large holes is holding me back. Yes, our men are probably worse, but at least we know them or have some kind of connection with them. Hanna is a complete stranger to us." Nearly all the men under our employment were connected to our bratva, so they weren't outstanding citizens by any means.

"We should really just give her a chance, I've got a really good feeling about her." Lev's voice lightened almost pleadingly when he stopped sounding like some salesman.

Jokingly, I sneered at him, "Yeah, a good feeling between your legs." I knew what he meant, but I still felt a little pissy.

Maybe I should have let it go and taken the higher road because Lev ran with the inch he got from me. "Well, can you blame me? She's feisty, got a killer body with nice ass tats, knows how to take care of herself, and her ass is something else man."

"And exactly how do you know she's got tattoos?" I couldn't control my apprehension as I jealously narrowed my eyes at Lev.

I only knew she had ink on her body because I happened to run into her at the club the other night. From my knowledge, she and Lev have never interacted outside of the office, and Hanna was always covered up around the place. So, how the hell did he know, or when did he get a chance to take a peek at her?

"Oh, we sparred for a while when you had your meeting the other day and her shirt ended up ripping in the middle of it because we were being too rough with each other. She can really pack a punch and kick by the way, still a little sore from where she landed a solid one on me." Lev's unbothered attitude with his little blip of giddiness pissed me off tremendously.

I shouldn't be feeling a tad bit murderous towards my younger brother for that, but I couldn't help the red-faced monster from making its appearance in me.

I was jealous and angry. Lucky little bastard got to lay his hands on her and see her artful body, things that only I should be doing.

It was so wrong to have all these intense feelings, though, all over some girl I've barely met. I'm fucking enamored with her, and I don't know why.

No, I do know why. The why was because she's a mystery, yeah, that's why. I'm a little obsessed with her because I need to fill in the holes of her life to sate my curiosity. I needed to know everything about Hanna to settle my paranoia.

I was just overly curious about her, which is why I wanted her, not because I desired something more. This morning was a fluke; my stupid hormones and pent-up sexual frustration clouded my mind. I just needed to figure her out. Figure out her background, her past, and her future. I wanted—no needed—to know every aspect of her.

To know her daily routines, frequented places, habits, and quirks. Then, I wanted to know what makes her happy and smile and how to make that happen. And more importantly, I needed to know how Hanna felt—particularly under me.

Unfortunately, all of the pondering in the world had to wait until after my collections run because I couldn't afford to be distracted, not unless I wanted to get injured or lose my life. The wisest option would've been to take Lev up on his offer to do the run for me, but I needed the fresh air to get away from the office, away from *her*.

Going on a collection run with a muddled mind might bite me in the ass, but I wasn't too worried. Too bad the same couldn't be said toward my older brother—Nikolai—who called me the moment I settled into the car with some of the other men.

With one annoyance off my mind, another quickly filled its spot. "Hey, you don't have to if you don't got the time, I can always send Arseny. Besides, you have that assignment later tonight too, or did you forget?" The brief and lighthearted greeting didn't last long after I picked up Nikolai's phone call. Granted, he wasn't one to sweet talk or beat around the bush.

The buildings outside passed by in a blur as the car sped down the streets. "It's just a quick collection run, I'll be fine. Besides, I've dealt with this idiot before, so it'll be a piece of cake. He won't get violent or gun happy, he's more of a runner than a shooter. His guards won't stand a chance against me or our men either, so don't worry. Besides, I needed this to get some fresh air." I admitted to him with an inaudible sigh. "And no, I didn't forget about tonight, and again, don't worry, we'll be fine."

"You know I'm never going to stop worrying about you all, especially you after hearing shit from Lev." Nikolai's deep and devious chuckle meant no good would come out of his mouth next.

"If this is about my little office crush then go shove it back up Lev's ass because he doesn't know what he's talking about." I groaned and rubbed my temples as I made a mental note to give Lev an ass kicking later for being a little snitch to our older brother.

"There's nothing wrong with liking a girl Stepan, just be smart about it is all I'm going to say. Turn up that charm and get her so Lev can stop coming to me for being a little shit towards you and her." Nikolai soft laugh made my eyes roll.

As if it was that easy. If it were, I'd spend time with Hanna instead of going on this collection assignment with my stewing thoughts. Sure, I probably did need to get my head out of my ass, but Hanna didn't make this any easier than it needed to be.

"Well, like you're the one to talk, you literally crashed into your wife's life then married her on second sight. Not exactly mister smooth yourself. As if you even had to woo your woman to get her." I would never stop giving him shit for the arranged marriage crap he pulled, even if it did work out fine after the fact.

"You make it sound like Angel doesn't give me hell herself or that since we're married I got it easy." Nikolai mused with a chuckle before the faint voice of Angel could be heard in the background, something about how she was a joy and the best thing to ever happen to him.

"Go appease your wife before she stabs you in your sleep." I remarked with a chuckle before we both bid each other farewell for now.

Well, I had to go anyway because I arrived at my destination. The curbside right outside the building doors was reserved for the owner, but I didn't give a shit. I was above him because our bratva supplied him with the means to keep his business running.

A single man remained at the wheel while the other three followed me into the building, where we walked past the line of people and beyond. "Excuse me, sir, you can't—" One curt glare was all it took for the receptionist to back off and let my men and I continue on our merry way up the elevator to the top floor where the C. E. O.'s office was located.

Pulling my gun out, I set my Korth NxR dead center of the beaten wooden desk before getting comfortable in the stiff office chair once I exited the elevator and booked it for the office. "You'd think he'd spruce the place up a bit with all the money we feed him." I thought out loud with a scoff.

"He's too busy wasting it away on girls above his pay grade." One of the guards mused with a ridiculing chuckle.

"Well, when you're a half-balding pig with a dick the size of a thumbnail, then you gotta pay for even decent pussy." Another chimed in with a snicker.

"If I ever have to pay to get laid then put me out of my misery." I joined in with my own scoffing chuckle. "Idiot's gotta get his priorities straight though, this is the third time he's been late with payment."

"Oh? Target practice for ya boss?" The others loved watching me shoot down non-compliant clients after too many strikes. "Think you can hit a running target from nearly a mile away?"

"Are you challenging me again Garett? After how much money you lost out on the last bet?" My eyebrow rose with my lopsided smirk as I leaned back in the chair with my arms behind my head and my feet kicked up on the desk.

"Quit making bets with him, you're only gonna stroke his already huge ass dick of an ego and make all the girls go to him." The guard next to him piped up, smacking his buddy in the arm.

"Well, whenever I do get a chance to snipe someone down again, I'll take another bet with you. One last chance for mister Hordile this time, but we won't leave without giving him one last proper warning so he won't be late next time or ever if he wants to continue doing business with us." I rather cut our losses with this slimeball, but Nikolai was adamant on keeping him strung with us until we siphoned all his assets.

Our conversation cut out from the office door swinging open with a fury to reveal an apple-faced man who huffed and puffed as if he would kneel over any second now. "You've some nerve Volkov! Marching into my business like this and breaking into my office!" Maybe the trip up here winded him so much that his brain suffered some damage from lack of oxygen because he was being a complete, brainless idiot.

Throwing my feet back to the ground, I leaned up and narrowed my eyes at him in warning. "Unless the next words out of your mouth are about the payment you owe the bratva, I don't want to hear it." To make my point clear, I reached over and placed my hand on my revolver on the desk.

The three guards by his side instantly pulled their pieces out and pointed them at me while my men took their aim at the guards in return. "I ain't paying you or your brothers shit anymore, so get out of here before I send you to your family in a coffin."

I couldn't help but laugh a little in mockery at his smugness. "I can shoot down all three before they get a chance at me, or at the very least my men would get them before they get me. As for whether or not you do business with us is not up to you at this point. Either you pay the protection fee and what you owe us, or we take you for all you have and leave you more homeless than a transient." Call me cocky and arrogant as fuck for tooting my own horn, but I didn't talk out of my ass; I'd very well back up my words without a shadow of a doubt.

"It'd be a shame for your wife's drug problems to be all across the internet. It would not look good for your little campaign of running for governor, nor would it do your precious children any good to have the rep of having a druggie mother and a corrupted father their whole lives. If you think I'd stop at just you then you better fucking think again Hordile." I overly dragged out my uncaring sigh as I let my fingers dance across the cold metal barrel of my gun. "I'd take every single penny from you and ruin you and your family for generations to come." It would suck for his family, but what happens to them would all be on him. So, he had no one but himself to blame.

It would suck the most for the children, but they'd learn to recover. Worst comes to worst, they create a whole new identity for themselves and turn their backs on their parents, who weren't really that good to begin with. Financially, they padded their spawns well, but other than that, mother was too busy with her head higher than the clouds while their father stuck his sorry excuse of a manhood into caverns of diseases with whoever he could pay off the street for a romp.

"You wouldn't... You're not a heartless bastard like your father." Oh, he wanted to pull that card now, huh?

My hollow chuckle trembled in the air before my dark, empty eyes settled on a rather nervous cue ball of a man. "You're right, I'm not as heartless. If I were anything like my father then we wouldn't even be having this conversation. You would have been flayed alive the second time you were late, your wife would have been thrown into a whore house, and you don't want to know what would have happened to your children. But if you for one second doubt what I'd do then I guess I have to step things up again."

Without a single sign of a warning, I lifted the gun and fired off three shots faster than a blink of an eye before training my aim on Holdile while the bodies of his guards dropped like flies around him. Using my free hand, I fished my phone out of my pocket to pull up one of our bank accounts. "If the money you owe us along with the interest doesn't show up in the next five seconds, you'll have the pleasure of meeting Nikolai's wife to find out why people fear her more than the Devil Volk himself."

The man trembled in his spot, but his hands and feet remained glued to his sides and the floor. "Five." My patient ran ice-thin. "Four."

That seemed to spur him into action with how he frantically fumbled for his phone in his pocket and began tapping away at it with shaky fingers. Seconds later, the numbers of the bank account on my screen jumped up in amount, bringing a somewhat satisfied smirk to my face as I got up from the ratty chair and walked over to him.

"Pleasure doing business with you."

BANG! BANG!

Chapter 12
Hanna

"WOW, IF BEING MARRIED changes you this much then I don't know if I wanna be married. I mean, my life is my life, I do whatever the fuck I want when I want. Why should I have to compromise with my partner and cut my fun?"

In all reality, Angel's husband wasn't shabby from what's been spilled to me so far by her, but I complained for the sake of it because Angel had decided last minute to stay home to not worry Nikolai.

I missed having my best girl next to me on the field, mainly because I didn't trust anyone but Angel fully to have my back. Even if I got along with all our men and players, it was only on the surface. Angel was the only person I trusted blindly without a single ounce of hesitation.

"Hanna, relationships, any relationship, is all about compromise. Even our friendship is full of compromises. I accept the fact that you love to beat people up, so I point you in the right direction instead of trying to stop you." Angel pointed out with a little raise in her voice that made her sound amused.

"Wha? Our friendship isn't filled with compromise, it just works because it's us." It was clear from my high-pitched voice that I wasn't convinced one bit, but I'll be damned if I let Angel take the win this early in our conversation.

It's not like I could argue with her either way because she was entirely correct.

"Now what is really bothering you bitch?" And there she goes picking at my life.

Sighing softly, I continued driving silently for a few seconds before responding to Angel. "I was just hoping you'd be here to lessen the surprise with Stepan and Lev." Also, there was another last-minute adjustment, which I wasn't aware of until about two hours ago.

"You're overthinking it, they ain't gonna flip out or anything, and they're coming in with the full mindset of following someone else's orders. So, don't worry about any conflict there. Besides, this is a very good time to show Stepan what you're really made of without any restraints." Angel still tried to lessen my nerves with her reassuring words and voice.

This would be the first time I'd see Stepan and Lev outside of work, not counting that one club run-in with Stepan of course. Both were still oblivious to my connection with Angel and the triad, so everything would come out of the bag tonight.

"Hanna, you've done a shit ton of things without me before without making a big deal out of it." Angel retorted with a soft chuckle that sounded a little muffled and buzzed through the phone speaker because my car didn't have the capability to have Bluetooth.

"I know, I know. I just..." I didn't know how to finish my train of thought without sounding like some brainless idiot.

"Hanna, Stepan's not going to run for the hills after seeing you beat a man's face off tonight." Angel half-joked with another chuckle, but this one sounded a little hesitant.

"I'm not worried about Stepan and what he thinks." I retorted almost instantly, scrunching my face in discomfort when images of Stepan's smiling and smirking face flooded my mind.

I might complain about not having anyone in my life, but it was meant in jest most of the time to give the others some grief. I couldn't allow myself to be vulnerable like that to anyone.

No matter how much my heart yearned for attention and affection, I would rather hurt myself by shutting the doors to everyone rather than suffer tremendous heartbreak.

I could hear a long sigh scratch at my speaker before Angel's drawn-out voice replied. "Hanna, you can't bullshit me. I know it's not easy for you, but if you're going to try with anyone then Stepan would be a great choice if you get the feeling that there's a mutual affection between the two of you." No doubt she had a small, sad frown right now from how she sounded. "Or, as I said before, fuck him out of your system."

My tense face twisted into a grimace as my hands gripped the steering wheel painfully. "No." No matter how much my heart ached to be denied, better me than someone else.

"Hanna, don't do this to yourself." Angel sounded like she chided me, disappointed almost.

"I'm doing this for myself. I know what I'm doing Ange. It's my life, and I'm doing what I need to preserve it." The curtness of my tone should be enough of an indicator for Angel to drop the subject.

A long, heavy sigh blared at my speakers before a few seconds of silence followed. "Good luck out there tonight. Give them hell." Her words sounded forced; I could still hear the underlying heaviness of her voice.

"Don't worry Ange, when do I not give them hell?" I had to force myself to laugh a little to better my mood.

"They're going to shit their pants the moment they see you." At least the dark chuckle was fully genuine.

"Alright, I'm pulling up. Rest easy Ange, we'll report back to you once everything is all done." I assured her with a smile before hanging up after she said goodbye in response.

Sighing heavily, I white-knuckled my steering wheel as I fought the discomfort furling under my chest. I had a little less than five minutes to pull myself together. I had a little less than five minutes to prepare myself to face Stepan.

Breathing deeply, I released one hand from the wheel to run it down my face. Groaning out of frustration, I let my hand linger against the right side of my face.

This is for your own good.

I had to remind myself the rest of the way as I pulled my steel walls back up.

As I pulled up to our meeting area, where other vehicles were parked, I saw that everyone had made themselves comfortable in one large group. They weren't loud, but I could hear their faint conversation and laughter the moment I parked and killed the engine.

"Finally, there she is! Oh man, you two are in for one hell of a night if she's coming out to play." I could hear one of the men say proudly when I opened my door.

"Hm? Who?" The one voice I could pick out from a crowded room with ease hit my eardrums, making me shiver from the pleasure of his deep voice.

"The Beast, that's who." Not sure if it was the same man from before who answered, but someone did with a twisted chuckle.

"I'm about to make you my bitch if you don't shut up." I threatened playfully with a sneer, shutting the car door and turning to look at everyone.

"Hanna?" Stepan's quick shock was expertly covered within seconds after his eyes landed on me.

"That's my name, don't wear it out." I teased cheekily with a wink and snicker.

Too bad this was no fairytale.

There's no Beauty to this Beast.

Chapter 13
Stepan

ONCE AGAIN, I ENCOUNTERED Hanna where I least expected it.

Unable to help myself, I let my careful eyes roam her body head to toe, taking in her strong and petite body clad entirely in black tactical gear. I didn't think anyone could make tactical gear look good, let alone sexy. I thought seeing her in the tiny black dress from before would be the cusp of it, yet she stood here so powerful and proud. I couldn't help the feeling of excitement from rushing down my body to my nether regions, making my member twitch to life.

Thank god for these thick tactical pants of mine. Otherwise, I'd be standing here awkwardly with a very obvious lump. Well, and thankfully, I happened to have my rifle positioned right across my body, so it helped hide my erection, too.

Hanna's thick, black hair was pulled back in a tantalizing ponytail. The sight of it and the sway of her hips as she approached us made me want to reach out and grab her by it. My fingers curled temptingly as I fought the urge to thread them through her black hair.

"Wait, you're *that* Hanna? Angel's best friend Hanna?" At least Lev saved me the embarrassment of not realizing it sooner.

Grinning and giggling, she stopped before us with her arms crossed loosely around herself. "The one and only, so don't you forget me." Glad to see Hanna was just as confident and boisterous outside of work.

"Damn, small world, I mean, what are the chances." Lev chuckled, reaching out and patting Hanna on the shoulder, only to quickly retreat his hand when he caught me glaring at him from the corner of my eyes.

"Why didn't you tell us you were Angel's friend?" Surely, she knew of us from Angel at the very least, so why keep that matter a secret?

"I didn't want it to possibly affect your guy's view of me. But don't take any offense to any of it, I just almost never mention my affiliation and relationship to Angel to keep the separation between me and the triad from people so I can live my life in peace somewhat. I mean, I have a bit of a reputation too, and not many people are keen on hiring someone known as The Beast in the streets." At least she had valid points.

Usually, I wouldn't let an applicant's affiliations affect my decision in their hire, but I would have in Hanna's case if I knew because anyone who worked with Angel had to be top-tier and solid. She would have been instantly hired on the spot if I knew based on what I knew about my sister-in-law.

"Fair, I won't fault you for any of it." I really couldn't, not when I would have done the same thing in her shoes.

It was honorable how she wanted to make her own name for herself, and I couldn't help but feel a little proud with a soft smile that I hid behind my hand after brushing it across my jaw.

"Well, seems like everyone is here, and I'm assuming you all heard the update from Bao or Greg at this point, but I'm in charge tonight bitches. So, you all better listen closely because I don't want to repeat myself." The atmosphere instantly weighed down gravely when Hanna's voice shifted from playful to stern.

"Simple assignment tonight. The police just need us to make a mess, take out some of the enemy's manpower, and make their case easy for them. I'll split everyone up into four teams, three ground teams and one sniper team who will take place in the guard towers. The ground team will enter and fan out to cover the perimeter and advance forward in a pincer movement to force the enemies to the docks. Snipers will be in charge of being our eyes and picking off stragglers. Any questions or problems so far?"

Yes, a very big, hard problem.

My clenched jaw remained hidden behind my hand which should just be glued to the lower half of my face at this point.

I could always appreciate a powerful woman or a woman in charge, but something about Hanna specifically made my body burn. Seeing her take charge aroused me so much.

It was funny, though, because I always liked to be the one in charge, and never have I ever been turned on by a woman displaying authority over anyone or anything, let alone over me. Yet, the brief thought of Hanna taking control over me made sparks of excitement bite at my body.

When no one made any indication of speaking up, Hanna continued. "Angel wants us to keep damage and causalities to a minimum, so out of respect for her let's keep that in mind. On the other hand, we all know what's best in the moment, and I rather have the enemy's body drop than one of ours."

The next few minutes were filled with Hanna flushing out the rest of the plan, splitting our group of sixteen into teams, and directing us to our positions on the map that Bao had brought.

Once everyone agreed with each other, we all busied ourselves around the vehicles to arm and stock ourselves properly.

Lev and I took less time than the others because we had already come mostly prepped, so the two of us checked our equipment while the others got ready.

Unfortunately, my rifle didn't distract me for long. I was quick to approach Hanna to lend a hand after pushing my rifle—which was slung across my body by a strap—behind me after seeing Hanna struggle a little with the straps of her body holster. As cute and amusing as it was, I could see her frustration grow with her tense and scrunching face.

"Hanna." I gave her huffing, pouty face a knowing look as I stood before her. "Arms up." I commanded sternly with a small upward lifting gesture of my hand.

Pursing her lips, she glared at me softly with defeat as she raised her arms above her head. "Thanks..." She muttered as I fixed her straps accordingly.

The innocent idea remained good until I invaded her personal bubble and touched her. If there was a wall behind us, then I would have shoved her against it, grabbed those tiny wrists of hers into one hand, and kept them pinned above her head against the wall while my other hand would have made quick work of her clothes.

I was so tempted to slide my hands down to her waist and grip her hips to pull her flush against me when I laid my hands on her curvy waist. The other tempting option would have been to go north and cup a feel of her delicate breasts. They weren't big by any means, maybe a good handful from a quick look, but not like I would complain as long as they were hers. Though on the smaller side, the straps of her holster framed them perfectly to where they popped slightly.

"Not too tight or loose?" Highly doubtful of the latter, considering how I cinched her in good, but I had to be sure.

"Nope, perfect, thank you." It was almost easy to miss how her breath hitched ever so slightly with how well she covered it with her confidence.

"Guns ready? Extra magazines stocked? Knives where they should be?" Fretting over her was second nature.

After all the years of looking over my brothers, it had become instinct for me to always ensure they were ready and to double-check their status before anything went down. It was a trait my father had drilled into me at a young age that never left. At least it was something good and not bad.

Being the second oldest meant I had to look out for Nikolai and my younger brothers. I had to have Nikolai's back and protect the others by being their cover. At least, that's all my bastard of a father ever drilled into me, along with making sure I would be one of the best snipers out there.

"Yes dad." Hanna snarked playfully with a roll of her eyes.

Keeping my mouth shut for both our sakes, I only offered my rolling eyes in response to her. I wanted to tell her to keep up the attitude so I'd have a damn good reason to bend her over my knee like the petulant brat she was.

Yeah, that would not have been good to say out loud, considering where we were right now and our standing with each other. I'd run her off before getting a chance at her.

"Bolt action? Wouldn't a semi be more faster and efficient?" She questioned curiously with a nod at my rifle.

"Typically, yes, but I prefer the accuracy of bolt actions, and it's what I was trained on. Never could switch over to semis after the bolt actions became ingrained into me. As for speed, I've got it down to milliseconds." More like I had to get it down to milliseconds to avoid getting my ass beat.

The phantom feeling of pain in my hands made me curl and uncurl them a few times to shake the feeling away. No matter how long it's been, memories of my father standing over me and beating me for not being fast enough always made my hands ache.

My hands and fingers would be shaking so badly because of my exhaustion, but he didn't care. Anytime I'd drop a bullet, it was a stomp to my hand. Couldn't pull the pin fast enough? Kick to the shoulder. Didn't hit the target good enough? My head would be in the ground.

No rest until everything was perfect to his standards.

Reluctantly, I started to shift my body away from Hanna. "Well, I'm going to head out with the other sniper and get into position. Be careful and safe out there."

"Always am, but knowing you're up and out there watching me makes me feel a hundred times safer."

Oh little tigress, I'll never take my eye off of you. Ever.

Chapter 14
Hanna

"TEAM ALPHA IS IN position. What's everyone else's status?"

There was a brief pause over the communications system following my question before a wave of shivers washed down my body.

"Snipers in position." Hearing his deep, smooth voice flowing through my earpiece was almost as good as having him beside me.

"Beta team in position." The familiar voice of my friend Greg was like a bucket of cold water, snapping me back fully to the situation at hand.

"Team Delta, status?" I asked tensely.

I had put Lev in charge of Delta, and he was usually pretty good with updates. The fact I've had radio silence from him since the teams have split was a little concerning.

"C...py..." The response was staticky and choppy.

"Looks like there was a small dead zone, hold on, let me try to correct it." My concern didn't die down one bit from Bao's response.

It only fully washed away with relief when I heard Lev's voice loud and clear. "Team Delta, does anyone copy?"

"This is Hanna, we can hear you loud and clear now." The worry about this simple raid going off the rails from the beginning was mute now.

It would have been a horrible impression on Stepan and Lev if shit hit the fan so quickly like that.

"Good. Well, Delta is in position." Lev's confirmation made my chest deflate from the large breath I had been holding.

"Stepan, how are things looking? Are we clear to advance?" I could only see so far beyond the scattered crates of the shipyard.

The last thing I wanted was to lead us straight into enemy fire or tip off the enemy of our presence sooner than needed.

"Everyone is gathered at the dock waiting for the ship, twenty total on the ground. Ship is a few yards out still, but it's coming on schedule from the looks of it. There are ten armed men on the ship guarding two cargo containers. There could possibly be more under that I can't see or account for. The teams are cleared to advance with caution, just don't go past the last row of cargo crates." It should be illegal for him to sound so damn good giving me a report like that.

"B-Boy chiming in, confirming all that Stepan said. Thermal sweeps from my drones confirms body count as thirty total, no surprises in the ship's haul." Bao's confirmation was all I needed to give the command to advance.

Bodies would need to drop to give us an advantage. There were only fifteen of us total, half of the enemy numbers. We needed to even out the playing field. Two snipers were in the guard towers, and the ground team was split into three groups of four each.

"Snipers, once they dock fully, take out the ship men, all of them." Taking out the ten should even out the playing field for us nicely.

"Copy that." My two snipers replied one right after another.

Silently and stealthily, my team and I weaved through the rows of cargo crates as we pushed forward. Thankfully, there weren't any scattered guards to deal with.

The faint chatter of the enemy became clearer the closer we got until every single word could be heard from our hidden positions behind the very last row of crates.

"Think they'll survive this time?" I heard one of the men ask.

"If they listened. I really hope they did because I don't want to get my ass reamed again." Another voice replied.

"It was a shame, they were pretty ones too." A third voice joined whatever conversation went on.

"Lost the girls and the drugs, Lady Qing was not happy one bit, same with the old fart she's working with." The second voice spoke up again.

Damn, Angel wouldn't be happy to hear about this later. She's had her suspicions about Nikolai's new business partner double dipping with the triad. If this conversation was what I assumed, things would get messy later on.

The eerily silent night was broken by the sound of multiple gunshots that cracked at the air like a whip. Panic from the enemy side broke out after the fourth shot. The sounds of their shuffling feet filled the air, along with orders to seek and shoot.

"Everyone cover your eyes and ears." I warned before throwing a flash bomb into the enemy crowd.

I waited for the telltale sign of utter chaos from the enemy, getting their sights stunned before giving the command to charge in.

Upon rushing in, my fisted hand instantly shot out at the first person in reach, clocking them in the face with a satisfied grin when I felt something give under the force. Throwing my leg out, I kicked the guy back, causing him to fall back into his comrade right behind him. Both of them went tumbling to the ground on top of each other, and I didn't give any of them a chance to recover to their feet by delivering a swift kick to their heads, knocking them out.

"Damn, wish I had a bat." I grumbled to myself while pulling my gun out to shoot at a man with his gun pointed at Greg.

Don't get me wrong, guns are fun, but just something about a good old beating settled nicely with me. There's nothing like pummeling a man down with my own two fists to get my adrenaline and anger out of me fully. Or a good old beating with a bat or crowbar works, too, but preferably my fists.

My eyes locked onto the barreling man charging at me. The reasonable thing to do would be to dodge the man because he was going fast and twice my size, but I've been known to be unreasonable. Besides, slamming into his midsection would be fun since the force would knock the wind out of him good.

When I dropped my weight to my hips and legs and braced myself to counter-tackle, my fun dropped dead—literally. A big bullet cleared the man's head, causing his heavy body to hit the ground at my feet when his life left his body.

"Okay, rude!" I whined annoyingly with a scoff.

Scowling out of frustration, I pulled out one of my daggers and leaped at a nearby man, securing my legs around him after jumping onto his back. Repeatedly, I brought the dagger down into his neck and chest area until his body dropped to the ground dead.

"Are you seriously pissed about me saving your ass just now? That man would have flattened you like a semi-truck." Stepan's voice brought me out of my little fit with a huff as I got back up to my feet and wiped the blood off my face with the back of my hand.

"Did I ask for your help asshole? I had him." I responded in an irritated tone before lunging at another man and burying my dagger into the junction of his neck, dragging his gargling body to the ground.

"Tigress, you weigh a hundred pounds soaking wet, that man's four hundred-pound self would have sent you flying into a crate if he somehow didn't mow you over outright." He retorted in a chiding tone which pissed me off. "It's simple physics."

"Well screw physics." I grumbled with a scowl.

"Not in this world little tigress." Hearing Stepan's amused chuckle made me huff again as I pulled my dagger out of the flesh bag I just killed.

"Hey, police are on their way, so round it up and start opening the crates people." Bao informed us, making us shift our priorities.

"Ugh." Frustrated, I swung my leg out and gave the man who rushed at me a roundhouse kick to the head, knocking him out.

"Alright boys, knock 'em out and tie 'em up!" I shouted while sheathing my dagger.

Out of the thirty enemy men, only eight survived the whole ordeal. The cops weren't going to be too happy about the amount of bodies we dropped, but they couldn't complain much if they wanted our help to continue. So, they would deal with the aftermath because we operated outside the law while they couldn't.

Once the survivors were rounded up and bound, I gave everyone a stern reminder before we got to work opening the crates. "Remember, no touching the shit we find, just leave it out in the open for the cops to use in their case." No need for a warrant if things were out in the open on public property.

Luckily, none of our men were dead or majorly injured, from what I could see after we regrouped some distance away before the cops arrived on the scene.

"Can't believe you took my target." I grumbled and pouted to Stepan after he approached me.

"Oh come on, you're still hung up on that little tigress?" Stepan inquired with a raised brow and small smirk.

"Hmp." Huffing with a pouting frown, I angrily crossed my arms and narrowed my eyes at him.

Sighing, Stepan rolled his eyes and reached out, unfurling my arms and settling them back to my sides. "I'll make it up to you tomorrow then, alright?" He offered with a soft smile while pleading with me for forgiveness with his eyes.

Tilting my head down, I let my eyes bore holes into his chest. "And just how are you going to make it up to me?" I did my best to keep my irritated façade, but I could feel my facial expression loosening up as a small smile threatened to break it fully.

"You'll see tomorrow, if you agree." I could see his chest rumble with his chuckle before my face was lifted by his finger curling under my chin, forcing me to meet his soft, sky-blue eyes that melted away at my resolve.

"Fine, but it better be good."

Chapter 15

Hanna

"Wait, you're serious about this? And this has nothing to do with last night?"

It was one hell of a coincidence I would get an official job offer the very next day after going on a night raid with Stepan and Lev.

"Believe it or not, but we had this written up before you even clocked off for the day. We just figured it'd be a nice surprise very first thing in the morning for you upon coming in." Stepan assured me with a firm and proud smile as he slid the papers closer to me.

"So, are you in?" Gently, he set the pen atop all the papers I had yet to sign if I agreed to be an official employee.

"Hope this isn't what you meant by making it up to me." I joked softly while picking up the pen to sign my name away through the various sheets of paper.

"Oh come on little tigress, you have to give me some more credit than that. What kind of man would I be if I gave you this crappy of an apology?" He seemed playfully offended with his little lopsided smirk.

"But if I give you too much credit then I might be disappointed." I shot back with a cheeky smile and giggle.

"Hanna, there are lots of things in the world that I can do, but disappointing you will never be one of them if I can help it." Smug little turd. I was tempted to throw the pen at him to get him to stop smiling like he'd won.

With nothing to say back, I quickly finished signing my employment papers and slid them back to him afterward.

"Well, everything seems in order, so welcome to the company, officially." Stepan chuckled proudly with a happy smile as he tucked the papers into a manilla envelope.

Getting up from his desk, he gestured for me to get up as he rounded it to my side. Holding his hand out, he waited until I gingerly placed mine in his before pulling me to my feet. "I'll show you your desk then drop you off with Lev for your assignment. I'll come find you after my meeting for lunch with you then I'll show you my apology for yesterday, alright?"

Humming softly, I nodded before letting my hand slip from his warm grasp. No matter how tempting he may be, I have to keep reminding myself that he was unavailable to me.

Sucking in a deep breath, I tensed my body to prevent it from shivering under his touch when I felt the warmth of his large hand devour my lower back.

"You okay? You didn't get hurt too much last night did you?" Stepan's eyes softened with worry as they worked my body from head to toe.

Quickly, I shook my head and averted my eyes from him. My legs ached to step away and put some distance between us, but the rest of my body, particularly my stupid brain, kept me rooted to further enjoy the tiny blip of serotonin his touch brought me.

"Just a little sore, that's all." It wasn't a full lie, so I slipped it through my reassuring smile easily enough.

"Well, lucky for you your new assignment doesn't require you on the field just yet, so take it easy at your desk today, alright?" He didn't seem thoroughly convinced with how hesitant he sounded, but at least he didn't push the matter either.

"Fine dad, I will." I replied playfully—and mostly innocently—with an equal smile.

It was subtle, but I caught the way his breath deepened briefly with his flared nostrils. The hand he had rested on my lower back tensed a little as he pressed it firmly against me.

I should stop. I was playing with fire, and I would definitely get burnt if I didn't stop. Hell, I shouldn't even be entertaining any of this if I intended to keep him at a distance. But I couldn't help it. The little reactions I got from him were too fun to give up.

Smiling innocently, I unwillingly stepped away from him, subconsciously shivering at the lack of warmth from his hand the more distance I put between him as I slowly made my way to the door. "Well, let's go?"

☐True to his word, Stepan left me to my own devices with Lev after showing me my desk, which happened to be right outside his office. Right outside, across a little ways from the door. I'm pretty sure the part about keeping me close to Lev because he would have me working closely with him was an excuse, but not like I could argue with him because I had no grounds for one.

It'd been a few hours since I'd been alone after Lev dumped our new assignment on me. As much as my body itched for some action, I was grateful today was seemingly effortless because my body definitely needed some downtime.

Letting out a long breath through my nose, I leaned back in my chair and brought a hand up to my shoulder to rub at it to get the tightening knot out. My brows knitted together with the tightening ache, and the corners of my lips kept pulling down and down with each passing second the more I dug my fingers into my muscles.

My body jolted at the tightening feeling of hands on my arm and shoulder, and I was about to jerk my arm back to whack the idiot who dared touch me until I caught a glimpse of who it was.

"Fucking hell, Stepan, don't sneak up on me like that." My head spun for a split second from letting out the breath I didn't know I held.

"Hanna, you're not going to get attacked in my building, so relax." He chuckled amusingly as he used the hand on my shoulder to brush away my own.

"You're going to wear yourself out fast if you keep your body in a constant state of fight or flight." There he goes again, chiding me like I'm some child. Well, he didn't sound like a lecturing parent, more of a concerned friend, but it sounded like the former coming from him.

"I'd be dead if I weren't." I retorted with a dry chuckle, grimacing with a hiss of pain when I felt him lift my arm into the air by my wrist while his fingers from his other hand dug into my sore shoulder.

"It's not healthy, Hanna. I don't want to see you tense and on edge while you're here in the office, alright? This is a safe space for everyone, including you now." His thumb digging into my stiff muscle made a soft groan slip from me as the tension grew and went.

"Are most of the people here bratva?" I didn't want to stay on the subject of my bad habits any longer.

"A majority, yes, but don't think you can slink away from me little tigress." Leave it to him to prevent an escape, too.

"Do you always dig so personally into your other employees?" I snarked back, not wanting to let him any closer to me.

"I know more than enough about my employees, especially those who are members of the bratva." His answer didn't confirm or deny anything, which was frustrating.

"Stepan, we can't be doing this." I deadpanned with a heavy sigh, leaning away from his hands.

I wasn't successful because his grip on me tightened, keeping me rooted. "Doing what?" His tone was a little apprehensive, making me feel small and cornered.

Steeling myself, I slightly twisted my body towards his hold to face him a little. With my free hand, I gestured between us with a disappointed frown. "This. You're my boss Stepan, we can't let it go beyond anything but a working relationship." I couldn't maintain my eye contact with him. My eyes had a mind of their own when they turned away from his face, no matter how much I fought my nerves.

The hand on my shoulder released and slid across my back to the other side before it curled around me, trapping me in his dominating presence. His hand slowly slid across my upper chest and upwards, splaying around my slender neck where my pulse was drumming madly. No doubt he felt it with how firmly his digits started to wrap around me.

His other hand remained wrapped around my wrist, slowly bringing my arm down across my waist so I was caged between him in my seat.

I could hear my heart thumping against my eardrums as my breaths picked up, making my body shiver with every inhale of his intoxicating scent. The crisp scent of morning dew brightened my senses and drew me into the freshness before his underlying warmth of spices—anise and cloves—ensnared me fully.

My eyes avoided him briefly before his grip on my jaw from his thumb and forefinger tightened to force my head upwards. I couldn't avoid his intense gaze if I wanted because he lightly jerked my face until my soft, chocolate brown eyes melted under his intense azure gaze filled with desire.

"Hanna, look me dead in my eyes with utter confidence and tell me you don't want this or anything between us, and I will drop it all and stop." His deep, smooth voice shook me to my very core, making me hitch my breath while I clenched at nothing.

Swallowing the lump in my throat, I forced it down the aching channel as I tried to regain my confidence. Sadly, nothing came out when I opened my mouth, even though the words were literally right there on my tongue.

"I don't want this." I practically had to force the words out of my mouth, fighting against the suffocation that squeezed at my chest when my heart seemed to ache at those words.

That should have been the end of it—the end of us.

But I made a grave mistake.

I let my eyes shift away and let my body melt into him.

My tongue fed him lies, but my body gave him the truth.

Chapter 16

Stepan

"Hanna."

One look was all I needed now for her to know.

"I took a few bites already." She argued back with a pout, hugging her coffee cup to her chest.

"Am I going to have to start holding your caffeine hostage like Nikolai does to Angel?" It seems like the two friends shared some of the same bad habits, fueling themselves with caffeine and no food in the morning being one of them.

Defeated, Hanna glared at me softly while letting out a huff, setting her coffee down and begrudgingly picking up the croissant I had gotten her moments ago.

Leaning against the edge of her desk with my arms crossed, I watched her like a hawk until she finished the food item slowly with a less-than-satisfied expression. Well, I guess I'd axe that option from the growing list.

"You don't have to hound me like a child," Hanna complained in a small voice as she gingerly cradled her coffee cup in her hands again.

"Start taking better care of yourself on a consistent and daily basis and *maybe* I'll consider stopping." I'd never stop if I were frank, but she didn't need to know that.

Hanna didn't need to know many things, at least for now. It'd taken a few days for her to return to baseline around me after that one afternoon, and I didn't want to scare her off again. So, I had to take it slow with her.

She may have denied me with her words that day, but her body told me all I needed to know.

It had been about two weeks since Hanna was officially hired, and it's been a week and a half since Hanna and I mainly returned to normal after she placed her line in the sand.

There's been a small distance between us, courtesy of Hanna wanting to keep this relationship professional. Out of respect for her, I've given her control and kept the distance she's placed. I'd work with what she was willing to give me.

She can deny it all she wants, but I knew the truth.

I would play things her way for now, slowly work my way into her until it'd be too late for her to pull back when she realizes what I've planned and done.

I'd already worked us into a small morning routine with her bad caffeine habit. For the past week, I've been getting her a small breakfast and making her eat it before she could have her coffee or energy drink. Something I've discovered about Hanna from her little slip-up was how she rarely ate anything for breakfast, only ever having coffee or energy drinks.

Hanna wasn't too happy with it the first few mornings, but she's come to accept it and not fight it by now.

"I'm going to be out of the office for most of the day today, so behave with Lev." Hanna's also gotten much more comfortable around us, particularly Lev—something I wasn't too happy about.

Lev knew to keep his distance from Hanna at this point, and I knew he'd never make any move on her after knowing I'd got my mark on her. The two got along too swimmingly for my liking and I was jealous because I wished Hanna would be as free around me as she was around Lev.

"Oh please, I feel like the babysitter between the two of us." Hanna chortled with a smug smirk thrown at Lev, who was situated across from her—their desks were connected.

"Oh fuck you." Lev snapped back with a playful scowl.

"Name the time and place." Hanna quipped back smugly, making Lev chuckle and flip her off.

"Alright you two, get back to work." I chuckled softly while pushing off the desk.

Before fully disappearing into my office, I turned my head to look at Hanna again. "Don't take off after work today, I have something for you."

The news brightened Hanna's face with a cute little smile as she wiggled in her seat while her sparkling, excited, and grateful eyes locked with mine. "What is it?" Though contained well, her excitement was still palpable and adorable to see.

Smirking mysteriously, I shrugged my shoulders softly. "You'll just have to be patient and see little tigress."

I never got the opportunity to give her the little apology present the other day after our little moment because she avoided me like the plague afterward for days. I'd planned on taking her out on a small lunch date before taking her to our weapons guy to have her fit for what I had in mind, but I got enough of a good feel of her hands to give my guy the correct measurements.

"How come you never give me anything?" Lev butted in with a fake, playful pout that had me chuckling and rolling my eyes at him.

Tossing a cocky little grin at my little brother, I responded to him. "Because all you give me is grief and paperwork. *Ne govorya uzhe o tom, chto ty malen'kiy der'mo.*" The last part had Lev scowling at me while flipping me the bird.

Unfortunately, the day went by at a snail's pace, much to my impatience and irritation. At least one of my meetings got canceled, so I had the chance to head back early. Hopefully, Hanna wasn't still out on her assignment so that I could steal more of her time.

My eagerness and excitement faded a little when I approached the top floor—her desk and workspace location—and saw her smiling at her phone. It wasn't the victorious smile she'd get when a source of hers panned out. No, it was too soft and wide, too giddy and dreamy.

"What's got you on cloud nine little tigress?" It was hard to maintain a cordial tone with her as I approached her, each step pressing against the barrier I'd placed around my irritation.

My fingers itched with a need to snatch her phone to see exactly what she was all smiley about, and I was oh so tempted the moment I stood a mere foot from her. Her cell phone was facing down on the desk when I stopped next to her, not allowing me any access to her screen, period, further vexing me.

"When are you going to stop calling me that? What happened to space and distance? Someone's going to get the wrong idea if you keep calling me that." Hanna sighed softly with a slight frown.

Leaning down with one hand on the desk and the other in my pants pocket, I smirked knowingly at her once I caught her gaze. "Then look me directly in the eyes and tell me you don't like it, that you want me to stop."

Hanna's jaw clenched, and the tension in her neck could be seen as her eyes hardened at me. "You're such an asshole." She strained through her gritted teeth before huffing and turning her chair around so the back faced me.

Amused, I let out a low chuckle before pulling my hand out of my pocket to pull out the small, thin box that rested inside the inner pocket of my jacket.

Teasingly, I held out the black box inches from her face after reaching around to nearly cage her between me and the desk. "If I'm such an asshole then I wouldn't bother with an apology gift now would I?"

Hanna's quick hands made a grab at the box, only to have me pull away at the last second. "Hey! Jerk! You can't just keep my gift away from me like that." She pouted with a slight growl and glanced up at me with eyes that could cut me with how sharp they looked. The fact her eyes already had a naturally sharp look because of her Asian heritage only added to the edge of it more.

"Technically I haven't officially gifted it to you yet, so I could withhold it until I see fit." I retorted calmly with a single-shoulder shrug while still practically dangling the box before her.

"Fine, I'm sorry I called you an asshole, dad." She replied mockingly with a roll of her eyes.

It'd be so easy to grab her by her luscious hair, bend her over the desk, and teach her a lesson until she called me something else. I didn't even know if she was into any of that, yet my brain couldn't seem to get the hint from the fantasies it concocted late at night.

The damn brat needed a firm hand, though, one I couldn't give, unfortunately. Well, unfortunately, for now. I won't stop my pursuit until I have her under my mercy with my name crying from her bruised lips.

Breathing deeply, I shoved my twisted thoughts away and put my mask back on before smiling down at her after pushing off the desk to stand up straight again. "One day you're going to regret being such a brat, little tigress." It wasn't a warning, not with the dark edge to my low voice.

Taking a step back, I reached down, grabbed her hand, and pulled her up to her feet. "Come on, I want to make sure you're fully happy with your gift." Gently, I tugged her along to the facility gym on the first floor and took her over to the boxing area, positioning her in front of a punching bag.

"What? Is it going to be a punchable picture of your face?" Hanna snickered mischievously, sticking the tip of her tongue between her teeth.

Rolling my eyes, I gently shoved her shoulder after letting go of her hand. "Close your eyes and hold your hands out." I instructed her.

"I swear, if you put a spider in my hands, I will make sure you never have kids." Her threat was playful, but the hardness behind her eyes meant she would make good on it if I did wrong her.

"Hanna, I'm not one for pranks; that's more of Lev's and Arseny's thing." Those two were the most playful out of the five of us. I never found any amusement or pleasure in practical jokes like my older brother Nikolai and my younger brother Alexei.

"Psh, you're not fun then." Hanna retorted before shutting her eyes and holding her hands out like an eager child for candy.

Rolling my eyes to myself, I internally chuckled before opening the box, taking out a pair of black, fingerless leather gloves, carefully slipping them onto her delicate hands, and tightening the strap around her wrist to secure them.

"Open your eyes and give them a go," I told her with a soft smile, stepping back and watching her face brighten up when she examined the gloves.

The pair she'd been using were torn up from what I've seen and didn't offer much protection. I had these special made to fit her hands as perfectly as possible with the right amount of padding around her knuckles to absorb the shock from impacts, along with a row of steel studs for extra impact against those on the receiving end. Her old ones had been too generic, chunky, ratty; I was surprised she hadn't hurt herself using them.

"How do they feel so far?" Visually, they looked to fit her perfectly like a glove.

"Fucking nice." She giggled with a wide grin before widening her stance and taking a few swings at the punching bag in front of her.

The elated smile on her face grew the more punches she delivered to the sand-filled sack—I didn't think it was possible for her to smile any wider. Seeing her so excited and happy brought a content smile to my face as I watched her go to town on the bag until she was panting heavily with the grin still on her face.

My breath was slightly knocked out of my mouth from the sudden impact of Hanna's body hitting mine in an unexpected hug—one I was more than happy to return. Looking down at her, I resisted the urge to hold her too tightly as she grinned at me. "If you're this happy with some gloves then you'd probably explode if I gave you a gun."

"Nah, I would explode if you gave me a nice bat or stick, but a gun would be a very close second." Hanna still bounced on the balls of her feet as she spoke with a joyful voice, which I found very adorable.

Pressing my lips firmly together, I resisted the urge to hold her face to bring it closer to mine. Instead, I tightened an arm around her to hug her more firmly against me. Leaning in, I settled my chin atop her head, moving a hand up to cradle the back of her head.

Gritting my teeth, I held my tongue back, not wanting to ruin this moment while it lasted.

God, I wished she'd let me in, let me take care of her.

"Thank you Stepan, thank you so much, you have no idea how happy I am right now, my heart is still racing a mile a minute." And she bounced on her feet like a bunny still.

I would do anything to make her happy, to keep her happy. She deserved so much to make up for the shitty life she's had to live through.

I don't know her full background yet, but from what Angel told me, Hanna had it rough until Angel's father took her in. Hanna lost her father at a young age and was then subjected to her mother's harsh hand. Angel didn't divulge much, but I could surmise enough with how grave her expression had been with her pain-laden voice.

My little tigress deserved nothing but the best, and I would give it all to her.

Chapter 17

Hanna

OH MY GOD, I'M really going to do this.

I should be excited, but why am I not? Why am I not more excited? I finally accepted a date with the hot guy I've been talking to for the past week, so I should be fucking elated. Yet, why did I feel somewhat icky?

My mind knew the answer, my brain pulling my eyes over to the open door just to my right.

Stepan fucking Volkov. The smug ass, handsome, sexy beast of a man who sat behind his desk with a head of tousled hair from how many times he's run his hand through it from the stress. Even when he was messy, he looked perfect.

He's the answer to why I tossed and turned late into the night until my hands ended up under my clothes for some relief and satisfaction before guilt set in.

I chose to put this wall between us, to shut and lock the door before he came close to it. So, I shouldn't fantasize about him at night and in the shower. Nothing good would come from letting my heart and mind run my desires. I just tortured myself at this point with forbidden thoughts about Stepan.

I needed to stop, but I couldn't.

I only ended up on the stupid dating site on impulse, hoping to fill in the void with another man to kick Stepan from my system completely. I just needed another handsome man who would be willing to give me the attention and affection I desperately craved and needed.

All I needed was attention and affection; anyone could give me that. It didn't have to be Stepan, so why should it be Stepan? There were tons of blonde-haired, blue-eyed men out there for me to snag up—with killer bodies, too!

My daily little breakfast didn't need to come from Stepan either. Any man could do that; I just had to find the right one and then figure out where the hell Stepan gets his little pirozhkis from. The damn asshole got me hooked on them, just those specific ones from only God knows where, because he refuses to tell me.

The other day, his little gift nearly had me tearing down the wall, but then I remembered that any man could give me gifts as long as I asked for them. Not like I ever would because then I would feel needy and greedy.

I really liked how Stepan gave me a meaningful gift, one I would actually use on a near-daily basis. I hadn't even complained about my old pair falling apart, yet he noticed and took action—I rather loved that. He paid attention when no one else had, maybe a little too close and much, but at least he noticed without being encouraged to.

But I could get all of that from someone who's *not* Stepan.

Of all the people in the rotten world to tug at my dried-out heart-strings, why did it have to be him?

Deep down, he's who I wanted, who my stupid fucking heart wanted. But I can't. I won't.

I have to forget about him. He was my boss, and he can't go anything beyond a friend for both our sakes. He may think he wants me, but they never do when they see all that's beneath. Even if they do see past my ugly, it's not like there was anything better underneath because my personality definitely won't be winning any awards anytime soon or ever.

Hell, I don't know what I'm even thinking with this stupid date and entertaining this man tonight. I'd also probably chase him off when I sensed him closing in. At least Stepan would understand and accept my mafia lifestyle, considering how he was mafia, so I guess there was an upside to Stepan besides his caring charm.

Still, no man wants a woman who could kick and beat their ass to the ground. No one wants a wild woman, a beast. I had no redeeming qualities. I was dark and twisted both inside and out. Emotional issues, psychopathy, delusional, crazy, strange, weird, violent, outspoken, arrogant almost. The list of qualities undesirable in a woman could go on and on if I had the time of day to list it all, and I'd check off nearly everything on the damn list.

Inhaling deeply, I held my breath until I felt my head spin before letting it out. I needed to get Stepan out of my mind, and I shouldn't be getting myself hung over a man I had no chance with. Besides, I had a hot date tonight. I should put in some effort, at the very least.

I wasn't even with Stepan, so why the hell did I feel guilty about going out on a date? I wasn't cheating on him because we weren't even together in such a sense in the slightest. Besides, not like he was exclusive to me either; a quick flash of the other day had me scowling spitefully in my spot when the image of him hugging and flirting with some leggy blonde zipped through my mind.

Who cared if she was some past employee he was friends with? He shouldn't have been such a charming bastard with her, flashing his heart-melting, knee-buckling smile. And how dare he touch her, too! Well, he didn't grope her or anything, but a hand on the shoulder counted as contact and that's all that mattered. He shouldn't be looking at anyone else but me if he was interested, nor should he even lay a finger on anyone else.

Rageful jealousy rose and fell with my breaths for a moment before reality set in. Even though my green-eyed monster tipped its head at me to ease the burden of my decision tonight, my mind and heart felt betrayed by my plans because they were already engaged with Stepan, and I hated that. He was the first man to notice me without effort on my end, and my stupid heart superglued itself on him.

Shaking my head softly, I mentally slapped myself and locked away my screaming heart. This was for the best. He deserved someone a hundred times better than me, a model, a kick-ass mafia bride like Angel, not silly old me.

I'm just a terror of a beast.

Chapter 18
Stepan

WHAT THE FUCK IS she doing here?!

Once again, the last place I expected to see Hanna was at Guilty. A fucking sex club.

I knew damn well she wasn't here for the dancing and clubbing scene because, again, this was a sex club—you don't go to a sex club for just dancing.

I didn't give half a shit about the fact she's a grown woman capable of making her own decisions. She shouldn't be here even though she had every right to. She shouldn't be anywhere other men could eye her hungrily, let alone at a place with a man glued to her side. Seeing her laugh or giggle at whatever the man told her after leaning down to her ear made the noise around me white out with rage. Saying I was livid would be a gross understatement.

Was he the one who'd been making her smile whenever she'd look at her phone? The one who'd been taking up her time? Time that should have been spent on me? On us? Was he the one she blew me off for? Was this the man with a death wish?

The crazed laugh bubbled in my chest as I hid my maddening grin behind my hand. If she thought this sorry replacement of me would be

112

good enough for her, she had another thing coming. If *he* thought he could take what's mine, then he would have something else coming after him.

My gaze remained locked on Hanna and the man with his arm around her waist. I couldn't focus on anyone or anything else but them. Everything faded into a blur with how my vision was pinpointed at them, following them as they made their way towards the stairs that led down to the playrooms.

Like a predator on the kill, I stalked after them with an eerily calm face even though a storm raged inside me.

People parted like the Red Sea as I advanced. No doubt they could feel the heavy, suffocating waves of rage rolling from me and wanted to avoid me like the plague right now. I wouldn't be surprised if a single look from me would drop a person dead if they dared garner my attention right now.

Keeping some distance, I followed Hanna down to the lower level, watching as she slipped into a playroom with the man.

Instantly, I recognized one of the rooms as a viewing room for those who enjoyed voyeurism.

Sucking a deep, sharp breath through my gritted teeth, I look over at the guard next to the door for the viewing room. "No one, and I mean *no one*, goes into this room until I'm gone. Is that clear?" I barely recognized my own voice when I gave the order. It was so low and grave with anger.

"Yes, sir." The guard knew better than to question an order from their employer.

Although the club technically belonged to Nikolai and Arseny, all of the Volkov brothers stood high up on the chain of command at all our clubs.

Entering the viewing room, I nearly slammed the door shut out of a fit of rage before standing right up to the two-way mirror, watching Hanna with narrowed eyes.

A huge part of me wanted to charge in there and tear her away from the man when I saw him strip her bare. No man should be touching her, no one but me. Those hands running down her toned body should be mine, not his. He didn't deserve to be touching her godly body.

Her haunting moans of pleasure echoed into the viewing room, sending shivers down my spine to my raging hard cock that strained painfully in my pants. The ache to be buried inside of her was excruciatingly painful, taking into account how she was right there on the other side of the wall, completely naked and wet, more than ready for me to slip the entirety of my thick length into her until her eyes rolled.

My fisted hands remained stuffed in the pockets of my tightened pants as I continued to watch Hanna let herself be taken by this chump with rageful eyes. As the session continued, I couldn't do anything but remain stiff like a board. This whole thing was practically torture.

It was only when Hanna's climax hit that my body loosened back up. Hearing her sweet, soft moan of pleasure when she orgasmed sent a shiver down my spine. Her moan nearly did me in as well; I almost came from hearing the height of her pleasure.

"Tsk." My teeth would fall out at this rate from how often and hard I gritted and ground them.

After snapping a quick picture of the man's and Hanna's faces, I swiftly exited the room and trudged out of the club to my car in the parking garage. The drive home went by in an angry haze because the only thing on my mind was what I witnessed at the club, which played on a constant loop.

My body bolted to my home office when I made it home in one piece. The stiffness and tension in my fingers begged to be relieved by my keyboard after I eagerly sat behind my desk.

Even when I needed my typically straight brain to focus on the research at hand, the damn thing refused to cooperate. No matter how hard I tried to reel it in to focus on the computer screen, it kept bouncing back to images of Hanna's tantalizing body in the throes of pleasure.

Figuring out the man's identity from a clear picture was child's play to me. At the speed at which my fingers flew across the keys on my keyboard, I had his whole life compiled in multiple windows on my computer. There wasn't a speck of dust of him that remained hidden from my raging fit to uncover him.

Logan Lockwood.

The son of a bitch who had a death wish.

Hanna picked this damned moron to entertain her? This plain, run-of-the-mill rich brat moron? I was utterly insulted because this was the idiot I lost to. She rejected me for *him*?! He's the one who got to take *my* Hanna to bed?

"NO!"

Slamming my hands onto the desk, I shot up from my seat, swept an arm out, and knocked the monitor off my desk, sending it to the ground with a *crash*. With a cry of anguish and fury, I clawed my hands across my desk from one end to the other, knocking everything off its surface.

Papers scattered with a flutter while denser objects hit the floor with thuds and clatters. The softer sounds of destruction became overpowered by the sound of my chair slamming against a display case after I had violently kicked it.

Unfortunately, the glass case stood no chance against the force of the chair. The sound of glass shattering briefly filled the room before a loud crash echoed the room from me wrenching the metal frame of the case to the ground while letting out another angry scream.

Nothing in my office escaped my furious wrath. Every single object, no matter how big or small, was destroyed either by force from being thrown or by a bullet from my Glock when I couldn't control the itch in my trigger finger.

A completely destroyed office and three spent magazines later, my rage finally settled.

Correction: my rage disappeared.

Just like that, there one second and gone the next.

THUMP! THUMP! THUMP!

It sounded like a drum beating at my ear when, in reality, it was my heart pounding in my heaving chest while I stood amongst the chaos.

Slowly, I dragged my heavy feet over to the floor-to-ceiling window at the back of my office and let my body fall against it with a winded breath. I didn't bother trying to control my sliding body when I felt my knees slowly give from the fatigue, letting it slide to the ground with a slight grunt.

Getting my breathing under control, I ran a hand through my messy hair, gripping it while I took some deep, controlled breaths to reset myself fully.

I should have been terrified of myself because of how fast it was for me to return to baseline, yet I wasn't because I'd grown comfortable with the fact. My fits of explosive fury used to be common in my late childhood and early teenage years, not that I would ever admit it to anyone. My brothers knew about my moments, only the surface, as that's how far I allowed them in.

They never knew—and still don't know—the full extent of the explosive episodes I suffered when my emotions would boil over like a pressure pot. I always kept a level head around them, always bottling up my anger and suffering until I snapped during moments of seclusion in the forests out back of our family home. My brothers didn't need to know about the bullet-riddled trees after I'd emptied countless magazines nor the mutilated animal corpses I'd tear apart physically with my own hands.

I only found myself flipping the switch after years of my father beating into me to be Nikolai's secondhand man and shadow. I was the contingency, Nikolai's replacement, if somehow he didn't work out. Being second meant I had to keep a level head at all times; at least, that's what my father beat into me.

To avoid my father's wrath and punishments, I learned to keep my emotions and feelings locked behind a flat smile and pretend everything was somewhat fine all the time. Things got harder when puberty hit, and the storm of hormones threw a wrench into my self-control for a few years until I reigned myself back in.

For the most part, some time at the shooting range, hunting, a quick spar with Lev, and more typical activities that weren't frowned upon were enough to run my buzz of emotions out of my system.

So, the fact I completely lost my shit just now over Hanna and her stupid little date, well, it was definitely something new in my adult life.

Although not going to lie, it felt damn good and cathartic. With how clear my head felt, I felt like a new, fresh man.

Chuckling and laughing crazily to myself, I let my head fall back against the window, my eyes taking an interest in my ceiling.

God, I haven't lost control like this since I was sixteen. Even then, my fits were never this destructive with personal property.

"Fucking hell, you see what you do to me, Hanna?" My frustration echoed through the closed room.

Fine, if she wants to play this game, then I'll fucking play, and I'll fucking win.

Chapter 19

Stepan

"SOMEONE SEEMS HAPPY THIS morning. You didn't sneak a coffee or energy drink on the way here, did you, little tigress?"

My irritation remained expertly veiled behind my friendly smile and voice.

The sight of Hanna still brought memories of the night two days ago crashing into me, but it wasn't anger or anything akin to it. No, whenever I'd get flashbacks of that night, all I could ever picture was Hanna's sweet face and delicious body. Then, after a brief bliss of a release from getting myself off imagining myself in the position of the man, my irritation would finally rear its ugly head the moment I realized the problem between Hanna and me.

A file of Logan Lockwood sat locked in my desk ever since that night. Everything about him at my disposal and abuse when I decide to act, *if* I act. Hanna hadn't been out again ever since that night, much to my delight. From what I've observed, it has been work and home for Hanna for the past two, nearly three days. At least having a simple routine made tailing her easy, but I doubt it would stay simple for long from how smiley she was being.

"No, Dad, I didn't sneak a snack. Just got a little problem figured out between my friend and I, that's all." The gall of this woman to lie to my face with a cute, innocent smile.

Okay, she didn't fully lie to me. She didn't sneak anything before showing up to work; that was genuine, but the part about her *friend* was a lie from the slight falter in her voice paired with her downturned eyes. Hanna had never been shy about naming anyone in conversation, even if she barely knew them. So, for her to elude me like that meant something was up.

"What friend?" I pressed with a smile, leaning against the edge of her desk with my arms crossed after sliding the little container filled with steamed buns.

"Just a friend." Yeah, something was definitely up. "That smells good, what is it? It doesn't smell like pirozhkis."

I would've accused her of changing the subject if I didn't know about her short attention span and how easily distracted she was as a person. No matter, it was too adorable and kept my irritation from rising because if we dug into the subject matter of her friend, then I would end up upset.

"Open it and see for yourself." I encouraged her with a chuckle while lightly pushing the container closer.

Eagerly, she opened the box with an excited grin, squealing softly with a clap of her hands and bouncing in her seat. "I've been craving these so badly. Is this just a coincidence or can you read my mind?"

"More like I can listen to you muttering to yourself about wanting to get some steamed buns the past three days." That and seeing her browse countless places for steamed buns whenever I'd glance at her from my desk or over her shoulder.

"Thank you so much." She spared me a quick, grateful glance before happily digging into the fresh, meat-filled buns.

After the first bite and some chewing, she leaned back in her seat, covering her mouth with her hand. "Holy shit, these are amazing, where the hell did you get these?"

A slow sigh of relief deflated my body when it was clear the shocked look on her face was a good one. Good to know I didn't fuck up the food.

Smiling teasingly, I reached out and pinched her stuffed cheek softly. "That's for me to know and you to find out, if you can."

"That's not fair, I can't let you buy me food all the time like this." Hanna pouted after swallowing her mouthful.

"You can and you will. I like spoiling you and making sure you are fed, happy, and healthy." I already enjoyed cooking as a hobby, but cooking for Hanna was a new enjoyment I looked forward to every day.

Yes, all the little breakfasts I've given her so far were nearly all made by my own hands in my kitchen. It was only the first few times that weren't because I had yet to get into the new habit of preparing food for Hanna.

"Well how the hell am I supposed to keep myself satisfied without you? You can't keep buying me food once you get a girlfriend or boyfriend to spoil." She retorted with a small scoffing chuckle filled with malice.

Amused, I returned her little chuckle with my own. "If that's what you're worried about then it's a simple fix." Pausing briefly, I leaned down until our faces were a few inches apart. "If you're my girlfriend then I get to continue spoiling you."

As if I'd entertain another woman when I had Hanna to hunt. No other woman could live up to her or come close to captivating me. No matter how good-looking or desirable, the sight of other females almost repulsed me because of the vice grip Hanna got me in. Other women didn't ignite an uncontrollable blaze of passion and lust within me anymore, but one glance at Hanna was all I needed to teeter on the edge of losing all my control.

If only Hanna could see and accept it all, but the nearly mocking laugh from her made it clear to me that she didn't or won't.

"Stepan, boundaries." She reminded me with a sad smile.

"Are meant to be broken." I added with a smirk before pulling back.

Oh, they'll be broken alright, broken and shattered beyond repair. Fuck her stupid boundaries, respectfully. This was the only boundary of Hanna's that I would ever overstep to open her eyes and heart to me, to us.

"But fine, I'm sorry if I'm pushing. You enjoy your breakfast, I have some work to do." Work as in figuring out a way to hack her damn phone and plot out my next steps regarding her.

Chapter 20

Stepan

THUNK!

Hopefully, Logan has more functioning brain cells than what I'm willing to credit him for and take my warning seriously. He's already been stupid enough to go on not one, but two dates with Hanna so far over the past week. Actually, three counting the one they were currently on while I busied myself with leaving Logan a *kind* warning at his door after breaking into his place and trashing it before leaving some roadkill I found scattered around his place. I might've also hidden some in places that'd take him a while to find, as in after they filled his place with the stench of death and decay.

My descent down the stairs of Logan's apartment complex took no pause when I pulled a phone out of my pocket when I felt it go off.

> Thanks for dinner and dessert tonight. We should do it again sooner than later :)

> Anything baby girl ;) but yeah we definitely should, you're the best dessert ever btw ;)

You don't taste bad yourself hehe ;) can we shoot for this Sat at Guilty?

Oh? You wanna do all that already?

Why wait on something good? Besides, I'm still calling your bluff lol!

We'll see how much of it you'll be calling between begging me lol.

Oh honey, I don't beg. I never beg for what I want, I just take it ;)

Good luck taking anything when I've got you bound and helplessly spread beneath me on the bed lol.

Good luck getting the ropes or cuffs around me in the first place buddy lol!

Buddy? Am I going to have to teach that sweet mouth of yours another lesson?

Can't be ANOTHER lesson if the first one didn't even stick hahaha!

I'm gonna have to beat that brattiness out of you.

Good luck lol! Well, I'm gonna get ready for bed and sleep, I've got a long day at work tomorrow.

Alright, sleep well baby girl.

Bile choked at my throat as my eyes read the messages on the tightly clutched phone in my hand.

Baby girl? Seriously? Out of all the things he could call her, that's just... No.

Seeing him call her that really pushed my control to not throw up because of how cringy and disgusting it felt. I don't know why he keeps calling her that either because she obviously didn't like it from the subtle shiver and flash of a frown I caught when I watched their date yesterday. Could he not see her displeasure at the nickname? Also, why hasn't Hanna flat-out told him about her dislike for soft little pet names?

Hanna hated the cliché terms of endearment, not all but most. She hated it when men would call her sweetie, sweetheart, cutie, cutes, and just anything soft sounding because it made her feel like a soft girl and not a strong woman. She verbally made her detest known to me after breaking the jaw of a guy who tried—and failed—to get her number and got a little too handsy.

She much preferred old-fashioned endearments, simple and not sappy ones, or something unique and personal like my little nickname. When I pressed, she didn't say she hated the nickname I gave her.

Tigress fit her quite well, given her level of cunning and danger. I only called her little tigress to get a bit more of a rile out of her and for sweeter, softer moments as it seemed fitting.

Hopefully, this stupid engagement of theirs will stop after Logan comes home tonight and finds the warning I—literally—stabbed into his door.

No more about him tonight; I've got better things to give my attention to.

The drive to Hanna's place sped by with how fast I drove. After parking the car a good half block from her place, I made the rest of my journey to her window on foot. The rickety ladder of the fire escape creaked and gave under my weight as I made my way up the thing warily. How the barely functional thing still stood after a few uses befuddles me. What few remaining rusted rungs seemed to be barely welded on, and I don't even know if the thing was properly attached to the building. I don't know how this damn fire escape came close to passing inspection.

Thankfully, her balcony was shaded enough to provide the perfect amount of darkness for me to sit undetected until daylight breaks. Although the flaw worked perfectly for me, it upset me greatly because of the thought of anyone else using this flaw to watch her. She didn't have functioning blinds or curtains, which meant the window of her fire escape remained wide open for any peeping Tom to view.

As I situated myself at the corner of her balcony, keeping myself entirely in the dark, the phone in my pocket went off again. Pulling it out, I could see it was an incoming call from Angel. I watched Hanna carefully, watching her search her little area for her phone before picking it up.

The call on the screen of the cloned phone in my hand picked up, and I held it to my ear, listening in on the conversation between Hanna and her friend Angel. Was this a complete violation of her privacy? Yes. Illegal? Very much so, yes. But I didn't give a single care because I needed to know every little thing that went out and came in with Hanna now.

Remaining quiet, I locked my eyes on Hanna, letting my blue orbs follow her enchanting body as she moved while talking to her friend about her date earlier tonight.

"Hanna honey, as happy as I am for you to somewhat find someone, I'm not because I can tell you're not fully genuine about this dude. Now, don't get me wrong, nothing wrong with exploring and shit, but you and I both know who you round back to at the end of the night. So, why are you wasting your time on this bozo? Not saying he's not worth the time, he sounds and seems like a great guy, just not a great guy for you." Angel's long, heavy sighs between her sentences were clearly heard on the other end. She sounded done, disappointed almost, though she sounded forced as if she tried to see the other side for her friend's sake.

"But you and I both know Stepan and I could never work. So, it's fine, I can settle." Hanna's voice dragged with disappointment and sadness, making me frown in the darkness as I continued to eavesdrop on their conversation.

"You need to quit that thinking. There is no law in the whole damn universe that says you and him can't be together or give a relationship a try. No, he's not too good for you, so don't even try to give me that crap. You are a kick-ass bitch who would be anyone's prized catch, and if for some asinine reason, Stepan can't see that, then shame on him, but he's not fucking blind or stupid last I checked. And I don't want you settling because settling is for idiots and losers, which you're not. Stepan's not perfect either, so quit putting him so high on the goddamn pedestal because he is on the same playing field as you." Angel continued to drill into her friend.

After a brief pause filled with some deep breaths, Angel continued, "Stepan's not going to judge you for your past, not with how him and his brothers grew up, as I said before. Stepan will understand, and he'll do right by you, promise. I'm not trying to set you up and shit, but even you can't deny that he looks at you with a fire in his eyes. Hell, even I can see it too when he's come to me about questions regarding you."

That last bit seemed to have caught Hanna's attention greatly with how she pipped up excitedly. "He's asked about me? What's he asked about?"

Angel's soft, mischievous giggle could be heard before her words. "He's so cute, like bitch let me tell you, this dude was trying to be so sly. He was all like 'so your friend applied for a position at my company, why didn't you tell me' and blah blah blah 'so can you tell me more about her like what is she usually like, where does she like to go, anything she particularly likes' and like he would not stop with the questions for small details, it was so cute."

Little snitch.

"R-really? What did you tell him?" At least Hanna was genuinely interested.

"The truth, I mean he was asking for things like your favorite desserts, candy, snacks, foods, hobbies, those kind of things. Girl, he's got it BAAAAAAAD for you. You should have seen the way his face lit up when I answered his questions, and when he'd talk about how good you were doing and all that, girl, trust me, he's like a goner for you." Angel's tone was soft and happy, and I wouldn't be surprised if she had a goofy smile right now.

"He's too good... Which is why I can't... I just can't. I'm too fucked up and broken for him. He's got his life together, handsome as hell, rich, smart, perfect really. And I'm just, here, boring me, broken beyond repair." I hated how Hanna couldn't give herself the credit she deserved.

"Honey, he's a bratva boss, he don't got shit together. You think Nikolai is mister perfect like the media portrays him? No one is ever perfect, the Volkovs would be low on the list with us. Honestly, sometimes I want to strangle Nikolai. Seriously, Stepan's not perfect as a man, but he'd possibly be perfect for you. Honestly, the Volkovs would be the last people on earth to judge others for shitty childhoods. You just have to remember where Stepan comes from Hanna." Angel reminded Hanna sternly with a soft sigh at the end.

"Fine, whatever, but what if his tastes in bed don't line up with mine? You know how hard it is to find the right partner in bed as a switch. And also, I don't want to embarrass myself in bed. He's probably going to laugh or be disgusted when I call him Daddy. And I mean, you know how embarrassing it is to admit to someone you have Daddy issues?" Hanna groaned, and I could see her burying her face in her hands through the window.

I wanted to burst in there and prove her wrong. I wanted to pull her into my arms and hold her, assure her that her worries are all for naught because they are.

Angel was right; I didn't—and wouldn't—give a shred of care in the world about her past or how broken she claimed to be. No matter how much she liked to argue otherwise, I didn't see her as damaged. I'd take her and accept her fully, no matter her condition. If she saw herself as broken, I'd fix her, piece her back together until she was whole and better.

I didn't give a shit about her issues; we all had our issues, me included. Hell, I'd probably be seen as a bastard for exploiting the knowledge about her having Daddy issues. I fully intended to use everything to my advantage, no matter how dirty the tactic.

"And he has Mommy *and* Daddy issues along with the rest of his brothers, so trust me, you'll be fine in that department." Angel laughed softly along with Hanna.

"What? Don't tell me Nikolai calls you Mommy in bed." Hanna joked teasingly with a snicker.

"Har har missy, that ain't our thing." Angel retorted playfully. "Not like you're into anything extreme even when you are in a switchy mood, at most is Stepan gets tied up or cuffed to the bed while you're a total brat."

Fuck that sounds hot as hell.

Suppressing my groan behind my tensed jaw, I reached down to my crotch with one hand to adjust my growing erection. I might not be a sub, but the idea of switching with Hanna had my brain feeling woozy from how all the blood rushed down to between my legs.

"God, you have no idea how many times I've fantasized about him begging under me." Hanna's groan grew deep and long, and I could faintly see her hand slipping between her thighs as she lay down on her bed.

"Oh, don't worry, I know. I have my very little moments where I do enjoy riding Nikolai and making him beg. Trust me, Stepan will probably be more than fine with the rare occasion of rope play involving him on the receiving end, and whenever you wanna cuff him and shit. Honestly, you only want to switch like two out of ten times, and not like you go full Domme or anything, you just like to have your little moment of beg me for my pussy if anything. You'll be fine, just communicate with him." Angel sighed playfully with a chuckle.

Okay, maybe a little too much information there I didn't need to know. It's no secret that my brothers have lives in the bedroom; it's only human, but I didn't need to know details beyond the fact they have sex.

"I don't know... Well, doesn't matter, I've pushed him away, so it's better that way. I'll just see where things go with Logan, enjoy my little run with him for a while, then just part ways on friendly terms with him."

Hanna sighed heavily, removing her hand from her legs and resting it next to her on the bed.

"Or, hear me out, or you can ditch Logan now and go figure your shit out with Stepan instead of wasting time and energy on a man who you don't even fully want." Angel remarked.

Huffing, she growled softly for a moment before responding to her friend. "I'll just see things out with Logan and have my fun, maybe I just need a good fucking to get Stepan out of my system."

Like hell I'd let that happen.

Oh, she's never going to be rid of me, ever.

"Well, as much as I want to keep chatting, Nikolai's home and he's—ah! Kolya, I'm on the phone." I could hear my older brother's faint voice through Angel's laugh before Hanna laughed and told her friend to go get some dick and hung up.

Tucking the phone away, I continued to watch Hanna in silence. This new routine I'd developed recently consisted of sitting and watching Hanna until she fell asleep for a long while. Then, it was home and bed for myself. Not tonight, though; there'd be a deviation once Hanna knocks out.

My expectations of her to throw back her meds and slumber away were disturbed greatly when Hanna started shifting, sliding her hands around her body, slipping one into her sleep shorts and the other under her shirt to her breast.

Fucking hell, is she seriously—fuck.

Gritting my teeth, I palmed myself through my pants, resisting the urge to stroke myself with her. I needed to keep my focus, and if I blew a load now then I'd lose my train of thought. Or I'd do something rash and regretful.

Torturously, I watched her with sharpened eyes, taking in as much detail as possible. The dim light of the lamp barely provided me enough illumination to see her squirming body through the window.

Every part of me wished my position was between her legs instead of outside her window. I wanted to reach out and touch her body, make it arch under my fingers when they'd inch down her body as a guide to engrave her body into my mind. I'd kill to have the chance to lean down and run my tongue along the length of her neck and down her body to have her taste seared onto my tongue.

Slowly, Hanna reached her peek, her tense body arching off the bed as she threw her head back with a pleasure-stricken face that was too good not to capture. Thankfully, I'd been fast enough to whip my phone out and snap a picture before she relaxed fully in bed with a blissfully content smile—which I also took a picture of.

With my phone in hand, I started to regret not videoing her like some creep to use for later. No matter, not as if this will be the last time I settle myself outside her window.

Hanna laid there staring off into space for a long while, though intentionally or not was unbeknownst to me. Seeing her zone out like so brought another issue to the forefront of my mind as my arousal ebbed.

The more I thought about it, the more I became convinced that Hanna was oblivious to her habit of spacing out. I played off the first few times as her being deep in thought and cataloged it as a cute habit in my endless file of Hanna in my brain. However, as time passed, I noticed it happening more often than not whenever she wasn't stimulated.

So, perhaps it wasn't intentional, bringing me to a different issue of what could be wrong with her. People don't space out consistently and so often, so there had to be some underlying problem causing the disassociation.

Hanna was different from other women in the past because I wanted to know her. I wanted to know everything about her, including all the bad and hideous things that make up the spunky woman I've become captivated with. I've never wanted to know anyone's past before, to understand what made them the way they are.

Yet, with Hanna, there was this need for more. It was never-ending with Hanna, and I would gladly let my madness consume me if it meant understanding Hanna fully inside and out.

Chapter 21
Hanna

"Hey, do you know where Lev went? I need to go over some details with him about our report."

I couldn't bring myself to cross the threshold into Stepan's suffocating office. Even if his door was wide open and everything was connected, his space right now felt like an entirely different world. I feared stepping in because I knew there'd be no escape from his gravitating pull once I did.

Keeping Stepan at arm's length proved more difficult with each passing day because I worked so closely with him and basically saw him for more than half my day. Unfortunately, I had no reprieve from his presence at night in the safety of my own home either with how he plagued my dreams. Well, more of graced, not plagued, because Stepan was always a welcomed sight and feeling, as much as I hated to admit it.

Stepan's gleaming blue eyes darted at me momentarily before peeling away as he straightened in his seat and leaned back in a relaxed position in the leather office chair. "He had to go on a quick run, should be back soon." If only that were all. "Are you okay? You seem kind of preoccupied over there at your desk."

"Just a personal thing, don't worry about it, and I won't let it affect my performance either, so don't worry." I assured him with a quick flash of a smile before turning around to try and leave.

Unfortunately, my steps faltered at his following words. "If Logan's not treating you right then Lev and I won't mind taking care of him."

Dragging out a sigh, I spun back around to face him with my arms crossed. "Listen, I said I was sorry for his sudden presence like that, I don't know how or why he even showed, not like I told him where I worked or asked him to come or anything." Yes, I appreciated the kind gesture of Logan bringing me some lunch the other day, but at the same time, I didn't because I didn't ask him to, nor did I appreciate being blindsided like that.

"And I told you there was no issue with it. There's no rule against employees having visitors now and then." Stepan's nonchalant demeanor chilled me to my bones with how sharp and angry his eyes were set on his smiling face. "What's he done this time to get you all frowny over there?"

My face instantly twisted with concern before a fake—and very unconvincing smile—tugged at my lips. "I'm not frowny, just got a little anxious thinking about what to wear for my date tonight." Whoops.

What came next was unexpected. "You should wear whatever you're comfortable in, don't overthink it." Once again, he still had that playfully fake smile on his face while his eyes raged.

"Are you okay?" A very loaded question, one I doubt I'd get a true answer to.

There was a brief silence from him before his eyes unexpectedly calmed down, which unsettled me greatly because how could someone make such anger disappear in the blink of an eye? "Yeah, just thinking about what I have to do outside of office hours, that's all. I was gonna ask you to go on a quick assignment, but I don't want to run the risk of keeping you late and having Logan wait when he comes picks you up later. So, I'll handle it, you just go sit your little ass down and finish what you need and stop fretting about your little date."

Stepan didn't give me a chance to say anything or question him about how he knew Logan would pick me up later because I sure as hell said nothing about my date to Stepan until the little slip-up earlier, but that was it. His hands grabbed my shoulders after he rushed out of his seat and appeared beside me with a few long strides. Spinning me around, he ushers me to my desk and sits me down in the chair before pushing me in fully.

"I almost forgot it's a time-sensitive assignment, so I have to go now." He jetted off after ruffling the top of my head, leaving me to wallow in my own confusion as to what just happened.

I didn't get a chance to question him upon his return either because he locked himself in his office when he returned. Judging by the way he beelined for his office with his taut face, I figured the assignment didn't go well. So, I decided to drop everything and let bygones be bygones. Besides, I had a date to look forward to, a date I should be getting picked up for any minute now.

During Stepan's absence, I finished my work for the day before using the employee area to freshen up and change into a dark, sleeveless denim dress that came down to mid-thigh with a pair of black leggings underneath and my trusty black combat boots on my feet. All I had to do now was wait for Logan to show up and pick me up, which should be any second now. Any second turned into any minute... This then turned into an hour until nearly three hours had passed since the promised time Logan had given me.

"You're still here?" I couldn't even bother glancing at Stepan, who'd left his office and stood by my desk where I'd laid my head down in my folded arms. "Wasn't Logan supposed to pick you up hours ago?" Yet he didn't sound concerned one bit. If anything, he sounded almost vindictive.

Disappointment filled my long sigh as I looked at my phone for the hundredth time, hoping to see some response from Logan flash across the screen. "I don't know what happened..." Was it possible that he stood me up? No, it wouldn't make sense for Logan to stand me up after we've hit it off pretty well.

A small yelp of surprise squeaked out of me when Stepan pulled me away from my desk by my chair. "Grab your stuff." His dominating tone softened with a playful edge.

No use fighting him, because either I listened and made things easy or he'd grab my stuff and drag me out of here himself. So, with a defeated sigh,

I stuffed my phone into my back pocket and got up. "Where we going?" It was way after hours, so anything work-related was out of the question.

"On a date." He stated nonchalantly with a soft smile as he settled his hand flat against my lower back to lead me out of the office to his car, where he buckled me in before I could utter a single question.

"Wha? A date? I don't remember you asking nor do I remember agreeing mister." We were already on the road when I got enough sense to sputter something out.

"That's because I didn't. I'm telling you that we're going on a date. Logan stood you up, so I'm making up for it to cheer you up because I don't like seeing you all mopey and sad." He sounded too smooth and rehearsed, which threw me for a spin because this didn't feel like some spur-of-the-moment.

Keeping my lips sealed, I look out the window to try and guess where he'd be taking me—with no luck until we stopped in front of a place.

Pit Pat Splat.

"Didn't take you for an artist." I teased with a snicker when we pulled into a parking spot at the front of the building. "Your idea of a date is to paint together?" I didn't mean to sound so conceited, but sitting and painting a scenic picture wasn't my thing.

"Have you been here before?" Stepan questioned as he killed the engine.

"No, because it's an art place, and I'm not exactly a painter." I remarked with a roll of my eyes before exiting the vehicle with Stepan before he could round around and help me out.

"A good all-around date spot if you've an artistic bone, but it's also a good place for what I've got planned for us." Stepan assured me with a smile before leading me inside the place with an arm around my shoulders.

Unconsciously, I leaned into him, and it was too late to pull away by the time I realized what I had done because it'd be too abrupt and awkward. So, I indulged in his hold with a warm smile. No matter how small or subtle, any gesture or touch from Stepan always caused heat to bloom within me. I shouldn't enjoy it as much as I should; it was a guilty pleasure, really.

"Are you going to paint me like one of your French girls? Or whatever that line is from The Titanic." Cheesiest line ever, in my opinion, but somewhat cute and silly.

"There won't be much painting done if your clothes come off." He mused under his breath before nodding at the man behind the front desk, who then led us around to a huge indoor area the size of a warehouse with various boxes and crates scattered about in almost an obstacle course.

"Though I'll find this will suit your fancy a lot more." Stepan leaned down and whispered in my ear with a low chuckle before directing my attention to a nearby table.

"Oh my God is that—" I couldn't contain my excitement as I bounced over to the table with glee.

"We got all night in here if you want, but maybe an hour before we get a late dinner and I take you home?" Stepan's voice grew closer with his footsteps until he was beside me. "I figured some paintballing would be enough to cheer you up. Ever paintballed before?" He asked while picking up the padded vest to slip it on.

Soundlessly, I shook my head as I picked up the vest to closely examine it. "I've always been curious, but never really tried it or anything. Oh my God I can shoot you and not get in trouble for it?" Okay, I shouldn't be getting so ecstatic about pelting Stepan with shots, but harmless fun was harmless fun, right?

"Tigress, you could shoot me with a real gun and bullet and I won't hold it against you." It sounded unbelievable, but the depth of his eyes meant his words were valid. He looked at me as if I could do no wrong in his eyes.

"What are we gonna get for dinner?" I doubt we'd spend more than half an hour paintballing.

I don't know about him, but I haven't eaten anything since the late afternoon, so I was rather famished. If it weren't for my excitement and the fact that I might throw up, I would've pressed him for dinner first. Well, there's nothing like a good run around and shooting to work up a good appetite.

"I was thinking we could hit up Stand Street since you love that place so much, and it has a little of everything so we don't have to decide on one thing." Smart man. At least he didn't answer 'It's up to you' or some shit like that, because I sure as hell wouldn't be able to decide for the life of me.

Stepan's smile widened darkly and playfully as he leaned down close to me. "Bet you can't get more than fifteen hits on me." Smug ass bastard.

"Oh? What's the wager then? Not that I need any motivation because I'm planning on painting you from head to toe." I chuckled with a challenging grin as I leaned up and puffed my chest out at him.

With a twinkle of victory in his eyes, as if he'd already won, he gave a soft snorting chuckle. "If you can get fifteen or more shots on me, then you and I will go weapon shopping tomorrow for any weapon of your choice. If you get under fifteen once the hour is up, then we go on another outing and dinner, my choice of course." Cheeky little asshole.

"Fine, you're on. Hope you're ready to cough up a brand new 1911 or USP 45 because ain't no way I'm losing this bet. So keep on dreaming about that second date, buddy, because that's the only place it's gonna happen." Although, if it was any fun like this one, I might throw the bet to see what else Stepan had up his sleeve. At least, that was my thought until reality kicked me in the ass to remind me why I couldn't be engaging with Stepan in any manner other than friendly.

"I was prepared to shell out for a tank, so that is nothing." Stepan's hearty chuckle filled the area briefly before a five-minute timer popped up on the scoreboard at the center of the place.

"May the best shooter win." With a flash of a smile, he disappeared behind the stacks of equipment.

Okay, maybe I wouldn't need to throw the game because my chances of losing were higher than I'd like to admit. My chances against Stepan weren't good, considering he was a world-class sniper all on his own. While my skills were good, they weren't *that* good compared to his.

I just had to stay hidden, out of sight, and somehow gain the element of surprise on him. Stepan may be one hell of a shot, but I was quicker, so as long as I could aim and react faster than him, that's all I needed. Besides, I could take the hits. He only said that I had to get fifteen hits on him and nothing about taking hits myself or anything. This would either be a game of cat 'n mouse or a game of patience, which he would win.

I had to take the offensive side of things, chase and hunt Stepan down if I wanted any chance of winning his little bet.

Do it for the gun. Do it for the gun.

The motivation repeated in my mind as my adrenaline worked itself throughout my body until my heart pounded in my chest like a rabid beast in its cage.

Snapping my head up to the scoreboard, I caught a glance at the time—forty minutes—before taking off in a random direction. The place was huge and littered with many hiding spots and vantage points. Wildly, my head snapped in every direction as I carefully stalked around the place. Left, right, up, down, everywhere.

Then, in a stroke of luck, a scurry of movement was caught out of the corner of my eyes, making me sharply change directions. My ears picked up the sounds of hurrying footsteps, and I quickly followed them until Stepan was in my sights.

Gotcha!

Not.

The paintball narrowly missed him by a damn inch. For a big guy, he was fast. Well, he was big to me, but compared to his brothers or others, he was a bit on the leaner side. As much as I appreciated Stepan's contrast from his brothers, I wished differently right now so that I'd have a bigger target to hit.

"God damn it, stay still!" I huffed when another shot narrowly missed him.

My hopes rose to new heights at the turn of a corner. A wicked grin spread across my face when Stepan's cornered body turned towards me. Shot after shot, the paintballs flew at him. Unfortunately, only three managed to stick, barely. I only got him because he was too busy climbing and vaulting over a stack of crates to escape me. Well, at least three was better than nothing; now I just needed to land twelve more hits on him, and I was golden.

Easier said than done.

Over twenty minutes, I only managed another seven hits on him after I tracked him down again and gave chase. Then he managed to slip away from me again, but I kept a close tail on him this time because the last ten minutes would fly by in a minute. I couldn't afford to hunt him down again.

Come on, just five more. Five more shots, and you get a shiny new baby.

"*Blyat*!" The reason for Stepan's sudden curse was apparent to me when I turned the corner.

Unable to help it, I let out a devious giggle before letting loose on poor Stepan, who got cornered again, this time with no escape because the only way out was through me since the other sides were the warehouse walls. Trapped, all he could do was try to dodge my shots until they became too much, and then all he did was hold his hands up in surrender while cowering and laughing in a corner. Too bad I have no concept of mercy because when the hell would I get a chance to freely shoot at Stepan like this?

"Ha! I win! You owe me a new gun!" I cheered with a crazed grin as I stood before him with my empty gun pointed at him.

Also, I had too much fun shooting Stepan in a nonlethal way.

Startled and taken aback, I let out a high-pitched sound and immediately raised my arms to shield myself when Stepan suddenly shot at me. Then, we were on the ground in laughter after I tackled him and grabbed the gun from his grasp, holding his wrists down as we laughed. "You're such a jerk for doing that," I managed through my fits of giggles while pinning him down with my body weight and trapping him under my legs and arms.

Stepan's laughter died down to soft chuckles as he reached up and took my goggles off with one hand while his other took his off. "Did you have fun though?" He asked through heavy pants as he looked up at me.

My head nodded in response while my lips grinned down at him. "I haven't had this much fun in... Well... I've actually never had this kind of fun before... So, thank you." Sure, I had fun killing people and beating people up, but never innocent fun like this.

A shiver snapped at my body when Stepan settled his hands on my thighs, digging his fingers into the back of it before stroking them slowly. Sucking in a sharp breath, I tuck my bottom lip under my teeth and chew on it to hold back my sound of pleasure as I looked down at Stepan pleadingly.

But was it for him to stop or continue?

Chapter 22
Hanna

I'M FUCKING LOSING IT.

Sucking in a sharp breath, I let loose another volley of punches at the punching bag, not giving a single care about the fact my knuckles ached for a break. I needed to vent in the best way I knew how, and since I couldn't exactly take a bat to a car or someone's face right now, this poor bag would have to do.

I don't know how, but my determination and goal of pushing Stepan aside had taken a turn for the worst.

After our little paintball outing and late-night dinner, things went astray for a bit. It was a great moment between us, too great. I nearly lost control that night in the warehouse with him; I almost gave into my urges and almost leaned down to kiss him. Guilt consumed me for a good night and day after I shut Stepan down and out that night before we both lost ourselves.

Stepan wasn't mine to have.

Apparently, my brain didn't get the memo because my dreams about Stepan occurred more often than not. Usually, I wouldn't complain be-cause anything was better than my nightmares, but the ones about Stepan started to become an annoyance because it kept him ever present in my mind—awake or not.

Also, my mind terrified me with how real it's made Stepan. They started as occasional dreams, but they plagued me more and more with time until now, where it felt like he was real. Yeah, I began to hallucinate him. It felt like he was physically in my bed with me, holding and soothing me.

It felt so damn real!

I knew I was crazy, but come on, even this started to make me sound like an insane asylum patient.

If things were different, then I might let it be because, well, I craved the safety and security Dream Stepan brought me. But I couldn't indulge myself this time, not with how I wanted to keep Stepan at a distance. I couldn't let myself become complacent with him, real or not.

"Fuck!" Pulling my hands back, I cradled my right one against my chest, groaning and hissing from the sharp pain tugging at the area.

I was about to push through the pain to give the bag another slew of punches, but a giant hand kept my hands firmly pressed against my chest. "Hanna, take a break, you're going to do more damage to yourself than that bag at this rate. Go to your desk and put some ice on that." Lev kept his concerned voice low as he looked at me with a soft frown.

At least I could enjoy Lev's company and attention without any guilt, something I've come to appreciate. Thankfully, our dynamic shifted into something good. It was a pissing contest between him and me for a small period before we somehow developed this strange best-friend-sibling relationship between us. Now, don't get me wrong, he's still an ass, but in a good way.

"I'm about to lock both of you in a damn closet if you keep tearing yourself up like this," Lev remarked with a sigh.

No, I didn't tell him about my stupid infatuation with his brother; shockingly, he somehow figured it all out on his own. I think he fried his little pea brain figuring it all out.

"And I would kill you after escaping, so think twice about that plan." I joked back with a chuckle.

At least he could always lift my mood up, and Lev, surprisingly, was good at that. He may seem like a big oaf of an idiot, but he was very attuned to people. Honestly, he could read people well, like his two older brothers, and doesn't realize it or credit himself enough for it.

"Man, if I locked you anywhere then there'd be no escaping. I mean, come on, I'm not an amateur. Besides, you'd probably be too busy shacking it up with Stepan to even try to escape." Lev teased with a deep and hearty chuckle, earning a kick to the shin from me.

"Seriously, Han, I don't know why you're beating yourself up over this shit. Just quit it with that stupid Logan dude and hook it up with Stepan. I mean, everyone can see that you both have the hots for each other, even you but you just don't accept it for some stupid ass fucking reason. I honestly didn't think you'd take Angel's advice about screwing some other dude to get over Stepan seriously." Even the idiot of the family could see my stupidity.

In all reality, yes, I should drop Logan and go spark something up with Stepan, especially since our attraction seemed mutual. Why won't I? Because I'm a stupid and stubborn bitch, that's why.

With Logan, I could keep him at a distance and not get so emotionally involved. On the other hand, if I got involved with Stepan, then I knew I would fall, hard. I was still convinced Stepan's attraction to me was fleeting or temporary. I don't have much going on for me, and no doubt he'd see that after being with me for a short time and losing interest. He's probably only chasing me because I'm not swooning at his feet or vying for his attention like most women he encountered.

I'm doing this to protect myself. Stepan will get over me sooner or later, so best we not get involved with each other and make it messier than it should be. I'd rather not unpack my baggage only to shove it back when I get kicked out.

Sighing disappointedly, Lev shook his head before placing his hands on my shoulders to turn me around. "If it were up to me, I'd lock you two in a place for a month so you two can get your shit together. Luckily, it's not up to me, so you just have to listen to me bitch about it to you whenever I see you being an ass to yourself about it."

Pretty sure if it were up to everyone, then they'd do exactly that, especially if my friends had any hands in the matter, given they knew how I am.

"Now," Lev said with a firm shove towards the direction of the door, "Go change and get your ass to your desk. I better see an ice pack on that wrist when I'm back."

"Ugh, fuck you." I scoffed in defeat with a roll of my eyes.

"If I wanted Stepan to put a bullet through my head then I'd take the offer." Lev laughed in response before giving my back a hard pat and shove.

Reluctantly, I went to the locker rooms to wash up and change back into my casual business attire, which consisted of fitted black pants, black ankle boots, a sleeveless, wine red halter neck blouse, and a black blazer thrown over.

At least Stepan wasn't in his office, so I had the whole floor to myself until Lev returned to his desk. The entire floor only consisted of Stepan's office, Lev's desk, and my desk, which was attached to Lev's, so I sat across from him. Only the three of us, besides any possible guards, were up on this level at any given time.

So, the time to myself was nice while it lasted, which unfortunately wasn't long—only about fifteen or so minutes.

"Hanna, why are you not icing and resting your wrist like you should?" Stepan sounded like a parent scolding their child when he posed his question to me. No doubt he had a stern look fitting his tone, but I didn't dare look over to confirm or deny my suspicions.

"*Malen'kaya tigritsa*, I asked you a question, so I expect an answer." So much for avoiding him because he positioned himself beside me at my desk.

"My wrist is fine, feels better now." I lied in a small voice, keeping my eyes glued to my computer screen while gritting through the pain as I typed on the keyboard.

I could hear his frustration building with his heavy breath and practically feel it suffocating me under his gaze.

I've never been one to shrink away from someone, but Stepan made me feel like a child right now for some odd reason. The underside of my desk started to look more inviting as Stepan bore his stern gaze into me.

Damn it, what the hell is wrong with me? He's just another man, so punch him in the face like you would any other man!

Steeling my nerves, I sucked in a slow, deep breath through my nose and then looked up at Stepan with hardened eyes of my own.

Shit.

"Why do you look like you want to take me over your knee?" I wanted to slap myself and jump to the bottom of the ocean after my thoughts left my mouth. I had no intention of actually asking him that!

Chuckling dryly, he pushed off the edge of the desk that he leaned back against to lower himself down and cage me in with his arms on the armrest of my chair. "Do you really want me to answer that?" The playful edge to his voice, paired with his stern expression, made it hard to discern whether it was a rhetorical question or not.

I don't know how, but he made me feel smaller by a simple question. "Better yet, why is that the question you ask? Something on your mind about me you want to share about, little tigress?"

That damn smirk of his is going to be the end of me.

Forcing the lump down my throat, I quickly slipped under his arm to try and make a run for the exit to go down to the employee lounge, but I didn't even make it an inch before he grabbed me by the back of my neck and threw me back down onto the chair.

Growling softly, I frowned deeply at him with a glare while throwing my fist at him out of instinct. Bad mistake, because of my sprained wrist. "Fuck!" I hissed under my breath when he caught my wrists with his hands.

"*Tigritsa*, stop, you're going to hurt yourself more." He sighed heavily with a slow blink before slowly getting on his knees before me.

Releasing my uninjured hand, he reached into his pocket and pulled out a roll of bandaging and a small pop-able icepack. After setting the pack on the desk, he popped open the ACE bandage wrapping, carefully and expertly wrapping my injured wrist up before placing a kiss against it, making me shiver involuntarily at the action.

If I had no self-control, then I would've grabbed his hand to keep the contact going. I was so starved for this man's touch, though I'd never fully admit it to myself and suffer in silence.

"Ice it until I come back, I'm going to run down to the med bay to grab a brace for you." He told me with a soft grunt when he pushed himself back up on his feet.

"I don't need—"

The hard look from him was all I needed to shut my mouth because that look meant business. "Thank you." I managed to force it out of myself, not wanting to seem like an ungrateful brat.

"You don't have to thank me for taking care of you, little tigress. I'll always do it no matter what because I want to." He gave me a soft smile filled with longing as he reached out and rubbed the top of my head softly.

"I'll always take care of you, don't you ever forget that."

Chapter 23

Stepan

Apparently, Logan lacked more brain cells than I credited him for.

He would've taken my threats seriously if he had been remotely intelligent. Instead, he goes on a date with Hanna even after I've given three warnings.

Logan only had himself to blame for what was about to happen. I had given him a clear warning when I left the office the other day. If Hanna knew about what I did to make our little paintballing date and dinner happen, then she'd probably beat me to a bloody pulp. Surely, I thought Logan would've gotten the message clear across his dense brain after seeing his tires slashed and watching his car blow up seconds after, but stupid me for thinking he had one functioning brain cell. Damn buffoon managed to sweeten his way into Hanna's graces the next day, so the façade of him standing her up fell into freezing waters.

No matter, the thought of him dying over the toilet from the poison in his food while his apartment burnt down brought some joy to my twisted heart. It's too bad I couldn't be around to witness the destruction and mayhem because I'd much rather spend it watching over Hanna. Hopefully, this will be the last warning I'll have to give him. I just needed him out of the picture so Hanna could be all mine for the taking.

Watching Hanna from the corner table I sat at was easy, but my positioning was the only easy part of this whole thing. Keeping myself rooted to watch her date unfold tested my self-control like the night at Guilty. I wanted to march myself over and throw Logan out of his seat—preferably out the second-story window—and take his spot across from Hanna. That or put a bullet through his head from where I was at and be rid of him forever.

Mine and Hanna's little lunch dates—at least I considered them dates—couldn't compare to her letting me take her out on an official dinner date to her favorite hole-in-the-wall place or wherever she fancied. Even with her tactic of distancing me, at least she still let me take her to lunch and give her breakfast, so I was grateful for that. However, it did irk me greatly whenever she'd ask me where I'd get the food I give her so that she could get some with Logan. The fact she even thought about him, let alone share anything with him, made the red-faced demon wake within me.

Pulling out my phone, I triple-checked with the men who worked in the restaurant to ensure things were in place as they should.

The place resided within our territory and paid us protection, so they were under Volkov control. Thankfully, Logan picked a place within our territory. Otherwise, this plan of mine wouldn't happen. Well, I could have paid a chef enough to do what I needed if they weren't already under Volkov control, but it was nice not to worry about keeping someone in check. The chef here wouldn't dare go to law enforcement with what I would have him do.

Dinner crawled by painfully for the next hour. I don't know what was more painful, watching their somewhat bland date or actually hearing their boring conversation. Hanna contributed little, mainly because she deflected nearly every question thrown at her. Logan was too self-absorbed and liked talking about himself and the successful company he inherited from his father.

Maybe I'd be less pissy if Hanna chose a better man than me to entertain, but this guy was as interesting as a brick wall. Scratch that; a brick wall had more going on than Logan. At least a brick wall could be colorful and artful with paintings and graffiti.

I never thought I'd say this, but I wouldn't even be mad if she hooked up with Lev instead of Logan. Granted, I don't want her to, nor would I let that happen, but still. Between my own brother and this moron, I much rather it be my damn brother.

I couldn't help but wonder if Logan was at home hugging his toilet at this point in time after I'd perched myself at Hanna's windowsill for the past hour. The poison—hopefully—should have kicked in by now after a few hours. In which the bomb should be going off in the next ten minutes according to the timer I'd set on it.

Well, no more of Logan tonight when I had Hanna to admire. Poor thing was passed out for the night already so soon after she came home from the date. No, she didn't knock out because she was exhausted with after-date activities. Logan had dropped her off at the corner right after the date, which pissed me off because he let her walk nearly a block home in the cold, at night, in a shady part of town.

Though to be fair, Hanna's never told Logan her exact location. I wasn't entirely sure why, but I had a few guesses. Maybe she didn't want to bring people back to her place or let others know where she lived; I was the same way with my hookups and dates, always at a hotel or their place if we were to spend the night with each other. Another thing I could think of was that maybe she was embarrassed about where she lived, but I couldn't see that from Hanna, given her personality. Another reason could be Logan himself not wanting to drive to a shady part of town to drop her off at her front door.

At least with me, she'd always be safe. I didn't give a shit about the damn area nearly being the slums. At the very least, I'd always walk her right to her door. Hanna's safety was something I'd never risk or play around with; she was much too precious.

Carefully, I forced her window open and slipped inside. I was mindful to keep as quiet as possible, even though I knew her meds would keep her knocked out well into the morning. If not, then she wouldn't remember anything if she stirred half awake.

I've slipped into her place nearly every night since her first date with Logan after their first time hooking up at Guilty. So, about two weeks now since I've developed this new nightly habit of breaking and entering Hanna's place.

Gently and slowly, I eased myself down next to her on the edge of her bed, sitting next to my sleeping beauty. Like every night before this, I let my entranced eyes drink in her body from head to toe, taking in every little detail her poorly lit lamp allowed me.

Sadly, I looked at her face, letting the tips of my rough fingers ghost her discolored cheek. I always wondered why she bought so much makeup, but after seeing her truly that first night, I connected the dots easily enough.

Now I wanted to know what happened to her, to know how the majority of the right side of her face got burned. Most of her right cheek was consumed by the scar, which had a very slight texture to it, just barely noticeable upon a quick touch. I only felt and knew the difference now after tracing every inch of her multiple times.

I could've easily asked her friends about it, but then I'd have to explain how I even knew of it in the first place. So far, my search for answers has led me to dead ends. There were no reports or articles with Hanna's name tied to it, so either the event never made it to any report, or it happened when she was a minor, so her name was kept out of the media. Well, the other option would be to—illegally—obtain her medical records; unless she never got official medical treatment, then nothing would be in any system.

Sighing softly, I leaned down and placed a kiss against her temple, letting my lips linger against her sweet skin so I could bask in her warm scent of ginger, honey, citrus, and dried tea leaves. If only I could spend every night and waking morning with her in my arms.

The soft sound of fabric scrunching under my fists softly scratched at the silence in the room. A dull ache gripped my tense muscles as I resisted the urge to scoop her up in my arms and hold her tightly against me. Her small body would fit and feel so nicely against mine.

A slight shake and whimper from my little tigress released the tension in my body with a wave of worry. Looking down, I watched Hanna's soft face twist with pain and fear as her nightmare took hold of her.

Nightmares were something Hanna suffered nearly every night from what I've observed, but they were usually fleeting. However, there were the rare ones that lingered, like this one tonight.

It was a clear indicator that her nightmare, this time, took hold of her with how hard her face twisted and gutted at me while her body started to toss and turn. Soon, her little whimpers picked up to full-blown words and screams.

Then, like the other nights before, I instinctively laid down next to her, wrapping my arms tightly around her waist and shoulders, holding her tightly against me as I shushed and whispered in Russian to her. *"Moya malen'kaya tigritsa, vse v poryadke. YA zdes', ya tebya poymal. Ty v bezopasnosti. Oni bol'she ne smogut prichinit' tebe vreda, tak chto vernis' ko mne. YA zdes' radi tebya, ya tebya poymal."*

Carefully, I turned her body to face me fully as I had been holding her sideways. *"Dorogaya, vernis' ko mne. Ochnites' ot svoyego koshmara. Tvoya mechta zdes', derzhit tebya. Prosypaysya ko mne."* I continued to whisper sweetly to her as I cradled her head against my chest, my fingers softly stroking her thick, voluptuous slate black hair.

My other hand held her lower back tightly, drawing small circles with my thumb to soothe her further. "My little tigress, fight it."

Much to my relief, Hanna's body started to calm shortly after I held her. I hated seeing her all twisted up in fear and suffering; seeing her go through the pains of her nightmares felt like a bullet to my gut while a knife twisted at my heart. I was helpless to her when it came to her nightmares. I couldn't make them go away, disappear forever.

At least my presence seemed to help her. The first few times I saw her go through the full motions of her nightmares wrenched at my heart; I don't know what came over me the third time I saw it happen, but I crawled into her tiny twin bed and held onto her for dear life. I'd half expected her to wake up and clock me one in the face. Still, I guess her medications did a better job than I thought because she calmed down in my embrace and peaked her eyes open momentarily to mumble something under her words before snuggling into me.

Just like now, her squinted eyes softened and opened halfway. Her brown orbs looked at me in a daze as her hands gripped the front of my shirt tightly. "I wish this was real, but I'll take what I can get. I want to have you so bad, it's not fair." Is it wrong of me to somewhat like her drugged up like this?

God, it'd be so easy to do anything to her right now, and she'd probably have no recollection of it. I shouldn't even entertain the idea, but I was only a human with needs at the end of the day. If it were anyone else, I would throw the idea out the window the moment it trickled in, but I festered on it when it came to Hanna.

I haven't acted much on my urges, maybe groping a feel of her ass or tits here and there the past nights at most, but something snapped in me tonight with how she pressed her body into me. So, unable to help myself, I slid my hands down to her bubbly ass and groped her until I got a small groan from her.

Fuck it, I need a better feel of her, to taste her. Just a small taste.

Ghosting my lips over hers, I tilt her head back by fisting the back of her head softly. My lips left a trail of kisses down her neck before I buried my face into the crook of her neck, groaning internally as I got a lungful of her intoxicating scent.

God, I really hoped she wouldn't fully wake. Otherwise, I'd be in really deep shit.

Cradling the back of her head with one hand, I carefully slip the other into her sleep shorts, muffling a groan by biting my lips when I felt the thin lace underneath. Slowly, I slid my hand deeper until I cupped her covered sex fully over her panties, letting my hand linger against her heat as I debated on whether I should continue; it wasn't too late to pull my hand back out and leave, but at the same time, I have my hands in her pants, literally.

Fuck it, not like I was a saint. As if I haven't been breaking her boundaries with what I've done so far.

Much to my surprise, Hanna's hips bucked at my hand, her sweet moans slipping out of her parted lips. God, she'd kill me in an instant if she knew what was happening right now.

"*Blyat'.*" I hissed under my breath when I traced a finger along the edge of her panties to part them—only to find it be the string of her soaked thong and not full fabric. "What's got you all this wet, *malenkaya?*" I muttered against her lips, suppressing my groan as I slipped my fingers between her folds and found her clit.

"You." Her answer dragged out with her moan as her hips rolled into me more. "I need to come, please."

Fuck. I can't deny her when she sounded so desperate, even if she wasn't fully aware of it. "Such a naughty girl." I growled into her ear as I slid two fingers into her tight pussy. "Fuck you're so tight."

Whatever control I had—if I even had any, to begin with—was ice-thin as I thrust my fingers in and out of her. I wanted it to last, but my urges got the best of me. My palm pressed and rubbed against her swollen clit as my fingers pumped in and out of her at a fast pace because I wanted to hear more and more of her melodic moans. "That's it, come for me, little tigress." Her soft face twisted with pleasure and bliss as her moans picked up with her squirming body and tightening walls.

"Stepan." Fuck, hearing her moan my name at the height of her pleasure was nearly enough to make me come in my pants.

Her body slowly relaxed as I helped her ride out her orgasm. She gave out a small whimper of protest when I slowed my fingers to a stop, pulled out of her completely, and fixed her thong back into place before pulling my hand out completely.

The urge to rip her shorts off and bury my face between her legs skyrocketed the moment her addictive taste hit my tongue when I brought my fingers up to my mouth to suck and lick them clean. I could do it and get away with it, but then I'd never leave.

"That's so hot." Hanna's dazed voice matched her melted brown eyes as she smiled at me with a wide smile filled with happiness and bliss. "Thank you, Daddy."

Fucking hell, this woman's going to be the death of me.

I let out an internal groan as I wrapped my arms around her again to hold her close and tight. I wanted to enjoy this side of her more before torturing myself by leaving her side for the night.

I loved Hanna for who she was, all her spunk, confidence, bite, all of it. I didn't care about having a mouthy woman or not, or at least I didn't care when it came to Hanna; I found her fire amusing and wanted.

However, I wished Hanna would let her softer side come out sometimes. I've only ever gotten bits and pieces of it when she'd show her gratitude with a smile whenever I'd drop her food off or take her out for lunch. I wished she'd let this hidden side of her out, make herself vulnerable to me so I could show and prove to her that I could protect and guard her and her secrets with my life.

Leaning down, I kissed the top of her head while wiping her stray tears away. "I am always here little tigress, always and forever. I am not going anywhere. I am going to wait for you, even if it means forever. Whenever you are ready, *malen'kaya tigritsa*, I will be here." Hanna is it for me.

I meant every single word. I will wait for her, even if it means forever.

I wanted no one else.

Only Hanna.

Chapter 24
Hanna

FUCKING STEPAN.

I should be enjoying sex with Logan, not like he was a bad lay, but no, I couldn't. I couldn't enjoy my time in bed with my boy toy because all I could think about was Stepan—fucking Stepan.

Logan's hands may be the ones running down my body, but all I could imagine were Stepan's hands and how they'd feel in place of Logan's. I wanted the fire Stepan's touch brought to my body, not this budding warmth from Logan.

I really should heed my friends' advice of cutting Logan off before I lead him on too much, especially since I really have no intentions of getting too deep or far with him. For some reason, though, I sensed he knew of my reservations about our relationship.

The two of us seemed complacent with what we've got going on, this casual relationship of sorts. We both enjoyed our time together; we made each other happy and all, and sex was good—not great but good—and all together, it seemed like a good relationship. But that was it; it was good, not great. If I really thought about it, we felt more or less like friends with benefits.

Of course, I was in a state of denial. Logan's a great guy, a little self-absorbed, but overall great. Was he up to par with Stepan? No, not even close, but I refused to admit it because I tried to make this relationship work for my stubborn sake.

As long as Dream Stepan keeps up his nightly visits, I'd be okay with sticking it out with Logan. In hindsight, that's probably fucked up on some level, but not like I was cheating on Logan because dream Stepan was just that, a dream, a figment of my unconscious imagination. I couldn't control my dreams.

Although, I wished I could have some kind of control over them. Recently, they've become *very* vivid, as in I feel like Stepan is physically there next to me in my bed, holding me tenderly while his low voice whispers sweet words into my eager ear. Even when I reach out to touch his handsome face, to trace my finger along his sharp features while losing myself in his illustrious blue eyes.

It all felt so real.

He felt so real.

But he wasn't. There's no way any of it could be beyond a figment of my overactive imagination—Stepan's only a hallucination, probably a side effect from my medication. I should get my meds changed, though, if the side effects got that bad, but a huge part of me didn't want to.

My meds before did an okay job with helping my sleep and anxiety and keeping my nightmares at bay—mostly. I still suffered the full brunt of the nightmares about my past more often than not. Ever since Dream Stepan made his appearance, they've been almost nonexistent. The nightmares would start and go away the moment I felt his presence and embrace.

Disappointedly, I found myself waking up to an empty bed every morning. The only part of my hallucination that remained were the remnants of his cozy and soothing scent of spices.

My mind toyed with the idea of him actually being there next to me in my bed, but I quickly shook the idea out of my head with a ridiculous laugh because it was beyond absurd. No way could such a thing be possible. I'd notice any signs of a break-in *if* Stepan were crazy enough to pull something like breaking and entering my place while I slept.

Stepan breaking into my place to watch me sleep or him putting such effort towards me was beyond ludicrous. He'd never stoop so low as to do something so creepy and wrong like that either; it wasn't in his character.

A sharp hiss of pain pierced my train of thought. My eyes locked back onto Stepan, who sat in his office chair with me between his legs, holding an icepack to his bruised nose. "I still say ya'll should've let Nikolai have a go at Lev for all he said. I mean, he deserves a good beating for saying that about Angel and all. Hell, I want to have a swing at him after hearing about everything."

Stepan and his brothers got into a minor tiff two nights ago when they gathered for their weekly meeting, and the subject of Angel's real identity came up. Lev dug himself a grave with their eldest brother by dragging his wife through the mud and making insinuations about her intentions and feelings regarding another one of their brothers.

Nikolai didn't take too kindly to Lev's words and nearly gave him a full-blown beating if Stepan hadn't stepped in with his younger brothers, a set of twins named Alexei and Arseny. Poor Stepan got headbutted in the moment and got his nose busted up good.

Letting out a deep breath through his mouth, he gave me a stuffed groan and shook his head. "Don't, tigress, he already feels bad enough, and he apologized and meant it. Just leave Lev to his own devices and let him come around on his own. You jumping on his back won't help any. Just leave him." At least Stepan's nasally voice eased some of the edge off because I couldn't help but find it funny.

"Are you okay? You seem kind of off, not in a completely bad way, but a little off." Even when he's the one hurt, he still worries about me when there's not much to even be concerned about.

"Didn't sleep too well last night, that's all, but don't worry, I'm still and always on my A-game." I assured him with a confident smile and a short giggle.

"Why didn't you sleep well?" For some reason, his question made me feel wary as a ripple of chills made my body erupt in goosebumps.

There was this glint in his eyes, and he almost sounded like he smirked with his words. Yet, I couldn't tell because of the icepack and my own hand, which covered the lower half of his face. But he sounded and looked like he knew something I didn't or something he shouldn't and was being a cheeky bastard and rubbing it in my face.

"Just an off night, nothing much. Plus I stayed up late talking to Angel, so my routine got thrown off." I half lied smoothly. No one, not even Angel, knew about my vivid dreams of Stepan, and I intended to keep it that way. So, telling Stepan was the very last thing I wanted to do. He'd probably think I was insane if he knew about my dreams about him.

"Go take a nap on the couch then if you're a little tired, Lev won't be back for a while on his end of the assignment, and you've finished what you needed for now." He sounded too encouraging with his suggestion when he nodded towards the black leather couch in his office.

Shaking my head defiantly, I narrowed my eyes warily at him. "I'll busy myself with other tasks. Sleeping on the job is frowned upon anyways." The act sounded nice and welcoming.

Strangely, the thought of him watching over me as I slept didn't creep me out. Maybe because I became used to my late-night visits from Dream Stepan. The notion of it was somewhat calming. For some reason, I got a warm sense of security to be able to sleep soundly with him watching out for me. Creepy, but sweet.

"Wouldn't be frowned upon if your boss tells you to or allows you to. I want you performing at your peek, and you can't do that if you aren't well rested." Stepan rebutted, this time definitely smiling or smirking from the lift in his cheeks.

"I can't, I'm used to the security of my bed." Now, that's a full lie.

My bed was a ratty-ass twin-sized piece of cardboard. I really should get a new mattress, but my laziness to get a new one has prevented me from doing so. Well, in all honesty, my current mattress wasn't *that* bad, it had an old charm to it.

"Don't worry, you won't need your bed to keep you safe. I'll be here to chase away the bad dreams." His eyes gained *that* glint to them again as his voice took an edge, making the hairs on the back of my neck stand up.

"What if I'm not tired anymore, hm?" I challenged him defiantly with a glare and slight frown as I pursed my lips a little.

Chuckling, Stepan reached up and grasped my wrist firmly, removing my hand and the icepack from his face to show me his dangerous smirk and burning eyes. "There's many ways to solve that problem, little tigress."

"You're not letting me leave your damn office unless I take a nap, huh?" I could make a run for it; the door was wide open.

It'd be easy to kick him away while he sat in his chair and put some distance between us before bolting for the door and shutting it behind me.

"What do you think, tigress?"

The cocky ass smirk on his face provided enough of an answer to me.

There was no escape, not unless he let me.

There was no escaping Stepan, not in reality or beyond.

Like every night for the past few weeks, he manifested in my mind and next to me as I lay in bed. His phantom touch felt surreal, as if he was physically in my bed, embracing me in his safe and strong arms. The breaths of his words hitting my ears felt as real as the shivers down my spine.

"What troubles my little tigress?" His concern was almost palpable as his hand wiped away the tears from my nightmare.

"Them, always them." Those cursed hands felt like acid on my skin with every touch.

Even if they could never touch me again, let alone harm me, I couldn't escape them in my slumber. Medications helped curb my nightmares, but they didn't completely cure me of them. No, nothing ever could. Or so I thought. Oddly enough, this strange presence of Stepan, something my insane mind probably conjured up, did well in protecting me from the horrors of my past.

His touch and words were what pulled me away from the burning flames that threatened to consume me like once before; they kept me safe from the other hands that sought to harm and scar me. If only this could be forever. If only this could be real. I knew for a damn fact that once morning came, I'd be alone.

I probably should get new medications if the hallucinations were becoming this out of hand, but if I did, then I wouldn't have this solace.

How the fuck did I even end up like this?

"I'm here, I'm always here for you." Such sweet lies threatened to shatter my dream.

"No you won't, you won't always be. You're not even here right now, just a figment of my fucked up imagination." My words slurred out of me because I was so heavily medicated.

"As long as you want me, I will always be here for you." His scent of warm spices melted my body as I relaxed into him fully.

"That's what my dad said, and now he's scattered somewhere I don't know." Man, it felt like someone shoved a handful of cotton into my mouth, and my head grew heavier and heavier with each passing moment because the meds were trying to do their job.

"You really loved your dad huh?" If my mind functioned as it should, or if I was awake, I would have quipped back at him. "You're always so happy at the mention of him."

"The best. Doted me like hell, spoiled me, but taught me well. He wanted a good life for me, encouraged me to pursue my dreams. I told him I wanted to fight people when I grew up, so he enrolled me in everything he could think of, from karate to MMA and everything. He spared nothing when it came to me." Yep, still a violent little shithead even back then, and I was proud of it.

Memories of my father teaching me to defend myself and letting me play fight against him flooded my mind and brought an uncontrollable smile to my face until the castle came crumbling down. "I miss him so much. Why'd he have to die? It's not fair." The tears streamed down my face whether I liked it or not.

I don't know what he said. If he said anything, it all sounded like incoherent mumbles to my muffled ears, but the vibrations of his voice were enough to calm me as he held me.

"Don't leave me, please." I begged as if I could control my own mind.

"I'm never going anywhere little tigress." The warmth of his lips branded my temple. "I promise."

Chapter 25

Stepan

THUD! BANG! SLAM!

The heavy door of my office swung open with a fury before being slammed shut. Some small objects within my office, small vases, and unsecured decorations shook and rattled from the force of the door slamming shut.

I didn't bother lifting my head to the furious Asian woman who trudged up and around the desk until she was next to me.

SLAM! Clink.

It was hard *not* to look up at her when she slammed a plastic bag right in front of my face on the desk. I took my sweet time, though, letting my eyes trail up her arm to her furious face. Her nostrils flared with her labored breaths while her sharp eyes sliced into me like daggers.

"Li—"

Hanna promptly cut me off by grabbing the collar of my shirt and jerking me closer to her as she leaned down until her seething face was inches from mine. "You better have a good fucking explanation." Her voice was low, raspy, and saturated with anger, almost like something possessed her and spoke through her.

Keeping my calm and relaxed demeanor, I lazily glance over the brass bullet briefly before locking my eyes with Hanna again. "That's a bullet, something that gets fired—"

Guess Hanna wasn't amused by my smart-aleck antic today because she shoved me violently back into my chair. Her tiny, roughish hand wrapped itself around my neck after she climbed into my lap, straddling it while leaning her weight into her choke hold.

With a growl, she picked the bullet up again, this time holding it right in my face. "You're fucking lucky I don't fire this through your leg. What the fuck was it doing inside Logan's car?"

This was the worst time to be turned on, but by God Hanna made it impossible not to. The little beast of a tiger finally let her claws out, and I fucking love it.

"Maybe your little boyfriend likes to collect bullets, ever think of that?" I continued to play dumb, plastering an innocent but cheeky and evil smile on my face.

A sharp breath was sucked through my nose when her grip on my neck tightened to where I could feel my ears buzz a little. "Don't be a fucking smart ass with me Stepan, you really don't want to piss me off more. So, answer the fucking question before I choke the life out of you and your dick."

"What makes you think I'd oppose to that?" I challenged with an edgy smirk, daring her to make good on her threat. I'd love to see her try.

Letting out an angry growl, she tightened her hand, actually choking me to where I could feel a full buzz from the lack of oxygen flowing up to my brain.

Groaning softly, I let out a raspy chuckle before grabbing Hanna by her hips and throwing her off me. I threw her backward, using the motion of me rising out of my seat to help shove her back onto the desk.

Grabbing her wrist, I tore her hand away from my neck with a firm yank and pinned it to the desk by her head as I leaned down onto her.

Hanna's other hand shot out across my face, landing a solid slap that resounded throughout the room when her hand connected, causing my head to snap to the side from impact.

Before I could fully recover and make a grab for her free hand, Hanna curled her legs up and used them to kick me off of her. With the opening, she instantly rolled off the desk and scrambled to the door.

Holding my cheek with a twisted grin, I mused a dark chuckle to myself. "Well, didn't expect to get *that* turned on by that, little tigress." The slap zapped a shock of pleasure straight down to my aching cock.

Like hell would I let her escape now.

With a quick tap on my keyboard, the door to my office locked with a loud click just as Hanna grabbed at the handle. After jiggling the handle a few times without success, she shouted angrily as her fist pounded against the door. "Mother fucker, let me out!" She demanded with a snarl, twisting her head around to glare at me harshly.

Slowly, without a care in the world, I stalked over to her with an unreadable expression. "You really want to know why my bullet was in your little boy toy's car?" I barely recognized my own voice because it came out so low and dangerously calm despite being filled with anger.

With every step, Hanna backed further towards the door until her back was flushed against it. Realization widened at her eyes, but before she could dart away to put some distance between us, I closed the distance with vast strides and slammed my hands against the door on either side of her head, caging her in.

"That bullet is his final warning after the faulty bomb," I growled darkly as I pressed my large body against hers, pinning and trapping her.

"You could have hit him you fucking bastard. The bullet grazed his cheek." She seethed back with a wavering voice.

"Oh please, if I wanted to blow his head off then I would have. I never miss, darling, never. His cheek was grazed because I wanted it to be, for it to fully hit home for him. I'm rather insulted you'd think I'd miss, tigress." I haven't missed a single target by a hair since my teen years when my father forced me to hone my skills to the utmost possible.

Unless I was utterly sick or other outside factors, such as the weather, interfered greatly, my shots always hit dead on. No one ever sees me coming, nor do they hear me coming. It was why everyone called me The Silent Volk. I might not be able to pack hard punches like Nikolai or Lev, but I made up for it being deadlier in stealth and deadly precision.

Some might see it as cowardly, hiding in the shadows and taking the kill shot when people least expect it. I saw it as being efficient. No point in pummeling someone to death if you're going to waste all that energy to get hurt and dirty in the process, not when a well-aimed shot took care of the problem faster and cleaner.

"Sorry, because it seems like you're missing quite a lot lately, like the hints I throw in your face about not being fucking interested." She spat spitefully before careening her head forward to butt mine.

My hand instantly slid over her neck to wrap my rough fingers around her slender neck. With a *thud*, her head bounced against the door when I pinned her neck abruptly.

Unable to help it, I let my wicked chuckle rumble in my chest. "I thought I already made it clear to you that I don't like liars, Hanna. You're lucky I don't punish you for all the empty lies you've spewed regarding your feelings towards me."

Hanna opened her mouth to argue, but I didn't let her get a word out. My grip tightened around her neck before pressing her more into the door while I leaned my lips down to her ear. "Your mouth moves mindlessly as does your tongue. I don't need your words to tell me all I need to know. Just one look in your eyes, at your body language, your reactions, your demeanor, hell even the subtle tones of your voice, is all I need to discern the truth from you."

"You're fucking insane Stepan." She seethed through gritted teeth as her hands clawed at my wrist.

"That's not a denial I hear." I smirked arrogantly in response while parting her legs with a knee. "Go ahead and lie to me, lie to me right now."

Using my free hand, I capture both her wrists and pin them against the wall. Then, I jammed my hips between her plush thighs until I was flushed against her covered core.

"Lie to me and tell me you aren't turned on by this, that if I stuck my hand down your panties right now then you won't be soaking wet, that you don't like being in this position with me." I challenged her cockily, hovering my face less than an inch from hers after forcing her head up by gripping her jaw with my fingers.

Slowly, I rolled my hips into her, pressing myself more than firmly enough for her to feel the raging hard-on I had under my slacks.

Hanna's sweet lips parted, but no words came out, only a jagged, gasping whisper of a moan as her eyes fluttered softly.

"Go on, fucking lie to me little tigress. I dare you to tell me right now that you aren't enjoying this, that you don't want my cock in you right now after feeling how hard I am for you. Go ahead, lie. Give me a good reason to bend you over the couch and fuck you raw until you scream loud enough for the whole building to know who you belong to." My raspy voice dipped lower until I almost growled under my breath.

My stormy blue eyes remained dead set on her endless dark pools from how blown with pleasure her pupils were. There wasn't a single ounce of resistance in her inviting eyes as her body ceased its struggle against my grip.

I couldn't help but smile victoriously when I felt the subtle movements of her hips grinding back against mine as I kept up the slow, torturous pace.

"Don't say what you don't mean Stepan." I barely caught her sweet, whispering words in my lustful haze.

"I am always a man of my words, Hanna." I wasn't some stupid boy or a teenager trying to talk a game I couldn't play and win.

"Fucking hell, I'm supposed to be mad at you right now." She whined with a pathetic but cute stomp of her foot against the door.

Taking in a shaky breath, she looked at me with tearful eyes. "I fucking hate you. Why can't you just let me be with Logan. You already know you and me can't happen. So, just fucking let me go." Her voice ladened with a longing sadness that made my lips flatten.

Sighing sadly, I leaned my forehead against hers and looked deeply into her eyes. "I can't, Hanna, I can't ever let you go. If you were truly happy with Logan then maybe I could, but even a blind monkey can see how you and him aren't a good match."

I leaned in ever so slightly on a whim to ghost my lips against hers. "I am done playing by your rules, Hanna. I've given you your damn space, respected your boundary for us, but not anymore. I am going to show you that you belong with me starting tonight, and I won't stop until you have my ring on your finger and my collar around your neck."

Reluctantly—and unhappily—I let her go and stepped back after unlocking the door. "That is a promise my little tigress."

"I'll just keep rejecting you until you grow tired and fed up." She retorted defiantly in a solid and confident voice as she straightened herself out.

Chuckling deeply, I looked at her with a raised brow and a confident smile. "I will never grow tired or fed up with you, Hanna. Never. And the sooner you come to realize and accept that along with us, the sooner the real fun and pleasure between us can begin. If not, then, well, don't blame me for all the punishments you'll be getting by my hands."

Turning around, she opened the door and stood there for a moment before turning her head back to look at me with hardened and narrowed eyes. "If I see your ass tonight at Guilty then I'm going to fucking kill you."

Her attempt to be threatening was adorable. I would've taken her seriously if she meant it. From her squared-back shoulders to her playfully hardened eyes, I knew she'd presented me with a challenge.

I dare you. That's what her eyes screamed at me.

"If I see you at Guilty tonight with Logan then you've no one but yourself to blame for what happens after I throw you over my shoulder and march out of the club with you." This would be the only warning she'd get from me.

Let the games begin.

Chapter 26
Hanna

FUCKING STEPAN.

Fuck him.

It didn't take me long to connect the dots after Logan had come clean with me about receiving threats ever since he became involved with me. Sure, hearing about the notes, the break-in, and the dead animals was somewhat brushed off because anyone could have done those as a stupid prank. When he showed me the bullet that blew out his car window after grazing his cheek, that's what made the dot to Stepan connect. I knew his signature at this point after seeing his personal stash of bullets.

Stepan didn't use mass-produced bullets; he made his own or, at the very least, had his special order. His bullets had a well-hidden but distinct pattern at the tip of the round. If I hadn't seen his bullets, I could've missed it myself because the patterned lines followed the bullet's length down to the tip. The V's carved into them could easily be mistaken as striations from the gun barrel at a glance. Hell, I would have played it off as striations myself if it weren't for Stepan, who'd explained the point of it to me when I questioned him about his ammunition long ago.

'Why are your bullets so weird? Are they used? What are these lines?'

'It's the letter V stripped down around the bullet. V for Volk 'cause that's what everyone calls me. I made it that way to throw people off because no one

is none the wiser. They think it's striations or manufacture error whenev-
er they find one of my rounds. Of course, my enemies know my signature,
so if they see it then they know they've got to watch their backs.'

Honestly, I had to give him credit for his innovative thinking regarding his signature. Really, if I hadn't known any better, or gotten that background from Stepan, I would have played the shooting off as some coincidence or some stupid idiot misfiring.

I found it hard to wrap my mind around why he would do that? I'd rejected him, made my rejection known, kept him at a distance, and kept my boundary strong. Did he do this out of spite because I rejected him? No, I couldn't see Stepan doing something so childish like that.

The answer was clear deep down: he did it to keep me to himself because he saw through my lies. His sharp eyes could cut through steel easily, so seeing through my defenses would've been easy for him.

As infuriated as I had been with him earlier, I couldn't argue strongly against him because he was right, yet again. My mouth uttered the lies, and my tongue weaved. I thought maybe I could fake it until I made it if I lied to myself enough. Superficially, I started to believe it, and I continued to live my lies about Logan and Stepan happily. I mean, I just had to keep to the surface because if I dipped my head down, the truth would devour me like a shark in open waters.

After what happened in his office earlier, the solution to my problem was clear, but I refused to take it because I was still so upset and angry at him for threatening Logan and making me face my true feelings regarding him and me.

So, I decided to do something stupid.

Just one last time.

I'd end it tonight, things with Logan, I mean. If Stepan wants to give chase, I'll give him one to see if he's worth it. After one last night with Logan, just as a middle finger to Stepan because fuck him.

Initially, I planned on forgoing my date with Logan tonight, but after the little argument with Stepan, I went fuck it. Might as well try to fuck my emotions out of my system and piss Stepan off while I was at it; kill two birds with one stone.

So, that's how I ended up here, in a private room at Guilty, rather than being at the gym beating my knuckles up.

The plan was simple: meet up with Logan at Guilty for one last night, and then we'd part ways forever. Unfortunately, the world had other plans by the name of Stepan.

Logan had left the room to get some water for me, and not a minute later, Stepan barged through the door with an eerie, dark, angry expression that sent a shock of fear and excitement jolting through my body.

I was fucked, royally fucked, like beyond fucked six ways 'til Sunday.

Stepan was seething as he stalked up to my retreating body. Every step he took towards me was another scoot back on the bed in response from my terrified body until I hit the headboard. I couldn't read him, couldn't predict him.

He may be seething with rage, but it was all tightly tucked beneath this overly calm and smug-like exterior. The storm raged in his eyes, making those soft, bright blue orbs of his darken; his mouth was curved in a twisted, knowing smirk as if he knew I would disobey him and go on my date with Logan but was extremely resentful that I did.

Swallowing my fear, I tried my best to harden my eyes confidently at him when he stood at the bedside. "Logan's going to be back any minute now, so leave." My body and mind knew the lie before it left me shakily. Logan wasn't coming back, not if Stepan was here.

Disapprovingly, Stepan tutted at me while shaking his head. "Oh Hanna, I'm really going to have to teach you a hard lesson about lying after tonight." Something about the edge his voice took on towards the end had my body spurring into action.

My body barely twisted to scramble off the other side when Stepan pounced in response. "Let me go!" His massive body pinned my struggling one face down on the bed, and his leg was thrown over the back of both my thighs to keep my legs pinned while his hands pinned my wrists.

"Get off!" I snarled, throwing my head back violently in hopes of catching his face.

Even though I fought him hard, he still managed to wrangle both my wrists into one of his hands before fisting my hair and jerking my head back at a harsh angle. "Logan's not coming back, ever. Him and I had a nice little chat before you even showed up at the club tonight. Now, here's what's going to happen, I'm going to take you back to my place where we'll work out our emotions, then we'll talk like civilized people in the morning over breakfast. How you leave this place with me is up to you, you can either be a good girl and walk out of here with me, or we can do it my way which involves some rope and toys. Either way, you're leaving here with me, so what will it be, little tigress?"

My heavy breaths heaved at my chest while my eyes strained to glare at him out of the corner of my eyes. "Fuck you." I spat venomously, jerking my body under him more violently in another attempt to get free.

"Oh, you will tonight, *tigritsa*." His deep, hot, breathy chuckle hitting my ear made me shudder involuntarily.

The feeling of his teeth grazing the shell of my ear brought another wave of arousal to my dying struggle. "What's your safeword, little tigress? Or do you want to use 'fire' for tonight?" His demeanor softened with his caring voice, making my insides purr delightfully at the sudden switch between his hardness and concern.

"Fire, that's always been my safeword." Considering how much I've been burnt in my life, it seemed fitting to use it as my safeword. Coincidentally, it was the club's universal safeword too.

"I'm giving you one chance right now to use it before I take you out of here. You can use it whenever you want with me whenever you want me to stop or slow down, but your first chance is right here and now. So, do you want to use it?" I could see his desire for me thundering in his darkened eyes, but I could also see his restraint as he placed my comfort and consent above his own primal wants and needs.

I wanted to melt under his gaze. I've never wanted to submit to someone so needily like now. How he looked at me made me feel safe and secure.

"No." Not an ounce of hesitation or reservation about my firm answer to him.

"I'm going to do so much to you, make you hurt all over with pleasure, make that line blur between pain and pleasure. I won't stop unless I hear you say your safeword. I won't push you far tonight, but I will push you even if and when you resist me. If you ever feel unsafe or uncomfortable at any point tonight, I want you to use your safeword, understood?" Stepan moved his head into my full line of sight, locking his serious eyes with mine.

Once again, there wasn't an ounce of hesitation as I gave him my. "Yes." This was insane, but my instincts were in control.

If I were being reasonable to any degree then I'd use my word right now and put an end to all of this, but my basal need for Stepan overrode my whole system. Something in me switched the moment he grabbed me and pinned me helplessly under him. The submissive part of me grinned and purred with complete delight at him taking me into his own hands.

"Ah!" The tension at my head tightened briefly with the jerk from Stepan.

"Yes, what?" His dangerously low voice echoed into my ear.

"Yes, dad." I quipped with a taunting smirk, earning another harsh yank from him that made me gasp.

"Try again, little tigress." His response was playful in nature, but baiting.

Give me a reason. That's what his eyes screamed at me as his hand tightened around my hair.

"Yes, sir." Another shudder shook my body from the warmth those words brought me.

Stepan pulled at my hair again, this time less harshly than the other two times. "Close, try again, *malenkaya*."

Feeling a little bold, I let my lips curl upwards in a soft, playful smile as I looked at him with hooded eyes. "Then I suggest you start showing me you earn the right to be called my Daddy."

That spurred him back into action.

Chuckling, he pressed a firm kiss against my neck before hauling me up to my feet. "Are you going to be good and come nicely? Or are we going to do this the hard way?" By the way his voice turned excited towards the end, I surmised he'd like a struggle from me.

Throwing my weight back entirely against him, I knocked both of us off our feet and onto the ground. Stepan landed with a winded grunt when I slammed back on top of him, and his hold on me loosened enough for me to slip and scramble away.

I barely made it a stride before tripping down to the ground because he'd grabbed my ankle and pulled my leg out from under me. "Asshole!" I groaned after catching my breath that was knocked from me.

Before I could get a deep breath in, the heavy feeling of Stepan came crashing down on me, winding me again. "Get your fat ass off of me!" I threw my arms back and twisted my body and kicked my legs to try and land a hit or throw him off.

On one swing, he caught my wrist and wrenched my arm back behind me, securing it to my back with one hand while the other grabbed my other until he had both my wrists pinned behind me.

"What are you—hey!" Something coarse but soft started to wrap and tighten around my wrists and forearms, binding them together tight and firm.

"You wanted to do this the hard way." Stepan grunted with effort as he pulled the two of us back up to our feet.

"Hey! Put me down!" I protested, flailing my legs when he threw me over his shoulder like a sack of potatoes.

Chuckling, Stepan tightened his arm around the back of my thighs before slapping my ass—hard—with his other hand, making me yelp from the sudden sting.

My struggling came to an abrupt halt at the feeling of his hand sliding up between the inside of my thighs. The short, lacy, black dress I wore did nothing to protect me from his searing touch as his fingers stroked along the length of my covered pussy, making me bite out a strangled moan.

The feeling of some object slipping under my soaked thong with his fingers had me jerking and squirming again for a moment before I went rigid at the feeling of something hard being pushed into my wet pussy. "Stepan! What did you—ah!" The sensation of vibrations against my sensitive walls had me shuddering and whimpering.

"You fucking asshole, take it out. You can't just shove a vibrator in me like that." I protested weakly with a shiver from the pleasureful waves washing over my body.

Smacking my ass again, he started for the door. "Says who?" Stepan's arrogant little laugh made me want to punch him. He's lucky my hands were bound, otherwise, I would!

"Says me you asshole." I groaned with another shudder from the feeling of my nipples stiffening under my dress.

The fabric of the dress shifted with each step Stepan took, rubbing against my sensitive nipples and stimulating them while the vibrator in me kept my pleasure afloat well. It wouldn't be enough to make me orgasm, but it was damn well an annoyance because it'd keep me in a constant state of arousal.

"Well, as I told you earlier in the office, I am done playing by your rules. I'm in charge now, so sucks to suck. If I want to shove a toy in your sweet cunt then I damn well will." I could hear the smirk in his smug voice as he continued to carry me out of the place to his car, where he settled me in the passenger seat.

The drive back to his place was torturous, and I swear he hit every little bump in the road on purpose because every little jarring movement jolted and shifted the toy within my tight walls. "Ah! Bastard." The latest bump caused the toy to press right into my G-spot, sending a shockwave of pleasure throughout my sensitive body.

"Won't be calling me that later tonight." Stepan chuckled lowly with a widening smirk.

"Oh? I'd beg to differ." I replied defiantly, smirking cockily in my seat.

His deep, dark chuckle sent shivers down my spine. "Then have fun not coming tonight, because until I hear what I want from your pretty lips, I'm not going to give you one single orgasm, nor am I going to let you come." The conviction in his voice meant his threat was a promise.

"Only good girls get to come, and you've been nothing close to good. So, I suggest you start behaving to earn back some points before I cash in and punish you."

Chapter 27

Stepan

"Fuck, I'm fucking sorry okay? Just let me come, please."

Well, she couldn't say I didn't warn her because I gave her ample warnings.

"You can cry and beg all you want, but you're not coming." I replied casually, keeping my eyes trained on the computer monitor while my fingers continued to play with her swollen and soaked pussy.

God, it was hard not to look over at Hanna's sweet pussy, though, especially with how I laid her on my desk next to my keyboard and monitor. I hadn't intended on doing any work when we got home, but Hanna was too much of a brat not to punish. So, begrudgingly, I forced myself to do some work to prove a point to her.

So, here we were, for the past hour now, with me behind my desk and her still bound atop my desk with an addition of a spreader bar between her legs to keep her from preventing me access. I'd kept her on edge with the use of the vibrator in her and my hand, driving her right to the edge only to deny her a release.

"Maybe if you apologize correctly and sincerely then I'll take some mercy on you for now." I hoped to all that's holy she'd cave soon because my self-restraint was ice-thin, so I feared I'd break before her.

This was torture for both of us. I denied both of us our releases, but at least she got to be stimulated while my throbbing cock ached very painfully in the confines of my pants, begging to be buried inside her sweet cunt. It'd be so easy to stand up and shove myself into her after freeing myself; she's so wet that I'd slide fully into her with no resistance.

But God, I couldn't cave though, not before her. I'd have no footing with her if I did.

Taking in a slow, deep breath, I quickly shoved my middle and ring finger knuckle deep into her soft walls, making her moan loudly and arch her back. "Please, please, please, I'm sorry."

Slightly satisfied with her change in tone, I look over at her with a soft smile, "Getting closer, but not quite, *malenkaya*." Slowly, I let my eyes drink in her image once more.

Hanna's toned legs were on perfect display with how I had her dress bunched around her waist to keep her lower half exposed to me. I couldn't wait to rip her dress fully off and get my lips on every inch of her irresistible body from head to toe until I could taste her from licking my own lips.

Pulling my hand away from her dripping wet core, I slowly danced my fingers along the inside of her thigh. "Come on little tigress, you're so close to getting that sweet release. You know what you need to do." I said with an overly sweetened smirk.

Slowly chipping at her like this was entertaining and such a power trip. When I initially situated her on my desk, she was still so feisty, fighting me tooth and nail. Slowly but surely, her firmness started to wane with each passing minute as I denied her orgasm over and over. I loved the little fight from her, and honestly, I had expected her to cave sooner than later, given how worked up she was. But my little Hanna surprised me by holding out this far.

Unfortunately, I had much more patience than she was willing to give me. Well, that and the fact I didn't want to lose to her made me hold out from throwing her onto my bed and taking her like a savage animal.

Hanna's sweet plea fell sweetly into my impatient ears. "Please, sir, I'm sorry, please make me come, please." There it was, the sincerity I'd wanted from her.

"Sorry for what?" I should take it easy on her and give her the sweet release I've denied her so far, but I held the power right now and loved it a bit too much to let go quite yet. Yes, I was being an asshole, and I didn't give a fuck.

"For calling you an asshole, a bastard, for not listening, fuck I'm sorry, please, please." Her body trembled under my touch as my fingers slowly slid back deeply into her and stroked at her sweet spot for a few seconds before pressing the vibrator right up against the sensitive spot.

"Stepan, please, please." She begged so sweetly with a voice overly saturated with need and desperation.

Getting up from my seat, I positioned myself between her legs and leaned down, placing my free hand next to her head and using it to hold myself up while I looked down at her arrogantly. "Are you going to be a good girl for Daddy?"

A look of frustration sharpened her eyes momentarily before they softened with defeat as she chewed at her bottom lip. "Yes." She whimpered with a shaky breath.

After giving her a few hard thrusts with my fingers, I withdrew my hand completely—removing the vibrator in the same action—and pushed off my desk to use both my hands to undo the spreader bar and toss it aside. Reaching down, I wrapped my hand tightly around Hanna's neck and pulled her up into a sitting position. "How do you want me to make you come, *malenkaya*?" I asked smugly, with my lips just a thread away from hers.

Snapping out of her little lustful daze, Hanna instantly wrapped her legs around my waist and locked herself against me with a soft moan. "Your cock, make me come with your cock, please." Desperation filled her pleading words as her hips slowly grind against me, letting me feel the heat from her arousal. "Please."

My throat ached with the growl that left me when I closed the distance between us completely. I didn't even try to be gentle with our first kiss; my hunger for her took over the moment her sweet taste invaded my mouth.

Hanna groaned when I took her bottom lip between my teeth, pulling and nipping at it until I could almost taste the iron from my vicious attack. With her lips parted, I took the chance to drive my tongue deep into her mouth, quickly seeking hers out and pressing against it feverishly as I tightened my hand around her neck to mash her lips harder against mine.

Fuck, I couldn't get enough of her. Kissing someone had never felt this hot or exciting before, ever. It's as if Hanna broke open some dam of fiery hot passion and lust—an intense desire only towards her.

Breaking the kiss, the two of us remained there with our heads together, our chests heaving with our heavy panting.

Concern softened my face when my hands ran along her tied arms, feeling the soft rope against her flesh. "Are your hands and arms feeling alright still, little tigress?" She'd been tied up ever since the club, and though she made no complaints yet, I wanted to have the peace of mind that she still had proper circulation to her arms.

"Yes, dad." She responded sassily with a slight roll of her eyes and a smirk, earning her a hard spank on her round bottom.

"Do I have to punish you again already?" I threatened playfully with a twisted, teasing smirk.

Her attitude quickly changed with her widened eyes while her head quickly shook side to side. "No, I'm sorry." She muttered briefly, her eyes averting from me until I grabbed her face to force her otherwise. "I'll be good tonight, I promise." She sounded remorseful enough.

Well, it was our first night together, so I should cut her the slightest bit of slack. I could punish her for all of time after tonight.

Smiling softly, I leaned in and kissed her forehead. "Let's get you into our bed before I take you on this desk." It was a slip of my tongue, but I don't think she picked it up. I don't know why I said 'our' instead of mine; it really just came out.

Sliding my hands down her back to her plush bottom, I gripped them firmly, digging my fingers into her softness for a good moment before lifting her up and off the desk.

"Drop me and I will kick your balls." She threatened me with full conviction and harsh, glaring eyes.

Chuckling out of amusement, I let her remark slide this time. "If I ever drop something so precious as you then I would deserve a kick there." Unconsciously, my grip on her tightened with the threat hanging in the back of my mind.

Hanna leaned into me as much as she could with her arms still bound behind her, her legs tightly wrapped around me in a vice grip.

Carefully, with a hand splayed on her bottom and my other arm tightly wrapped around her shoulders, I carried her to the bedroom. Then, I unceremoniously tossed her onto the bed with a soft laugh when she squealed and glared up at me.

Climbing onto the bed, I cage her in between my arms and legs before leaning down and capturing her lips in another bruising kiss full of passion. "Fuck, I am never letting you leave me or this bed, ever." I rasped against her lips with a deep growl.

Shifting my weight to my knees, I balanced myself before moving my hands to the front of her thin, lacy dress. Bunching the material of her neckline, I gripped it firmly with both hands before tearing it apart right down the middle until the whole thing was split from top to bottom.

"Stepan!" Hanna's panicked protest shot out at the sound of fabric ripping.

Unable to help it, I let my deep chuckle free as my eyes roamed down her nearly bare body. Her thong had been disposed of earlier in the office with scissors, so only her strapless bra remained.

"You can't just rip my clothes like that." She pouted, bringing her legs around to try and kick at me. "I don't have an unlimited budget for clothes like you, you jerk."

Before she could land a solid hit, my hands had grabbed at her ankles and held her legs wide open in the air. "Yes, you do, and I was going to replace it. Wouldn't be fair of me to ruin your clothes and leave you with nothing."

Actually, now that I think about it, that wouldn't be so bad. Hanna walking around the house naked and ready for me to take her whenever I pleased; that was more than a lovely thought.

"I ain't rich like you, or did you forget?" Hanna's eyes rolled at me before she tried to pull her legs free.

"That might have been the case before tonight, but my wallet is yours now too." She would be dead wrong if she thought this was a one-off thing.

No, tonight was only the start of us.

It'll all have to wait until tomorrow, though; no use in spoiling the mood right now with a long-winded conversation.

Wrapping her legs around my waist, I freed my hands and snaked them behind her to unclasp her bra and discard it over the side of the bed as I lowered my body back down to hers. Cupping her face, I stoked her cheek tenderly with my thumb while looking at her adoringly.

After observing her wary eyes for a few seconds, I lowered my body down firmly against hers before sealing her lips in another kiss. This one was different from the others before, not rough and demanding. No, this one was deep, tender, full of longing and happiness. Reluctantly, I parted my lips from her to let us breathe properly. "We'll talk more about things in the morning, I have much more important matters to attend to."

Tangling my fingers into her hair, I pulled her head back fully to expose her neck to my hungry mouth as I eagerly left open-mouth kisses along her jawline to the sensitive column of her neck.

Not so carefully, I grazed my teeth—roughly—down the length of her sensitive flesh until I got to the crook of her neck, where I brutally sank my teeth into her, making her soft sighs of pleasure turn into whimpering yelps. Her body writhed under me, but I held her firm by her hair and a grip on her shoulder next to my mouth.

Besides the metallic taste of iron, I got a mouthful of chemicals. Definitely had to talk to her about that in the morning too, but I stored away that mental note for later to refocus on the task at hand.

Letting go of her, I moved my way down to her breasts, peppering kisses with the occasional love bite to mar up her beautiful body as mine. When I finally made it to the swell of her breast, I slid my tongue and ran it along her skin until I reached her hard nipple.

Trapping her hard bud between my teeth, I pulled roughly, making her moan softly and arch under my ministrations.

I'd be gentle with her another night; I couldn't hold back tonight. All my pent-up frustration with her will be unleashed onto her poor body tonight so she could feel a fraction of the torture she'd put me through the past weeks.

Taking her little, light brown nub into my mouth, I sucked at it hard while rolling it between my teeth and with my tongue.

"Oh fuck." Hanna whimpered and trembled under me when I slid my hand from her shoulder to between her legs, quickly finding her little bundle of nerves with my fingers and stroking it with the pad of my finger.

"Please, let me come, please." She begged needily through her desperate moans of pleasure.

Removing myself from her tit, I looked up at her as I moved to her other breast. "No, you said you wanted to come with my cock, so you don't get to have your orgasm until I'm fully inside of you." The cruel smirk pulled at my lips whether I wanted it or not. It was too much fun to mess with her and watch her respond with whines and pouty kicks against me.

Chuckling darkly, I used the length of my tongue against her neglected nipple before taking it into my mouth and giving it the same rough treatment I did to the other.

Pulling myself off, I sat back on my knees to quickly strip myself completely of my suffocating clothes.

The sight and feeling of her lustful eyes devouring my body with awe made my chest swell with pride as an arrogant grin played on my face. I regretted having her hands tied now after seeing her starved eyes on me. My hot body prickled with the need to have her hands run all over it.

"You can admire me all you want later baby, this is all for you and only you for now and ever." I wanted to get back down and dirty.

"Just relax and let Daddy take care of you for now."

Chapter 28
Hanna

TEARS STUNG AT MY eyes from his words.

I wanted that so badly, for him to take care of me, and I knew he would for tonight. But what about after? Did he know the depths of his words? I shouldn't dwell so deeply about all of it now, but I couldn't help it.

Forcefully, I shoved my worrisome thoughts away and locked them away for later, not wanting to ruin this only moment of ours. I'll save my disappointment for after the fact.

Focusing my attention back on him, I let my eyes follow his body carefully as he slowly moved back over me. I couldn't get enough of him for some goddamn reason. I felt like a kid on Christmas getting their much-anticipated dream gift. Why was Stepan so different? Why couldn't I tear my eyes away from his well-built body? From his firm pecs to those nicely cut abs that sat right above and between the dip of his dangerous v-line.

Stepan wasn't built like some tank like his brothers being leaner and athletic, but I was fond of his slight difference. Big and bulky was nice, but I always preferred those slightly slimmer, the happy medium between above average and enormous.

My mouth watered with a need to lean in and mark his body from head to toe with my tongue. God, I wanted to run my sharp tongue along every curve and dip of his muscles, especially that tantalizing v-line of his that would lead me to my grand prize.

Now, a dick was a dick to me, a stupid little male appendage with the means to get myself off, but one look at Stepan's thick, curved goodness, and I could feel myself melting with appreciation and want. I'd never wanted a cock in me so badly until now. Never before have I ever wanted to worship one either, yet I'd gladly get on my knees for him and love his member with every inch of my mouth and tongue.

Blowjobs were a motion for me to go through in the process of sex, but I avoided them because I wasn't keen on the act much. So, never have I ever felt a *need* to suck a cock, until now.

Hungrily, I licked my lips at the sight of his precum beading the very tip of his swollen length. I wanted to know how he tasted so badly, another thing I've never been inclined to do before. Yet, I wanted him to shove himself into my mouth, use me to get off, and stuff my mouth with his creamy goodness.

My face instantly scrunched softly with a pouting frown when I saw his thumb swipe the creamy, white bead away. Looking up at him, I opened my mouth to protest but was promptly silenced by his thumb being shoved into my mouth. Instinctively, I wrapped my lips around his finger and let my eyes flutter shut with my delightful moan when the taste of his seed hit my tongue.

Slowly, his finger slid out of my mouth as his hand traveled downwards to my breast, where he cupped my mound roughly in his hand.

Firmly gripping my waist, he slowly rolled his hips into me, making me moan at the feeling of his length rubbing against my aching sex. I thought he stroked himself along my slit to get his member nicely coated in my juices for lube, but after the fifth stroke—and the shit-eating grin on his face—it was clear that he was teasing me.

Fucking bastard, I knew what he wanted with one glance. I could play the long game and drag things out for both of us on any other night or time; my stubbornness was nonexistent right now. I knew from his clenched jaw with each thrust of his hips that he needed to be inside of me as much as I needed him in me, but I was so pent up and lost in the haze of my pleasure that the thought of holding out made my body ache with a painful need.

"Stepan, please, I need you in me, please." The sheer desperation in my pleading words surprised me because I'd never sounded so needy with anyone, even if I was yearning for relief from them.

My wanton eyes locked with his when his hand suddenly wrapped around my neck. Hovering his face dangerously close to mine, his stormy eyes kept firm with mine as his thumb ran back and forth along my jawline. "Are you going to give yourself fully to me and let me take care of you? Are you going to stop this game of push and shove with me? Are you finally going to let me be your fucking Daddy? The one you *need* and crave for in your life?"

Oh God, was he serious about this? Or was it a spur of the moment? No, Stepan wasn't the kind of man to act or speak without thought. His voice didn't hold his usual playful edge. He wasn't teasing me or simply dirty-talking in the moment. He was earnest with how full of conviction his voice carried. Beyond the lust in his darkened eyes was a slurry of desperation and longing.

Fuck it, I'd deal with the consequences in the morning after. I wanted to believe him fully, let myself be lulled into his comforting arms and words of promises, but I was too scared. What if that was it after tonight? That somehow I misread him in my clouded lust, and it really was just all for show.

But, again, fuck it, I'd deal with it come tomorrow.

Shuddering, I let the dull ache from my heart drown in my lustful pleasure before answering him. "Yes, Daddy." Those two words felt like a scorching hot knife through my stomach.

I just made myself vulnerable to him, and that scared me to no end.

"Fuck!" He hissed through gritted teeth with a strained groan.

His voice sounded so far away because of the buzz in my ear from the sudden, immense pleasure that slammed into me like a raging bull when Stepan thrust into me fully in one go. Immense pleasure shocked my body like a cold ocean wave before the inferno of heated passion countered it.

My scream remained caught in my throat as my body arched from the rapture attacking it—a silent scream of unbearable pleasure. A pleasantly painful ache gripped at my tense muscles as my orgasm washed over me along with the aftershocks of it.

"Tigress, you're squeezing at me too tightly, you need to relax." Stepan's strained voice barely cut through the white noise.

I couldn't help it. His thick cock shoving apart my tight walls snapped my last thread of control, especially when his tip hit the sweet spot deep within me. Shuddering with a shaky moan, I forced my body to relax back against the bed while keeping my legs tightly wrapped around his waist until he pried them and forced them onto the bed on either side of me.

The strength of his fingers dug into the sensitive flesh of my thighs as he pinned my legs down and open. Whining, I gave a slight pout while looking up at him pleadingly. "I want to feel close to you, keep you against me."

Chuckling, Stepan leaned down and kissed me softly with a smile and a small thrust that had my face twisting with pleasure. "After I get myself fully in you." He whispered against my lips before leaning back up and pressing my legs open more before giving me another firm thrust, sending a wave of pain with the pleasure.

Warily, I let my eyes fall between my legs. A trembling gasp escaped my parted lips with my widening eyes. I felt so stuffed already, yet he wasn't even fully in me, only a little over halfway. "You're going to ruin me." I whimpered nervously with a small jitter of excitement at the thought of him forcing my body to take him fully.

"What are you thinking about, little tigress? You just fluttered around me just now." He prodded with a curious and playful smirk as he slowly moved his hips to steadily work more and more of his girthy member into me with each thrust.

With my inhibitions lost to the rising pleasure, I had no control over my words as they rolled off my tongue. "About Daddy's big cock fully stuffed in my tight pussy." The moment my words registered in my ditzy brain, a wave of heat warmed my cheeks from the embarrassment.

Another wave of shivers hit my body at the sound of Stepan's deep chuckle paired with the sight of his wicked, cocky grin. "Good," he said with a hard thrust, forcing a good portion of him into me and making me yelp from the sharp pang of pain when I felt the burn of him stretching me. "Because my cock is the only one you should ever be thinking about from here on out. Your pussy belongs to me now, just like all of you. My cock is the only one that can ever be inside of you, and I am going to fuck your pussy until it knows that."

One more hard thrust and his hips were flushed against my body, and the painful burn of his full-length filling and stretching my tight walls had me moaning loudly as my hands gripped at the sheets under me.

"Too much, it's too much." Both his hands grabbed at my hips when I tried to squirm away from him, keeping me firmly pressed against him, forcing me to adjust to him.

"You can and you will, you're already taking me so well already, *malenkaya*. Just a little more, I know you can do it." His strong voice turned softer towards the end as he moved one of his hands up to cup my face and stroke my cheek lovingly. "Relax, little tigress, relax."

Running a hand along my leg, he slowly moved it around his waist. "Wrap your legs around me, baby, and move when you are ready." It was sweet that he gave me control, kind of.

His hands were loosely around my waist, with his thumbs drawing lazy circles on my skin. If I moved to pull away too much, then he steeled his grip to keep me rooted. He wouldn't let me pull away completely for a reprieve, unfortunately.

It took me longer than I'd like, but I adjusted enough to where there was more pleasure than pain. Slowly, I locked my ankles behind him and started to grind myself against him to get more pleasure from our position. It was only until my breaths drew out longer and longer with my moans that Stepan took back over.

I'd thought he'd start slow, ease us both into the motions. But no, he dug his fingers into me, pressed me down into the bed, and started to wildly buck his hips, filling the room with the sounds of our bodies colliding with each other.

Stepan showed me no mercy as he began to give me longer, deeper, and harder strokes that jerked my body with each thrust. "Oh God." I whimpered with a sobbing moan as I orgasmed.

The high of my bliss was cut short due to my senses hitting a wall because of Stepan's hand around my neck. "There's no God here, so try that again, *malenkaya*." He choked me harder as his pace became more punishing, slamming into me harder to where I was sure he'd bruise me.

"Fucking try that again, Hanna. Who am I? Hm? Who am I to you?" Fuck, I *will* have bruises from him fucking me so brutally. "If you don't answer then you're not allowed to come."

Cheeky bastard then proceeded to roll his hips into me, making his delicious dick hit my sweet spots that had stars filling my vision. My body shook in response to the new onslaught of intense, mind-numbing pleasure, and my throat scratched with my pitched moans and sobs.

It only took a few thrusts for him to push me right to the edge of the cliff again, this time dangling me off of it by a foot. I could come if I really wanted to, but my body refused to cooperate. My body clung to his unspoken threat of punishment and held my orgasm back.

Just fucking great; even my own body betrayed me by obeying him mindlessly.

Shuddering, I pushed away the wave of aching pain from my heart again before giving in to him. "My Daddy, you're my Daddy." And I wanted it that way beyond tonight, but he'll probably forget it all after getting his fill tonight.

Yesterday's trash, that's what I'll be after tonight to him.

Groaning deeply, Stepan released my neck and slammed his hand next to my head as his body hunched forward. The taste of his lips invaded my mouth the moment he pressed them against mine in a deep kiss, making me swallow his groan as he reached his release.

My scream of ecstasy became muddled and lost with his groans as my own orgasm violently ravaged my body when the tight knot in my stomach snapped painfully. "Stepan, fuck, shit, shit. Daddy!" Then an incoherent string of curses and mumbles left my trembling lips as the aftershocks of my orgasm hit me while his cock pulsated against my tightened walls, his seed spilling into me.

"That's right, I'm your fucking Daddy, and don't you ever forget that," he said breathlessly against my lips before giving me a chaste kiss.

He slid his hand behind me, pulling at the ropes until they loosened up enough for him to unravel the lengthy material from my arms completely as I came down from my high.

Tossing the rope aside, he slowly slid out of me with a sharp intake of breath through his teeth. Reaching out, he pulled the covers back and pulled them back over us after he settled down next to me. Tightly, he wrapped his arms around my waist and pulled me atop him as he lay on his back.

Holding me tightly, he busied one of his hands by groping my ass, gently molding my softness in his big, rough hand; the other slowly rubbed at my back soothingly as he rested his chin at the top of my head.

"Satisfied yet, little tigress? Or do you still want some more orgasms?" He asked with a soft chuckle, tilting his head to the side to look down at me with a caring smile.

Through my panting, I gently shook my head as I couldn't find the energy to respond verbally to him in the moment.

"No, as in you're not satisfied, or no, as in you don't want more orgasms?" Stepan asked for clarification with a cheeky smile.

"No more." I replied in a small voice with another shake of my head.

The butterflies in my stomach fluttered to my chest when I felt Stepan's lips against my forehead. "I'm going to get you some water and snacks and a cloth to clean you up." He murmured against my forehead before shifting me off of him onto the bed.

Lazily, my eyes followed him as he got off the bed and left the room momentarily before returning with a big glass of water and a small plate filled with some pirozhkis. I couldn't help but grin goofily at the sight of the food as the delicious scent filled my nose.

With a smile, Stepan sat at the edge of the bed and pulled me into his lap after setting the water and plate on the nightstand. Then, in a peaceful silence, he fed me until I turned my head away when I grew full enough. Gently, he set me back down to leave for the bathroom, where the sound of running water crackled through the air briefly before he reappeared at my side with some washcloths in hand.

Wincing, I started to push myself up fully, only to be stopped by Stepan pushing me back down on the bed with a firm hand on my back. "No, I made a mess of you, so it's only fair I clean you up." He told me with a chuckle before gently wiping at my face.

The familiar smell of makeup cleaner—my makeup cleaner—had my hand darting out to grab at his wrist. I could feel my eyes grow cold and tense as I looked up at him nervously.

"Hanna, I am not leaving you to sleep in a face full of makeup. I don't care for your burns if that's what you're worried about. I'm not some shallow bastard." The warmth his eyes held with his smile made my grip on him loosen enough to where he resumed wiping my face.

It took a few, but it clicked in my mind eventually.

"How do you know about my burns?"

Chapter 29

Stepan

IT'S BEEN NEARLY A week since we first slept together, and Hanna still avoided me like the black plague. I don't know how it happened, but things did *not* go the way I'd intended the morning after when I refused to answer her question about her burns. I'd deflected her question about how I knew about her burns, not wanting to confess to her about how I'd been basically stalking her for over a month. I wanted to enjoy our night of bliss, not toss a nuclear bomb into it.

I thought things would be fine the following day, but I woke up to an empty bed. Come to find out, Hanna had taken off before I woke. My Lexus LX was still missing from my garage, but I couldn't care less about her taking it and using it. I'd been more torn about her running away from me.

Then, I thought I could catch her at the office and pull her away to talk about things, but she'd somehow managed to successfully avoid me there, too. It was like I'd broken down the wall and closed the distance between us, only to have her put me on a rocket ship to the moon and build the wall of China between us.

Perhaps she needed space, so I gave her some space to give her time to process things and have a small break from me before trying to work out our relationship. That plan blew up in my face because the space did nothing but further the distance between us with how cold she grew towards me.

"What did Lev do this time for you to make such an ugly face?" Nikolai's playful jab pulled me from my thoughts.

Sighing heavily, I ran a hand through my hair and looked over to my older brother as he sat down at the seat across the patio table from me. The sharp scent of vodka hit my nose as Nikolai poured into a shot glass before me. "Not Lev." I sigh exasperatedly, burying my head in my hands for a moment before taking the shot, letting the smooth liquor go down like water without a twitch of my face. Setting the glass down, I ran a hand down the back of my head and gripped the back of it with an annoyed scowl.

"Oh? Really?" Now Nikolai was really interested because I had never had any trouble besides our brother Lev.

Letting out another heavy sigh, I tilted my head back and looked up at the sky momentarily, wondering how I ended up at Nikolai's place on a whim. It wasn't unusual for me to randomly visit him; our family was tightly knit with each other, always sharing nearly every aspect. We're also well involved with each other because we helped Nikolai run the family bratva, so there was that, too.

Slowly, I let my head fall level and looked at my older brother for a moment before speaking up. "How do you do it? I mean, I know you chose to chain yourself to Angel the night of the treaty, but how do you do it? How do you guys make your relationship work?"

"Ah, girl problems." Nikolai laughed teasingly at me before taking a drink himself. "I honestly don't know what to tell you *bratik*. Angel and I just make it work somehow. I mean, there's a lot of compromise. *A lot*. I give her a lot more space than I'd like, but she's an independent woman who doesn't enjoy having her space and life impeded on. We've just kind of learned to live with each other and appreciate each other."

"Okay, but when do you know when to not give her space? I'm giving Hanna so much space, but she just pulls away the more I give. I don't want to force my hand with her because she's not going to react well to me grabbing a hold of her life." I hadn't meant to let it slip that it was Hanna who's been the thorn in my side, but my frustration got the better of me.

Nikolai nearly choked on his drink when he heard the name slip from my mouth, coughing a little with a chuckling laugh. "Hanna? As in Angel's best friend Hanna? The crazy female Lev?"

I groaned, hanging my head into my hands. "Yes, *that* Hanna." The sting of pain was quick to bite the back of my head when I gripped at it with my fingers to vent out some frustration.

"Then just treat her like you would Lev, simple as that. You and I both know how things go with Lev. Yes, space is good and needed with him, but we also need a heavy hand with him after a while otherwise he shuts off completely. Just do the same with Hanna. Obviously if she's pulling away too much with the space you're giving her then that means it's time to grab her by the back of her neck and drag her back whether she likes it or not." Nikolai stated simply before his wife interrupted us.

"Grab who by the back of their neck and drag them where? You better not be talking about me or I swear I'll—"

He didn't give his poor wife a chance to finish her sentence. His hands shot out the moment she was within arm's range, and he pulled her squealing body into his lap with a smirk. Grabbing her face, he held her firm to his darkening gaze. "You'll what, *lisichka*?" The underlying edge to his playful voice made Angel shiver and shrink in his lap.

"N-nothing." She sputtered with a blush before settling in his lap, tucking her small body into Nikolai's overbearing one.

Looking over at me, she cleared her throat and recollected herself before speaking. "What are you guys talking about? I heard Hanna's name. Did she do something? Did she get into trouble?" The sincere concern Angel had for her friend warmed my heart.

I shook my head in response, chuckling softly before smiling at her reassuringly. "Hanna's done nothing wrong, and she's still perfect." Even if she pulled away faster than a rabbit making a run for it.

"Stepan's having trouble with his little crush on her, that's all." Nikolai shot me a smug smirk, making me narrow my eyes and cuss at him under my breath in Russian.

Angel's head tilted with her furrowed brows. "What's happening between you and Hanna?" Angel questioned with genuine curiosity.

"Did Hanna tell you about anything that happened a few nights ago?" I knew Hanna and Angel were tight as thieves, but I've also noticed how little Hanna tells her sometimes.

"Well, all she said was that you guys hung out after she cut things off with Logan. She didn't really want to go into any details when I pressed, so I just left it. Although, she sounded off, now that I think about it. All she really told me was that things were great and amazing, but that she really had to think about everything again because she doesn't want to get hurt." Angel replied to me after a moment of recollection.

"We slept together." I deadpanned, instant regret smacking me in the face like a bag of hammers when Angel looked at me with wide eyes as if I'd sprouted an extra head. Even Nikolai's face twitched with surprise when his eyebrow raised up.

"Stepan, what did you do?" Okay, now she looked and sounded like she wanted to spring across the table and rip my throat out.

Keeping my calm façade on, I gave her the whole—not detailed—truth of what happened that night.

"Stepan." Angel let out a long sighing groan as she ran her hand down her face. "I'm going to kill you if Hanna doesn't do it first."

"Listen, I am trying to understand her, so help me." I pleaded desperately because I needed answers no one else could give.

"Hanna's..." Angel paused for a second, her face twisting in thought before biting out, "Complicated."

Another pregnant pause staled the air before Angel's heavy sigh broke it. "Even I have to admit that, so you really don't have it easy when it comes to Hanna and relationships and attachments. She does likes you, plain and simple, but with all the trauma she's been through, it makes it hard for her to form a relationship in a typical manner. She's guarded, like very guarded, and it's not going to be easy, but you need to force your way in with her. You need to tear down those walls and keep to her to prevent her from putting any back up. Yes, distance is good and nice, but with Hanna, distance is often not the answer because that gives her the time and excuses to push you away and build those walls back up."

Letting out a deep breath, I quickly poured myself another shot and downed it before setting the glass down with a heavy hand. Basically, I fucked up, but at least she said it nicely. So, that was greatly appreciated. She could've called me a total idiotic asshole and left it at that.

Angel continued after I gave her a slow nod of my head once things started to sink into me a little more. "You need to be persistent with Hanna, even if it seems counterintuitive, that's how you need to be with her. As much as I don't like it, but Kolya's right, you need to grab her by the back of her neck and lead her where you want. I mean it, you're going to have to be a little forceful with her and be in her face. Show her that you're serious about her and keep reassuring her day in and day out because she's the kind of person who needs constant reminders. Even I have to do that with her more often than not with our bond, even if she knows better because she practically grew up with me after my father took her in after the incident."

"What incident?" Most of Hanna's life remained a mystery to me, so Angel's words instantly piqued my interest and curiosity.

Sighing sadly with an apologetic smile, Angel shook her head softly at me. "It's not my place to tell." Her lips were locked down tighter than Fort Knox on the matter.

"Does it have to do with how she got her burns?" It was the only thing I could think of at the moment, and I did plan to bring up the subject of Hanna's burns with Angel for more insight.

Unexpectedly, Angel's soft face hardened with sharp, narrowed eyes as her upper lip curled slightly with her scowl. The hostility from my sister-in-law came out of nowhere. "How do you know about her burns?"

Very touchy subject, got it.

I noted mentally while leaning back in my seat with my arms crossed guardedly. "I saw them." It wasn't a lie; I did see them last night after cleaning her face off.

Scoffing, Angel rolled her eyes at me, "No shit Sherlock, I meant how. Hanna never, and I mean *never* shows anyone her scars, not even me."

"I cleaned her up after we had our fun and saw them." Again, not a lie, but I omitted a huge part of the truth.

Unfortunately, Angel saw right through me. "She wouldn't have let that happen, nor would she let you clean her face. You better start spilling your guts right now before I spill them for you and have Alexei shove it all back in so I can do it again." And there's the well-feared bratva bride.

Looking over at Nikolai, I raised a brow at him in a silent question. "Don't look at me for help, she'd gut me in my sleep if I try to stop her."

"Well, thanks for having my back, asshole." I playfully spat at Nikolai with a chuckle.

He may be the big, bad brute of a bratva boss, but he was putty for his wife. Which I found funny and cute because he's the Dom between the two of them, yet Angel called the shots more than he'd care to admit.

Their marriage might've started out unconventionally. It might be hard to believe, taking in the fact Angel and Nikolai were strangers courted into an arranged marriage out of the blue, but one look at them and the chemistry between them shined brighter than the stars on a clear night. Was it a fairytale love story? No, not even close, but the two loved each other deeply as if they were in one. They weren't much for PDA, but seeing how they looked at each other with such warmth and adoration was more than a clear indicator of their true feelings for each other.

I couldn't help but wonder when that'd be me and Hanna. Yes, when, not if. If what Angel said was true—and I have no doubts about it—then Hanna will be mine. I just needed to play my cards right.

A plan quickly brewed in my mind, one that'll either make us or break us.

Taking a deep breath of fresh air, I zoned my focus back to Angel, who glared at me with dagger-like eyes. "I might or might not have seen her through her window..." I admitted sheepishly.

The urge to duck my head away from Nikolai and Angel's widened eyes filled with disbelief and disapproval threatened to crane my neck. "You what?" Don't know if Angel's question was rhetorical or not.

Groaning softly, Nikolai brought his hand up to his forehead and rubbed at his temples with his thumb and middle finger. "Stepan, what did you do?" Nikolai sighed heavily with a scrunched-up face.

Okay, how was I going to put this in a non-creepy way? Or, at the very least, in a way where Angel won't stab me twenty-thousand times because she was going to kill me; that much was clear from her piercing glare.

"Why the fuck are you Volkovs so... Ugh! I swear, you are all a bunch of idiots sometimes. Is it too much to ask for some normalcy in you guys?" Angel exclaimed with a long groan after hearing my confession about stalking Hanna and breaking into her place nightly. Obviously, I didn't go into detail, but I gave them the bare gist.

"Y'all need therapy, I swear." Angel muttered with a roll of her eyes.

"So do you." I retorted with a playful scoff and smirk.

"I do not, I am perfectly fine." Angel argued weakly with averted eyes.

"Angel, you're married to Nikolai and love him, nothing about that is normal. That's not even mentioning the fact that you're a triad princess and have a penchant for pain and torture, you little sadist." No one, and I mean *no one*, in our family was remotely normal, and that included Angel.

"Nikolai is perfectly fine." I couldn't help but burst out laughing at her statement, receiving a glare from my older brother for my reaction. "At least he didn't stalk me."

"Angel, he did for a moment, did he ever show you the pictures he's taken of you before he decided to push you onto the back burner?" Oh, I was in deep shit now.

Nikolai glared at me with a 'cut it out' look running through his sharp eyes. Guess he never told her about his little stint then from the reactions I got from both of them.

"I'm sorry, what?" The saccharine smile on Angel's face, paired with her deadly eyes, meant that it was time for me to take my leave.
"Good luck *bratok.* "

Chapter 30
Hanna

Panting heavily, I continued to push my protestant body to punch at the sand-filled sack even though my aching arms screamed at me to stop. I had too many pent-up emotions to vent, so stopping wasn't an option, not until my body gave out on its own.

I stopped feeling the blows after a while, my knuckles numb to the sensation. Hell, I wouldn't be surprised if I found my knuckles bloody under my gloves from how hard and much I'd been going at the bag for the past hour almost. I'd already burned through my legs, which were stiffly locked under me because I had kicked the bag until I was content.

Sleeping with Stepan didn't get him out of my system, but I'd already figured as much after feeling the depth of his kiss the moment he sealed us together.

Don't get me wrong, the sex with Stepan was beyond amazing, and him taking care of me afterwards by cleaning me and feeding me snacks before holding me tightly until I drifted off was wonderful. However, the tension between us grew when he avoided and deflected my questions.

I should have stayed that morning, waited until he woke up to talk to him because he did say we'd discuss things after a good night's sleep. But my anxiety got the better of me. Stepan probably got me out of his system. Our sweet little moment ended that night after our eyes closed. He probably would have sent me off after waking as if I was just another lay.

Why else would he keep on pushing my questions off? He obviously didn't want to answer them and get involved with me. It was the only thing that made sense to me, and my suspicions were somewhat confirmed by how distant he'd kept me the past week at work. He treated me like I wasn't there, no more bantering or teasing; he still gave me breakfast and lunch, but there was nothing much beyond very brief conversations about work.

Stepan was done with me. I should have known better than to make myself vulnerable to him like that. It might have been a game for him, but it wasn't for me. So far, he's made no move to prove me wrong otherwise. All his talk that night was just that, dirty talk.

How could I have been so fucking stupid?

Thankfully, no one was around the gym this late to hear my cry of anger as I punched the bag one last time.

I felt so enraged at myself and Stepan. I can't believe I let myself get played by him even after being so cautious to keep him behind a steel wall. I shouldn't be angry at Stepan for pursuing me; he had every right to do as he pleased, but he shouldn't have done me dirty like that after I'd told him what I did.

I'm such an idiot. A fucking idiot.

I made such an embarrassment of myself to him. I can't believe I let myself fall to his stupid charms.

Breathing heavily, I threw a pathetic punch at the bag when I turned around to leave the employee gym for the locker room.

After a quick shower to freshen up, I left for home with a heavy mind and heart.

The distance hurt, a lot. Just the thought of it right now felt like a knife to my clenching heart. A part of me was glad for the distance, a tiny part, but the majority of me was sorely disappointed and anguished by it.

He truly didn't want me in the end, and that thought hurt like hell. He got what he wanted, now I'm yesterday's news.

God damn it, fuck him. Screw him. Fuck Stepan.

Like a messy roller-coaster, my sadness swung back to rage within a moment.

Why the hell am I hung up over him?

Because you're fucking obsessed with him and like him, a lot.

Fucking heart and emotions.

As I approached my apartment, I held my phone to my ear after dialing Angel to hit her up for a night out. I needed to blow some more steam off, so what better way than to dance the night away after getting myself shit-faced drunk. Besides having a buddy to drink and dance with, I needed someone to vent to and get comfort from.

"Well, do you really want to go to White Out again after what happened?" I asked my friend with a chuckle as I opened the door to my apartment. "Well, we can go anywhere as long as we can drink and dance the night away. I just need to get Stepan out of my mind and system and hopefully out of my damn bleeding heart."

SLAM!

Clatter!

Everything happened in a blink of an eye.

The moment I crossed the threshold of my place, the door slammed shut with such force that everything around me shook. By the time I'd blink once, I found myself shoved and pinned against the back of my door.

My phone practically flew out of my hand when my wrists were grabbed and forced to the side of my head.

I couldn't budge one bit from the weight of a body pressed up against me, and whoever pinned me was smart enough to pin my hips and legs with their own. I was effectively trapped, unfortunately.

It took a second longer than I'd like, but my vision cleared back up enough for me to see my assailant, which brought a deep scowl of anger to my face. "Stepan, what the fuck! Get off of me! The fuck are you doing here!? How'd you—"

Stepan inched back briefly and slammed his body back into mine, making me let out a winded grunt when my body hit the door again.

His raspy voice shook at my body with the raw anger and lust that muddled it. "I'm done dancing around you, we're going to work this shit out between us tonight, right now. Now, there are two ways this can play out, whichever is up to you. The first way is we sit down and talk like civil people, as in you sit and listen to all I have to say without being unreasonable in return. Or, we can have this conversation with you on your knees choking on my cock. Your choice."

"Fuck you, Daddy." I spat harshly, the words flying out of my mouth before I could even think about controlling them.

"Oh, you will later if you're a good girl." God, I wish I could punch his arrogant smirk right off his handsome face.

"I swear, if you don't let me go right now and march your ass out the door then I will personally kick it out myself. I want you gone." Yet my words did not reflect an ounce of that want. My voice lacked any kind of conviction because my emotions spilt over.

"No, you don't, and even if you really did than too fucking bad because I'm not going anywhere. I already made that mistake this week, and I'm never making it ever again. You're going to have to learn to put up with me from here on out because I am not budging from your side. Now, take your pick, tigress. Are we going to be civil or not?" Stepan wasn't playing around. His darkened eyes were firm as they held mine captive.

I was torn between wanting to cry or scream at him because of the turbulent emotions crashing around inside of me like a violent ocean storm. After a brief moment of debate, I settled on anger and rage, not wanting to cry and become a weak, sobbing mess right now when I wanted to keep a firm footing with Stepan.

"I have nothing to talk to you about, so get the fuck out and go stick your dick in a blender." I seethed before spitting in his face because I couldn't punch or kick him due to him restraining me.

"Fine, hard way it is." Stepan's tongue softly clicked with annoyance before his eyes darkened completely, making me tremble under the dominating gaze.

I barely managed to suck in a full breath when he pushed away before I let out a yelp of pain and surprise when his hand fisted the back of my head, hard. "Let go of me!" I demanded venomously, reaching up and clawing at his arm to get him to release me. "Fucking bastard!"

I spat every name in the book at him as he forced me to the ground with a dark, unreadable expression on his face that made my nerves stand on edge. Stepan dragged me over to my bed, forcing me to crawl on my knees to avoid being fully dragged by my hair.

"Stepan, I swear to God, if you shove your pathetic dick in my mouth, I will bite it off." I was half tempted to go through with the threat because I was so angry at him.

"Try and I will shove a gag in your mouth before I fuck it." His voice dropped low and gravelly, making me tremble with pleasure.

Stupid body, fucking traitor!

I was supposed to be angry at him, not turned on!

Sitting down on the edge of the bed, he positioned me between his legs before quickly undoing his belt and pants to pull his throbbing cock out. Then, without warning, he yanked my head forward and forced himself into my mouth after pulling my head back painfully until I opened my mouth to gasp from the sting.

Hissing and groaning through gritted teeth, he took a second to breathe before speaking. "Now, you are going to fucking listen to me and listen to me well. I am fucking done with this game of push and shove with us. I don't know what happened after that first night with us, but I was hurt and sad when I woke up without your beautiful body next to me. I thought you needed space, which is why I hung back this whole week, but turns out that was a wrong move on my end. I wasn't trying to push you away or distance you. I am not done with you, I never will be, so get that through your thick skull."

His grip on my head tightened as he started to fuck my face, forcing me to deep throat him despite my gagging, groaning softly as he leaned onto his free hand after gripping the edge of the bed. Sucking in a sharp breath, he closed his eyes for a second to breathe deeply before continuing.

"I meant all I said that day and night. You belong to me. You are mine. I will take care of you until the day we take our last breaths on this damn earth. Then I'll find you in the afterlife and care for you again. Until my ring is on your finger and my collar is choking at your neck, I am never going to stop hunting you. You think I made you admit and say all those things in the spur of the moment? Hm?" From the way he looked at me demandingly, I knew he wanted an answer.

With my mouth stuffed full, all I could manage was a whimpering moan and a slight nod of my head as I looked up at him with my teary eyes.

"Who am I to you Hanna?" He asked, pulling me off of him and forcing me to look up at him with my tear-strewn face.

I didn't hesitate to give him the answer he wanted, "My Daddy." But it was also the truth.

Stepan's body shuddered at my answer, his eyes softening momentarily with adoration before they became stern again. "And what does that mean? Hm? What do good Daddies do?"

Shivering, I reach out and take his pulsating cock into one hand, making him suck in a breath through his teeth when I start to stroke him. "It means you're going to take care of me because good Daddies take care of their girls."

In a swift movement, he picked me off the floor and laid me down on the bed, his hand making quick work of my clothes until I was completely naked with his head between my legs. "Wait, Stepan it's—ah!" A violent tremble of pleasure shook at my body when his hot mouth latched onto my aching cunt and gave me a long, hard lick.

One, two, three long licks, and he stood at the edge of the bed to strip himself before climbing onto the bed and caging me in with his huge body. Belt in one hand, he gathered my wrist with the other, bound them together with his belt, and pinned them above my head. "Don't move them."

"Yes, sir." My voice came out breathy as his lips ghosted down my body.

Spreading my legs wide, he parted my pussy lips and stroked my slit to slicken his fingers up before shoving two of them into me and instantly latching his mouth onto my clit. His fingers pumped in and out of me hard and fast as his tongue and teeth assaulted my poor clit.

It didn't take long for me to feel the familiar knot of an orgasm tighten in my stomach from his ministrations. "Daddy, I'm gonna come, I need to come, please." My body ached as it held out for his permission.

Breaking his seal on my pussy, he lifted his head to look up at me with a satisfied smile. "Then come, come for me." His words snapped at the knot, my whimpering moans filled the room as my orgasm shook at my body. "That's it, come for me, that's it, good girl." His fingers kept up their hard pace, coaxing out a second orgasm out of me and making me nearly scream with pleasure.

My hands gripped the sheets above my head, fisting them until my knuckles hurt. Painful aches of pleasure grabbed at my writhing body as I rode out the aftershocks of my orgasms, my loud moans quickly dying down to small sobs.

"Daddy, I need your cock in me, please." My aching walls clenched around his finger needily when he slowly removed them.

The hot, lustful air grew heavy with a chill of seriousness as Stepan hovered above me with his hands on either side of my head. "Then no more running away, no more distance, no more pushing me away. This isn't going to be some temporary thing, nor is it moment by moment. I am serious about this, about us. You are mine, for now and ever, understand?"

Worrying my bottom lip between my teeth out of habit, I looked deeply into his awaiting eyes. "I'm afraid to say yes." I admitted with a cracked voice, letting my vulnerability out into the open.

Settling his forehead against mine, he kissed me softly but deeply. "I swear, you are it for me Hanna, no one else. I am never going to leave you, let alone hurt you intentionally. I will cherish you forever, I swear." His soft voice was firm with promise.

Cupping my face, he wiped away my tears and peppered my face with loving kisses, covering nearly every inch—and spending a longer time at my burn scar—before kissing me deeply and passionately.

Breathing shakily, I looked deeply into his eyes. "I am yours, Stepan." They weren't words on a whim; they were a promise to him.

A deep moan pulled from my throat at the feeling of his thick length slowly sinking into me fully until I felt his hips flush against me.

Though amazing, the sex tonight was different than before. Our first night was one filled with unadulterated desire, lust, and pleasure. Tonight, his slow, deep thrusts, gave a much different feeling.

I've fucked a ton of people in my life, but never before have I ever made love with someone. I never understood the difference. Sex was sex in my mind, and from the look of it all, making love was sex in the end.

Fuck how wrong I was.

The pleasure ravaging my body as Stepan took me so sensually was a new sensation altogether. I never knew pleasure could be heightened this much to where my body felt as if it was submerged in lava.

"Stepan, coming." My whimper of a warning was the only thing I managed before I lost control to the passion. "Oh Daddy." White hot pleasure blanketed me fully as I endured an intense orgasm like never before.

The feeling of his release being poured into me almost went unnoticed in my suspended state of pleasure. Still, my body seemed to have its own mind and responded to him with another orgasm that made me float higher to where I was on the cusp of blacking out from the sheer pleasure.

Something warm and strong embraced me, and a deep, soothing voice uttered words that sounded like they came from every direction. "*Ty sdelal potryasayushche, malenkaya. Vernis' ko mne. U menya yest' ty. Ty v bezopasnosti. Vernis' ko mne, malen'kaya tigritsa.*" Did he always sound so hot speaking Russian before? It felt like his voice took a deeper turn and edge than usual in my joyful state of mind.

The drop came like a bucket of iced water.

"Don't leave me, please. I'm sorry for being a bitch and running away. I just don't want to get hurt. I like you too much and won't be able to handle the heartbreak. I'm so much baggage, so much. I'm not good enough for you, I don't look hot or anything, I've got anger issues and every kind of issue in existence. Please don't leave me after all of this, please." Everything broke out like a dam.

All my insecurities and anxiety hit me harder than a train with broken brakes. "Half my body is burnt and scarred and ugly. My personality is just as ugly. I can't help but kill because I like it. I love violence too much. I won't make a good girlfriend or housewife, I don't know how to do any of that shit nor do I want to. I'm just an ugly, broken person who isn't worth a second of your time."

I didn't even notice when Stepan moved us under the covers or released my wrists from his leather belt. All I knew was that I was tightly curled against Stepan in his strong arms.

"Hanna you are perfect to me, burns or not, psychotic or not. I fell for everything that is you. Your scars don't drive me away, they make me more drawn to you because it shows you've been through hell and back and still you're a kickass woman. All I want to do is love your body the way it is, kiss every inch of it until the feeling of my lips linger even while I'm away from you." Stepan spoke soothingly as his hands rubbed at my back and shoulders.

"I will never leave you, and I will remind you of that every single second of every single day. I will shower you with every bit of affection I can muster, to show you the tender love you deserve. You don't have to worry about anything anymore, I got you, so just let it all go, give it all to me to burden so you can be free." Stepan's lips pressed against my forehead in a long kiss.

Could I do that though? Open myself fully to him like that? It didn't feel fair, but I was so tired on the inside.

"Let Daddy take care of you, *malenkaya*." His words fanned over my lips after he moved a hand to my face to cup it and tilt it up towards him.

"Yes, Daddy."

Chapter 31
Hanna

Shooting up from the bed, my hand instinctively went for the gun I hid under my mattress.

The racing of my heart matched the erratic rattling of the doorknob, pumping my adrenaline through my heightening body.

Glancing over to the stovetop, I saw it to be 3 AM.

"Tigress?" Stepan's groggy voice sounded behind me after shuffling off the bed. "Expecting company?"

Stepan quickly pulled his pants on, as he'd only been in his boxers.

"At three in the fucking morning?" I deadpanned with a downward tilt of my head at him.

"You are so not living here after tonight." Stepan groaned tiredly, running his hand down his face before bending down to pick up his revolver and readying it. "And that is one issue I'm not compromising on. Come morning, you're packing your shit up and moving into my place."

"I think the fuck not." I argued with an angry pout.

"You have people attempting a break in at three in the fucking morning. Also, the security of this place is worse than shit. I could pick the damn locks with no hands. Hell, I'm surprised the damn locks even remotely work. I am not risking your safety living here, so I am not compromising on this issue one bit. Besides, you're going to be living with me either way, doesn't hurt that it's sooner than later." Stepan kept his voice down as he spoke, probably to avoid tipping off the person on the other side of the door.

"You can't just start dictating my life just because we had mind blowing sex. Who said anything about engaging with you any further than bed?" Okay, pretty sure I did earlier when I agreed to give him the reigns to my life, but I was pissed at him for making such a huge decision so soon and wanted to argue with him for the sake of it. "You're not in charge of me."

Oh, that did it. Stepan's face tensed for a moment with annoyance before relaxing darkly. "Remember this later when you are getting punished. For now, put a shirt on before I have to shoot out the eyes of whoever is beyond that door for laying eyes on is mine." He wasn't done, far from it.

A chill ran through my body at the realization of my nakedness. In my rush to grab a weapon to defend myself, the thought of throwing something on flew over my head. Well, the element of shock would have been good to use against the enemy when they see a naked woman pointing a gun at them.

Now, it would be reasonable to put some clothes on before the person successfully picks the lock and breaks in, but I wanted to shove it in Stepan's face right now.

"You don't got what it takes to shoot both their eyes out." I egged him with a grin. "You can't do it, your aim isn't *that* good."

Though well hidden, I could see that my words still got to him by the subtle twitching of his eye and the corner of his lips when it threatened to fall into a scowl. His eyes narrowed slightly at me as a warning for me to cut my shit out.

"*If* you can even take out one eye, I bet you can't get the second one." I continued to goad him with an uppity attitude and smile.

"Little ti—"

Stepan didn't get a chance to finish his sentence as the door flew open. Two quick gunshots tore and shook the air not even a second later, and the poor man who'd been the first to show his face ended up with two bullet holes through his head, specifically his eyes.

Holy shit. That was hot.

I couldn't help but admire Stepan in that instant. The way he barely glanced over before his muscles flexed from pulling the trigger twice in a hair of a second. God, he looked damn sexy, so much that I couldn't help my pussy from clenching in arousal.

"Clothes. Now." He demanded in a dangerously low and gravelly voice before kicking his discarded shirt up from the floor at me.

"Yes, sir." My free hand caught the shirt as it fell.

Quickly, I slipped on the forest green button-up and haphazardly buttoned the thing up so it could swallow my tiny body before rolling the sleeves up to free my hands.

A look of hunger and appreciation crossed his face before his cool, calm façade replaced it. His head snapped towards the door as five men filed in, warily stepping over their buddy whose brains were blown out.

"Wow, would have been appreciated to have a heads up about a gang bang, I might have put out the fun toys if you did." I joked with a dry chuckle while aiming at one of the men.

"We just want the girl, so walk away." One of the men spoke up, the only one not shaking in their pants.

"H-hey man, maybe we should forget this, do you know who they are?" It seems like one of them has a brain cell working, or at the very least, a sense of self-preservation.

"We outnumber them you idiot, so why would it matter who they—"

The arrogant man stopped midsentence when Stepan took out three of the five men in less than a second. "Rude, didn't even leave one for me to shoot," I grumbled under my breath in mock disappointment.

"You'll have those two for yourself, torture's not my thing. So, loosening their lips for info is all for you to enjoy, tigress." Stepan assured me with a faint smirk and glanced at me before his face straightened sternly at the man who definitely bit off more than he could chew.

"You know, we only need one of you for questioning." The paling faces of fear brought a crazed smile to my face as I lazily bounced the gun between the two remaining men. "So, who wants to die first?"

The smart choice was the less cocky man because he seemed somewhat competent. He wouldn't be fun to torture, though, not with the little backbone he had. Unfortunately, he also seemed to be the brains between the last standing.

"Wait, you'll let me live if I talk?" The weaker man quickly asked, holding his hands up in surrender.

Smiling sweetly, I shifted my aim to his unfortunate partner. "Obviously, it'd be cruel of me to kill you after you give me all I want."

"Wait, you bastard, you can't just toss me to the dogs like that." His partner protested with a hateful scowl.

"Oh, don't worry, we have plans for you too bud. So, be patient and let the adults talk, then we'll address you." The only plan I had for him was to turn him into a punching bag in hopes that he'd give me something good. If not, then oh well.

"Now, both of you get on the floor, on your knees, and slide your guns over to Stepan." I demanded, my smile sharpening to a deadly curve.

The two men looked at each other for a moment before dropping to the ground, disarming their guns on their way down, and sliding it over to Stepan's feet when their knees touched the ground.

"Who sent you after me? And for what reason?" It was my place they broke into, so I doubt Stepan was their intended target.

"Some Asian lady, older looking, kind of like you. I mean, not that you're old looking, I meant she looks like you or very similar." The wimpier one spoke up with averted eyes.

"Wow, trying to crack a bad joke about us Asians all looking the same?" I joked dryly with a dark chuckle at the man's panicked reaction to my words. "Why did they send you after me then? Better be a good answer since you already couldn't tell me *who* hired your sorry asses." My voice sharpened to an edge.

"She didn't give us much information, just told us how much she'd pay us and who to take back to her alive and untouched. The woman's rich and powerful, she's with Lady Qing, close friends or something I don't know, but they seemed close when I saw them interacting with each other at the meeting." The man quickly rattled off.

Hearing the temporary triad head's name brought an intense scowl to my face to where I thought it'd become permanent.

Nothing good ever came from Lady Qing's involvement. Angel's stepmother was an evil snake, and even though her downfall had been set in stone with our plans to shut down her black market auction and underground arena, she would remain a huge problem until a bullet went clean through her head.

Lowering my gun, I looked at Stepan with a nod and he aimed at the rat. "Wait! You said you'd let me live!" His panic saturated the air sweetly, bringing a twisted smile to my face.

"Yeah, *I* am letting you live. I didn't say anything about him." My evil smile would be the last thing he sees on this earth.

A single gunshot went off, and the man's body slumped fully onto the ground, eyes wide open and trained on me still.

Turning my attention to the surviving man, I walk over and squat down to him. "Lucky you, you get to live to be my messenger."

Grinning crazily, I pressed the head of the gun into his hand that was flat on the floor. "You return to your little employer and tell them to go fuck themselves. If they want me then they can grow a pair and come get me themselves and save me the trouble of hunting them down."

Pulling the trigger, I put a hole through the man's hand and quickly moved to the other hand to make it match the other with another shot.

Whoever this person is, they're fucking with the wrong person.

"You tell them The Beast will paint the city with their blood."

Chapter 32

Stepan

A WINDED GRUNT FORCED its way out of my body when Hanna shoved me back onto my bed with a wild look in her eyes. *"Malenkaya—"*

Her soft lips fell on mine tersely, cutting my protest before it even got a chance to begin. "Fuck that was so hot how you shot those men. I need you so badly right now, Stepan." Her nimble fingers worked quickly to undo my suit jacket and pants to expose most of my body to her.

The rough pads of her fingers left trails of fire in their wake when she started to feel me up, taking her sweet time to leave no inch of my upper body untouched. "Hanna, fuck." The feeling of her tight pussy gripping around my length had me sucking in a sharp breath from the hit of pleasure when she fully seated herself on me.

"It's late, we need—fuck!" Groaning deeply, my hands instantly went to Hanna's hips, gripping them tightly as a violent shudder shook my body.

"I need Daddy's cock, that's what I need." She replied happily with a blissful sigh as she kept herself fully seated on my cock.

Once the guy ran off after being shot by Hanna, I practically dragged Hanna out of her place, threw her in my car, and drove us back to my house. I barely gave her enough time to pull on a pair of sleep shorts under my dress shirt she still wore before forcing her to leave. I grew too impatient regarding her safety to ask for my shirt back in the moment, too, settling for my suit jacket to cover my top half to keep decent.

When we'd gotten back to my place, Hanna kicked her shorts off the moment we set foot inside and dragged me to the bedroom. Guess her panties went with the shorts, too, because I felt nothing but her bare pussy when she rocked her hips against me earlier.

Releasing her hips, I grabbed my shirt—the one she wore—and tore it open, not caring about ruining it as some of the buttons flew off. Instantly, my hands went to her breasts, cupping the small handfuls and molding them in my big hands while my fingers pinched and pulled at her taut nipples.

Gritting my teeth, I thrust my hips upwards to try and get her to move some more, only to have her giggle and sit down firmly on me, pinning my hips down. "Nah ah, use your words Daddy." She grinned cheekily at me, barely moving her hips to tease me.

"Little tigress, move." I demanded needily, bucking my hips at her to try and move her myself.

Then, much to my surprise, her hand ended up around my neck. "That wasn't nice Daddy, try that again." Her face leaned close to mine, her smirking lips inches from mine as her hand tightened around my neck.

Besides being surprised about the fact she managed to get her small hand around my neck enough to choke me, I was surprised to find myself enjoying this little exchange more than I expected.

Sliding my hands down her body, I rested them on her hips, stroking them with my thumbs as I admired her for a moment longer. "Hanna, move, please. Ride my cock to your pleasure. Ride Daddy til he comes, please." Never in my life did I ever think I'd be begging my girl like this or begging anyone in this manner in general.

Hanna shrugged my open shirt off her body entirely and discarded it off the side of the bed before kissing me deeply with a soft moan. Her tongue tentatively ran against my bottom lip before she forced her way into my mouth, making me chuckle softly as I fought back against her until I shoved her tongue back into her mouth and filled it with my own.

My hands slowly slipped down to the globes of her ass when she started to lift her hips and bounce, gripping at them tightly until I heard her groan. God, I couldn't wait to bend her over and mark her ass up, turn it cherry red, and spank her until she couldn't sit.

It didn't take long for Hanna to slam herself onto me hard and fast, her hips lifting until only my tip remained before they were brought down firmly against me.

My exhaustion, paired with the feeling of her tight walls clenching at me with her orgasms, became too much too fast for me. Groaning deeply, I looked up at Hanna knowingly and adoringly. "Hanna, I'm close."

Tightening her grip on my neck, she squeezed for a few seconds before releasing me fully. "I know, I can feel you swelling." She giggled deviously, slowing her hips down with an evil smirk. "Is there something you want Daddy?"

Fuck this little tigress of mine is going to be the end of me.

"Tigress, please." I huffed defeatedly, my cheeks flushing a little from the notion of all this.

"Please what Daddy?" She was enjoying this too much; the giddy little shit-eating grin on her face said as much.

"Let me come, please. Let me fill up your sweet cunt with my cum." None of this was ever going to see the light of day or leave this damn room.

Satisfied, Hanna smiled widely as she kissed me hard and passionately. Her hips quickly resumed their pace from before, making my balls curl with my release until I felt myself erupt into her waiting walls.

Groaning, I let my eyes travel to the clock on the wall. "Fuck it, we're not going to the office tomorrow." It was nearly 6 AM, and we'd only gotten three hours of sleep at most.

☐"No, stay, cuddle." Hanna's sleepy voice demanded cutely, her hands tiredly gripping my arms to keep me from slipping out of bed.

I didn't bother trying to stop the smile from curving at my lips as I leaned down and kissed her temple. "It's nearly noon, little tigress. I am going to wash up then make us lunch, I expect you to be downstairs in a hour."

"Or what?" Her sleepy, half-opened eyes glared at me, making me chuckle amusingly at her adorableness.

"Or Daddy will have to teach that ass of yours a lesson a lot sooner than later." My tone might have been playful, but my threat wasn't.

Sticking her tongue out, Hanna flipped me off before turning herself into a burrito with the covers.

All the softness fell from my face with my deep breath. Sitting up, I shot my hand out and fisted her hair, dragging her protestant self off the bed when I slid to the edge of it. "As cute as your little stunt was, it's earned you an attitude adjustment."

Using her hair to control her, I dragged her up and over my knee, locking her in place by throwing one of my legs over the back of hers. Then, with a firm tug, I forced her to crane her neck before leaning down to nip at her ear. "Twenty-five, and you better count each one or I start over."

"What!? You can't spank me twenty-five times, that's so many, what the fuck." Hanna's struggle intensified until a solid crack against her bubbly bottom caused her to stop with a yelp.

"I can, and I will. If you want to be a little brat then you better be prepared to take the consequences." I loved that she was a brat, and I wouldn't want it any other way because it fitted Hanna perfectly. Also, her being a brat meant ample reasons to punish her.

"Fuck you Daddy." That little spat earned her another hard smack against her pinkening cheek.

"You're going to have a lot of learning to do, *malenkaya*. And I am going to enjoy teaching you." I could already picture her little spitfire later when I'd show her how bad girls get fucked. For now, she had some spankings to take.

"Just so you know, those two didn't count. So, start counting, otherwise I start over." The wicked grin spread across my face the moment I pulled my hand back and brought it down—hard—on her ass, making it bounce from the impact.

Hanna's sharp tongue lashed at me with a good run of curses before she finally relented after the twelfth hit. Of course, being the little bastard I am, I added more to her punishment for her defiance just now.

"Twenty-five. Fuck. Ow! Wait—ow! Why are you still spanking me?" She bit out between her sobs of pain and pleasure. "Fuck, Stepan my ass hurts so much already, no more, please."

Settling my hand on her hot bottom, I slowly groped her, making her groan and squirm under me. "It was twenty-five until you decided to get mouthy with me, now it's until I think you've learned your lesson." Or until I became satisfied.

With a firm squeeze that made her whimper, I pulled my hand back and brought it back down on her burning ass where the imprints of my hand started to become very prominent.

My hand stung by the time I finished delivering twenty more spanks to her. In a teasing voice, I asked her, "Should I give you more, little tigress?" The tips of my fingers caressed the bottom curve of her ass where it met her thighs, patiently waiting for her answer.

"No, Daddy, no more, please, I learned my lesson, I'll be good, I'll listen, I won't mouth off, just please no more, please." Her sweet pleas, filled with remorse and desperation, were music to my ears. I'm pretty sure she could feel the effects her words and tears had on me with how my rock-hard cock pressed into her belly.

Sliding my hand down between her legs, I couldn't help but smile when I felt how drenched she was. I probably shouldn't indulge her anymore. Otherwise, we'd be stuck in bed forever, but fuck it. I already went too long without getting my fill of her from before, so I might as well start making up for it now that she's mine.

Lifting my leg off of her thighs, I shifted my hand from her hair to the back of her neck. Firmly, I pulled her onto the bed fully and positioned her on her back with a pillow nestled under her hips to elevate them.

Teasingly, I ran my fingers up and down her soaked slit after pushing her legs wide open. "Who made you this wet?" My fingers slowly circled her clit as I looked at her with a cocky smirk.

The defiance in her eyes melted the longer her eyes held my dominating ones. Slowly, her reservations faded until they were filled with trust and longing. "You did Daddy." Her sweet whisper, paired with the way her body fully relaxed into me, brought a warm smile to my face. "Take care of me, please."

Leaning down, I cupped her face with my free hand to hold her firm and kiss her wholeheartedly. "I will always take care of you, Hanna, in every aspect of our lives." I whispered my sweet promise to her before easing my hips into her, groaning softly at the feeling of her warmth wrapping around my length.

Steadying myself on my forearm, I kept my other hand firmly planted between her folds to keep my fingers busy with her clit while my cock worked her insides. "That's it little tigress, come on, come for me like a good girl, cream all over my cock baby." I wasn't surprised at how fast Hanna approached her orgasm because of all the stimulation I gave her.

"You're taking me so well, such a good girl, my good girl." I whispered sweetly against her lips as my eyes held hers deeply.

Her eyes fluttered shut as her orgasm reached its peak, and her strong body trembled under me, with her melodic moans escaping her lips. "More, please, I need more." Her nails raked down my chest and snuck around my waist until her hands gripped my ass.

I could feel the pressure from her hands urging me to thrust faster and harder, but I held firm in my long and sensual strokes for the time being until she rode out her first orgasm completely. I wanted her to settle a little before pulling her down under the deep end.

My fingers pinched and strummed at her clit the instant I picked up my pace and slammed into her without mercy. I don't know how many orgasms I wrung out of her screaming body, but by the time I'd reached my climax and filled her, she was a blissful mess of smiles and incoherent moans and mumbles.

We definitely weren't getting anything done today, not with my insatiable girl around me. I didn't think she had it in her when I pulled both of us into the shower, but she surprised me by convincing me to engage in some shower sex. So, my plan for a quick shower went out the window the moment she bent over and eased herself onto me after sucking me off to get me hard again.

Then, after the shower, we went for another round shortly after lunch. Thankfully, I wore her out enough on that round for her to take a small nap, giving me time to do *some* work.

Unfortunately, I didn't get as much done as I wanted because my mind kept getting distracted by the events of last night with the men who broke into Hanna's place. My men who cleaned up reported back to me about the dead men and their affiliations, so I couldn't help but go down the rabbit hole with research and calls to my connections.

After three hours of work on the couch with Hanna's head on my lap, she finally woke. Upon waking, Hanna remained quiet for a good while, content with laying in my lap with my hand petting her head. "Something on your mind, little tigress?" Though happy, I could see something else behind her chocolate orbs.

I pushed my laptop aside fully after shutting it to give Hanna my full attention, looking at her with a soft smile while my fingers continued to thread her thick locks. With careful eyes, I watched the conflict storm within her, slowly working its way to her face that twisted and scrunched. "Hanna, I can't read your mind, so you need to tell me using your words. If we're going to make this work, then we need open communication."

The worry sagged the corners of her lips as she pulled herself up and climbed into my lap, straddling it with her arms looped loosely around my neck. "This. Us. What are we now? Are you actually serious about me? Because I'm telling you now, if this is some short-term stint for you then I want out, now."

"You are mine, and I am yours, that's what we are now. If you want official terms then you're my girlfriend, my girl, my woman, my tigress, and eventually you will be my wife. You should already know by now that I'm not the kind of man to play around at this point in my life." Wrapping an arm around her waist, I used my other to hold her face tenderly as I kissed her lovingly. "I am serious about us with every fiber of my being from my soul to my heart and everything humanly possible. You have captivated me ever since you walked through my office door and flipped Lev off." I couldn't help but chuckle at the memory as it flashed through my mind. "I've been a helpless moth drawn to your fire ever since. I love the fact you aren't like most woman out there, your confidence, your power, your skills, your fierce independence. Just everything about you is so damn fucking perfect. I cannot imagine my life with anyone else by my side besides you. Only you. Now that I've finally got you here, with me, I am never. *Never.* Ever. Letting you go."

No escape for her now. Even if she wanted to leave, I won't let her. I'm a greedy dragon who finally got his gold, his precious sought-after treasure; no way in hell would I ever let my claws loose for her to slip. If she ever dared to run, then I'd chase her and bring her right back and chain her to the bed.

"Wife?" The shock starkened her eyes, but wonder and joy softened the edges as she fought back a smile with twitching lips.

"Yes, wife, because like I said, I am never letting you go. Can't have you as my girlfriend forever. Wife is a lot more permanent and binding. If I was crazy enough then I would call some favors in and have us married right now and we'd be off on our honeymoon by tonight. The thought and idea seemed tempting, not gonna lie, but I know you'd hate me if I forced you into something like that." It will happen eventually, so I didn't care whether it was now or later—but my preference would be now or a lot sooner.

"For your sake, we'll take things one day at a time. I know this is new territory for you, so I don't want to shock you. We will take things at your pace for the most part, and I will be there hand in hand with you throughout it all because we're going to go through this together." Smiling confidently and happily, I place a quick kiss on her forehead. "For now, we'll just start here, with you getting settled in your new home, our home, and get comfortable with each other, alright?" There will be some things I'd push and pull with her, but I needed her to set the pace; otherwise, I'd scare her off.

"Yes, Daddy." A wide smile brightened her face with her sparkling eyes as she looked at me adoringly. The soft moment lasted shorter than I'd like though. "But also, aren't we comfortable with each other already? Or do you screw stupid everyone you meet and pick up off the streets?" Her soft smile gained an edge of mischievousness with her little quip.

Rolling my eyes, I quickly slapped her sore ass, making her jump and yelp. "You're the only one I've fucked dumb and taken over my knee like the little brat you are." I've had my fair share of partners, but the relationship was more of an exchange.

I've never been so emotionally involved or wanted to get emotionally involved with anyone until Hanna. Sex with my previous partners was just that, sex, a means to get things out. I've never been inclined much to drive my partner to the brink of insanity with pleasure like I do with Hanna, just enough orgasms to satisfy them.

It's also true that I've never taken anyone else over my knee. If I ever wanted to do some impact play, they were on the bed or bent over furniture. Having someone over my knee always felt a little too intimate for some odd reason.

Hanna's face slowly morphed into an angry pout. "Have you ever been anyone else's Daddy?" Her attempt to hide her jealousy was amusing and adorable.

"Oh, *malenkaya*," I said with a chuckle while stroking her stuck-out bottom lip with my thumb. "No, only you." I've always shoved that inkling of myself into the recesses of my mind, but it fast-tracked right to the forefront after finding out about Hanna's tastes.

"Hmp, good." Her pout lifted to a victorious smile that she tried to hide by tilting her head so her hair would cascade over her face.

"Maybe I should make you jealous some more, you're kinda cute jealous." Maybe that's why I liked to pick on her more often than not.

Seeing her get riled up and pouty always made my chest feel light with butterflies.

"If you're prepared to hide bodies left and right then go for it." Her face sharpened with narrowed eyes full of playfulness.

Chuckling, I leaned in and gave her another full kiss with a quick slip of my tongue before pulling away, tugging her bottom lip with me and making it swell. "I'll never pay any attention to anyone else but you. I've got the perfect woman by my side. There's no point looking at trash when I've got the world's most precious treasure in my arms."

Chapter 33

Hanna

"YOU CAN'T—ANGE, YOU KNOW damn well why I can't be involved with her."

My friend's face fell with an apologetic frown, "I know, and this wasn't easy for me to decide either, but you're the only person who can carry this assignment out successfully. I know your history with her, and if there was anyone else better, then I would go with them in a heartbeat. Please, you're the only one who can do this, the only one I trust to not fuck this up."

Clicking my tongue with a heavy sigh, I leaned back in my seat with my arms crossed. Running my tongue across my teeth, I let out another frustrated sigh. The tension from my clenched jaw threatened to shatter my teeth as my fists tightened painfully with my fingernails digging into my palm.

"Han—" Angel's hand reached across the table for mine, but I quickly slapped her hand away out of anger before abruptly standing up, knocking the chair over. "Ask me to jump over a cliff into a bottomless ravine, to jump out of an airplane with no parachute, down into a volcano, hell anything but this." My emotions were already storming at the mention of *her* name. "You know what she did to that little girl, what she made me witness." My mind threatened to pull me back to those dreadful moments, but I stood my ground with my rage to defy the pull.

I didn't shove Angel away this time when she got up, went over to me, and pulled me into a tight hug. "Then it's time for you to avenge that poor girl. We couldn't touch her before, but now we can. You and I both know it's only a matter of time before she flees because of the Qing Triad's disbandment. We need to end her now before she sets up operations elsewhere and ruins more lives. She's already ruined yours and that girl's. It's time you give her what she deserves for fucking your life up like that, for what she did to that girl."

Chuckling dryly, I pulled away to look at my friend with slight disbelief. "Aren't you supposed to be the one talking me out of all of that?" Sometimes, I forget how twisted Angel can be.

Although, ever since she married Nikolai and took her role as his bride seriously, she's changed—for the better, in my opinion. Angel had tried to leave the mafia life behind, to deny her true self, but Nikolai's brought it to the surface. She's truly the mafia queen she has always meant to be now.

"Please, I need to sit on it." Though I had a good idea of what my answer would be either way, maybe some time would make it change.

"I wish I could tell you to take all the time you need, but..." Angel gave me a sad smile before sitting down with a wince and a hand on her growing stomach.

"I know, we don't have the time. I won't take long, promise, I just need to process it before seeing if it's something I can commit to." I had to talk to Stepan about all of it, get his input, and see if it would help my decision any.

Squatting down, I hovered my face with Angel's stomach. "You two quit bugging your mom, she already has to put up with your dad and so much more shit right now."

It'd been about a month since we'd executed our plan to take down Angel's stepmother. Angel had taken up the mantle of Dragon Head and merged the triad with the Volkov Bratva, putting everything under Nikolai's rule before disbanding the triad. Although we'd successfully shut down Lady Qing and her black-market auction, her partners were still at large. And we won't stop until all of them—Lilian Wu, Ramon Cortez, and Ivan Petrov—were all taken down fully.

Although Nikolai and his brothers handled most of the merge and all the stress that came with it, Angel refused to take the backseat. Even if she was over two months pregnant with their twins, she still partook in mafia matters as if she wasn't, which stressed Nikolai out more often than not.

I wondered if Stepan ever stressed out about me like that. I was a capable woman; he knew how well I could handle myself. Yet, a part of me wondered if he cared for me deeply enough to have some unconscious or instinctual worry for my safety. Was I that important for him to worry?

"*Lisichka*? Everything alright? Do you need me to get you something? Do I need to call the doctor or Alexei?" Speaking of her worrywart of a husband, the bratva brute appears and instantly wraps his arms protectively around his wife.

"If you can get him to get off my ass then I'll forget about asking you to handle Lilian." Angel joked with a slight roll of her eyes before looking up at her husband lovingly.

"Don't know if that assignment would be worse or not." I joked back with a dry chuckle, pushing myself upright again. "Well, I'll leave you two lovebirds alone, I gotta head into the office for work soon anyways."

"How are you and Stepan by the way?" Angel asked with a teasing smirk, giving me her curious and playful eyes.

"Well, if you'd stop telling him shit about me then I'd much appreciate it. I still haven't picked your bones about letting him know about my burns." I hadn't brought the question back up with Stepan since that night, and maybe I should for a straight answer instead of assuming Angel told him. But I settled for the latter because it was the only possible option.

"Your burns? Hanna, I've never mentioned anything about your burns to Stepan, or anything personal. All I've ever told him was that you love food but you're mildly allergic to mint and berries, like very mildly, and that you have a very bad and traumatic past. Oh, and that you need a firm hand and persistence rather than space, which I heard very clearly how he followed that piece of advice." Angel gave a slight snicker while looking at me smugly.

She'd heard a good portion of the night Stepan ambushed me in my apartment because the phone didn't hang up after I'd dropped it.

Wiping her expression back to serious, she looked at me questioningly. "But I really don't know what you're talking about, Hanna, with your burns. You know I'd never tell anyone, even my own husband because those are your secrets to keep and tell." She was sincere, and I had no doubts about her in my mind.

"Did you tell him anything besides what you just said? My favorite foods? Products? Routines? Anything?" Ever since Stepan and I settled at his place—my new home, or our home as he labeled it—he's been perfect with giving me everything I need to a tee.

It didn't occur to me how strange it was for him to know me so well, chalking it up to him being overly observant. The more I thought about it now, though, the more unsettled I got. How'd he know the exact brands of the products I used? Or that I liked certain things with certain foods, like no cilantro with my noodle soups? Or that I liked to get up at 7 AM every day to work out before he even saw my daily routines? Then my burns, if Angel hadn't said anything to him. Same with my nightmares and medications; he knew about them before I even told him anything, now that I thought hard about it.

"No, nothing besides what I listed off." Angel replied with a firm shake of her head.

Fucking asshole. I'm gonna kill him.

Breathing heavily, I delivered another solid punch to the pad Lev held, making him grunt a little. "It's already dead hothead, but I'm not, so could ya ease up?" Lev joked with a forced chuckle before lowering the punching pads and looking at me with concern. "Do I need to kick Stepan's ass?"

"What?" I couldn't help but give out a chortle at his question. "No, no, it's not Stepan, no." For the most part, at least.

"Then whose got you all pissy?" Lev shook the pads off and gave me a stern look as he tossed my water bottle at me.

Catching it with a sigh, I took a few sips before looking at Lev with a forced smile. "It's nothing, I'm just taking it too personal, just something stupid." I didn't want to open my can of worms with anyone, not even myself, let alone Lev.

"It's not nothing stupid if it's got you that angry to where you're going to go into a fury." Lev chuckled softly with a raised brow. "I know how you are Hanna, or have you forgotten that you're basically my long-lost twin?" He furthered his smugness with a damn smirk that made me want to punch him across the face.

"Then you should know that I don't want to talk about it until I've simmered enough." I remarked with a winning smirk.

"Before or after you rip someone's head off?" Lev scoffed with a roll of his eyes. "Go wash up, Stepan will have my balls if I keep you again."

"So ridiculous, still can't believe he's jealous of his own brother." Sure, Lev and I spent a lot of time together, sometimes even more than Stepan and I, but still. The lack of chemistry between Lev and I was clear as day.

Although I could understand where he came from, so I didn't hold it against him. If he hung out with a female friend more than me, sibling or not, I'd get jealous eventually. Well, scratch that, I'd be jealous instantly, no matter who the female is. He's not allowed to give anyone else but me his attention, and I'm not afraid to cut a bitch if she gets too close.

With a huff, I left for the locker room and quickly freshened up before heading up to Stepan's office with a happy little smile on my face. I know I should still be upset at him for my little paranoia earlier, and don't get me wrong, I still was, but I could take it out on him later when we got home.

I missed him just a tad too much to rip into him right now. Besides, maybe I overthought it all; maybe he knew because he was overly observant, or I had let something slip whenever I'd ramble. Either way, I'd bring it up to him later in a civil manner. Besides, the training with Lev helped me unload a lot of steam.

The trip to his office zipped by with how fast my feet practically skipped up the stairs and down the hallways.

"Ste—"

My chest tightened at the sight before me, all my happiness and excitement leaving me in shock like an ice bath.

"What the fuck is she doing here?"

Chapter 34

Hanna

SLAM!

"Hanna! What hell is going on with you? You're being ridiculous without an explanation." Stepan slipped through the door before I slammed it shut in his face. Shame.

A pair of hands grabbed my arms and spun my scowling self around. "What is going on? Talk to me, little tigress." His expression twisted with genuine concern as his eyes studied my face for an answer.

Unable to respond because my tongue remained stiff as a board in my mouth for some goddamn reason, I settled for turning my gaze away from him. That only worked for a second before a yank on the martingale collar around my neck forced my attention back to Stepan.

"*Malenkaya*, we can either do this the easy way or the hard way. The easy way is you sit your ass down on the couch and talk, the hard way involves you going over my knee or tied down to the spanking bench. Which will it be?" All hints of softness eroded with his stern, dominating presence.

"*Poshel ty, papochka.*" I spat with a glare, crossing my arms and jutting my chin up at him.

Logically, I should take the easy way out, and maybe if I was in a better mood then I would have. Unfortunately, I was in a piss poor mood, so I lashed out at him. Would I regret this sooner than later? Probably, but fuck it.

Sighing disappointedly with a shake of his head, he softened his face briefly before it hardened darkly, making me feel the instant chill of regret. Before I could spew my halfhearted apology, Stepan grabbed my hair by the base of my ponytail, forcing me onto my hands and knees.

With a firm pull, he forced me to look up at him. "Since I'm feeling a little generous, I'll let you pick where you'll get punished. Over my knee or the bench? If you don't answer then I'll pick and you won't be getting any orgasms tonight. Now, apologize and pick."

Clenching my thighs, I rubbed them together in response to the growing ache between my legs. Swallowing my pride, I let my eyes soften with my apology, "I'm sorry for snapping at you Daddy... I want to be punished over your knee." God, it humiliated me to pick like that, yet I got so wet from making the choice.

Stepan made his way over to the couch in the living room, dragging me behind him until he was comfortable on the couch. Then he laid me across his knee and locked me down with a leg thrown over the back of my thighs. "Take my belt off, *malenkaya*."

His grip on my hair wasn't firm like earlier, allowing me enough room to whip my head back at him. "What? But I'm over your knee." A soft worry rang in my voice as I looked up at him with wide eyes and a slight pout.

Chuckling deeply and darkly, he brought his free hand down onto my bottom, making me flinch with a sharp gasp. A small whimper left me despite biting my bottom lip when I felt his hard grip on my ass cheek. "Oh little tigress, I only gave you a glimpse of *where* you will be punished, not *how* you will be punished. No, you have no choice in that matter."

The temptation to spite him bit at my tongue with my teeth, but he had played me; I had to accept that. But by God, the urge to glare at him, hiss a string of curses at him, and maybe flip him the bird for extra effect was so fucking tempting.

"Unless you rather the paddle." That threat got my hands moving faster than I could think.

With half my body locked down by his leg, I had to twist my upper half at an odd angle to maneuver my hands enough with the bit of space I created. The bratty side of me tempted my fingers to be slow in undoing his buckle and slipping it off, but one look at his disapproving gaze meant he knew what went on in my little head. So, I behaved and made it quick, shivering at the sound of the leather rubbing against the fabric of his pants when I pulled it loose and placed the belt into his waiting hand.

"Why am I punishing you, *malenkaya*?" He asked in a stern voice as he released my hair and moved the same hand to my nape to hold me down firmly after repositioning my body.

Stubbornly, I chewed at my bottom lip for a moment to swallow my pride yet again. "Because I cussed at you and didn't listen the first time when you were being nice to me." I mumbled with a hung head, letting my eyes mindlessly follow the lines on the wooden floor.

"I'm not punishing you for being upset, just how you reacted and chose to act out because of it. Talking and communicating your feelings and emotions isn't easy for you. I understand that, but that doesn't make it an excuse for you to misbehave when I give you the right options. Understand?" His voice softened enough to where I could feel his care for me touch my soul.

"Yes, sir. I'm sorry. Please, punish me." I deserved it, and I'd take it as I should.

"Sixteen, you know what you have to do, little tigress." He said, pulling my leggings and panties down to bare my bubbly bottom to him.

"Yes, Daddy, count each one." Or risk more than needed.

The sound of the leather slicing the air was the only warning my ears got before the bite came, right on my sit spot—the area where my thighs met my ass cheeks. "Fuck!" I squealed from the sudden pain, unprepared for how hard he came down on me. "One!"

It didn't ease up from there. Sixteen wasn't a lot compared to what I usually got on a near-daily basis, but I guess he won't take it easy on me because it was less. Every snap of the leather against my burning cheeks made my eyes burn with my tears while my throat scratched from my yelps.

"Daddy it hurts, stop, please." My plea won't be heeded, but I had to get it out of my system.

He wouldn't stop just because I begged; I could beg all I wanted and mean it, and he wouldn't stop. We wanted it that way though, as twisted as it was, I got off on fighting him, begging him to be denied, to be forced by him. If anything ever got too much, he would stop instantly if I used our safeword, which I've only ever had to use once when we were testing my limits. The moment the word 'fire' left my lips, his whole demeanor changed, and everything ended instantly.

Stepan knew my limits at this point, and I trusted him with my safety. He never gave me more than I could handle, even if it sometimes seemed outrageous. The sixty lashes I'd gotten nights prior paled compared to the measly sixteen currently; even though the count was greater, he didn't go as hard, unlike now, making the whole thing more than bearable.

Pausing, he rubbed and groped at my sore ass, shushing me soothingly while massaging the back of my head with his strong fingers. "You're doing so well *malen'kaya tigritsa*, so well, we're almost done, just five more, you can take it. Daddy's good girl can take it." This was a break for me to pull myself together for the last bit and change my mind if needed.

Relaxing my body, I gripped his legs to brace myself, flinching and yelping when the hit came. More tears spilled from my eyes, joining the small puddle on the floor. Well, only four more, I could take it. I've handled worse, taken worse; four more lashes won't kill me or break me.

God, I can feel the welts without actually reaching back and touching them.

The clatter of his belt, along with the feeling of his leg lifting off of me, brought a sense of relief to me. A shiver crossed my body at the feeling of the cold air hitting my bare legs when Stepan pulled my leggings off entirely.

Confused, I looked up at him, only to have him hook his finger into the loop of the collar and pull me fully into his lap by it. "Take my cock out and sit on it." He commanded before letting go of the collar to grab the hem of my top and lift it off my body, leaving me in my bra that didn't stay on much longer after my top was disposed of randomly somewhere.

Glancing down, I quickly undid his pants and pulled his thick member out. With my legs on either side of him, I lowered myself down and nestled him between my soaked folds, grinding against his full length with a soft moan, coating him in my juices before sinking myself down on him fully. Struggling to hold my orgasm back with ragged breaths, I gripped at his shoulders tightly as I let my eyes flutter shut.

"Good girl, good to see you finally learned your lesson about Daddy owning your orgasms." His praise and proud smile went straight down my spine to my aching walls, causing me to tighten around him. "You can come, *malenkaya*, you were such a good girl taking your lashes, so good and amazing, you made me so proud."

I didn't even need to move for additional stimulation to orgasm. Being fully seated on him like this, having his girthy cock split me open with how aroused I'd gotten from the spanking, was more than enough to give me an orgasm.

Shuddering, I tightened my arms around his neck and pressed myself tightly against him, burying my face into the crook of his neck to inhale his scent as my orgasm took its course.

He embraced me in return, holding me close with a hand tangled into the back of my hair while his other hand slowly rubbed my back. "Good girl, come for me. Use Daddy's cock to come all you want, you deserve it for taking your punishment so well." He whispered huskily in my ear, making me shiver with renewed excitement. "But," he chuckled softly, pulling my head back to look at his smirking face, "We're going to talk about everything. Alright? Otherwise, I won't fill your greedy little pussy or mouth tonight."

If he were anyone else, then I'd laugh and tell them to go ahead because why should I care as long as I got my fill of pleasure? Stepan was different though; I cared about his pleasure as much as mine. Besides enjoying the feeling of him filling me, I found myself enjoying the high I got from making him reach his release. I'd miss out on the total satisfaction if I didn't get his climax.

"Hmp." I nodded in response with a pout.

Leaning back, I steadied myself with his shoulders after moving his hands down to my waist and having him hold me there. Slowly, I rocked my hips and let myself ease into the pleasure of his length pressing and hitting all the sweet, deep spots within me.

"We'll start with the obvious: why did the sight and presence of Lilian Wu flip a switch in you?" Even though he sounded and mainly looked put together, I could see his resolve threatening to break from the strain of his jaw and muscles.

My hips started to slow; just hearing *her* name was enough to get me out of the mood to fuck. Unfortunately, Stepan won't have any of it because he grabbed my hips and made me move, so I was constantly stimulated.

"Do we really have to do this now? I don't want the mood to be ruined." Talking about torture was hotter than this subject.

"If you want me to drop the subject then I will, just remember what happens if you go that route." He reminded me with an arrogant smirk, making me narrow my eyes at him.

"I hate her." I replied bluntly with a huff.

From the way Stepan rolled his eyes in response, he held back a snarky response. "I'm going on a whim and am willing to bet that she has a lot to do with a bad past, particularly your trauma since you unconsciously rubbed at your burn areas, something you only do when you get extreme-ly uncomfortable, more particularly whenever anything about your past comes up."

"How do you know about my burns?" The question he's vehemently avoided so far.

"We're talking about you first, then we can move onto me if you can think straight after I'm done with you." Damn jerk, he has no intentions of answering any of my questions tonight; that much was evident by his jaded voice. "Now, elaborate."

Huffing with a pout, I narrowed my eyes at him for a moment while I remained still on his member, the only movements being the subtle rocking of my hips because of his hands moving me. "Don't think too much on it, *malenkaya*, stay focused, stay with me." Easier said than done.

I never thought about *those* moments in my life, at least not actively. Anxiously, I chewed at my bottom lip while playing with the back of Stepan's hair in an attempt to distract myself enough so I wouldn't fall into a flashback. The pleasure from him filling me provided a good focal point, but I needed to touch something, to feel him, more of him.

"You know, I think the reason why Angel and I get along so well and understand each other so well is because we both have fucked up families but good fathers." Not the answer he wanted, but I wasn't done.

I had to keep my head above the water first, to breathe and take my breath before diving under. "Lilian's my aunt, her and my mother made me work in a brothel... I was only ten years old. They didn't care though, all they saw were the dollar signs, the stacks of cash... For two years, I had to..." I had to pause to force the bile that choked at my throat back down. "The things they made me do, the things they did to me, what I was forced to witness..." I had to pause again otherwise I would throw up right this instant. "Two years until my only friend in the place got into an accident that burned the place down. I shouldn't be this traumatized over it, others were there a lot longer than me, two years would've been nothing to them. So, I shouldn't be complaining or be traumatized by any of it." I finished in a shaky voice.

I hadn't realized how tight my grip on Stepan's hair got until he hissed with a soft wince. "Sorry." His neck suffered at my other hand, my nails having dug into the back of it.

"Hanna, no, don't feel guilty for feeling the way you do. You were just a child when all of that was forced onto you." Leaning up, Stepan slid his hands up my body and held my face gently, swiping away the tears that fell from my eyes uncontrollably. "It doesn't matter how long or when you were subjected to such horrendous things, anyone would be traumatized by it no matter what." His strong arms suffocate me in comfort before his next words sweetened my ears. "You have every right to feel broken, that's okay, that doesn't make you any less of a person, nor does it damage your image any."

Pulling away, he gave me a proud smile as he held my face adoringly. "If anything, seeing how far you've come, how far you've built yourself back up into this badass woman who doesn't take no shit from no one, even me, is amazing to see. You have to give yourself more credit tigress, I mean it. Not everyone can recover and bounce back like you, and don't feel guilty for the others just because you managed to recover faster. Everyone does things at their own pace and time, and some are savable while some aren't, unfortunately."

Stepan's comforting touch and words kept the icky memories at bay enough to keep me from going under. However, there was this darkness, an anger, a resentment of sorts burning deep in his eyes below the comforting look he gave me. "I shouldn't have dismissed you so coldly back in the office, forgive me?" His expression softened with appeal, and his lips ghosted mine for a second in an attempt to get on my good side.

"I can't stay upset at you for that, not when you didn't know anything. Besides, I already forgave you after our little tiff in the parking lot." His cheek had a pink hue to it still from where I'd slapped him good after missing my punch.

Smiling victoriously, he leaned in fully and captured my lips in a hot kiss.

I'd expected the weight to lift off my shoulders once I confessed to him, yet why did I still have this nagging feeling?

Chapter 35
Stepan

WITH HANNA SOUND ASLEEP in my arms, I lazily stroked her arm and back.

Even though she came clean to me about her past earlier, something didn't feel right. Her eyes were clouded with uncertainty when she spoke. There was an element of truth to her words, no complete lies, but there was something very off. She had a distant look in her eyes when she spoke; I could hear the hurt in her voice, but it wasn't deep. It was as if she disassociated and went on autopilot.

I didn't doubt Hanna, no. Again, I sensed some truth to her words, but something deeper existed. And I intended to figure it out whether she likes it or not. I wasn't upset with her though, not at all, because she didn't do it on purpose from what I picked up.

Sighing softly, I looked down at my sleeping beauty with sadness and concern. Well, at least I avoided having to confess my side to her; she was too tired after I took her for a few rounds after dinner to bother bringing her questions back up.

Breathing deeply, I took in her scent to calm myself and lull myself into a deep slumber with her, only stirring awake when I felt her warmth leave me.

"*Malenkaya*, not yet, just a little more." I whined needily, pulling her back against me and locking my arms around her waist. "It's Saturday, stay in bed with me a little more." With a long groan, I bury my face into her hair while spooning her tightly.

"I wish I could, hon, but I need to go run some errands for Angel that are time-sensitive," Hanna replied with a tired chuckle, prying my arms off and bringing a hand up to her lips to kiss the back of it.

Letting out another long groan, I pull her on top of me with a cheeky grin. "Were you really gonna leave without giving me a morning kiss?" I pulled at any string I had to keep in her in my arms for moments longer to ease this creeping feeling in my chest.

Giggling, Hanna turned her body to face me with pinked-tinted cheeks. "You are so beautiful." I couldn't hold back my smile as I stroked her burnt cheek with the back of my fingers and hand. "Uniquely you."

"You're just saying that." She fought me with a pout while trying to hold back her smile.

"Have I ever lied to you, tigress?" I questioned with a raised brow while tracing patterns on her cheek. "Just know that I will never tell you anything but the truth."

"I still don't see what you see in me." She sighed sadly with a smile.

"Everything." I breathe out with an uncontrollable smile. "You are perfect to me in every way. Even if you are broken, I'm helping you piece yourself back together to be better. You are so confident and spunky, so carefree, it's refreshing to see. You really aren't like most people or any woman I've encountered, and that intrigues me, but what really captivates me is you yourself. I'll spend every day of our life caring for you and cherishing you until no more doubts remain." I whispered against her lips before kissing her slowly and deeply with a groan. "I've caught my little tigress, and I'm gonna make her live in her little caged paradise with her Daddy."

Before I could try to slide her down to sneak my morning wood into her, her phone went off. With a giggle, Hanna slapped my chest softly before pushing off of me to pick up her phone. "Hey... Yeah, I'm about to... Yeah, I know, be nice to Benjamin... No, I really was about to go until *someone* tried to keep me in bed... No, I'm not sitting on his dick right now... Oh don't worry, he's taking the best care of me... Yeah, he's the best... Yeah, I'll catch up with you later after the assignment, go enjoy your time with Nikolai, I can hear him trying to get at you... Bye take care."

Sitting up, I leaned over, hugged her from behind, and kissed the back of her head. "Join me in the shower? I'll make us some breakfast afterwards." I mumbled against her neck, trailing little nips and kisses along her succulent skin, leaving a small trial of love bites.

"I'm so sore Daddy." She hissed with a wince when my fingers brushed against her bare pussy.

"Since when has that stop me?" I chuckled deeply, nipping at the shell of her ear and playing lazily with her sensitive clit. "Gonna be a good girl for me and let me fill you up before you go? Fill you up so that when you're out there you'll have a constant reminder of me dripping out of you, staining your little panties and thighs with my seed and scent."

Her resolve fell away with every shudder, and with every word until she leaned back fully against me with her legs wide open for me. "Good girl." I purred with delight, letting out a small growl as I sank my teeth into her shoulder.

"Ow! Daddy!" She yelped and tried to pull herself away from me, which made me bite her harder until I tasted blood.

"Have to mark what's mine for all the other fuckers out there to see and back off. You're mine. No one else's."

I'm pretty sure I made Hanna late for whatever she had to do with taking her in the bed before going another round with her against the shower wall until the water ran cold. I certainly didn't mind keeping her around longer, but I was biased in that department.

"Well, you look too happy to be in the dog house. I'm taking it your talk with Hanna went better than okay?" Angel asked with a soft groan of discomfort as she sat down across the patio table from me. "What did you want to talk to me about anyways?"

Needing answers to questions Hanna won't give me, I went to the only option I had besides my brothers. Unfortunately, my brothers wouldn't be much help if what I gave them to work with was shoddy.

"About that..." Rubbing the back of my neck nervously, I let my eyes draw away from Angel's scolding glare.

"Stepan, I swear on my children, if you do not tell her soon, I will. It's not right for you to hold such a secret like that from her." Angel threatened while mean-mugging me.

She'd been pestering me nonstop about coming clean to Hanna about how I stalked her and violated her privacy and personal space with my late-night antics and of course, how I threatened her last boy toy. Hanna only knew about the near-miss bullet, but not all the other things I did to Logan behind her back.

Scoffing softly, I looked at Angel challengingly. "Oh? You're the one to talk, or need I remind you about you withholding your real name from your own husband?" That was a big little issue not too long ago now.

Nikolai had married Angel under a false name. Now, she did come clean to him about that part, but she never told Nikolai her real name—he had to get that from her half-brother. All her skeletons came tumbling out of the closet rather messily once we got our hands on her real file.

"That is not the same. Kolya never asked me about it. I would have told him if he did, but he didn't. You and Hanna, on the other hand, she's asked you and you've been avoiding it like fucking COVID." Angel snapped back with a harshening glare. "Why didn't you tell her yesterday like you'd planned?"

"Well, that's part of the reason why I'm here. I did plan on telling her, but then she flipped out when she saw Lilian Wu in my office, and it was just a dumpster fire all the way home until I made her talk. I didn't find a good opportunity to tell her the rest of the night because of how vulnerable she became and how she regressed." I replied with a tired groan that became muffled by my hands running down my face.

Angel's face unfurled as she settled fully in her seat. "What happened? Tell me everything from the start of the day to wherever." A soft sigh of defeat and a look of understanding crossed her face.

"It was a normal morning, normal day at the office, we were all doing our jobs, and I was getting ready to call it a day when Lilian Wu showed up at my office unannounced, demanding protection from the bratva along with other bullshit." Angel opened her mouth, but I held a hand up to stop her. "And no, before you say anything, I wasn't going to entertain her request given the information about her. I was about to send her away until Hanna showed up and bat shit hell happened."

Just the memory of yesterday evening brought a pounding headache to my tense head. "I don't know what she said to Lilian because it was in another language, but she was pissed and upset like never before. Hanna's usually so put together no matter what, that seeing her go off the bat like that was a little concerning to me. Lilian had a few spats with Hanna too before turning her attention back to me and saying she wasn't done and would be back, which Hanna did not take kindly to at all."

Groaning, I ran my hands through my hair and leaned over onto my elbows on the table. "Hanna got all pissy with me at the office then went silent, angry silent, until we got home and I made her talk. I forced her to open up about her and Lilian, and she told me about her past, but something about me doubts half of what she said. I know she was telling me the truth, or some semblance of the truth. She had this distant look to her eyes when she spoke, the dulled over eyes whenever she disassociates or regresses." I didn't bother mentioning how cold Hanna got with her emotions.

Angel let out a long sigh with her sagged shoulders. "What exactly did she tell you?" She sounded so worn, like some parent asking what trouble their child got into this time.

Taking a moment, I reiterated what Hanna told me about her past, furrowing my face at Angel's saddening expression. "It's mostly true, yes, and don't hold anything against Hanna because to her, it is the truth."

Angel looked off into the distance for a moment, and I could see the gears turning in her head as she slowly sipped at her glass of water. "Everyone processes trauma differently. I dealt with the trauma of my ex by trying to move on, put him in the past, ignoring him and lived in a weird state of denial for the longest while. Hanna... She... How do I put this..."

Sighing heavily, Angel ran a hand across her jaw and rested it there in thought. "Hanna copes by disassociating or regressing, mainly, but the main thing is her memory itself of everything. Sometimes people concoct stories to fit their narratives. Hanna's the type to refuse to be a victim, which is why she's overly confident and expressive, to mask her insecurities and basically trick herself. Fake it until you make it basically. But sorry, I lost track, the memories, her memories. I don't want to say much because like I said before, it's her story to tell, but it's obvious she won't tell you the whole story because she can't."

"Can't or won't?" I pressed quizzically.

"It's a strange mixture of both because to Hanna, the story she tells you is the truth to her and her mind. She's grown comfortable with her own lie of the events to where it's what she believes to have happened. Yes, she was forced into a brothel by her mother and Lilian, her aunt. Yes, she was subjected to the stuff of the devil's nightmares in the place. And yes, a fire burnt the place down. My father found out about the place because of the fire and took Hanna in afterwards and exiled her mother who took the blame for everything to leave Lilian to run her business with the triad still." Even though she finished speaking, I couldn't help but feel something amiss.

"But?" I pressed sternly, not liking to be kept in the dark if there was information amiss.

"But the way Hanna presents it is a little skewed... In her version, there's always a little girl with her, her friend in the place. We searched the whole place from underground and up, combed through every bit of ash, and we found no trace of this girl who died in the fire. We accounted for everyone dead and alive, and when we questioned the bastards who were regulars with Hanna, they told us there was never any other girl. The girl never existed, at least not to us or anyone else but Hanna."

Oh Hanna, I'm going to make this right.

Chapter 36

Hanna

"HANNA!"

I startled with a jump when a pair of hands grabbed at my shoulders and pulled me away from the stove.

Zoning back in, I took notice of my wet hands. "*Malenkaya*, you were going to burn yourself." Stepan sighed with a concerned look. "Go sit down on the couch with your wolf, I'll finish dinner up."

"I'm sorry." I mumbled with a hung head as I handed him the handful of spaghetti noodles I'd planned on putting into the boiling pot of water.

Sweetly, he held me tightly and kissed my forehead. "I'm sorry for yelling at you, but you weren't responding the first few times I called your name, and you were holding your hand too close to the water. I'm not mad at you or anything, just worried about how distracted you are." He spoke against my temple before placing a kiss there.

"If you wanted me out of the kitchen then you just had to say so." I joked dryly, forcing myself to chuckle painfully.

"Hanna, I know how your cooking skills are, and I really appreciate you wanting to make dinner for us tonight, but you really are too distracted. You nearly cut yourself too many times earlier with chopping up the veggies for the salad, and now the boiling water. Let me take care of it, alright? Go decompress on the couch, turn on a show, I'll bring the food out once it's done," he said with a nod towards the couch in the living room that was in clear view from the kitchen thanks to the open floor plan of the house.

"*Malenkaya*." His urging tone became stern when he noticed me lingering and debating. "I know you wanted to make dinner, maybe tomorrow okay?"

Sighing in defeat, I nodded softly before turning my head to give him a quick kiss. "Can you eat me out later, Daddy?" Don't know why I got a little shy asking him as if he doesn't try to shove his head between my legs nearly every damn morning and night.

His chest shook with his chuckle. "I was gonna eat you out regardless for dessert." He whispered hotly in my ear, making me shiver with excitement. "Now go be a good girl on the couch." His hand gave my bottom a few firm pats before he turned his attention away from me.

Cheekily smirking, I gave Stepan's delicious ass a quick swipe, giggling and running away before Stepan could grab me. Going over to the couch, I tuck myself comfortably onto the soft leather sectional and hug my giant stuffed wolf that Stepan got me for when he'd have to leave me alone; he even sacrificed—unwillingly—one of his shirts for me to put on it so his scent would be present.

"I swear, sometimes you love that thing more than me." Stepan joked with a chuckle from the kitchen, making me look over to see his jealous eyes.

Snickering playfully, I stick my tongue out at him before grabbing the remote to turn the TV onto Criminal Minds. Moments like these were so lovely, and I only wished our lives could be more like this. To come home from the office to the comfort of home life. "Hon? Do you ever think about leaving the bratva life behind?"

"Do you want me to?" He responded with a question.

Keeping my attention trained on the TV, I hummed softly in thought before answering him, "No. Well, not fully... I don't know why I asked, it's stupid." He'd never leave his brothers high and dry. Even if Nikolai didn't force his brothers to partake in the bratva, they all chose to be involved because of their respect and love for their older brother.

Stepan doesn't particularly care for the family business much, but he has made his wishes for a normal-ish life known occasionally. I don't blame him because I was the same. I never cared for my future much until Stepan happened to it. Now, I had us to think about, as strange of a notion it was.

"This won't last long, tigress. Once everything is sorted out then it'll be smooth sailing again." Stepan assured me confidently.

Merges were always messy, and not everyone under triad command was too keen on coming under the rule of the Volkov Bratva when Angel made the announcement. Lev and I, along with most of the other enforcers, had been dealing with those unwilling to cooperate with our fists while Stepan and the rest of his brothers handled the business side of things.

"I know... I'm just tired."

A lot more than usual.

"Oh fuck, Daddy! Coming!" Again, for the hundredth time, it felt like.

A high-pitched moan fell from my lips as my body convulsed from the mind-shattering pleasure ravaging my body. Aches clawed at my body with my orgasm, my body tensing from the waves of my release that drenched Stepan's face as he continued to torture me with his tongue, mouth, and fingers.

The towel under my hips was soaked entirely through from how much Stepan had made me squirt and gush over the past hour. "Daddy no more, please, I'm so sore, I don't think I can come anymore." I whimpered pleadingly while trying to buck my hips away from him to get a rest from the overstimulation against my aching sex.

"One more *malenkaya*, squirt one more time for me." He encouraged me with a hungry look as he curled his fingers in me, making me squeal and lift my hips. "Soak Daddy's face one more time, you can do it."

The sound of the TV sounded miles away compared to the sounds of my wet pussy being finger fucked by Stepan. I don't exactly remember how we ended up like this. After dinner, we cuddled on the couch, and I remember dozing off. Next thing I know, I'm waking up to Stepan's head between my legs; the lewd sounds of him eating me out like I was some juicy apple filled the living room along with my cries of pleasure. Then there was a brief period where he fucked me with his cock before he went back to feasting on my cunt like a starved man after giving me a creampie.

Painfully, my abdominal muscles tightened with another orgasm, sending my juices spraying out of my trembling body for Stepan to lap up like a thirsty beast. "Daddy, please." I begged through my cries of pain and pleasure.

Climbing up, Stepan steadied himself with an arm next to my head as he slowly pumped his fingers in and out of me. "Shh, ride it out *malenkaya*, ride it out. That was the last one, so ride it out fully. You did so good for Daddy, so good." He soothed me with soft kisses on my face and lips.

Coming down from my high, I let my head lull over the back of the armrest to look at the clock on the wall across from it. "Why did you let me sleep?" It was a little past midnight if I read the clock correctly.

"Because you were too cute to wake up." Stepan chuckled with a teasing smile, earning a pointed look from me. "You needed the rest little tigress, a small nap won't kill you."

Sluggishly, I grabbed Stepan's shirt and threw it on after untangling myself from his arms. "I should just have a rule where you can't wear anything but lingerie or nothing." He joked with a playful chuckle while looking at me with a goofy smile. "You look so sexy in nothing but a collar or clad in sheer." He reached out and ran his finger along the edge of the black leather and lace collar that adorned my neck, playing with the loop hanging off the center.

"And who says I'd follow that rule, hm?" I challenged him with a daring smirk, leaning up to get in his face.

Running his tongue across his teeth, he chuckled lowly. His finger hooked around the collar's ring, and he pulled me down and off the couch to his feet. "Don't be crying to me when I punish you if that's how you're going to be. Or maybe do, you know how much your tears turn me on, especially when I'm causing them." The corners of his lips curved deviously as he looked down at me. "And you know damn well it won't be a funishment. It'll be the bench and paddle."

A chill of fearful excitement bit down my body at the image of his words. "No, I'll be good Daddy." I wanted a fun spanking, not an actual one after the last punishment I got left marks for days.

Softening his smile, he grabbed my neck fully and dragged me into his lap fully so I straddled him. "What's on your mind *malenkaya*? I can see something brewing in your eyes." His eyes searched mine for an answer as he gingerly stroked my face with a finger.

Taking a moment, I let my eyes linger longingly on his, debating whether I wanted to do this now or later. I intended to bring the subject up after dinner, but that went out the window after the food coma hit while I was in the safety and comfort of Stepan's arms. It was late, so maybe I should hold off until tomorrow. Then again, if I push it off then who knows when I'd get an opportunity next.

Fuck it, we were both wide awake still, obviously. Might as well rip the bandage off and get it over with.

"How did you know about my burns? My meds? My nightmares? I never told you about any of it, nor would anyone tell you about any of that if you'd asked. And none of that 'oh I'll tell you later' shit because I want an answer, right here, right now." It was rare for me to demand anything of Stepan in a stern manner like this, and the severity of my tone made it clear that I wouldn't be pushed out of this like usual.

Stepan's chest deflated with a heavy sigh as he ran a hand through his messy hair. Nudging me off his lap, he settled me next to him on the couch to pull his pants back on and to pull my shorts—with my panties—onto me.

I didn't push his silence because I could see that he was deep in thought with how clouded his eyes became with distraction. He'd answer me once he got his thoughts sorted out, or at the very least, his lies straight. Well, doubtful he'd lie to me; he hasn't yet from what I know, and hopefully not ever.

Omission was a huge issue with Stepan, though. I've never held it against him, though, because most of the time, he withholds information about his bratva business to me, which I could care less to be privy to half the time. Still, sometimes I wonder about pushing that limit with him so we could be fully open with each other. I didn't want any kind of secrets between us, spoken or not.

"Stepan." I urged sternly while maintaining a soft voice when he tightened his lips.

Another heavy sigh left him as he looked at me with a crestfallen expression and guilty eyes. "Stepan Kirillovich Volkov, answer me. Now." The way he flinched and shied away from my scolding tone made the emotional storm in me come to life.

"I saw them." He bluntly stated while averting his attention from me to the floor.

"How?" Was he peeking at me in the employee showers? That's the only place he could have seen them because I kept them covered good otherwise.

"At night, after you get ready for bed... And after you sleep when your medications kicked in..." He admitted shamefully, like a child being caught with their hand in the cookie jar.

"And exactly how did you see all of that?" The answer was pretty clear, but I needed to hear him admit it.

"I used to follow you home, to make sure you were safe and sound... Nearly every night... I'd climb the fire escape and hide in the blind spot of your escapes balcony and just watch you," he said with a nervous bob of his Adam's apple. "Then I started to climb through the window to make sure you were safely tucked in and safe, and I couldn't bring myself to leave you when you'd cling onto me or when you'd have nightmares and my embrace made them go away."

So, I wasn't batshit crazy, good to know. But fucking hell was I pissed as fuck at Stepan right now. How dare he violate my privacy and space like that!? Fucking stalking me like some creep, then played the peeping Tom. Oh, he'll regret what he did.

With an eerie calm, I got up from the couch and walked towards the patio door to slide it open. Then, I headed to the armor cabinet next to the patio door, unlocking the coded safe and grabbing a handgun from inside. Pulling out a box of rubber bullets, I popped the magazine out and pointed the gun at the open doorway. "You have until I finish loading this before I come after you, so I suggest you fucking take it because I am going to make you regret everything you've done the moment I catch you and shove your face into the dirt." The low growl in my voice shook my nerves to the core because of how dangerous it made me sound. Also, I didn't know I could sound unhinged-ish.

Stepan didn't even bother trying to argue, his body bolting right out the door like a caged animal with a chance at freedom. As he cleared the garden and ran for the tree line, I kept my eyes carefully trained on him while I meticulously loaded the magazine. And yes, I had full intentions of using the damn thing on Stepan.

After clipping the loaded magazine in place, I pulled on my boots, grabbed my handcuffs, and took off after Stepan. At least the moon was nearly full tonight, and the skies were clear. Made following his tracks a whole lot easier, especially since his trail was easy to pick up with the disruption compared to the forest's surroundings. Footprints, broken branches and twigs, disturbed bushes, and the ground painted a perfect path with how the fallen leaves had parted from his fleeing.

Grinning and giggling like a maniac, I slowly turned around in my spot to carefully survey my surroundings when I came to a stop with the tracks. "Stepaaaaaaan, come out, come out, wherever you are hon. You can't hide and run from me forever!" The calm fury from before came out unhinged now. "How does it feel, huh? To be stalked like some piece of meat?"

I could see where he tried to cover up his tracks, going around in circles and making a mess of the surrounding place. We had all night to play this little game of hide and seek, but my patience with him ran thin.

A grim smirk graced my lips when I caught a glimpse of movement in the tree branches.

To predictable.

It was no surprise he'd take to the high ground, given his affinity for sniping and stalking. Always have the higher ground for a better view and to hide from those on the ground.

With no hesitation or reservations, I aimed and pulled the trigger. Stepan's hissing cuss meant I hit him, along with the sounds of the branches rustling. "*Blyat!*" Stepan froze in place when his eyes locked with mine.

Slowly, I stalked up to the tree with a wicked smile, taking my sweet time as I knew I'd won. "Come on down here darling, I just want to talk."

About how I'm going to fuck you up and hand your ass to you.

He didn't need to know that part; he'd only experience it when I'd get my hands on him. He couldn't stay in the damn tree forever, not like I'd let him anyways. When he made no indication of coming down, I raised the gun and shot him in the leg, making it buckle and sending him tumbling down a few branches before he caught himself.

"Don't make me start throwing rocks at you." I growled through gritted teeth. To further push my threat, I bend down and pick up a stone by my feet, tossing it and catching it in my hand repeatedly.

"*Malenkaya*, let's talk about—*blyat!*" The stone chipping at the tree trunk right next to his head tersely cut him off. "I'm sorry, alright? I'm sorry I followed you around like a fucking creep, and I am sorry for violating your personal space and privacy with my actions. I am sorry, but I will never regret or take back any of it. If I hadn't followed you around then I wouldn't have gotten the chance to ensure your safety every night, nor would I have been able to see all your little quirks, habits, and other stupid shit that is valuable information to me."

"That's so sweet and fucked up. Still not going to change the fact that I'm going to fucking kill you." He could and should have gone about it differently.

Yes, it was nice that he paid that much attention to me like no other guy has before. Yes, it was nice that he made an effort to remember all he observed about me. And yes, it was nice knowing he had my back and safety.

Still doesn't change the fact that it's all fucked up like a mauled body.

"Either get down here or I will start chucking stones at you. You don't want to face my wrath if I have to climb up the fucking tree myself and drag your ass down." I seethed lowly.

"*Khorosho, khorosho, khorosho*, I'm coming down, just don't shoot me." Stepan's wary eyes bounced between my face and the gun, waiting until I lowered it to descend fully to the ground.

The moment his feet touched the ground, I lunged at him, tackling him to the ground onto his front side. Both of us struggled against each other for a moment, him trying to escape me while I wrestled his arms behind him to cuff them. It took more out of me than I expected, but I eventually managed to secure his arms behind him.

Once the cuffs were tightly on him, I stood back up and pushed him onto his back using my foot. Standing above him, I keep my foot firmly planted on his chest to prevent him from squirming away.

Leaning down, I shifted my position so my knee dug into him and got face down close to his. Pressing the gun into his body, I slowly ran it up to his temple, reveling the way his body shivered and erupted in goosebumps while his lips parted with a sighing groan that died out into soft, pleading whimpers.

"Look. At. Me." I demanded harshly, choking him until his breaths became shallow. "You better not pull that kind of shit with me again, you hear me? I will not hesitate to cut your dick off and feed it to you. Am I clear?"

"Yes, tigress." He gasped under me, his body squirming in a slight struggle.

"Now, fucking beg for my forgiveness, and beg for me to let you come." There was no way of denying our arousal from this little chase and hunt. His hardon tented at his pants, painfully from the looks of it; likewise, my panties were soaked to the point my own juices dripped down my thigh.

Ghosting my lips over his, I teased my way down his shuddering body, letting my tongue slide out between my lips to lick the delicious dips of his muscles. His half-naked body was scuffed up good from his little tumble down the tree earlier. The rough bark scratched at his bare chest as he'd only thrown on a pair of pants earlier after our rounds; his shirt was still on my body currently.

Setting the gun down, I used both hands to undo his pants and free his hard member. Teasingly, I dragged my nails down the underside of his shaft, making him bite his bottom lip and drag out a groan. Roughly, I cupped his balls, fondling them while my other hand squeezed at his length with hard and slow strokes.

"Hanna, I'm so sorry, please, I really am. I am so fucking sorry, and I will spend the rest of our lives apologizing, but I need you right now, please. I need your mouth, your tongue, your pussy, anything, please, I just need anything of you, please." He whimpered breathily while bucking his hips at my hands. "Hanna." He continued to beg needily while imploring me with his lust-filled eyes.

Climbing on top of him, I push my panties to the side and sit on his length after laying it flat against his abdomen. Slowly, I rocked my hips, humping him as a means to tease him. I could easily get off like this—it wasn't ideal, but for the sake of torturing him, it'd have to do.

Steadying myself on his chest, I bit back a moan as I dug my nails into his pecs, causing him to suck in a sharp breath. "Hanna, please, I'm sorry, please forgive me, please. Fuck, please forgive me and fuck me, please." I didn't think I could get any wetter until I heard his raw desperation and need.

"No. Not good enough yet." I wasn't letting him off the hook that easily. No, he had to earn it.

Stepan begged desperately for a long while as I teased him endlessly. I threw everything that came to my mind at him: raking my nails down his body, using my teeth to add more marks to his beat-up body, choking him, slapping him, even sitting on his face and making him eat me out for brief periods and pulling away before he could enjoy himself too much.

Of course, it was all to teach him a lesson; I'd already forgiven him with the first sincere apology. "*Malenkaya*, please, it hurts." His hips shamelessly thrust at me as I hovered my hips over him. "Please, I need you so badly, please, please fuck me and let me fill your sweet cunt, please."

Well, guess I've tortured him enough. His poor, throbbing cock was so swollen. So, using my hand to angle it up, I slam myself down on him with a loud moan from the delicious burn of him stretching at me again. "Oh fuck, Stepan." My orgasm shook at my body as I remained seated on him.

Throwing his head back, he gave out a desperate whimper. "Fuck, let Daddy come, please, ride my cock and make me come, please." He begged with a guttural groan.

"Not until I say." I grinned deviously at him after a short recovery.

Wasting no time, I lifted my hips and bounced on him like a rabid rabbit, filling the forest with the sounds of my wet pussy taking his cock and our bodies slapping together. "Not yet, Daddy, not yet." I could feel his length throbbing more and more, indicating his approach to his release.

"Hanna, please, fuck I don't know how much more I can take." He gasped with ragged breaths and groans. "Please."

"Almost, just a little more, please, I want us to come together." I knew I was close, just a little more. "Fuck! Now!"

Stepan's body stiffened under me as I my tight walls trapped his pulsating cock within me in a vice grip, milking him for all he's got.

Moaning deeply, I clawed at his chest reflexively. Unable to control my own strength in the throes of my orgasm, my nails dug into him hard enough to draw blood. "Fuck, Daddy... Fuck I hope you learned your lesson." I sputtered through the aftershocks of my orgasm.

Leaning down, I kiss him deeply through my heavy pants, tangling my tongue with his after forcing my way into his mouth.

"Fuck, I don't want this to end, but we can't spend all night out here like this. Uncuff me, so we can head back," he panted heavily between kisses.

Pulling away, I look down at him with a nervous, lopsided grin and a sheepish chuckle.

"About that... I don't have the key.... "

Chapter 37

Hanna

"I SEE HE FINALLY slipped it on your fingers."

Lev's chuckled teasingly, making my smile widen as my fingers unconsciously brushed over the cold metal across the base of my fingers.

"Look at you, so happy about some metal around your hands." Lev continued with a soft shake of his head.

"You're just jealous you don't got someone to spoil you with shiny shit like me." I remarked, sticking my tongue out at him while hugging my hands close to my chest.

"Oh please, there's nothing I can't afford to get myself. If I want it, I get it." Lev scoffed with a chuckle.

"Oh? Then where's Nicole?" I jabbed with a snide smirk and a knowing roll of my eyes.

The sound of his latest target flipped his face upside-down, and he let out an exasperated groan. Seems like he's still salty about losing to his target in their little game of cat and mouse. I could have warned him beforehand about how crafty my friend could be and helped him, but my lips were sealed in the matter. "Why's Stepan so beat up looking?" He changed the subject.

"Hunting accident." I replied casually with a shrug of my shoulders.

Lev didn't need to know precisely what kind of hunt took place, nor *who* the hunter and hunted were. Also, that was the story Stepan wanted to go with to explain why his face was scraped up from his tree tumble and when I made him eat dirt on the ground.

Upon entering the office with Lev—we were out on an assignment—we could feel the staleness of the place. The floor was quiet; Stepan's door was shut with two men in suits standing on either side and at the small meeting table off to the corner sat a cowering girl with four men surrounding her.

"Leave, there is an important meeting in progress." One of the men by the door spoke up gruffly while stiffening his body.

"Do you know who we are?" Lev challenged with a scowl, stepping up to the man, who was close to his height, with his chest puffed out. "You know whose building you are in?"

"Obviously they don't otherwise they'd speak to us with a lot more respect and not look at us as if we are sewer rats." I sneered distastefully at the two men before leering over at the four in the corner.

Slowly, I trudged up to the four men, who instantly made a grab for their guns. So, they were trigger-anxious idiots; good to know. Not like it mattered to me. So, what if I was outgunned? One shot and Stepan would burst out of his office to stop things—or put some holes in these men—before things would turn deadly for Lev and me.

"I suggest you take your hands off your guns. He won't take too kindly to you all pointing such a dangerous thing at his woman and brother." I warned them in a low and deadly voice before softening my face at the trembling girl. "Move. I want to speak to her."

Something wasn't right with the girl. One look at her, and I could feel my hackles ready to raise, my body ready to spur into action to pull her behind me. Something about her screamed for help, something in her body language, her eyes specifically. Her eyes sliced into me like daggers; something about them felt familiar.

"No one speaks to her but Mr. Hwei." One of the four men spoke up, holding a hand out to stop me from stepping closer when I was right in his face.

"And I don't give a shit about that. Either you move, or I break your face at the very least. Unless you want me to scream and have Stepan come out here to demonstrate how deadly his aim can be with you as the target. You are in his building, therefore under his control, and mine since I am his fiancé." Okay, that last part was a lie, but I wanted to drill my importance to Stepan into them for effect. "I only want to talk to her."

When they made no indications to budge, I rolled my eyes and reached out, grabbing the girl who let out a yelp of surprise when I pulled her behind me protectively. The man closest to me grabbed his piece, but the one behind him stopped him with a hand on the shoulder. "If you fuck this up for Mr. Hwei then it's over for you. Just leave it, it's only a talk."

Pulling the girl aside, I moved to the other side of the room and sat her on the couch, handing her some water, which she nervously took from me. "How old are you?" I asked softly, keeping my voice low. "Hey, don't look at them, look at me. They can't hurt you, they can't touch you, not in this building, not ever."

The girl looked at me with much confusion before mumbling under her breath in another language. My Cantonese might be rusty, but I knew enough to be conversational and to understand most things said.

Doing my best to look comforting—which was hard because I had splatters of blood on me and sported a pair of brass knuckles—I switched my tongue. "Hey, I won't let them touch you. I promise, you are safe with me." My words were so stiff since it'd been a long while since I'd spoken Cantonese. "So, how old are you?"

Nervously, her eyes kept bouncing between me and the men around the room, who bore holes into her with their harsh gazes. "If you all don't look away right now then I will put bullets through your eyes." I threatened in English, not bothering to look at them once I had turned my attention back to the girl.

"Take your hand off your fucking gun and look away like she said. You fuck with one of our women and we will descend on all of you like the pack of wolves we are and rip you to shreds." Lev backed me up in a strong and threatening voice.

Taking the girl's hands into my own, I stroked the back of it soothingly. "Please, I really want to help you, I can see it in your eyes." Eyes that still haunted me for some goddamn reason.

"Fourteen." She answered me in a voice barely above a whisper as she hung her head.

"Is he your father?" I doubt it because the poor girl seemed ready to piss herself from how terrified she looked. "Is he hurting you?"

Tears filled her eyes as her hands shot out and grabbed onto my arms. "He... He bought me... P-please don't let him keep me, I don't want him to touch me again, it hurts, please help me, please."

Looking over to Lev, I waved him over and instructed him to call for backup and watch the girl. Then, I went over to the office doors, glaring up at the two men when they tried to block my way. "Move, or I will cut your limbs off. My position in this place is as high as Stepan and his brother, so either you let me through or things get ugly for all of you." At least my threat was good enough for them to act accordingly.

I was more than ready to rip this Mr. Hwei a new one when I threw the doors open and stepped into the office like a damn queen, but one look at him and everything came crumbling down like a house of glass being smashed by a wrecking ball.

Even though he sat across the desk from Stepan a few meters away from me, it felt like he was right beside me. I was back *there* in half a second; in *that* hellish place which broke me. It'd been over fifteen years, yet it felt like yesterday that his grubby hands grabbed at my body, at my friend's body.

"Nana."

When did the room become so suffocating?

My mouth felt drier than the Sahara Desert, and every struggling inhale burned at my airways as if I sucked in a lung full of fire. Then everything felt so big as if I shrunk into an ant. Fear turned my legs to stone as the ground swallowed me like cement, and bile choked at my throat from the feeling of my heart twisting at my insides.

"How's my favorite girl been?" Mr. Hwei's voice echoed as if he was miles away.

'My favorite girl. Always so good.'

I'm gonna be sick.

By some God-given miracle, my feet moved. The sound of Stepan's private little office bathroom opening and shutting flew over my head by a mile. Acid burned at my throat as I hunched over the toilet, and the uncontrollable sobs forced more vomit out of me as I hugged the toilet.

Not even my mind was safe from being seared because memories I'd long locked away flooded through the weakened barriers and spread like wildfire in my mind. I became consumed by the flames of my past to where it felt like I was actually back in the damn building as it burned down around. Everything hurt so much, yet I felt so numb at the same time. My body burned even though I was drowning in the subzero Arctic waters.

My body nearly shut down for some reason at the feeling of human contact until I realized it was Stepan because of his voice and safe embrace. "*Malenkaya*, come back to me, you're not there anymore, you're here, safe with me. I got you. Daddy's got you." He shushed softly while stroking my hair.

"Make him go away, it hurts to see him. He did so much bad to me, to *her*. He did so much bad things to Nana." Even after all these years, the hatred I felt for all the men who'd hurt me and my friend—Nana—in the brothel wasn't enough to spur me into action.

I thought the dark feeling would be enough for me to enact some form of revenge against the men who'd harm me and Nana if I ever saw them again. Instead, I shut down and cowered away like a damn fool after puking my guts out.

"How about we make him go away forever, together." He suggested, well more so commanded because his stern tone meant he wanted me to be involved. "I'll be right there by your side." He said with a voice full of promise. "You need this Hanna, you need to be the one to plunge the knife into him or put the bullet through him. It's the only way you'll be able to fully free yourself."

"I can't do it, Daddy, it's too much." I couldn't face those memories again, and I might not survive a second wave.

"Yes, you can, tigress. Get your anger out on him, beat him to a bloody pulp, make him suffer as he did to you." No matter how much Stepan tried to convince me, I couldn't do it. I couldn't work myself up enough.

"Stepan, I can't, please, I can't." I begged him with uncontrollable tears as I clung to the front of his shirt. "I'm sorry, I can't."

Shushing me softly, he kissed my forehead. "It's okay little tigress, it's okay, you have nothing to be sorry for, so don't apologize."

"I'm fucking pathetic, weak and pathetic." Why couldn't I do it? Beating him up and killing him would be no different than killing the men on my raids, so why couldn't I bring myself to act on the thought?

Comfortingly, Stepan cups my face and brings my attention to him. "You are not, my tigress, you are anything but. This is a lot, he's not some simple man to you, he's a root of your suffering in your childhood. So, don't apologize or think otherwise of yourself. Why don't I send you home with Lev and Benjamin so I can take care of the trash? Does that sound fine to you, *malenkaya*?"

"You'll do that? You'll take care of my problem?" I shouldn't be pawning off my dirty work to him, but I didn't want to let the man go unscathed either just because I chickened out.

"Hanna, you are mine to protect and care for, so of course I will take care of all your problems. I meant what I said, I will take care of you *malenkaya*, forever and always."

Chapter 38
Stepan

"I THOUGHT YOU WERE a reasonable man!" Mr. Hwei spat as he struggled against his bindings.

"I am a very reasonable man, to the fair people. Scum and criminals don't get such treatment from me, especially vermin like you. Now, I was going to play the long game with you, use you to expand our list of targets, but that was all before your connection with Hanna came up. I can't let the man who assaulted and raped my woman to live a second longer than he should." My brothers and I already had plans to end his miserable life after using him. His name had been on the roster of members who partook in Lady Qing's black market auction.

Bratva or not, we had our line in the sand: drugs, murder, sex, all fair game to an extent. My brothers and I drew the line at anything involving innocents, children, women, and the elderly. Lady Qing didn't have the same idea because she took part in everything deplorable under the sun as long as it meant padding her pockets well.

Mr. Hwei here was a happy family man with a successful financial institution under his thumb—and a serial child molester. We planned on robbing him dry before turning him into the hands of the law, and if that failed, then *we* would be the *law*. The plan went out the window the moment Hanna revealed to me who Mr. Hwei was to her, along with the fact that he brought a child—his current victim—into my establishment.

His days were numbered right here, right now. He won't survive me tonight, and I'm sure he knew that with how he eyed the flipping bullet in my hands—the one with his name freshly carved into it.

"How many?" I dawdled, keeping my form relaxed in my seat across from him.

After sending Hanna away from the office with Benjamin and Lev, I rounded up some men to deal with Mr. Hwei's guards before dragging him to The Catacombs, a newly acquired holding area out in the desert, courtesy of Nikolai's wife after taking down her stepmother.

Currently, Mr. Hwei was bound to a chair with me opposite in a chair, leg crossed with an ankle on one knee, and the rest of my body was lazily leaned back with a bullet twirling in my fingers. After I tied him down in the chair, I made quick work crafting a bullet in front of him, making it a point for him to see me carve his name into the jacket of it.

"Huh? How many what?" Mr. Hwei asked for clarification in a perplexed voice.

"How many times did you visit Hanna? How many times did you touch her?" I wanted to aim my gun at him and pull the trigger already, but not this time. I wanted to toy with him, draw this out to see him squirm. I needed to torture him and make him suffer for Hanna.

"I don't know, a lot, I didn't keep track, and why does it matter if I tell you if you're just going to kill me?" He had a good point; if I were in his position, then I would keep my mouth shut or lie.

"Your answer will determine your death. It can be quick and painless, though not my preferred choice, or very drawn out and painful." Drawing out a sigh, I smirked darkly at Mr. Hwei with my next words. "Now, the last isn't my forte, but I've got a lovely sister-in-law and my twin brothers who love the game of torture and are far more patient than me." I wasn't one to get my hands dirty much, hence why I preferred to stay and shoot from afar. As much as I hated sniping because of my introduction and training, I found a love for it after the fact.

"I don't know, maybe thirty times?" His face twisted with worry and concern, and his chair clattered more against the ground from his bouncing knee.

Remaining silent, all I do is flash him a flat smile before getting up to prepare my rifle in a drawn-out manner. "Do you know about anyone else who came and saw Hanna? Other patrons who had their eyes on her or her little friend? Also, what can you tell me about Hanna's friend?" I paid him no attention as I carefully inspected my weapon.

"I can give you a list of who I know and those who came with me, but I know nothing about this friend of hers. Hanna was alone there, always, she had no one." One silent, deadly glare made him flinch, but he didn't attempt to correct his words as he remained firm.

"The other girl, I won't repeat myself." I pressed, further narrowing my eyes harshly at him.

Mr. Hwei remained unwavering in his answer. "There was no other girl. I won't lie, I touched Hanna and many others in my life, but I swear on everything I have and own and everything on my horrible life, there was never another girl with Hanna."

SLAM!

"Liar! Nana was always there with me whenever you 'visited' me! You touched both of us, made me watch whenever you touched her!" Hanna's sudden appearance and outburst took me aback because she was supposed to be safe at home.

Mr. Hwei kept his stern eyes on me as he shook his head and denied what Hanna said. "I know she is yours and you want to believe her, but you have to believe me because I was the one who dealt the bad hand to her. There was no other girl. Nana, the girl she is referring to, that was our nickname for her." He kept his voice low to where Hanna wouldn't have been able to hear from the distance she was at.

Going over to Hanna, I gave her a tight hug and a kiss on the forehead before sending her away with Lev and Benjamin again. "Let me take care of this for you, I'll see you at home." I whispered into her ear before I let her go completely.

Once Hanna was gone, I returned to Mr. Hwei and freed a single hand of his before tossing a pad of paper and pen into his lap. "Names, start writing. Anyone and everyone who you know or think came into contact with Hanna at the brothel." I demanded, leaning against a nearby table with my arms crossed.

Minutes later, he had nearly a full sheet filled out with names—too many names. After tucking the paper away safely into my pockets, I cut his ropes with a knife and nodded towards the exit. "You have thirty minutes to get away." The way his face brightened up before he scrambled away was almost laughable.

There was nothing but barren desert for hundreds of miles, and I'd already stuck a tracker onto his back. So, he wasn't getting away. But it was riveting to give him that moment of false hope only to know that I would be taking it away in less than thirty minutes.

Picking up my rifle, I slowly leave to the guard tower outside for the vantage point. As I made my way there, I called up my brother, Arseny. "I'm going to send you a list of names, and I want everything on every single one of those names. I also want you to put out word to our men and forces to not touch any of those men on the list. They are mine and Hanna's to kill, no one else's." The folded paper felt like a weight in my pocket.

Every single one of those bastards will pay for harming my Hanna, even if they only looked in her direction but didn't touch. Fuck keeping my involvement with the mafia to a minimum. It's time to show everyone just how ruthless the Volkov Bratva's second in command can be and burn my name into the city.

"You sure I can't cut them up a little? Give them a little chase? You know I won't kill them, as if Angel and Alexei would let me." Arseny somewhat knew about Hanna's jaded past because I'd asked him to help dig into her and to find anyone connected or responsible for her suffering before.

"No, they are to not be harmed, much. I want to give Hanna the option for closure through their deaths or harm by her own hands." She might not take too kindly to having her demons taken from her without an opinion in the matter.

"Good to see you didn't pull something like Kolya." Arseny chuckled, making me roll my eyes at the memory of us helping our older brother kidnap Angel's ex.

"Oh please, we all know I'm the one with the functioning brain out of the lot of us." I joked with a tense chuckle.

"Hey now, Alexei and I are up there with you, or did you forget who the doctor is? Med school is no joke." My younger brother playfully chided with a soft chuckle.

"You two are psychopaths, not smart." The twins may be the youngest, the babies of the family, but underneath their charming smiles were fucked up things.

Honestly, the twins should be the most feared out of the five of us. At least with Nikolai, Lev, and me, a person knows their outcome and path toward it; with the twins, though, they were unpredictable with their psychopathic tendencies.

"Go avenge your girl, I'll start digging," Arseny told me with a chuckle before we said our goodbyes and hung up.

Once I was settled in the guard tower and in position, I pulled up the tracking app on my tablet to get an idea of where to search for my target. It didn't take long for me to locate the pathetic man through the scope of my rifle after referencing the tablet.

Not gonna lie; it amused me a little to watch him run with nowhere to hide. The panic on his sweaty face brought a sick smile to my face because, no doubt, he realized his fate by now.

I quickly glanced at my watch and saw that thirty minutes were almost up. The seconds ticked by in my mind while my finger rested comfortably on the trigger with budding temptation with each passing second.

BANG!

One well-aimed shot and his body dropped to the ground like a sack of bricks. I barely felt the satisfied smile stretching at my lips until the buzz from pulling the trigger simmered down after I ejected the casing and pocketed it for later. Then, I couldn't help but wonder how long it'd be until the pristine desert sand would be soiled with red iron as I culled the list.

Wonder if the pristine desert sand would be soiled with red iron by the time I combed through the list.

"Leave the body for the vultures," I commanded the guards in the tower, and I told them to pass the message along before descending.

Scum like him didn't deserve to be buried or dumped anywhere. If I were more into torture, then having animals eat him alive would have appealed to me more. No matter, a headshot at a good distance gave me the same thrill.

Hanna's head popped up from the couch when I entered the area. Silently, she watched me with big, curious eyes as I approached her and sat down next to her on the couch, where she was curled up in her little blanket burrito, hugging her stuffed wolf. I almost didn't want to disturb her because she looked too cute and comfortable.

Keeping the peaceful silence between us, I reached into my pocket, pulled out the shell casing along with the bloodied rifle bullet, and held it out to her in my open palm.

Her eyes furrowed a little as she reached out and took the bullet and casing to inspect it closer. "H-he's really gone?" Her heavy eyes brightened with hope and excitement as she sat up fully.

"Being picked apart by coyotes and vultures as we speak." I nodded softly and reached out to pull her into my lap.

A soft, grateful smile graced her lips as she hugged me tightly. "Thank you." Her muffled voice cracked softly as she continued to bury her face into me.

Kissing her head, I stroked her hair in silence for a few moments. "The desert will be a boneyard by the time I'm done crossing everyone off the list he gave me." My voice was full of firm conviction.

Pulling her head back, she frowned at me. "List?" Her head tilted softly to the side as her eyebrows bunched together.

Shifting a bit in my spot, I fish out the folded paper and give it to her, watching her carefully unfold it and run her eyes over its contents. "I don't know their names... Only their horrible faces." She muttered with a sad and grim frown.

"I'll have Arseny throw something together so you can confirm the targets, then I'll carve each and every single one of their names into the bullets that I'll send through their heads." It was a promise. If her demons were too much for her to handle, then I'd deal with them—I'd be her black knight in bloodied armor.

"You don't have to, it's my problem, you shouldn't..." Seeing Hanna so broken up like this hurt me so much, but there was a sense of gratitude and happiness under it all. Hanna trusted me enough to show me this side of her, and I will never take her unconscious act for granted.

"Your problems are my problem, tigress. I will take care of it all, take the weight off your shoulders." I assured her with a kiss against her forehead.

"Thank you, Styosha." She rubbed her face into my chest while curling up tightly into me. "Can I watch? I want to see their bodies drop with my own eyes."

"Of course, you can do whatever you want, and you can participate to any degree you want." Though I made it my personal mission to put down each and every single person on that list, Hanna still called the shots. If, for some insane reason, she asked me to abandon this little manhunt of mine, then I would—begrudgingly.

"You're really going to do this? For me? You'll put down everyone who ever touched me?" She sounded so hopeful but, at the same time, empty with disbelief.

"Hanna," I said, grasping her chin to make her look up at me. "I will do anything for you. Anything. You are my priority. I will do anything to make you happy, to defend you, protect you, avenge you, anything and everything. You are my life now Hanna."

Leaning down, I capture her lips in a deep, heart-aching kiss.

"I love you, Hanna. I love you so much."

Chapter 39

Hanna

I LOVE YOU, HANNA. I love you so much.

"I'm scared." I squeezed through my trembling lips.

I was fucking terrified. Commitment was never my thing, only flings and fuck buddies. The most emotionally involved I ever got with anyone were Angel and my friends, but that was a friendly love.

This though, this relationship with Stepan. He made it clear from the get-go that he was serious about this, about us. He never had to say anything; I already knew, from how he looked at me with such deep devotion, held me as if I were to slip away any second, and cherished me like I'm his world. It's always been this unspoken thing between us until now, and I thought when the time came for those three little words to be uttered into existence, I'd take it better or feel a little indifferent since I already knew his true feelings towards me. Yet, hearing him say it just now felt like a bucket of ice water to the face.

"I know, and I'm sorry for springing it on you suddenly like this, I wanted something more mellow before I would say it, but I just had to let you know. It pains me so much every day to hold back those words. I know they aren't enough to convey the depth of my feelings for you, nothing ever could, but I just had to let you know. I love you, and I'm here for you, always. You don't have to say it back, I don't expect you to, and I know this is new territory for you, so take all the time you need to process it all, I'll be here." He was too damn sweet and good to be true, but he's as real as ever right now in my hands.

As much as I wanted to repeat the exact words to him, I couldn't muster it up. Judging by his face, he understood and wasn't upset. So, settling for the next best, I hugged him tightly and buried my face into his neck.

Sighing somberly, I shoved the subject aside to speak the thought in my mind. "I wish Nana could be here to relish in their deaths too."

"Mhm." The warmth from him chilled over in a second.

Leaning away from him, I narrowed my eyes accusingly at him. "You don't believe him, do you? You know I'd never lie to you, especially about something like that." Now, the warm fuzzy feeling in me flared dangerously into anger.

"Let's not talk about that right now. What do you want for dinner?" He deflected with a question.

"No, we are going to talk about this right now because how can you believe him over me? What gain would I have to lie to you about any of it? Why the hell would I lie about my friend?" There goes our sweet little moment over this stupid shit again.

Scoffing sharply, I shoved him away and got up to my feet. "You know what, thank you for taking care of Mr. Hwei, but I'm going out. I need some space."

Stepan's objections fell on deaf ears as I went off to our room to change out of his shirt, throwing on some tactical gear and slipping on the brass knuckles that Stepan recently gifted me. It wasn't a shiny new gun, but I much preferred these over one.

"Move." The hostility in my snarl made him wince and freeze in his spot.

"Hanna ple—"

"No! I don't want to hear any of it. Now, move." I seethed inches from his face with my hands clenched at my side to prevent them from shoving at Stepan.

Reluctantly, he sidestepped to let me trudge through a few steps before stopping me with a grab of my arm. "I'm coming with you. I'm not letting you go out there alone like this. I won't get in your way, but I can't stay home knowing you're out there doing something dangerous."

One look at his pleading eyes, and I knew I couldn't say no. "Five minutes, if you're not ready by then, then I'm going solo," I grumbled and relented with crossed arms.

Five minutes later, both of us were on the road. The car filled with suffocating tension—mainly from my side—within seconds of the doors closing. I had nothing to say to him unless I wanted to get into a shouting match with him.

Out of the corner of my eyes, I could see him shift around uncomfortably in his seat. "This girl... Tell me more about her... You've barely mentioned her, and I only got a name today. I'm in the dark here Hanna, so give me something, anything, please." His voice was heavy as he begged me.

White knuckling the steering wheel, I took a moment to breathe deeply and gather my thoughts. "Nana was the only friend I ever made in the place. She arrived at the same time as me, we were forced to share a room together, not that we minded because we kept each other company perfectly. Honestly, she was the perfect friend, discount the shitty place we were in of course."

Thinking back, Nana was perfect. A little too perfect? Maybe, but we were stuck together and made it work. "She was a spitfire like me, both of us with ambitious dreams of being adventurers, archeologists, anything that will let us go out there and get sweaty and dirty. We loved the same foods as well, same allergies too, same hobbies, just everything. Honestly, it's as if we were the same person sometimes, or long-lost twins."

"And she was lost in the fire?" His pitiful voice weighed my heart down with a frown.

"Yeah... It was a freak accident, one of our client liked wax play and had a candle lit. There was a jug of gasoline that had spilt earlier in the day and wasn't cleaned up properly, and when the candle got knocked over, everything just lit up." The flash memory of that night made me shudder as my body erupted in goosebumps at the phantom feeling of flames licking the scarred areas of my body.

I tried to keep myself together, but my voice cracked. "I tried to save her, but the flames took her before I knew it. She was just there one second then gone the next. I didn't think I was going to make it out of there, to be honest. I got blocked in by some collapsed beams. I crawled into a corner, cowered, and accepted my fate before I passed out because of the smoke. So, it was a damn surprise to wake up, alive, in a hospital." I forced out a dry chuckle as the survivor's guilt started to pull me under.

"Hey." My body jolted at Stepan's touch on my thigh. "Don't. There was nothing you could do if she wasn't there. You tried. You're here and she's not, and that is fine. Don't feel guilty. If she's not here to enjoy life then enjoy your life for her. She's probably out there watching you, so live a good life for her to watch." His strong fingers stroked at my inner thighs as he squeezed me softly.

Unable to help it, I let my smile spread. Dropping a hand from the wheel, I laid it over his and held it tightly. "You know, you make it hard to be mad at you." I remarked before reaching over blindly and smacking him on the chest.

"Good, because you can be terrifying when you're angry." No doubt our chase left a good lesson on him. "Where are we headed anyways?"

"Into the city. There's been a problem with one of the new businesses not wanting to comply with the new rule. So, just gotta bash a few heads." And get these pent-up emotions out of me before I blow; if I did blow, Stepan would most likely be the receptacle.

"Is it just you or are you meeting others there?" Stepan continued to question, his hand finding mine and interlocking our fingers.

"Just me, it's just a small little crew if anything. No one should be around the business but the boss and some stragglers. Going in there shooting would have been more than enough to get their compliance, I mean, that works most of the time." I've only done this a hundred times.

Besides, my reputation was usually enough to have people backing down when I set foot somewhere.

"Chertov ad. YA rad, chto zastavil tebya vzyat' menya s soboy." Stepan muttered in his spot.

"What?" Unfortunately, my Russian was very limited still, and probably for a long while because I was never a good learner. Hell, I'm surprised I retained what I have learned, which were a bunch of cuss words and hot things to rile Stepan up.

"Nothing, just glad I'm with you then." He spoke a little too quickly for my liking, but I could do nothing about it.

In hindsight, going alone was probably a bad idea. Even though I wasn't too ecstatic about Stepan tagging along earlier, now that my head was out of the clouds, I could see it was a good decision on my part.

BANG! SLAM!

"Gospodi, blyad', Gospodi." Stepan uttered in shock behind me after I kicked the man into the door, breaking the door down in the process.

Everyone, meaning the five men playing poker at a round table, turned their heads towards me and reached for their guns, only to stop short when Stepan released a warning shot into the table they sat at.

I'd already pumped myself up in the car before entering the area; the adrenaline had buzzed and dulled my senses to where I felt as if I'd fly into some roid rage. But all of that disappeared in a hair of a second when my eyes landed on a particular man at the table. Dread drowned me like a tidal wave, and I felt myself grow sick to my stomach again.

"Oh my, Nana, you've grown so much." The man spoke with a sick smile that further churned my stomach.

"D-don't call me that! That's not my name... That's not me." I snapped with a backstep, bumping into Stepan, who wrapped his arms around my waist to steady me.

"*YA tut, u menya ty malen'kaya.*" He whispered soothingly in a low voice that made his chest rumble. "You want me to put a bullet through his head now or later?"

"Later. I want him dead now. But I wanted to burn him like he loved to do to Nana." I could barely get my words out in an audible voice as I shook like a leaf against Stepan.

"Who's in charge and who's the idiot who's been giving my brother and his wife grief with business?" Stepan's strong voice took command of the room in a suffocating manner.

Silently and shakily, a man next to my nightmare raised his hand. The moment his hand went up in the air, three shots rang out in succession of each other, and the other three men slumped over onto the table with holes through their brains.

"Are we going to have a problem with you and your business going forward?" Judging from the smugness in his voice, Stepan probably had an unhinged smirk and look in his eyes.

"N-no, no problem from me, I swear." The man looked ready to piss himself, and I wouldn't be surprised if he did from how terrified he looked.

"You." Stepan trained his gun onto the other man, making him flinch. "Get up, you're coming with us."

"Listen, Nana—"

The name made me wince involuntarily. "I said to stop calling me that. Stop calling me her, I'm not her."

Why does everyone keep calling me that? Calling me her? I'm not her!

Chapter 40

Hanna

THE SOFT *CLICK* OF the front door meant Stepan was finally home.

Betrayed by my own body, I felt my head dart up like some bird towards a sound, giving myself away.

"Love, you're supposed to be asleep." He noted aloud with a sigh as he made his way over to the couch, where I remained bundled up in my blanket burrito.

"And you know how it goes all the time." I couldn't sleep without Stepan next to me; my mind and body had been conditioned to have his presence embrace me to slumber.

Besides, this had been our new routine for the past month after we compiled a list of my offenders to the best of our knowledge and capabilities. Nearly every weekend, Stepan would go out after dinner to cross someone off the list while I remained in the safety of our home, awaiting his return, bundled on the couch with my stuffed wolf. Sleep never came for me during this time because I'd be too anxious about Stepan's return, where he'd give me the spent bullet and casing with the victim's name etched on it—a sign that the deed had been done.

The exchange was always silent, and nothing much would come of it after I gave him a silent sign of my gratitude, usually through a tearful hug or kiss before we moved on.

But not tonight.

Stepan's once bright blues were darkened with a storm, which unsettled me greatly. Apologetic, pity, sadness, regret; why were such things reflecting in his eyes? No question left my lips because I was too busy studying my lover with wary eyes, watching as he took the bullet and casing from me to tuck them away before situating himself on the couch.

Soft sounds of shuffling filled the air when I immediately crawled into his lap to seek out his warmth and comfort, but I felt none as he fixed my position with his strong hands so that I straddled and faced him. Immediately, my eyes avoided his face out of fear for what was to come, but I had no choice but to face him when he commanded me in his dominating voice, "*Malenkaya*, look at me." Conditioned, my body obeyed, nor did I fight it.

Unlike his even breathing, mine was erratic with anxious energy. "We need to talk." His voice was as calm and leveled as his controlled breathing, which surprisingly calmed me even though I felt like some petulant child being reprimanded at the moment.

"What about?" I spat with a scowl, not liking where this was going.

"Nana." At least he didn't seem pleased about it either, but at the same time, why bring it up if it brought both of us no joy.

"There's nothing to talk about." Oh, there was a shit ton to talk about in regards to that subject matter, but I'd rather eat rotten shit than swallow that subject ever. "Besides, I already told you, Nana was my friend in the brothel when I was forced there for my two years. I don't know why everyone keeps calling me *that* when they see me. All of them, not just one, all. It's stupid. Can't they fucking see that I'm not Nana? I'm not her! I'm me!" My raising voice cracked with rage and confusion.

A long sigh passed out of Stepan as he held me tightly and kissed my forehead longingly after whispering, "*Mne ochen' zhal' za to, chto ya sobirayus' sdelat', no eto dlya tvoyego zhe blaga. YA tebya lyublyu.*"

The shock of his following words cut off all trains of thought in my brain. "Yes, you are."

The bastard. Anger and betrayal grit at my teeth achingly as I shoved at him. "Not you too! You know damn well I'm not!" How could he do this? Of all the people in my life, the only one I trusted to have my back through it all, even he turned on me in the end. He didn't deserve to look so hurt and broken at my reaction, not when he was the direct cause and knew damn well the reason.

His grip on me didn't falter, though, no matter how much I pushed and shoved at him. "Yes, you are. You're Nana. Nana was your name in the place, what they called *you*." He insisted firmly with a resolute voice.

Snapping back with as much bite as I could muster, "No! It's not! That was *her* name!" I don't care how much I cared for him; his neck would be wrung for this.

Grunting through my hits, he wrestled with me slightly to keep me from escaping. "Her who? Tell me who this 'her' looked like then. What was she like? Who was Nana, Hanna? Put yourself back there and tell me what Nana looked like and how she was as a person." He continued to press despite my increasing discomfort and fight.

"Why the fuck does this all matter?" I wanted to shut myself in a dark room and brood alone, not answer his stupid questions.

"Just answer me and I'll let you go." He wagered while tightening his hold on me.

If that's what it will take to get away from him, then fine. "A girl, I told you, she was a girl there who was my only friend in that God-forsaken hell hole." The answer came out nearly robotically, but there was pain breaking my voice as tears stung my eyes.

He urged in a soft voice, "Keep going." Slowly, he lowered my hands into my lap and bear hugged me. "What did she look like Hanna? What was she like?"

All the fight I had left me the moment my mind went back to years ago before I shut down completely to preserve myself. "Why are you making me do this? What did I do?" Was this a cruel punishment for something I did? It had to be. Why else would he bring this shit show up and shove my face into it?

Whispers of a sigh ghosted my ear before the chill of warmth from his lips touched my temple. "I'm not punishing you, *malenkaya*. I'm doing this for your benefit. Now, answer my question. Put yourself back there, immerse yourself and tell me everything the day of the fire after you tell me what Nana looks like." What was his plan here then?

Tightening my lips, I fought the memories that threatened to bust the door down to flood me. In a silent plea, I looked at Stepan with desperation. Unfortunately, he wasn't having any of it. "I am right here love. I got you, and I will keep you rooted. You won't go through it alone, I won't let you." His eyes softened with his own plea for me to continue.

The mere thought of reliving that day spiked my heart rate and caused my stomach to churn my dinner up. "No, I can't, don't make me, please." I needed to make it to the toilet, or the sink, or some container to vomit in.

Erratically, my eyes darted around the area as my chest tightened uncomfortably. "Hanna." Stepan's voice boomed, making my attention zero in on him. "You can, and you will. Do it for me, you can do it. Tell me what Nana looked like, start there." He spoke in a softened voice as his arms released their constriction around me so he could hold my face tenderly.

"Daddy, I'm gonna throw up," I whined before the dry heaves hit me, causing my body to jerk as I did my best to hold back my vomit.

Tightening his arms around me, he quickly carried me over to the trashcan in the kitchen, where I proceeded to hunch over it and empty my stomach's content into it. Well, at least I had Stepan comforting me by rubbing my back while he held my hair back, even though this was all his fucking fault.

After I got done hurling my life out into the trash and rinsed my mouth, Stepan carried me back to the couch and situated us like earlier before coaxing me to open up about Hanna with words of comfort and reassurance in between until I relented.

My hesitation waned enough to where I felt myself slip back to *that* day. Just a quick glimpse and I could—no! They were there, I didn't want them to be, but they were there. They touched me, grabbed me—the pain, it hurts, it hurt so much! "No! Nonononono! Stop touching me! It hurts!" I was back in the mold-filled room on the ratty mattress with a monster on top of me; his alcohol-filled breath was all I could taste all the way into my lungs.

"H...a!" A familiar voice, but who? My body moved, but not because of this horrid bastard in front of me. "It's not real, not anymore, you're not there, you are here, safe, with me. Focus, find Nana and tell me what she looks like. I am here Hanna. I am here, and I have got you."

Pain, all the pain I'd felt, staled out as my eyes searched the plain room. Where was Nana? She was usually right here, right—there! There she—no... Yes? "Nana?" The blurry figure of a girl faded like a ghost until all I saw was my own reflection on a floor-length mirror across from the mattress.

"No! Nana come back!" I pleaded until my throat became raw.

Lashing my hands out, I clawed my way towards her fading figure, towards the mirror. Then, I touched something solid. Splaying my hands against the warm surface, I blinked a few times before snapping out of it to face Stepan's concerned but comforting face.

Hot tears burned my face like trails of lava as they spilled over uncontrollably. "What did you do? She was there but then she disappeared. I can't see her." What trickery did he play on my mind? What fucked up mind games was he playing at?

"What did you see then, tell me." The air around Stepan shifted as he wiped the tears away with his thumb.

"A ghost of her, but then she disappeared..." Words lumped and lodged at my throat, choking my own voice from coming out any further—preventing the truth from surfacing.

"Then what, Hanna? Then what did you see after that?" He urged me in a desperate voice while his eyes comforted and coaxed me.

My mouth opened and shut like a fish out of water as I struggled to get the single-word answer out. Instead of answering him, I did something stupid. I went back. Maybe it was a fluke. Maybe I remembered wrong.

Very bad idea. Worst I ever had in my life.

Acid like breath hit my neck and ear as the man reappeared before me. "Nana, you're such a good little doll."

Well, I definitely remembered why I hated being called doll by people. That was not the point, though; I needed to find Nana. Shutting the man out, I searched the small room again, only to have my attention jerk back to the man because of something he did.

"Nana."

"No! Stop calling me that! And stop touching me! It hurts! Please stop! Please! Just stop!" Viciously, I threw my head from side to side in denial as I lashed out with my fists and kicked my legs.

A slam into something solid caused my mind to fully snap back and realize that I'd lashed out at Stepan when I noticed how I tried to pull my wrists free from his grip. "I'm so sorry, I didn't—"

Releasing me, Stepan shifted me against him and soothed me with long strokes up and down the length of my back. "Shh, you don't have to apologize, you've done nothing wrong, it's just an unconscious reaction, you weren't here fully. It's okay." His lighthearted tone meant he held nothing against me for beating at him just now.

Continuing to soothe me, he whispered something in Russian to me as he peppered my face with loving kisses. "Whenever you're ready, tell me where you went and what you saw." He encouraged, not letting up with his kisses while he threaded his fingers through my thick hair.

There was a moment of understanding silence between us as I worked up the nerve to relive the moment through my words. "I was back there, in that horrid room, some man was there, I don't know who, just a gross man. He was touching me, he had his hands all over me, and I was naked. He kept calling me his doll, kept calling me Nana. I tried to look around for her, but all I kept seeing was my own reflection in a stupid mirror. But why? Why can't I see her? Why do I see myself? It makes no sense." Confusion gripped and choked at me, causing my anxiety to rise again with every quickening breath.

Stepan's eyes softened with sadness as he stroked my face with the back of his finger. "Breathe, in and hold then out. Breathe. Tell me about the fire now, what happened that day? How did you start the fire, Hanna?" Down then up, just as I calmed enough, his question threw me for a loop.

"What? What you? How *I* started the fire?" I'd already told him the fire wasn't my doing! It was Nana...

...Who didn't exist...

Embracing me, he covered me in his presence of safety and comfort. "Tell me what happened, *malenkaya*," he urged me warmly and softly, "It's okay. The truth won't hurt you, it will set you free."

Memories of the fateful night came flooding in, memories I barely had any recollection of.

It's done, it's over, breathe.

My tiny body shook with every trembling breath as I lay curled on the mattress, paying no attention to the man as he dressed himself. But something caught my attention: a small box. I don't know what came over me, but I lunged for it on a whim, snatching the box into my tiny hands and cradling it closely to my chest like a lifeline.

"Oh Nana, it's okay, I'll be back tomorrow, you don't have to beg at my feet." The man's chuckling words echoed out with his fading footsteps, and they shut out completely with the opening and closing of the door.

Alone, I pulled my hands away to study the box of matches closely. I decided at that moment, no idea what, but I made up my mind about something dire.

My limbs moved on their own accord, as if someone pulled the strings and I was a puppet. Through the door, I made my way down to the kitchen, where some of the workers looked at me with empty eyes. Everyone here was dead on the inside, just like me.

Usually, my trips to the kitchen were quick, but not this time. I took my time studying the place and making notes on certain items for later. Like all the other times, though, I had no appetite. The small bun I grabbed and forced myself to consume was an automatic action as a means to keep my broken body going for some bizarre reason. Well, and if I didn't eat, then they'd tie me down and force-feed me.

Time passed by a blur, and by the time I realized it, I'd snuck into the kitchen sometime in the night and grabbed a jug of oil and a can of gasoline before retreating to my room. Then, I struck the match after dumping the oil and gasoline onto the mattress, the pile of clothes, and the room. The small flame consumed the wooden match stick, charring it along its path.

Whoosh!

Then, match after match, I lit them and threw them into the growing fire that blazed around me. Hot waves of flame and blazes grabbed at my body, but it only hurt for a moment. I felt something, then nothing.

I'd accepted my fate.

I didn't try to escape.

All I did was lay down on the floor and curl up into a tight ball, waiting for death to come and take me.

"It was me... I did it. The fire. It was me. But... I barely remember it, just the fire, the flames, the pain, then the bliss of freedom in my grasp. I couldn't wait to see my dad again, to have him smile and hold me." Words no longer came out as all I could do was sob into Stepan's chest.

All this time, it was me. "Why am I so fucked up? Why did I do that? Why did I lie about Nana? About the fire, nearly everything." The abuse did happen. None of what happened to me was a lie, but the day everything ended and the strange girl which stemmed from my nickname in the place, all those details were some fabrication.

Pressing a kiss against my forehead, Stepan spoke against my temple, "You were a child still, tigress, your mind did what it could to protect you, to preserve whatever was left of you. Eventually, you just believed it all, and it became the truth to you. You were protecting yourself, to survive and persevere. You are not fucked up, you are perfect. You had fucked up things happen to you, but that didn't screw you up."

Holding me tightly as if I would fall away any second, he held me longingly in a peaceful silence before continuing in a proud voice. "If anything, you became a stronger person because of it all. Even if you concocted a false memory to live by, it didn't damage you. You still built yourself up into the strong and confident woman you are today, and I couldn't be more proud of you." Pulling back, I looked up to see his equally proud smile that made a warmth bloom in my chest. "You didn't let your trauma turn your life down a different path of destruction, so own that and be proud of it. I just wanted you to see the full truth and start living with it, that's why I did what I did. I couldn't stand the thought of you having a break down every time anyone tries to challenge your fabrication, and I can't dance around it forever." He finished with an apologetic smile and regretful eyes.

Cliché, but a weight lifted off my shoulders and chest. For once in my life, I felt as if I could actually breathe. This unknown tension between Stepan and I eased, too. "I don't know what you see in me. I'm just a burnt mess." I gave a dry chuckle as I leaned away to wipe away my tears.

Stepan's lips instantly widened into a loving smile as he rested his forehead against mine. "Everything. I see a good day, a good future, a good life with the most amazing woman in the world. You are my everything Hanna, I mean it. I wouldn't want you any other way. Scars and trauma and all, I want all of it because that is you." His lips sealed mine in a deep, passionate kiss filled with everything—that's the only way I could describe it.

"I love you Hanna, forever and always."

"I know."

Chapter 41

"I WANT ATTENTION."

I demanded with crossed arms and a stomp of my feet like some petulant child.

Sighing heavily, Stepan looked up at me from his desk. "And I told you, I will give it to you once I am—"

CLATTER!

My arm remained extended after knocking over his little stationary on his desk, smirking at him defiantly because I could see the irritation and annoyance twitch on his face. "No, now." I continue to demand, not caring about the punishment for my brattiness later.

"Last warning, if you don't start behaving, your ass will hate you later tonight." His blue eyes stormed over with lust and promise as his fingers drummed against the top of his desk. "And you won't get to orgasm."

My face dropped at the last bit because I could take whatever spanking he had in mind, no matter the method of delivery, but to be denied my orgasms knowing how close to the edge he'd get me, yeah, no.

"Kneel." He commanded, pointing his finger at the floor between his open legs.

"Yes, Daddy." I knew what he wanted by now, and I was already in deep shit with him for later. So, might as well be good and see if I could earn any mercy.

Settling between his legs under the desk, I quickly undo his pants and pull out his hardening cock. "What's taking your attention from me?" I asked, looking up at him through my lashes as I stroked him.

"Trying to pinpoint Lilian Wu's operations to shut down. She's been playing it safe and retreating, so we've been a step behind. I just don't want her—mhmm fuck." Stepan's hand fisted the back of my hair when I took him all into my mouth and down my throat in one go. "Fucking... Ugh... Don't want her getting away."

Well, guess this was one way to get his attention. Maybe I should have done this earlier; doubt he would have punished me for getting down on my knees and giving him a blowjob to ease his stress while he worked. Oh well, pissing him off was more fun anyways.

Though speaking about Lilian, I couldn't help but feel a tad guilty because Stepan shouldered the responsibility for shutting Lilian Wu down after I told Angel I couldn't take the assignment. As much as I wanted to accept, I couldn't, knowing I couldn't give it my full attention and effort.

I harbored too much hatred for my estranged aunt; I knew for a fact if I got involved, then my emotions *will* get the best of me. I'd be too much of a liability than help. At least no one gave me any grief for it, so I was thankful for that.

Easing off with a soft pop, I look up at him fully while evenly stroking his entire length. "Have you located her safe houses and back-up storage units?"

As much as I hated the knowledge, I knew how my aunt operated. Even if it has been years since I last had contact with her, she was a creature of habit. I also knew she was a lousy gambler because she put everything into one pot once she got too comfortable with no form of contingency. Her safe piles and backups were everything to her last I remembered, and I was more than willing to bet my damn life on them.

"Wasn't even aware she had any, so no." Stepan looked at me with torn eyes before shaking his head as if he had dismissed his own thoughts.

"What is it?" I probably shouldn't pry, but I couldn't help but want to pick at his brain because of my curiosity.

Stepan muttered a quick "Nothing" in response with a shake of his head, making me pout angrily and grip at his family jewels—not too hard, just enough to give him a jolt.

"Tell, or I'll give you blue balls." I threatened with a serious glare.

Sighing heavily, Stepan stroked my hair momentarily while looking at me in thought. "I know you already said you wanted nothing to do with Lilian, given your past with her, but you'd be so much help because you're the only one who knows her and how she works. I don't want to ask you to assist because you already made your displeasure known. And there are some things I will force my hand with, but this won't be one of those."

But they were stuck in the mud if I didn't help. They were fighting a losing battle without the proper knowledge and information. Usually, I would be okay with it because eventually, our friend Bao would be able to dig a lead-up, but not with Lilian. Bao could access anything as long as it had an electronic trail. Unfortunately, Lilian was very old school—pen and paper and no cash at the bank old-school. She was very distrustful of everything and everyone but herself, which is why she's been able to remain so elusive.

"What if I screw up? She's the start of everything bad to me. I know she's in the past, and I shouldn't let her affect me this much, but I still haven't gotten over my loathing." It was stupid because I wasn't one to hold grudges. Well, more like I dealt with the problem before I could have a grudge. "I don't want to make some kind of rash decision in the moment."

"I won't let you, tigress. I'll be your voice of reason in those moments." Stepan assured me with a smile. "I'll drive, and you can be in the backseat. You don't have to become directly involved per se, could just work in the background. If you never have to see her or interact with her then would that entice you any?"

"Can I think about it?" I wasn't in the mood to weigh the pros and cons at the moment with Stepan's dick in my hands.

Rolling his eyes, he shoved my face closer to himself. "Of course, I don't expect an answer right away, so get busy sucking like a good girl while I finish up." To make his point, he shoved his tip against my lips, smearing his precum on me.

Well, not sure how much work he got done because after a few bobs of my head, he gave out a growl and took my face into his hands, stood up, and face fucked me until I gagged and choked on him with my hot tears streaming down my face. "Fuck your mouth feels so good, little tigress." He groaned with a chest-rumbling growl.

Slowly, his hands shifted, so one fisted the back of my hair while the other held my throat. "Such a good girl for Daddy, letting him use your filthy mouth to pleasure himself. Fuck I can feel myself going down your throat. You have any idea how much I love it when you choke on his cock baby?"

My grip on his hips tightened to where my nails dug into him, pulling another groan from him. I loved it when he used me for his pleasure; the nights when he'd come home and throw me around like a doll and fuck me until he was satisfied were the best. Then, when he'd drag me around using his collar around my neck, God, being led around the house was enough to get me to orgasm if I was aroused enough.

I trusted Stepan, though; even if he fucked me until I cried and begged for him to let up, spanked me until I couldn't walk, tied me up in the most uncomfortable positions, I knew he'd never harm me. He had my life in his hands every time we entered our space, and I trusted him wholeheartedly. No matter how many bruises and marks—and he always left a lot of marks—he graced my body with, he always tended to me carefully after all. From feeding me, washing me, and applying various balms and medicine to ensure I healed correctly, he cared for me well and showered me with all his love.

"*Blyat*!" Stepan hissed and groaned with his release, burying himself fully deep down my throat so my face pressed flat against his pelvis.

Groaning with a happy smile, I eagerly swallowed to milk his cock as it throbbed, making him gasp and shudder. With a firm yank, he pulled me off of him completely and forced me to look up at him. "Open your mouth."

Shuddering through my panting, I opened my mouth wide and stuck my tongue out for him to see nothing went to waste. "Good girl." His praise brought a happy shiver to my body, along with a smile to my face.

"I love you so much, *malenkaya*." He whispered with a soft, happy, goofy smile.

"Mhmm."

Yet, no matter how much I trusted him, I still couldn't bring myself to say the words back to him.

The hairs on the back of my neck stood rigid at the sound of the familiar voice. "I have to say, I'm disappointed I didn't hear the news about your engagement, Hanna."

The corners of my lips followed the pull of gravity until they ached. Acting on an instinct to preserve myself, I pulled my gun out as I whipped around, pointing it directly at the vile woman a few feet from me inside Stepan's office.

"That's because it's none of your fucking business. Just like how you have no fucking business here at Stepan's office, so I suggest you leave before I put you in a body bag." This was exactly why I couldn't be on any assignment related to Lilian, unless it was an assassination assignment.

I was too unpredictable around her. Even if I liked to think otherwise, I knew the moment her presence would be made known to me then everything went overboard. No matter how much control I had over myself, nothing was fair game when it came to her.

Sometimes, the mere thought of her made me want to go into a murderous rage, while other times, it made me want to retreat and blow up in silence. One thing's for sure: she'd end up dead with me around, whether I want it or not.

Forgive and forget.

Let bygones be bygones.

Leave the past in the past.

Be the better person.

I've heard it all, and my response to all of it will always be the same: fuck that shit. Fucking hated it when people shoved all of that good shit in my face, which is why I didn't bother with therapy. I didn't want to be the better person; I wanted to be the worst; I wanted to become my tormentor's nightmare, the demon to drag them to hell to burn.

It was all bullshit to me how people tell those who've suffered to move on as if it was an easy thing to do. Why do I have to suffer while those who traumatized me got to live their happy life? Do people not know the constant pain victims suffered? The never-ending nightmares that plagued every inch of our lives?

Yes, I know I was one of the lucky ones to recover and live a primarily functional life, but that didn't mean I was normal again. Normal is something I can never be again. Normal died with my father the day he was gunned down in a drive-by. The little girl with dreams died in the brothel, along with what sanity I had.

Stepan might be avenging my lost innocence by killing those who broke me, but both of the two sole people responsible still lived and breathed. Maybe I should kill the greedy bitch, and give myself the peace I deserved. But I can't, not yet.

If I killed her now, then I'd be damning so many victims. Unfortunately, Stepan and his men haven't found all her safe houses and storages yet, so she needed to stay alive.

But by God, was it tempting to twitch my finger and send a bullet between her eyes

"Such an insolent brat. You should be thanking me and speaking to me with respect. You wouldn't be here if it weren't for me. If I didn't take you in after your mother begged me to, then you'd be dead in the streets or homeless and starving. I gave you a roof over your head, a warm home, three meals a day, and all you had to do was work a little in return, that's all. So, you should be kissing my feet for shaping you into the woman you are today." Every word of hers felt like acid on my body to me.

It sickened me how she could never see anything wrong in her actions, always displacing the blame or twisting the situation to make her stand in a good light. She was the type of person to murder someone and get away scot-free because she managed to talk the jury into seeing her as some victim. That or she'd place the blame on some innocent soul and convince the judge to sentence them instead of her.

"I would have been better off in the streets than in your stupid whore house. None of what you gave me would ever be worth the indecencies inflicted upon me. I suffered for two fucking years, two fucking years of endless abuse and rape." Rage trembled at my body, my restraint stiffening my trigger finger because murdering her right now would do no good—I had to keep the reminder on a constant mental loop.

Her dark chuckle brought a scowl to my face. "Did I keep you prisoner there? Lock you in the room? Chain you to the wall? No, I didn't. You had free roam of the place, the doors were always unlocked for you to come and go as you pleased. Nothing kept you there but you. No one, let alone me, forced you to stay and take those men who adored you. You have no one to blame for your suffering but yourself my dear."

"I was a fucking child!" I snarled with my upper lip peeled back.

"You still had full autonomy." She retorted apathetically, shrugging her shoulders while giving me a smug expression.

"You'd punish me until I complied. Fucking branded me as your property!" I raised my shaky voice.

"Well, I wanted to make sure you were safe, so I had to place my mark on you for others to know whose protection you were under. As for punishment, I never did such a thing, only reprimanded you for not following rules as I saw fit." Another thing I hated about her was how she had a damn answer for anything, no matter how fucked up it may be.

Honestly, if she weren't a triad businesswoman, she'd probably make a damn good lawyer, or a demon, or a demon lawyer. The damn snake who convinced Eve to take the forbidden fruit paled in comparison to Lilian; she was just that conniving and crafty in a very devious and dark way.

"Face it Hanna, you have me to thank for the strong woman you've become today. I mean, look at you, working for the Volkov Bratva, marrying one of the Volkov brothers, you are set, and you are only here because of me. So, you owe me." The nerve of this bitch.

My maniacal laugh plucked at my vocal cords uncontrollably. "Owe you? I don't owe you shit! Thanks for the fucking trauma but that's all I'm ever going to thank you for. I sure as hell don't owe you jackshit. If anything, the only thing I owe you is a bullet to the head because you sure as hell don't have a heart for me to stab or shoot at." A vile being like her couldn't have a heart; I was pretty sure if she were to be cracked open, then there'd be a void where her heart would be.

Sighing, she shook her head at me in a manner meant to chastise me. "I never should have let that stupid man take you under his wing after the fire. Obviously, he couldn't raise any of his children right, so it's no surprise you turned out so ungrateful and ill-mannered."

Beyond Lilian, I watched Stepan's body appear in the doorway of his office after the faint sounds of his footsteps echoed through the tense silence. "I thought I made it clear that you are not welcomed here." Stepan's powerful voice chilled the area from the entryway as he leaned against the doorframe with his arms crossed.

Lilian's attitude changed completely into a sickly, sweet, fake persona. "Is it wrong to meet my future nephew-in-law and talk business?" The sweet venom in her voice made me want to yak my lunch up in her face, which would have been a massive waste because it was a good lunch.

"Even if you weren't estranged from Hanna, I still wouldn't agree to any business deals between you and I, let alone you and the bratva. As I told you last time, I have no interest, and it would be in your best interest to surrender before things get ugly." Pushing off the doorframe, he looked at Lilian pointedly and spoke in a stern voice, "Now, unless you're here for us to take you to the cops or to The Catacombs, I suggest you run before one of us hunts you down." At least one of us could keep a professional and threatening front.

I still wanted to empty my magazine into her at the very least; preferably, I wanted to beat her to a bloody pulp and vent out all my rage at her. Unfortunately, her death now would be more trouble than good. I might know some locations of her safehouses and storages, but not all of them. So, unless we can get one of her men to squeal like a pig, we need the source itself, aka Lilian herself.

"I don't take to threats kindly Volkov." Lilian's demeanor darkened as she turned her full attention to Stepan.

"When it's a threat from me, you really shouldn't." Stepan's eyes narrowed slightly in a harsh manner as he pushed off the doorframe and stalked up to her. "Now, leave me and my woman alone, and get out. If I see you near Hanna ever again then your head will meet my bullet." Even though I didn't need his protection, having him shift in front of me protectively warmed my heart.

"You're going to regret this Volkov." The acid in her tone sent a chill down my spine.

Her words weren't an empty threat. Knowing my aunt, her threats were never empty. Stepan and I would regret turning her away, and it was only a matter of time. The unfortunate part of it all is that we won't see her coming. She's a snake through and through, always striking when you'd least expect it. I don't know my aunt's dirty tactics enough to predict her well. Stepan and I would need to watch our backs on the streets and sleep with one eye open.

We weren't safe until she burned in Hell.

No one was safe.

Chapter 42

Hanna

"You know, I don't exactly remember you proposing to me, or vice versa."

I knew Stepan wouldn't let that tidbit go, even though it had been a week since my aunt's ill visit.

"Because it never happened. I just said that shit to one of Mr. Hwei's guards a while back to try and get through them because saying I'm your girlfriend wouldn't have the same effect. Fiancé carried much more importance." He didn't need to know how natural it felt to address him as such.

I wouldn't admit any of it out loud, though. Yes, I love Stepan to death, but marriage? Married life wasn't for me. On the other hand, would it even be any different than how we are now? We already lived together and had our own daily routines catered around each other, and it was apparent where our feelings were for each other. Wouldn't marriage be some weird official declaration of our relationship? It wouldn't change anything, right? Or it shouldn't?

Husband and wife. Wife and husband. Yuck.

But boyfriend and girlfriend seemed too juvenile, too temporary sounding. Could we break up? Yes. But did I particularly like the thought? Fuck no. I hated the idea of us splitting. I'd grown so comfortable with having Stepan in my life, and not complacent comfortable, but happy comfortable to where the fire of life within me burned brightly because of him in my life as a lover.

The thought of not waking up in Stepan's warm arms and his annoying snoring made my chest feel uncomfortable as if something had reached in and gripped my heart. Then, the thought of us not together as lovers tore at my heart.

As the days stretched to weeks, then months, I found it harder and harder to picture a future without Stepan in it, and maybe it was just me being fearful of an actual commitment to someone. I wanted something permanent and solid with Stepan, but why change a stupid label when what we had worked so well?

"Where are you going?" I was curious when I noticed him decked out in tactical gear. "It's 11 PM. Also, why was I not invited?"

Chuckling, Stepan came up behind me and wrapped his arms around my waist, holding me close and resting his chin on my shoulder. "Bratva business, *malenkaya*, nothing you need to worry about. Besides, I thought you were going out to beat up some pimps for Angel?"

"I was, but then he got wind of me and ran to the police to turn himself in, so there went my night. Can I go with you since I got my fun ruined?" I asked with a pout.

"Not this one, sorry tigress. Maybe next time or when it doesn't involve your aunt." He sighed softly, turning his head and kissing my cheek before pulling away completely. "I might take a while, so don't wait up for me, alright?"

"Fine," I agreed with a huff. "But you know I can't sleep without you next to me." A habit that's formed since Stepan became entangled in my life, or at the very least when he started spending some nights with me.

Sleeping in a cold, empty bed felt lonely, and as cheesy as it was, Stepan chased my demons away. I haven't had to take any of my meds ever since we started sharing a bed, and the rare nights without his comfort engulfing me were—more often than not—filled with nightmares of my past.

"You have your little Wolf Stepan." He remarked with a teasing smile.

Crossing my arms, I stomped my foot and looked at him flatly. "It's not the same and you know that. I'm waiting and that's that, hmp."

"If it gets past 1 AM then I want your ass in bed, got that?" Stepan sighed exasperatedly with a slight roll of his eyes.

With a defeated sigh, I relented. "Yes, Daddy." If I weren't so tired, I'd push and not cave, but I could already feel the tiredness settling into my bones as we spoke.

"Good girl." Chuckling, he leaned in and kissed my forehead quickly before grabbing my face and giving me a full-blown, knee-buckling kiss on the lips.

"Be safe out there and come back to me alive." My words ghosted his lips the moment our lips parted.

"Always. Can't have any other man taking my place with you." As if any man could if Stepan met an unfortunate end.

"Never." I assured him with a smile before kissing him.

The moment he turned around to leave, I couldn't help but swat my hand at his framed ass with a cheeky giggle and grin.

"You're lucky I have to get going, otherwise I'd bend you over the counter." He remarked with a single look at me before leaving altogether.

A calm yet eerie silence filled the home once the sound of his car faded entirely into the distance. The soft *pitter-patter* of my feet against the hardwood floor echoed through the place briefly until I settled myself into the corner of the sectional with my blanket and stuffed animal.

I couldn't be bothered to turn the TV on because my mind was more than enough to keep me distracted—in a bad way.

Not to sound like a bitch, but I've never worried much or whenever Stepan went out on business. Yet, a nasty nag gnawed at my chest as if someone dug and rubbed their fist hard into my sternum. It also felt like someone had their hands in my guts and twisted and kneaded at it like dough.

Fuck, I'm gonna be sick.

Nervously, I chewed at my bottom lip until it hurt as the feeling of dread pulled me under. I needed to calm myself down before I'd go into a full-blown panic attack, which was ridiculous because I shouldn't be this anxious about Stepan going out.

"Fucking hell." I snarled, shooting off the couch onto my feet to pace around like a madwoman.

Stepan had his gear on, so he was mostly protected. He knew what he was doing; he was a pro. I shouldn't worry, especially since this was probably the thousandth time he's done something like this. Also, he'd be away from most of the action because he always stuck afar to snipe; he never went into the fray unless necessary.

So, why am I so anxious!?

I shouldn't be having a panic attack over this. Never have, never should.

I heaved my tightening chest as breathing became harder and harder. I needed to calm down, but I couldn't, not with how the room shrunk and spun. My body fell onto the couch after I stumbled and tripped over my own two feet.

I can't breathe, why can't I breathe? Why can't I feel my hands? Or my feet? Did someone poison me?

"...Nna... H...Nna..." The airy voice sounded so distant that I couldn't decipher whether it was real or not.

Instinctively, my mouth opened in a cry for help, but nothing came out but whimpers. Help, I needed help.

Someone, help me, please!

Pressure surrounded me suddenly, and I could feel my body being rocked—or maybe it was me shaking. "Shh, you're okay. Breathe." The lighter male voice sounded real enough.

"Keep holding her, the medication should kick into effect any moment." Was it the same voice? No, very similar, but something about this voice sounded more somber than the first.

"Hanna, you gotta breathe or you're going to pass out." It was the first voice again, this time softer.

"Arseny, you're squeezing her too tightly, she can't breathe you idiot." No wonder the voices sounded familiar.

"Shut up, she's calming down." Arseny's face came more into focus as my panic subsided.

Drifting my eyes over to the shadow next to me, I made out the other twin—Alexei—with a needle in hand. "What'd you give me?" Whatever it was, it kicked my ass.

"Same thing I gave you last time you had a total panic attack, valium. Which by the way, you're welcome." Alexei answered with an unbothered shrug of his shoulders before shifting around to sit on the couch.

"Wow, where's your compassion doctor?" Arseny bit out sarcastically, rolling his eyes as he released me and settled me comfortably on the couch.

Once again, Alexei replied unbothered, "It's there when it needs to be." The psychopathic doctor; I would say it was a joke, but it wasn't.

Believe it or not, the youngest Volkovs were certified psychopaths. Initially, I was surprised, but after I saw how they were overly charming, arrogant, manipulative, and sadistic—combined with their gross lack of empathy—I understood. Now, I still find it ironic how Alexei's a doctor given his psychopathy because I always imagined doctors needed a good amount of empathy to function successfully in their profession, but Angel said something about Alexei faking enough remorse and empathy to pass way under the radar. Although, psychopath or not, Alexei was one hell of a doctor—err surgeon.

"What are you two doing here?" Wow, I felt sluggish and wondered if my words even came out coherently enough.

"Stepan asked us to come over and keep you company and to make sure you're in bed around 1 AM," Arseny replied in his usual playful voice.

The more time I spent around the twins, the more of their little nuisances I picked up. Granted, I still couldn't tell them apart half the time unless Alexei wore his scrubs or white coat. Still, between the two of them, Arseny was outwardly more charming and playful than Alexei, always having this little uptick to his voice that made him sound just a tad happier, almost while Alexei had a more serious undertone to him.

Huffing out a pouting whimper, I looked up lazily at Arseny, "I'm not a child, I don't need to be babysat."

"Well, if we weren't here then you might have gone into a mental crisis." Alexei pointed out with a dour expression. "Why were you even having a panic attack in the first place? It's been months since your last one."

"I don't know." I instantly replied in a nearly slurred manner. "It just came on before I knew it."

"What were you thinking about?" Great, just what I needed tonight, Alexei playing shrink.

"I wanna sleep." I deadpanned, not wanting to engage with Alexei tonight—or ever—on the subject of my mental health.

"Then sleep, makes our job easier." Alexei remarked with a—failed—repressed smirk.

My arms moved slightly from Arseny tugging playfully at my stuffed animal. "Hey, you think Mia might like one of these?" Arseny asked no one in particular, probably in an attempt to change the air in the room.

"You're still entertaining that cop? I'm telling you, she's a waste of time and effort." Alexei replied with a roll of his eyes and an annoyed scoff.

"Mia's okay, but Alexei is right Arseny, she's a cop in the end, it won't end well for either of you guys. She's not gonna leave the force, nor are you going to leave your bratva life behind." My words felt like a mouthful the more the medication took its course to where fighting it became more difficult.

A mafia man and a cop, yeah that Romeo and Juliet story's one as old as time. I didn't hate Mia; she was a good cop and a good person with a good head on her shoulders, but she was a cop in the end. I didn't want Arseny to end up hurt in the end because whether I fully admit it or not, I cared about every single one of Stepan's brothers.

"Don't worry about me, I always got plans that work out." Arseny didn't sound fully confident with his assurance, but I couldn't argue with him currently with my foggy mind.

The world zoned out to blackness within a few blinks, and I'm pretty sure my eyes closed on their own accord. I wanted to wait for Stepan, but no fighting the meds. At least I wasn't out for long; at least it didn't feel long. "Where are you two going?" My voice was soft and groggy as I sat up from the couch, trying to rub the sleep from my eyes.

"Shit, thought you said she was supposed to be out until morning!" Arseny hissed at his brother, slapping his arm with an audible impact.

"She is, I dosed her right, maybe her body's just too used to it and got it out of her system faster than average people." I heard Alexei reply flatly with a glare at his younger twin.

"What's going on?" I could see their frantic faces now that my vision had cleared up.

"Nothing, just go back to sleep, I just got called that's all." Alexei tried to reassure me with a fake smile, which I saw through like an x-ray.

"You really should rest Hanna." Arseny tried his hand at steering me away from some silent problem.

"Not until you two tell me what the fuck is going on. If you don't start talking then I'll start swinging." Whatever weighed down my body fleeted as my adrenaline rushed through my body.

"Go!" Arseny shoved Alexei towards the door, the action setting me off.

With a few long strides, I closed the small distance between Arseny and I threw my leg out to kick at him. My foot connected with his midsection, knocking him back onto the couch behind him. Then, I grabbed the nearby vase off the side table and chucked it at Alexei, who made an escape for the door, nailing him right in the back, knocking him off balance and onto the floor.

I tried to make a run for Alexei, but a pair of solid arms ensnared me, and I was lifted off the ground. "Son of a—let me go this instant and tell me what the fuck is going on or so help me I will beat your asses into next year!" My kicking legs flailed hopelessly in the air as Arseny kept me lifted with my arms pinned in his bearhug.

"Why the fuck do all of you Volkovs have to be built like damn trees!?" Even if the twins were the shortest out of the bunch, it wasn't by much, and they were still big and tall compared to me.

Ding! Ding! Ding! Ding! Ding! Ding! Ding!

God damn it, who the hell was spamming me at this hour!?

Chapter 43

Hanna

"LET ME GO!"

If this were an actual hospital, then I'd be thrown out for my throat-scratching shouts.

"Hanna, stop!" Angel's shout of protest fell on deaf ears as I struggled against her and the others.

"*Lisichka*, stop it, she's going to run you over." Between holding me back and avoiding an injury from me, Nikolai tried to shove his pregnant wife out of the way to safety.

"I swear to God, if you don't let me see him right now." All I could manage was a strangled cry of frustration as I jerked against everyone's hold.

To say I was pissed would be the understatement of the year. When I saw Angel's messages earlier about something happening to Stepan, I practically charged my way through the twins. I booked it to Nikolai and Angel's place, where they had a little medical house for emergencies like these where a trip to an actual hospital would raise too many flags.

No one would tell me anything, though, just that Stepan was in surgery, hence why Arseny tried to get Alexei out of the house earlier before I threw a vase at him. Alexei was currently in the operating room with some more of their staff and Angel before she decided to come out here to try and talk some sense into me.

Fueled with rage, I decided that I'd had it. If they weren't going to tell me jack shit, then I will just barrel my way through into the room to see for myself. I didn't give a damn about the fact three of Stepan's brothers were on me. Fucking Hercules could be on me right now, and I'd still find a way through him.

Letting out an angry growl, I gritted my teeth and threw my head back, smashing it against Arseny, who was bear-hugging me from behind. The shock of the impact barely dazed me because of my anger and adrenaline. Then, when Arseny's arms still refused to budge fully, I repeated another headbutt, succeeding the second time.

Arseny released me with a muffled curse in Russian. By the sounds of his nasally voice, I probably broke his nose. I would feel sorry if it weren't his fault; he refused to let me go, and I did somewhat warn him.

With Arseny off my back—literally—I turned my attention to Nikolai, who had my right arm in a hold. Nikolai instantly leaned out of range for me to headbutt him, not that I planned to. Instead of throwing my head at him, I leaned over and sank my teeth deep into his arm.

"*Blyat*!" Nikolai hissed in pain while trying to pry me off.

"Hanna, stop it." Angel pleaded, grabbing onto my shoulders to help pull away. She wasn't successful though.

"Angel, please step back, I don't want you getting caught up and getting hurt." Nikolai begged his wife through gritted teeth.

"Hanna, just listen to me, please. You don't want to see Stepan like this. Seeing him right now in his current condition won't do you any good, trust me. If this is the last time you see him then you don't want the final images of him to be less than ideal. Please, we're doing this for your own good." Angel looked at me with a soft frown and down-turned eyes as she pleaded with me.

Releasing her husband's arm from my jaws, I looked at her with pleading eyes. "I need to see that he's okay, please."

Frowning further, Angel shook her head slowly. "He's not okay right now, that's the thing. Alive, yes, but I really don't want you seeing him in that state. It's for your own good."

Feigning a sigh of defeat, I forced my body to relax while I hung my head. I couldn't muscle my way through this, not against three bratva bosses and my pregnant friend. I had to play it smart.

When their holds on me loosened and released, I sprung like a tightly coiled spring. My first target was my friend; my hands shot out and grabbed her shoulders, shoving her—gently—at Nikolai, who immediately braced her and fretted over her to pay me much attention. Then, I swung my elbow back and cracked it into Arseny's face, stunning him enough to grab him by the front of his shirt and pivot him into Lev to stop him from going after me.

With that little mess going, I turned on the balls of my feet and booked it for the closed door, throwing the heavy door open with a huge slam when it impacted the wall.

It never bothered me to see a body on an operating table being sliced into with tubes sticking out of them, but the sight of Stepan brought a frigid shock to my system. "Alexei, why does he look like that? He's not going to die is he?" The heart monitor was beeping steadily at a good pace, I think, but seeing all the tubes going in and out of Stepan while he was opened up on an operating table did something else to me.

"You really think I'm going to let my own brother die?" Alexei scoffed back, glancing up at me with a quick glare as if to tell me, 'How dare you question my abilities' or some shit like that. "Go lay down before you pass out, you're as white as a ghost. The others can tell you what happened."

Yet, I couldn't budge with this heavy dread chaining me to the ground. If I forced myself to move, then my body might fall apart and crumble into nothing. I also couldn't bring myself to take Stepan out of my sight; no matter how horrible he looked, I needed to ensure with my own eyes that he was alive. On the other hand, if I didn't leave now, I'd hurl, and I didn't want to think what Alexei would do to me if I threw up in his operating room.

"Hanna, come on, let's go sit down." Angel's usual comforting touch sent a shock of chills through me when I felt her hands on my shoulders.

"No, I don't want to leave him." I was afraid he'd cease to breathe the moment I took my eyes off of him.

"He's in good hands Hanna, Alexei's not going to let anything happen to him. I know it looks horrible, but he will be fine after he gets patched up." My legs felt like stiff sticks when Angel forced me to move back outside.

The emotional turmoil threatened to break my body as I sat outside the door with the others. I wanted to cry, scream, throw a huge hissy fit, go berserk. "What happened?" I demanded in an emotionless voice, locking my cold gaze at Nikolai, who was being tended to by Angel.

"He got hit." He stated the obvious, which made my eyes roll out of annoyance.

Gritting my teeth, I balled my hands up into fists. "No fucking shit Sherlock, now answer the fucking question before I rip your throat out." I seethed with a growl.

"We don't know the details, just that he was covering us one minute and the next he said he was hit and needed backup. We got to him as fast as we could when he called for help. When we caught up to him, we saw the damage. He passed out on the car ride back. All we know is that he was shot three times, a bunch of contusions, broken ribs, punctured lungs, that's it." Lev sighed heavily with a groan, hanging his head and holding it in his hands as he paced his erratic breathing.

"You better have gotten the fucking bastards that did that to him." If not, then I'd burn the whole fucking world to ashes to make sure I got every last one of those motherfuckers.

"Of course we did, they weren't too keen on retreating even after we showed up." Nikolai grunted with a hiss when Angel pressed something against the fresh bite mark. "But we kept some alive and captured for questioning." He added quickly.

"I want them, I don't want anyone touching them for questioning but me." Even if they couldn't give me the information I wanted, I'd still get a kick out of beating them up for what they did to Stepan.

With a heavy sigh of worry, I switched back to the important matter at hand. "Why is he open on the table like that if it's just a few shots and injuries?" Digging out a bullet didn't require opening someone fully up, so what the fuck was going on?

"One of the bullets traveled from his abdomen all the way up into his chest cavity, so we have to repair the damage and fish the bullet out." Angel answered me with a disheartened smile.

"He's going to be okay though, right?" It sounded more like a demand than a question.

"So far, he is stable. He got lucky and no major arteries were hit, nor was the internal damage *that* bad. We'll have to see what Alexei says 'cause he's the doc, but given my experience, that's what I assume." That wasn't the answer I hoped for from Angel.

"Ange, I need you to give it to me straight, as a friend, not a nurse. Is he going to be okay?" I hated it when she got all medical and professional with me. I understood why she'd default to that side of her, and I appreciate her attempts to prevent my hopes from being raised or crushed, but still.

Angel let out a long exhale and looked at me for a moment with conflicting eyes before caving. "From a medical standpoint, he is stable in there, odds of him surviving are high right now given his condition, but you and I both know that things can take a turn for the worse out of nowhere and for no reason. So, you know why I can't give you a definite 'yes he will be fine and dandy' and shit, not when I know he could just crash for no reason. Even if he does make it out of the OR, he still has to wake up and recover, which brings up a whole different bag of bullshit with it. He might have dodged the bullets to major arteries but he still lost a lot of blood, and we don't know the extent of his full injuries because no one witnessed what happened fully."

"Thanks... I'm going to step outside for a moment." I needed to move and get some fresh air. Otherwise, I would shut down right now. Well, I needed to go outside to scream out my anger at the world; no way in hell would I do that in here in front of everyone.

Well, I would if I could move. I felt like I had anchors tied around my ankles right now. "Hanna." My body jerked from Arseny grabbing my shoulders. "You need to calm down, breathe."

Why did he sound so distant?

Why am I feeling so disconnected?

Why is everything fading?

My chest hurts, why?

Is there a leak? Why is there raindrops?

Ouch!

"Hanna, come back, it's okay, breathe, just come back to us, just breathe."

The voice sounded so distant, and maybe it wasn't even real.

"Hanna, in, hold, and out. In, hold, and out." The instructions repeated God knows how many times, and I wanted to tell Angel to shut up. I was tempted not to listen, but my body seemed to follow her on its own accord because I barely registered the rhythmic rising and falling of my chest as it happened.

My head spun as the oxygen fully flooded it again, as if I had gotten out of bed too fast. Then I noticed the cold chill on my cheeks only when my senses returned fully. Numbingly, I reached up and brushed my fingers along my cheek, picking up the trail of tears that streamed from my aching eyes.

"Close your eyes for a bit Hanna, it's okay, it'll be okay." Angel continued to shush and soothe me, her fingers running through my locks.

"No, I want to see Daddy." I whimpered with a sob.

"Stepan will still be here after you wake." Angel assured me, tightening her arms around me as she slowed her rocking.

Vehemently, I shook my head in defiance and tried to push Angel away, but she held firm. "It's not going to do you any good to exhaust yourself like this Hanna. It won't be healthy for you either if you keep going into panic attacks in the meantime. We can't keep on dosing you like this."

She gave an exasperated sigh and paused for a moment before continuing. "How about this, if I promise to put you next to Stepan when he's out of the OR then will you rest?" She bargained with me in a very sweet tone.

Huffing, I gnawed at my bottom lip stubbornly for a moment before reluctantly nodding.

As if I had any choice.

I could feel my body crashing, badly.

He needed to live, he can't die, he's not allowed to, not until I tell him.

Fuck, I never told him.

Chapter 44

Hanna

I WOULDN'T EVEN BE mad at myself if this massive headache was from a hangover after a fun night out, but no.

"Fucking hell..." I groaned groggily as I forced my eyes to blink open.

Groaning out a whine, I buried myself into the familiar warmth next to me with an unconscious smile that lasted all about a second before reality crashed into me like a wrecking ball to a glass building.

Startling up into a sitting position, I frantically ran my eyes over Stepan, who remained dead asleep with a tube in his mouth, wires to his body, and an IV line in his hand.

"Hey, careful, you don't want to knock anything loose." My head snapped over to the voice, relaxing a little when I saw it was Angel.

Frowning, I settled my hand against his chest, feeling it rise and fall in a slow, steady rhythm. "Why does he look like that still? Why is there a tube in him? Why isn't he awake?" The questions flew out of my mouth before I could control them.

"He had quite a bit of damage to his lungs from the broken ribs puncturing them, he broke seven ribs, Hanna. And then, the bullet that traveled through his abdomen into his chest cavity caught some of his lungs as well, so the tube is to help him breathe for now. We're keeping him sedated for comfort and for him to recover easier. He'll be out for a while

I'm afraid. He has some head injuries to from the bruises and bumps we found on his head when we examined him, but we won't know the extent of the damage until he wakes up." Angel gave me a quick rundown while I sat there like a sad child holding Stepan's free hand.

"Can I be alone with him, please?" My voice softened and cracked as I laid back down next to him, setting my head on his chest and cuddling him.

"Yeah, I'll tell the others to give you some space for a bit." Angel smiled warmly at me, patting my arm as she passed.

I lay there like a statue for a long time, letting the buzz and beeps from the machines fill the room while I collected my thoughts. "Styosha, don't leave me please, please don't leave me. You're not allowed to leave me, not like this, you stupid idiot, how dare you go get shot like that? You're not supposed to be laying in bed near death like this, you asshole! You weren't supposed to get hurt out there."

As if he had any control of any of it. None of it was his fault. He didn't ask to get shot, nor did he purposely put himself in the line of fire—at least, I hoped he didn't do something that stupid. Also, I just wanted to know what happened to put him in this state. Stepan was *always* careful, nearly overly so. So, how did a group get the jump on him like this? He wasn't a part of the leading group raiding with Nikolai and Lev; he hung afar to snipe, so he should've or would've seen an ambush coming.

"Don't you dare fucking die on me, or I swear I'll find a way to bring your ass back to life and kill you myself for leaving me in this rotten world. I can't fucking live without you, so please, please, please, don't leave me alone." Well, at least he wasn't awake to see me ugly sobbing and getting my snot and tears all over him.

"I have something important to tell you, so you can't leave me until I do." To think about Stepan dying before... No, I couldn't even thoroughly think about it.

"I'm gonna make them pay for doing this to you." I didn't plan on stopping even after I couldn't feel my hands when I met the fuckers who were a part of the crew who did this to Stepan. I *will* beat them to death, not would or could or should or if; I. Fucking. *Will.*

"Hanna, we don't have to do this today if you aren't in the right mindset. They aren't going anywhere, and none of us will touch them." Arseny spoke beside me as we descended the stairs to the holding area of The Catacombs.

Hissing out a sigh, I glared over at Arseny as I put my brass knuckles on. "I'm in the fucking mood to break some faces, whether that be yours or theirs, I don't care." Yes, I was still a little pissed at him for trying to prevent me from seeing Stepan the night the call came in.

"Now, unless you want some plastic surgery from Alexei, which cell are they in?" I demanded with a stern galre.

Defeated, he shook his head with a sigh before pointing at a cell with two raggedy-looking men in them. "Want me to set up a room for you?"

"No, I'm setting a fucking example of them for everyone here. Don't fucking mess with me, don't even think about it." I let out a short scream to startle everyone in the area as I lunged at the cage, pounding my fist against it to let the sound of metal against the metal ring out.

In one fast motion, I reached through the bars and grabbed the unfortunate man who was too close. Fisting the front of his shirt, I yank him against the bars with a loud thud and bang. "You're gonna regret ever thinking about pointing your gun at Stepan." I seethed right in his face before banging him against the cage again and shoving him back onto his ass.

Spinning around, I nod at the cage after locking eyes with Arseny. "Open the cage." Then, I looked at Lev, "Hold the shorter one while I deal with his buddy first."

Arseny seemed hesitant, but he budged after I harshened my glare at him. "Should I call the cleanup crew at least?"

"No, I want everyone here to have a constant reminder of what happens if they dare to entertain the idea of crossing me or anyone in my company." There's nothing like watching a good old death beating to really knock the point into thick skulls.

I had a sadistic streak like Angel, but I also enjoyed death, unlike her—death by my hands that is.

Once Arseny opened the cell door, I trudged in, grabbed the taller, lankier man by the front of his shirt, and hauled him out to the center of the holding area where everyone else pressed up against their cells to get a close look at the commotion.

"Wait, why does it have to be me first? Why can't it be him? Listen, spare me, please, I'll give you the money she paid me, I didn't even spend it yet." The man begged me with desperate eyes as he groveled at my feet.

Unfortunately for him, I didn't have a heart like Angel—he didn't have to know that, for now. "What do you mean the money she paid you?" I sweetened my voice as I bent down to his level. "You weren't just protecting the warehouse?"

If I had any ounce of empathy, then I *might* feel a little bad for the hope that crossed his eyes at my change in demeanor. "The business tyrant, Lily Woo or something like that, she gave us money to hunt down the blonde brother. We were gonna run him off the road, but when we saw him splitting from the group, we followed and ambushed him."

"This 'Lily Woo,' did she happen to look somewhat like me only a lot skinnier, very bright red lipstick, and very sharp eyes?" The silent anger dripped behind my saccharine smile like venom off of fangs.

"Man, just shut up! She's gonna kill you either way! She's—mh-mmpfh!" Lev's big hand instantly slapped over the other man's mouth, shutting him up.

The man before me looked up at me with shaky eyes after eyeing his buddy for a second. "Y-yes, only she didn't look hot like you." Cute, his attempt to get into my good graces was almost laughable given his fate.

"Flirting will get you nowhere, but I appreciate the compliment." The edges of my smile widened twistedly. "Do you know who I am? What they call me?" He probably wouldn't be flirting with me if he knew.

The man's throat bobbed with his hard swallow as he looked at me closely. Then, slowly, his head shook. "I'd remember a hot chick like you..." Oh, he kept digging himself deeper and deeper.

With an exaggerated smile on my face, I darkened my eyes at him. "Tell me, have you heard about the story about how you should never cross the triad's princess? Or more of why you should never cross or harm her?" I questioned with a tilt of my head.

"B-because it's a death sentence." His breathing started to pick up erratically.

"And why is that? Besides the fact her father would have sent a squad after you." There was a huge reason people kept their distance from Angel, and it wasn't because of the hidden guards or her father.

By the way, his face dropped and paled as if he faced Death itself, he knew the answer. "Y-you? You-you're The Beast? The Beast is a man, a brute of a man capable of ripping people to shreds. There's no way... No." He stared and shook his head at me in disbelief, jerking away from me as if being in my presence burned him.

"Don't underestimate the strength of a woman. Then again, that's how I get people because they never see me coming. I'm the last they ever expect when they hear about this 'rageful beast of a person with sharp teeth and claws with a deformed face' and a bunch of other shit. I mean, my face is fucked up, but that's about it." Tightening my grip on him, I jerked him towards me and got right up in his face with a wicked smile the devil would be proud of.

"I'll give you a chance to fight for your freedom." As if he stood a chance in the first place, but he didn't need to know that.

Pulling my arm back, I swung a punch across his face, knocking him to the ground. "Get up." I scoffed as I stood up straight with my hands clenched into fists by my side.

Scowling, I gave a hard kick to his stomach with a grunt before grabbing the back of his shirt to help haul him up. "I said up." I growled, waiting for him to stumble up to his feet and assume a wary fighting stance.

Taunting him with a smirk and wave of my hands, I held my arms wide open. "Come on, I'll even give you a free swing."

He was reluctant, but he went for it. He closed the small distance between us with a long stride and swung his arm. I quickly deflected by side-stepping and grabbing his wrist to redirect his forward motion, and his body fell forward with the momentum, landing his face right into my fist with a sickening crack and scream of pain. Then, shoving him upright, I ran an uppercut to his chin, causing him to stumble back a bit. Relentlessly, I went at him, throwing a flurry of punches to his abdomen with interruptions of right hooks.

I didn't give him a chance to fight back.

Teeth scattered around the floor with the occasional blow to the face, and blood painted the cement flooring with lovely red splatters. "Really should have thought twice about taking that fucking assignment. I'm almost tempted to let you live and recover so I can hunt you down and shoot you when you least expect it."

Saying it out loud made it really tempting. Imagining the fear and panic in his face as he'd run and hide, oh I'd get such a rush from that. Then the pumping adrenaline from the hunt itself, oh I'd be so fucking giddy like a kid on Christmas.

"What do you think? It is your life, so it's only fair you pick how it ends." I grinned like a madwoman down at him after I laid his ass out and stepped a foot on his chest.

After a few sputtered and gargled replies, I figured him to be a goner. Oh well, at least I still had the other one to play with. His chances of survival without any immediate medical attention—which he won't get—were practically zilch. Pretty sure if he were cut open right now, then blood would spill out instantly because of the internal bleeding. If he was somehow saved, he'd probably be a vegetable because of how much damage

I caused to his head—pretty sure he had a different head shape than when we started.

One final kick to the downed man's face, and I was done with him. Leaving him there to his own demise, I turned my attention to the man held by Lev. "You know," I said, stalking up to him, "If wasn't so fond of the idea of a hunt, I'd just use you as a human pinata. So, luck you, you get to live another day or two, or until I decide to let you out to chase."

"Lick my hand one more time and I'll cut your tongue out." Lev threatened the man who struggled against him.

"Let go of his mouth, I want to hear his pathetic excuses and pleas." Maybe he'll give me a good reason to remove his tongue.

The moment Lev removed his hand, the man spat in my face when I stopped a foot away from him. "Fuck off, I'm not going to play in your stupid fucked up games you psychotic bitch! I don't know why she even wanted you back so bad! You're fucking nuts! Any idiot who chooses to be with you is either stupid or equally fucked up! Your stupid aunt is just as crazy, fucking lied to us, saying the stupid Russian was keeping you against your will after kidnapping you to be his little bitch and babymaker. He already collared you like a dog, so how the hell were we supposed to know Lilian was making shit up?"

Flattening my face, I wipe the spit off—along with some blood—with the back of my hand before lashing out at him with a brutal backhand across his face. "Oh, how fucking noble of you to think about saving the poor captured princess. Tsk, as if that excuse to shoot Stepan down makes it any better. It's also fucking hilarious to think that you'd do something so noble, as if it'd forgive your horrid sins. Saving one girl doesn't make what you do in Lilian's whore houses go away." I'm not entirely sure about the other man, but I've seen this one around the brothels Lilian ran when I've done surveillance on the places.

His sour scowl meant I had him. "Do whatever the fuck you want, I'm not participating. I won't run if you hunt me like some animal. I won't fight back if you chose to beat me to death like Troy over there. I ain't gonna give you any satisfaction." Cute, he thought he had the game won.

A low, evil chuckle shook my shoulders briefly before they relaxed with a long, satisfied sigh. "Then I guess I'll just call Angel in for some help, surely you know of her reputation. Triad heiress, then the Bratva's Bride, and her oh so infamous Princess of Pain, surely you know how she coined that last title." I couldn't help my smirk from widening at the man's paling face. "If you don't entertain me, then I'll just let her have a go at you and watch with a bucket of popcorn, and trust me when I say you'd rather me than her." I'd rather go through a meatgrinder alive than be subjected to Angel's methods.

Either way, he was royally fucked.

Chapter 45

Hanna

Henry Gor.

My dead, cold eyes bore holes into the man who trembled before me in his bindings. His erratic eyes kept bouncing between me and the bullet I twirled between my fingers.

"Please, you don't have to do this." Nothing. I felt nothing in response to his pathetic plea.

Lazily, I drifted my eyes to the carefully crafted bullet, holding it still to trace the etched name on the casing. "Funny, I said the same thing back then before you laughed in my face and forced yourself onto me after you dislocated my legs to keep me from kicking you. You're lucky I don't have more patience, otherwise I'd dislocate every possible thing in your body. Fortunately for you, I only have enough time for your arms and legs. But it hurts, doesn't it?" If only I had Angel's penchant for torture.

Without a care in the world, I slowly load the bullet into the rifle—Stepan's favorite go-to rifle, to be exact. He couldn't be here to kill my demons for me, so the least I could do to have a piece of him be involved was to use his trusty weapon along with the specially-made bullets.

As I raised the weapon and took aim, the man gave me a smile of relief, letting his head fall back against the ground. I held my laugh back because he probably thought this would be his easy end. Instead, I let the laugh bubble in my throat while my lips stretched to a freakish smile before pulling the trigger with a gleeful giggle.

The horror and shock on his face when he realized he wasn't dead had me grinning madly as I watched him scream out while holding his abdomen where a fresh bullet hole was made. "If only I had the patience to inflict a fraction of the suffering you placed on me." Pausing, I feigned a half-disappointed sigh, "Shame you won't survive long enough to suffer the burns for the rest of your life."

Ignoring his panicked sputters and pleas, I stepped over his bleeding body and picked up the bullet after locating it. Can't forget my trophy and proof of the deed.

My head lifted to look at Lev, who waited for me at the exit, flicking the lighter cap on and off. "Is everyone relevant cleared of the building? We have the evidence too?" I wanted to double-check before torching the place to the ground.

"Yep, victims are on their way to the safe haven, clients are let go, and Bao and Nicole are setting up the mass media release for tonight. We also got lucky and scored a list of, what I think are, locations. I'll have Nicole and Bao look over it when I get back." He replied curtly, handing me the lighter once I was within arm's reach.

"Good." With one last look around the horrid brothel, I took one last inhale of the gasoline-filled air before backstepping outside to safety.

"One more off the list." I muttered to myself, flicking the lighter on and tossing it into the pile of gasoline containers in the corner, setting the place ablaze with the screaming man inside of it still. "I'm assuming the fire department and law enforcement know to delay their visit?" Our efforts would be for naught if they responded promptly.

"Yep, nothing some Benjamins won't fix." Lev chuckled, patting my back as we returned to the car.

His face took a serious, concerned turn the moment we reached the car, and he opened the door for me. "Go home and rest Hanna, and for fuck's sake eat an actual meal. You're starting to look like a stick and sick.

We've basically got the whole city and the outlying ones on lockdown, so none of your targets or Lilian will escape without us knowing."

"I'm fine." Probably the lie of the century, I really did feel—and probably looked—like utter shit. I ate, slept, and cared for myself, but to the bare minimum. Most of my time was spent next to Stepan in his little hospital bed while doing research on my targets—the men on the list Stepan created—and Lilian. If I wasn't researching, then I was actively out seeking and hunting; I stuffed my face with small, fast food meals here and there, and a lot of packaged ramen, slept handfuls of hours here and there before insomnia or my nightmares would keep my eyes wide open.

Sighing with a shake of his head, Lev clicked his tongue at me, annoyed. "Hanna, even a blind man can see how you're spiraling. Everyone's worried about you, rightfully so, and we're all this," he held his thumb and index finger a mere millimeter apart, "Close to locking you inside the house and forcing you to do shit."

"Listen, I know you want to vent out your anger and frustration on those who wronged you, prove yourself to Stepan that you can handle yourself without him by going down that list of offenders, but if he saw you like this, he wouldn't be happy. He wouldn't want you slowly tearing yourself apart like this." Sometimes, I wish Lev could be an idiot all the time and not get soft and worrisome like this.

"I'll be fine." At this point, it seemed more like I tried to convince myself of this than the others. "I just want to go back to him right now. I'm tired." A nap with Stepan sounded lovely right now, after a shower of course.

Defeated, Lev sighed with another shake of his head before ushering me into the car and taking us back to the Volkov Estate, where Stepan still resided in one of the medical suites.

It'd been about three weeks, and Stepan still hadn't woke. Both Alexei and Angel reassured me, and so far, Stepan was by all means stable, but the longer he remained in his little coma, the more worried I grew.

I didn't want to lose him. Besides my only friends in life, he was the best thing to ever happen to me. I never knew the warmth of happiness nor love until him; I thought those warm fuzzies were gone forever with my father's last breath on his final day. Yet, Stepan brought everything back to life in me tenfold. "Styosha, come back to me, please. I know you're there, just please wake up, don't leave me. If you leave me then who am I supposed to chase through the forest? Who am I supposed to be a brat to? Who am I supposed to annoy the shit out of? Who's gonna discipline me and give me the best orgasms of my life? Who's gonna love me?"

Who am I gonna love?

The exhaustion forced my emotions to boil to the surface. Holding Stepan tightly, I bury myself against him, shoving my face into the crook of his neck to inhale his soothing scent. My shoulders shook with my sobs as the tears fell from my eyes uncontrollably.

Fuck I really am a mess, but I didn't know how even to begin fixing myself—if there's even any fixing.

"Don't leave me, Stepan." To have it all crash down after I've bled my heart to Stepan, I'd definitely break.

Everything faded fast as my lack of sleep caught up to me, pulling me down the dark pit of slumber.

Well, at least I didn't have a nightmare this time. At least, when one started, it quickly faded into a rather vivid dream of a different kind.

However, the pressure in my tightened stomach felt real enough, along with Stepan's fingers curling inside of me. Oh well, even if it's relief in a dream, I'd take it over nothing. "Styosha, *yeshche pozhaluysta.*" I begged with a groggy croak, lazily bucking my hips out of instinct.

"Love it when you call me that, but try again, *malenkaya.*" Oh God, his voice sounded so real, like the shivers raking my body.

"*Pozhaluysta, papochka.*" Feeling my release so close, I reach a hand down to finish myself, only to startle fully awake when I grab onto a very solid and tangible object.

Blinking hard a few times, I broke into a wide smile and squealed as I hugged him tightly and threw my arms around Stepan's neck. "Daddy!" My happy laughter quickly turned into sobs of relief as I slumped fully into him. "I fucking hate you, you almost left me, you got hurt and almost left me."

Stepan said nothing in return as he held me tightly, whispering sweet nothings—I think—to me in Russian while petting my head.

The two of us remained like that for a long while until my cries subsided to little hiccups.

I can't wait, I have to tell him.

Pulling away, I looked at him in earnest.

"*YA tebya lyublyu.* I love you, Stepan. Marry me."

Chapter 46

Stepan

"I—WHA?"

Stupefied, I could only stare at her like a full-blown idiot.

After waking up from a near month-long coma, the last thing I expected was to hear a profession of love from Hanna. I never had any doubts about her feelings for me as I could clearly see the adoration and affection in her eyes whenever she looked at me; the intensity in which her eyes shined whenever I told her I loved her was more than enough for me. She didn't need to express her feelings verbally to reciprocate my love for her.

I wasn't complaining, though. I just never thought it would hit me so hard. After all, they were just three words. Yet, hearing Hanna say them had me feeling like a love-struck fool, an awkward teenager getting their first kiss ever from their hot crush, or a horny virgin getting laid for the first time.

If it weren't for the annoying beeping of the machines, I would've thought I died and went to Heaven. Well, that and Heaven was *way* out of reach for me because of my life.

"Say that again." I demanded, still stunned and wondering if I'd misheard her.

"I said I love you and to marry me." Hanna replied in a sure voice with a soft huff.

"You're asking me to marry you?" Now, that part caught me more off guard than the confession.

"I'm not asking, I'm telling you, demanding. You are going to marry me as soon as you get out of this damn place. I don't want to spend another second as your girlfriend, I want to be your wife. I am going to be your wife." She was definitely demanding it, almost as if she stated a fact.

"Well, someone's certainly gotten bold in my absence." I joked dryly in an attempt to ease my nerves away.

Warily, I studied her stern face. "Are you sure? We don't have to do or change anything if you aren't ready, tigress." I was more than ready to sign my life away on some damn papers to be tied to her for the rest of our lives, but I wanted Hanna to be completely sound with it all; I didn't want her making this decision because of my near-death experience.

"Yes, more sure than anything in my life. I want you Styosha, for now and ever. I've had a lot to think about the past three weeks, and I've made up my mind about us when you were to wake. I want you as my husband, and I your wife. I fucking need it." Her words grew softer and softer the closer her lips got to mine until there was no space left between us.

A growl ripped from my throat as I tangled a hand into the back of her head, pressing her lips harder against mine as the heat in the room rose from our pent-up passion exploding.

"Wha—hey! You're not healed up enough yet, quit being so fucking aggressive." Alexei's scolding made me break away from Hanna with a chuckle. "I do not have the time or energy to dig around your body again to put you back together."

"Oh go get laid and stop being a sourpuss." I chuckled with a pained groan from the sudden aches.

"If it turns me into idiots like you lot then no thanks." Alexei bit back as he urged Hanna off to examine me.

"Can I leave?" I'd been awake for hours before sticking my hands down Hanna's pants when I noticed her slipping into a nightmare from her whimpering and twisted face. So, I was rather impatient to leave already.

"If you promise not to strain yourself, as in no *physical or strenuous* activities. You might be out of the woods for now, but your body still needs to recover, and that's going to take weeks to months." Alexei narrowed his eyes knowingly at me with his arms crossed.

"Alexei, I'm not an idiot, I'm not going to let my dick make decisions for me." Would not have survived this long if I did.

Granted, nothing ever went accordingly when it came to Hanna.

Never in my life did I ever thought my own wedding would be in my own backyard two weeks after waking up from a coma. Hell, I never thought I'd have a wedding, period. Yet, here I stood in the gazebo in my backyard with Hanna in a lacy little white dress, me in a pair of black dress pants and a white button-up, and Angel's half-brother Greg as our officiant.

I never really thought much when it came to my nonexistent love life before. I had my flings and visits at the club, but that was about it. The past few girlfriends I had in my younger years didn't last too long, and I gave up on relationships when I entered my thirties. I'd come to accept the lonely bratva life as Nikolai had before his and Angel's arranged marriage.

Nikolai got lucky with Angel, and I was a little jealous for a moment because he got lucky and won the lottery with Angel; he'd been crushing on her ever since she saved him from a car wreck one fateful night. It just so happens she had a thing for him as well, so it was almost a match made in Heaven.

All five of us had resigned to the fact we'd be lost causes in the game of love and relationships; from gold diggers to those who couldn't handle being with a mafia man, we eventually gave up in that area of our life and stuck with no strings attached flings.

So, when Nikolai ended up going back on a promise and got hitched in an arranged marriage, I was kind of peeved. Granted, it all worked out in the end, and after the initial shock of everything, I was genuinely happy for Nikolai and Angel. He deserved his little piece of happiness given the shitty life he'd been dealt by the hands of our father. I might have gotten it bad, but Nikolai got it a hundred times worse, being the oldest and the one our father groomed to take over.

Well, not like any of it mattered now; things went down how they did. He was happy with his wife and soon-to-be sons, and I had Hanna—my soon-to-be wife—the one who held a very familiar-looking bouquet of roses. "Did you—" Before I could finish my sentence or fully turn my head to look at the rosebush behind her, Hanna grabbed my face to keep it centered on her cheeky face plastered with a big grin.

"We have our wedding to worry about, hon." She knew fully well what she did; cute how she thought she'd get away with it by using our wedding as an excuse.

The ceremony started and went in the blink of an eye, and by the time I knew it, it was time for our vows. "Now, do you, Stepan, take Hanna to be your lawfully wedded wife?" Greg asked, looking over at me from his little book.

"I do." These two simple words change everything.

Taking Hanna's lovely face into my hands, I look at her with all the love in the world. "This wasn't how I'd imagine our wedding to go or happen, but nothing ever goes accordingly when it comes to you. You threw my world off kilter when you stepped into my face, now it revolves around you. No matter how hard I tried to keep away from you, I always got pulled back to you. You are the center of gravity to me, my sun, my moon, my seas, and my skies. My everything. I'm obsessed with you, Hanna, always have, always will." With a big, uncontrolled smile, I leaned in and rest my forehead against hers, and looked deeply into her warm eyes. "I swear, I will cherish and love you as the precious treasure you are. I will always care for you and be there for you, through hell and back, through sickness and health, through everything." Leaning back up, I give her a promised filled look and smile. "I will always have your back, always have you in my sights in the darkest of nights and the brightest of days. I love you so much, Hanna."

Turning to Hanna, Greg repeated the same question, getting the same answer from Hanna before she started on her little piece.

"Well shit, make me feel like the asshole for having something short prepared now would you? I wasn't expecting a whole ass speech from you given everything." Hanna chuckled with a soft cry of happiness. "God, I really don't know what came over me to demand this marriage, it just felt so right, it still does. I'm not one to do labels and shit, but I didn't like the thought of you being anything less than my husband if worse comes to worst. I wanted to be yours, your wife, and I wanted you to be my husband. Just saying we're together isn't enough, nor was saying you're my boyfriend because that sounds immature and not so serious. I'm not perfect in any way, shape, or form, but you make me feel perfect, and you treat me like a damn queen. I swear I will do my all to reciprocate all you give me in earnest to show you how much you mean to me, how much I love and appreciate you. Through thick and thin, rich and poor, through sickness and health, and life and death, I'll be by your side through it all, as your wife. I love you so much, Stepan, my Styosha."

"Alright, alright, hurry up and kiss already and sign the papers and make it all official, come on." Greg laughed softly, shoving us together. "And by the power vest in me and the state of California yada yada I pronounce you husband and wife, Mister and Missus Volkov."

Grinning, I tightened my hold on Hanna's face and pulled her into a lip-smashing kiss.

"Mrs. Volkov." I murmured against her lips.

The reception went off without a hitch, as in no one got into a drunken brawl or broke anything. I wasn't worried, though; my brothers knew how to hold their liquor, and our men knew better than to get blacked out drunk or do anything stupid.

Unlike Hanna, I kept my alcohol intake to the bare minimum to keep a clear mind; Alexei and Angel were also on my ass about drinking too much, given the fact I'd recently woke from a coma and was still in recovery technically.

I was mindful not to let Hanna drink too much once it got later into the evening; I didn't want to bed my wife for the first time with her in a drunken state. Hanna wasn't too happy about being cut off, but after some whispered promises of what was to come, she was more than willing to comply.

Once it got pretty late, Hanna and I bid farewell to everyone and left them to enjoy the after-party while we retired to our bedroom. "Stay." I commanded after walking her to the foot of the bed and sitting her down on the edge.

Leaving Hanna's side for a moment, I went to the dresser and pulled out a small, long, rectangular box from the top drawer. A small smile graced my face at the sight of Hanna's eyes lighting up when I stood before her and opened the box to reveal a black, leather O-ring collar with a center row of purple diamonds that started and ended at the platinum plate which had my name in Cyrillic engraved on it.

Lifting the collar out of the box, I carefully set it next to Hanna on the bed before lifting the bottom of the box to reveal a thick, black leather bracelet with three spaced-out O-rings and a platinum plate between two of the rings that had Hanna's name in both English and Cyrillic engraved on it.

"Stepan." Hanna looked up at me in wonder and awe as she took the bracelet carefully.

"You might have asked me to marry you, or more or less demanded it, but I'm asking you the more important question." Holding her awestruck face in my hands, I stroked her cheeks with my thumb. "Will you let me collar you?"

Her tears had never worried me before, but when she burst out in a sob from my question, I couldn't help but feel my anxiety hike to new heights. It didn't help my nerves with how long she took to answer.

"Yes, a thousand times, no a million, billion, gazillion, infinite times yes." She sounded as if I asked her to be the ruler of the universe with how gleeful her voice was. "Oh God, did you think I was gonna say no? You look like you're about to pass out." Her face dropped with concern.

"Not gonna lie, yes, I did for a sec when you took a while to answer and just cried." I chuckled nervously, letting out the shaky breath I held in my aching chest.

"Oh, Styosha, no, those were happy tears, I couldn't believe it for a second and then it just hit me." She sniffled with a smile, placing her hands over mine and stroking the back of them with her thumbs.

Smiling uncontrollably, I leaned down and kissed her wholeheartedly with a deep groaning growl, stealing her breath away fully with my own before pulling away and kneeling before her. Looking up at her with a softened face, I quickly slip her flats off—because she refused to wear heels, even to her own wedding—and ran my hands up her legs to her back, where my fingers searched for the zipper of her dress and undid it in one smooth motion. "Stand up." I commanded, scooting back a few inches to give her room to rise to her feet.

Once she was up, the strapless dress naturally fell from her heavenly body to the floor. "Hold onto my shoulders so you don't fall." Reaching out, I bunched the sides of her panties in my hands and slowly pulled them down and off before getting back up on my feet.

Standing before her, I reach out and tuck her hair behind her ear. "Kneel." The way her eyes melted with lust and bliss made me shiver involuntarily as she slowly got down to her knees before me, bowing her head and keeping her hands in her lap.

After savoring the picturesque moment for a few seconds, I reached over to the bed, carefully picked up the collar, and held it before her. "If you chose to accept my collar then you vow to be mine and only mine even beyond death. In return, I vow to always treat you right and do right by you, to love and cherish you as my little brat until the end of time, to provide you a safe space where you can be free, to punish and discipline you when necessary, and to give you all of me in return."

Her cheeks rose with her smile as she kept her head down. "I accept your collar, Daddy." There was no hesitation or reluctance, which brought warmth to my heart. "I vow to cherish your mark on me for now and ever, and to never take it for granted. I wholeheartedly accept all that you are willing to give me. I will always do right by you, and I give you all of me to use and do as you please. You have my mind, heart, body, soul, and submission. Everything. I am yours, only yours."

No going back now.

I thought I felt the height of my pounding heart during our wedding ceremony, but somehow, it raced harder against my chest now as I wrapped the leather around Hanna's succulent neck and latched it.

Mine.

The wave of possessiveness stirred within me like never before. Seeing her with *my* collar around her neck uncaged a different being in me. All her collars before held no value now in light of this custom one I made for her.

Fuck, she was all mine now. Fucking, mine.

Gritting my teeth with a low growl, I reeled myself back in because we weren't done quite yet. Grabbing the bracelet from the bed, I knelt before her, curled a finger under her chin to lift her face for a chaste kiss, and gave her the bracelet before holding my wrists out to her. "I vow to belong to you and only you, that bracelet will serve as your collar and mark on me, and will hold the same equivalent to my mark around your neck. I am yours as you are mine. Mind, body, soul, and submission."

With a tearful—happy tearful—smile, Hanna wrapped the bracelet around my wrist and latched it shut. "I accept, and I vow to never take this for granted either. I will always treat you right and respectfully in our moments, to cherish, love, and support you whole-heartedly until the end of time."

Locking my soul to hers fully uncaged the beast I'd been holding back. Hooking a finger into the ring of her collar, I pulled her into a hard kiss, keeping our lips locked as I dragged us up to our feet before backing her onto the bed. Upon feeling the bed hit my knees, I broke the kiss to shove her down and pin her by her neck. "So fucking beautiful. God, you're all mine, my little tigress, my lovely wife." Leaning down, I settle my arm above her head. "My little brat."

Hanna's tongue swept across her plush bottom lip before taking it between her lips in a muffled groan. "I love you so much, Stepan. Make love to me, please. Make love to me then fuck me like your whore."

Grinning darkly, I took her lips in a possessive kiss. "There's my little tigress." I chuckled deeply against her lips before pushing off to strip myself bare.

Climbing back onto the bed, I pushed Hanna up so we were at the head of the bed before giving her one deep kiss and working my way down her body. "Daddy, I need you now, please, don't make me wait any longer."

Pressing my tongue against her sex, I ran my tongue up the length of it as I lifted my head. "Patience." I chided with a smirk.

She was more than ready with how soaking wet she was, but I wanted to prep her some more before taking her all night long.

Pressing my hands to the back of her thighs, I kept her legs open as I dipped my head back down to her pussy, wasting no time slipping my tongue inside of her entrance. Moving my head, I press myself close to use my nose to rub her clit with the motions of my head while my tongue worked her walls, getting every bit of her delicious nectar with a satisfied groan that dragged out louder when I felt her constrict around me and bathe my tongue more with her juices.

Removing myself from her, I sat back on my knees and delivered a quick slap to her pussy, making her yelp and jump. Smirking, I gave her two more spanks before shoving two of my fingers deep into her, causing her to arch up off the bed with a deep moan. "Just once, *malenkaya*, you can do it. Be a good girl and soak the sheets, squirt for Daddy and you'll get his cock."

I knew what spots set her off after all this time, so it didn't take me long to get her body shaking with her release. Pushing her through her orgasm, I slammed my fingers harder into her sweet spot to overstimulate her, my palm working her clit to keep her riding the edge.

Abruptly, I pulled my fingers out and unrelentingly rubbed her clit to make her squirt. Hanna's body jerked with the shocks of her orgasm, and her fingers clawed into my arm in her attempts to pry me away. "Daddy." She whimpered between her moans.

Her spasming body fell against the bed after her release took its full course. A sheen of sweat covered her heaving body as she panted. I was tempted to thrust my fingers back into her and pull another squirting orgasm from her, but I decided against it because what kind of a husband would I be if that's how I started our first night as husband and wife together off.

Leaning down, I caged her between my arms and kissed her heavily, shoving my tongue into her mouth with ease—not like she fought me. Then, shifting my weight onto one arm, I reached down and took ahold of my stiff member, stroking it along the length of her sex to slicken myself up with her juices before entering her fully to the hilt in one, hard thrust that got her coming instantly.

"Are you gonna be a good wife and come undone on your husband's cock?" I teased with a strained chuckle.

I needed to hang in there enough to not make an embarrassment of myself. My body was nowhere close to healed, so I needed to be careful before I kneeled over and ended up with a hospital trip tonight.

Bracing myself with one arm still, I slipped the other under around her hips to lift her a little to thrust into her at a better angle. For once, I went slow with Hanna, pulling out nearly all the way before sinking back into her with long strokes. We've fucked, a lot, but never once had we taken a step back to take things nice and slow like this.

Of course, it didn't last long, as I expected. "Styosha, more, please. *Trakhni menya krepko, papochka. Blya, isporti menya svoim chlenom.* " She demanded with a moaning whine, wrapping her legs around me to pull me closer and to use me as leverage to buck her own hips at me.

"Holy shit." That was the last thing I expected to blurt out of her mouth. "Such a filthy mouth on you. I'm not even going to ask where you learned that." Chuckling softly with a shake of my head, I let go of her waist to use my hands to gather her wrists up and pin them above her head. "I'm gonna have to teach you some manners later."

Easing some of my weight into her, I sucked in a sharp breath from the sudden pain shooting across my body when I started pounding into her at a hard and fast pace. Using the junction of her neck to hide my pained face, I took some of it out on her by sinking my teeth into her, easily breaking the skin from how hard I bit.

Hanna's body writhed and moaned under me as I continued to fuck her as if there was no tomorrow. "Stepan, gonna, come, Daddy, fuck." She shuddered under me before going tense and still.

"Fuck." I wanted to hold out more, but she squeezed me so tight that I couldn't control my own release from following.

It took me a moment to recover from the shock of my release, instantly regretting so once I felt the pain of my body hit me all at once.

"Styosha? What's wrong? Oh my God, are you hurt? Shit, Stepan, why didn't you tell me?" Hanna immediately moved me off of her and forced me to lie down on the bed. "Hon, if you were in pain then why didn't you tell me?"

Well, now I felt like an asshole for shoving my body aside for the sake of making love to my wife; the deep concern wrinkling at her face tugged at my guilt. "I barely felt anything in the moment, I'm fine, don't worry. I just need to take a break, rest a little." Unfortunately, there probably won't be a round two tonight.

Smiling happily and adoringly, I reach out and cup Hanna's face. "I love you so much, Hanna."

"No more tonight, just cuddles and sleep." Hanna huffed with a roll of her eyes before turning her head to kiss the inside of my palm. "I love you too, Stepan."

"Daddy." Hanna moaned under me as I thrust in and out of her slowly.

"Go back to sleep, little tigress." I chuckled deeply next to her ear, grazing the shell of it as I pressed more of my body weight into her to keep her squirming body pinned under me.

"Not fair." She whined into the pillow with a groan as her walls tightened around me.

"One more, *malenkaya*, come one more time for me." I was close from her orgasm, just one more tight squeeze, and I'd blow my load into her for the morning.

"I can't, tired." Her mouth might be saying one thing, but her body responded otherwise; the subtle shiver and goosebumps with how her soft moans picked up in pitch and pace meant she was close again.

I couldn't hold it against her, though, since I decided to be horny first thing in the morning and slide into her. On the other hand, I couldn't help myself. Waking up to my lovely little naked wife made the temptation too great. So, I couldn't help but pin her onto her front side and bury myself deep into her.

God, I still can't get over the fact she's my wife.

My. Wife.

Two months later, I still think I'd wake up one day without the rings on our fingers.

"Fuck! Styosha!" She cried out in pleasure under me, her body tensing and trembling with her release.

Gritting my teeth with a groan, my hips stilled against hers after a few sloppy thrusts as my own release rushed out of me. *"Chert, vot i vse, khoroshaya devochka."*

Threading my fingers through her hair, I fisted the back of her head and pulled her head up off the pillow for a heated kiss. "Such a good girl for me." I groaned against her lips after breaking the kiss.

"Not fair, my brain's always mush whenever you fuck me awake like this." She whined with a pout, letting her head flop back onto the pillow after I let her go. "You little somnophiliac." Her voice was muffled by the pillow slightly.

Rolling my eyes, I let out a short huff of a chuckle before kissing her temple. "Rest, I'll make us some breakfast and leave it on the table for you. I'll be in my office if you need me."

"Mhmmtay. Love you." Hanna hummed before dozing off.

Just like every day for the past two months, I'd wake up to Hanna in my arms, then fucked her—or she fucks me—before going about my usual routine and cooping myself up in my home office. I'd been stuck at the house since I was cleared to be released home. I tried to return to the office a few times before deciding to work from home when I couldn't find the energy to last the day. No matter. I have had Hanna home most of the time nowadays since she shifted her focus onto hunting her aunt down. I also might've put her on more research-based assignments to keep her from going out much.

However nice it was though, we—mainly me—were getting stir crazy. I wanted to go for a nice run or a chase through the forest, but unfortunately, I was still under restrictions. As embarrassing as it was to admit, I could barely have sex with Hanna currently.

Hanna certainly got a kick out of this whole recovery situation, though. Damn brat enjoyed the fact I couldn't fully punish her because I had to take it easy; granted, I proved her wrong after she pushed my buttons too much. I had Hanna at my mercy with some rope and remote controlled toys.

Just like now, after she decided to be a little brat and talk back to me after making a small mess by knocking things over, I had her hogtied on the couch in my office with a vibrator strapped against her clit.

I had to give her some credit, though; she lasted well until after lunchtime before she started to act up. "I'm trying to do work over here, little tigress. If you can't keep quiet then I'll have to gag you." I playfully threatened her with a lighthearted chuckle.

"You're so mean, Daddy." She whined with a soft sob before squealing from her orgasm.

"You're the one who wanted to come, so that's what I'm giving you. You could have been patient and waited until I was done with my work, but you decided to strip and finger fuck yourself to an orgasm even after I warned you what'd happen if you disobeyed me." I couldn't help the smugness from showing through in my voice and on my face.

"I'll behave, I won't be bad, just please no more." She begged with a sobbing groan.

"You see, I would show you some mercy if you actually meant it and I actually believe you. We've done this song and dance before, little tigress." Especially with how much of a brat she'd been lately, the moment she got her second wind after I released her, she'd be all up in my face.

With one last look at my lovely little brat of a wife, I went back to work, taking my sweet time to drag out her little punishment. She didn't want to wait for her orgasms, so I gave her what she wanted. Granted, now she had orgasms whether she wanted to or not.

My eyes dawdled over to her from my desk, smirking widely behind the hand I'd placed over my jaw to prop it up. "Are you ready to apologize genuinely?"

"Yes, please, I'm sorry, I'm sorry, I'm sorry for not listening to you, I'm sorry for being a brat, I'm sorry, just please, please, I won't get uppity again like that, please." Her words came out frantic between her panting moans.

Slowly, I got up and went over to her, watching her eyes grow hopeful with relief the closer I got. Standing next to the couch, I let my eyes drink her beauty in as I lazily trailed my fingers down her tantalizing figure, taking in every little dip of her toned muscles, the swell of her breasts, the lines in on her abdomen, all the way down to her throbbing pussy.

Fingering the harness straps, I smirked at her playfully as I purposedly dragged out the process of undoing the straps. "What have we learned?" I questioned with a raised brow.

"To listen to Daddy." Hanna whimpered with a remorseful frown. "And that everything belongs to you, even me, all of me. My body, my pleasure, my orgasms, everything, belongs to you, Daddy."

Unable to help it, I smiled proudly at her and leaned down to kiss her deeply. "Good girl." I praised with the same smile before removing everything from her soaked cunt.

"One more," I said in a deep voice, sinking two of my fingers into her deeply and curling them against her sweet spot. "Come one more time for Daddy."

Hanna didn't fight it as I finger fucked her—hard and slow—into one more release, only slowing down to a complete stop after her clenched walls finally released my fingers. "*Takaya khoroshaya devochka dlya papy. YA tak toboy gorzhus'.*" I chuckled lowly against her lips before capturing them in a bruising kiss.

"I love you, Hanna." And I'll never, ever stop.

"I love you too, Stepan, so much." The blissful smile and adoring look in her eyes brought a happy smile to my face.

"I know, and I'll never take any of it for granted, ever. I'll spend every day for the rest of our lives showing you just how much I love you and how grateful I am for you and your love." I promise her with a deep, passionate kiss after taking hold of her face.

BANG!

"*Blyat'!*" Frustrated, I let go of the rifle to step back and shake out my hands.

The recoil from the shot shook at my aching body to the point where I couldn't keep hold to continue. Hell, I couldn't even pull the pin to disengage the spent casing from the damn thing because my hands shook so much from the blowback.

"*Bratik*, I think that's enough for today." No doubt Lev's eyes were as concerned as his voice if I were to look back at him.

"I still can't fucking shoot for shit." I gritted out, lashing my arm out and knocking over my rifle that was set on the table.

I didn't even need to look at the target up close to know I missed my mark. Even though I had everything lined up perfectly, there was a slight tremble by the time I pulled the trigger because of my weakened body; I didn't handle the recoil well either—as in, I didn't handle it at all.

"Stepan, you're even lucky to be up and shooting a damn rifle in the first place given that you're barely three months out on recovery. You're lucky you're not getting knocked on your ass with the recoil. So, stop taking it so hard on yourself." Nikolai chided me with a sigh and shook his head. "Honestly, take it easy."

"I fucking can't!" I snapped, banging my fist onto the table with a growl. "I'm sick and tired of being cooped up at home, I can't fucking work out or go for a run like I want, I can barely handle a handgun again, I can't fucking shoot a damn rifle like I'd been doing since I was fucking eight! I'm tired of being weak and useless!"

My chest heaved heavily with my angry breaths. "I should have been more careful that night, I should have seen the ambush coming from my position and warn you guys. I should have seen it all coming and act accordingly."

"Stepan, you really need to stop beating yourself up for it. Shit happens, and you noticed it in time to effectively take out a whole lot of them before shit went down on your end." Nikolai's attempt to get me to ease my shoulders went in one ear and out the other.

I still blamed myself for that night. Everything happened because I didn't keep a close enough eye out. If I'd noticed the ambush against the main group, then I wouldn't have been so distracted with my slight panic, and I would've noticed the group of men approaching me from behind; I didn't even notice the shooter right under me from my perch in the tree until he shot the first bullet into me which knocked me out of the tree.

"*Bratik*, take a break, go out to the cabin with Hanna for a few days or weeks, just get away from all of this." Lev's suggestion sounded more like a command, which irked me slightly in my current state.

Widening his stance and crossing his arms, Nikolai gave me an authoritative look. "Lev's onto something, you just need to remove yourself from any kind of work with the company and bratva business. We'll be more than fine with you taking a little vacation, and Lev can handle the company just fine with the rest of us as backup in your absence. You're going to be no good to anyone like this, so go reset yourself." With the stern tone he used, it meant 'go, or I'll make you' with no room for debate.

"Styosha?" Hanna's voice snapped me out of my budding anger.

"Hon." My body broke out in shivers at her touch on my bare arm. "We're just all worried about you. I know you're frustrated, I understand, but you can't keep doing this, you're only going to make things worse and draw out the recovery period if you keep pushing yourself like this. I understand you want to get back to normal, but this isn't the way to go about it."

Letting out a heavy exhale, I place my hand over Hanna's and stroke the back of it with my thumb as I let my eyes settle on her worried face.

Well, this would be the best forced vacation ever or the worst. Either way, I was going whether I wanted to or not.

Fuck it.

Chapter 47
Hanna

"HANNA! THIS ISN'T FAIR!"

Humming cheerfully to myself, I pretended to ignore Stepan's protests from the bedroom where I had him tied to the bed frame. I might be the brat, but sometimes he needed a kick in the ass as well.

"Unless the next few words are 'I'm sorry' or 'please forgive me' or something along those lines, I ain't listening." I reminded him from the kitchen as I busied myself making breakfast for us.

I couldn't help but chuckle to myself when Stepan let out a long groan. "Are you seriously going to leave me tied in here if I don't?" Two could play the stubborn game, and I always won when push came to shove.

"What do you think? You left me tied to the bench for nearly the whole day until I became delirious from orgasming as a punishment." Leaving him tied would be child's play compared to the punishments he doled on me.

Stubbornly, Stepan held out for longer than I credited him for; I finished with breakfast and got in a quick workout before he finally caved. I expected him to last until about halfway through my breakfast, but I guess I underestimated him.

"*Malenkaya*, I'm sorry, okay?" He groaned with a deflated huff.

With a triumphant smirk on my face, I made my way to the bedroom up on the second floor of the cabin from the living area and leaned against the doorframe with my arms crossed. "For?"

"For disobeying doctor's orders and trying to push myself when I shouldn't, now please let me go, please." Stepan weakly tugged at his bindings while looking at me with pleading eyes. "Tigress, please."

My smirk widened into a devious smile when I noticed a shiver run down his body when I stalked up to him with my head held high. "Something tells me you don't want me to untie you quite yet." As if pointing out the obvious, I snapped my eyes to the tent in his sweatpants. "What were you thinking about?"

Slowly, I trailed a finger up his leg, stopping right at the base of his hardened member to draw lazy circles up and down his covered length. "You know it was supposed to be a punishment, so why are you hard, hm?" Laying down on the bed next to him, I propped my chin up on an elbow while keeping my other hand occupied with teasing his throbbing length.

"Hanna, just untie me please, I already apologized and admitted my fault, so please." Stepan's eyes averted from mine as he dodged my question.

Letting out an audible sigh, I began to palm him through his pants, causing him to suck in a sharp breath as his hips rolled at me. "If I let you go then what are you gonna do with this hard problem of yours? You weren't thinking about stroking one out in the shower were you? Or were you going to bend me over somewhere and screw my brains out, hm?"

When Stepan refused to answer or look at me, I grabbed the back of his hair and forced his head in my direction. "I expect an answer, hon." Gripping him through his pants, I gave him a firm squeeze and stroke. "If you don't answer me then I'll just ride you until I'm satisfied, without letting you come." I threatened with a playful leer and smirk.

"No, don't do that, please." No doubt his last punishment ran through his mind right about now with the tortured expression on his face.

"Then be a good Daddy and answer me." I replied in a sweet voice and smiled as if I didn't just threaten to give him blue balls just now.

"I was hard 'cause I was thinking about you on top of me or sucking me off while I was tied, happy? I was going to ask you to do one of the two for some relief." He admitted with flushed cheeks and averted eyes.

It was adorable how he still got embarrassed whenever our positions were switched. Also, I loved that I had such power over him. Our dynamic wasn't stark black and white, which I found amusing because I never expected Stepan to be a switch like me when we first got into things. I couldn't explain the rush I'd get whenever I'd top. To have such a strong and powerful man under you at your mercy, obeying your every word and whim. I might only sometimes like it, but the occasional change in dynamic momentarily was nice.

Getting on top of him, I straddled him and flashed him a cheeky smile as I grind my hips against his hard-on. "See, now was that so hard?" I teased as I leaned down and hovered my lips over his. "What do you want? For me to suck you off? Or for me to ride you?"

Stepan's body arched at my touch when I raked my nails down his bare chest and abs and slipped a teasing finger under the waistband of his pants. "Suck me off, I want to see you swallow me." He pleaded in a voice filled with desperation. "Please, tigress."

Quickly pecking his lips, I ran a tongue down his body while my hands pulled his pants down to release his cock. Ghosting my lips down his length, I gave his balls a slow, firm lick before taking them into my mouth as I wrapped my hand around his girthy shaft.

Peaking up, I watched Stepan lay his head back and tense his muscles as I sucked and licked at his balls while stroking him. "Hanna, please, I need to feel you, please." His voice came out breathy and needy with his bucking hips.

Pulling off with a soft *pop*, I give his length a slow lick up from the base to the tip, swirling my tongue around his crown and then his tip, picking up the bead of precum that leaked out with a delighted moan. "What? My tongue? Lips? Mouth? Hands? Pussy? You gotta be more specific, Daddy, otherwise I won't know." I teased with a smirk, sticking my tongue out and giving his tip some soft flicks.

"*Malenkaya*." He whined, looking down at me pleadingly. When I made no move to do anything but tease with little touches, strokes, and licks, he threw his head back with a defeated groan. "Your mouth, please, I need to feel your mouth around my cock."

A quick smirk of victory graced my lips before I took him fully into my mouth, only stopping when I felt him hit the back of my throat. "Take more of me, please." He breathed out shakily.

Holding his hips down, I ignore him—for now—and start to bob my head. He could shove himself down and face fuck me when he's in charge, which was not now. I wanted to enjoy him a little longer before choking on him.

As my head moved, my tongue swept along the underside of his throbbing member. Stepan kept begging me to take in more as I kept my leisure pace, but again, I didn't heed his pleas. His desperation picked up faster than I anticipated, which brought a smile to the corners of my lips as I continued to blow him off.

"Ple—ah!" Stepan gasped sharply when I deepthroated him suddenly, his body flexing under me as I swallowed his cock. "Shit." The metal bars of the headboard creaked under Stepan's force when he gripped and pulled at the ropes that bound him.

With an arm across his hips to keep him from bucking at me too much, I used my other hand to cup his family jewels and play with them while I continued to move my head, nearly pulling off completely before taking him all the way down to the base each and every time.

A small moment passed before Stepan's groan caught in his throat with the warning of his release, which I pulled back enough to where only his tip remained. With a strangled groan, he came in me, filling my mouth with his cum. My hand stroked at his pulsating cock as I sucked to milk him for all he had before pulling off completely. Carefully, while looking at him, I opened my mouth and stuck my tongue out to show him my filled mouth before swallowing everything and repeating the action to show him not a single drop remained.

"Fuck, I'm never gonna get tired of that." Stepan let out a satisfied chuckle and adoring look as his body slackened against his restraints. "Now are you done with your little power trip?"

Rolling my eyes, I leaned down and kissed him softly before undoing the bindings around his wrists and ankles. I let my hand and fingers linger around his wrist with the bracelet, smiling unconsciously as I traced the edges and engraving on the metal plate.

The wedding was fun and lovely, but our private collaring ceremony will forever be my life's most memorable and important event.

Unknowingly, my fingers brushed against my own collar, the one Stepan puts on every morning after we shower. I've no shame wearing it out; why should I be ashamed about showing the world who owns me? Who I chose to give myself wholly to. I was rather proud of it, and having his collar adorn my neck gave me a sense of security and belonging.

"I love how happy you always look whenever it comes to your collar." Stepan noted out loud with a happy smile of his own, pulling me from my thoughts.

"Because having your collar on my body makes me very happy." I assured him with a genuine smile before kissing him passionately. "Now, go wash up, I'll heat up your breakfast then we'll pack up and head back." I murmured against his lips after breaking the kiss.

"Bossy, bossy, but yes, *malenkaya*." Stepan replied with a roll of eyes before patting my ass to urge me off.

Two weeks came and went in the blink of an eye; it felt like yesterday that we arrived, Stepan much more reluctant than now. It was a pain in the ass to deal with his sour ass the first few days, but he adjusted with some help of a firm hand. As lovely as it was, there were moments when I wished we could cut the getaway short because living out in the forest doing nothing—felt like nothing to me—was boring.

Also, spending nearly every waking second with Stepan was, well, let's say I've had my fill of him for a whole year. I needed some space, badly.

I love him, but by God did he become intolerable. I thought working at home with him was bad, but at least we remained occupied with our own work for certain amounts of time; here, we literally only had each other. Stepan was supposed to take it easy, but him going out hunting was the only break I got from him, so I let him go for some peace of my sanity—or whatever I had left of it.

Seems like Stepan was more than eager to get back home as well because he kicked his ass into high gear right after his meal and packed the car in record time. We were on the road by the time I knew it.

It didn't take long for his hand to find my thigh and claim it once we were on the road. "I'm curious, and been wanting to ask but never got around to it, but where did your title, The Beast, come from? You don't seem too bothered by it either."

A confident chuckle shook at my body as I took his hand off my leg to intertwine his fingers with mine. "Besides the fact I look like one, it's because of my violent streak. I used to look bad before I got tattoos to cover up most of my scars, and paired that with my level of violence and craziness, it just kind of stuck. Although, it was more of a joke at first that Angel made after seeing how crazy I got with beating people up. The little moniker never bothered me, I actually like it because of the shock and fear I see in people when they see me or hear about me."

Although I've no shame about my title, a small aspect of it fitted illy. "And it was just kind of fitting. I looked hideous with a piss-poor attitude and personality. Ugly and doomed to never be loved."

A flinch snapped at my body in reaction to Stepan flicking my forehead. "None of that kind of thinking and talking. You have a great group of friends who are your family, and you have me now. So, I don't want to hear any of that shit or I'll start tallying." Well, it's a good thing my self-doubt was nil to none at this point in time, so at least I'd be avoiding that lot of punishment.

Tension pulled my eyes back and around as I grabbed his hand and held it in mine again. "Tell me something about you since you just found out something about me. Might as well kill the time." As dandy as we were,

Stepan rarely—never—talked about his past or anything too deeply about his family. Hell, I knew more about his family from his brothers than him.

Though true, I knew he was messing around with me by how jovial his voice was. "Not much to know about me. Father was a bastard. Mother was an angel. Obviously I got fucked up along the way hence why I'm the way I am." That earned him a playful smack to the chest from me.

"Tell me about your family. I mean, I know about your brothers, but your father and mother I know nothing about. Even if it's a bucket of shit, I want to know everything about you." I knew it was a sore subject; even with his brothers, I couldn't pry any of that information from them.

"Well, my family immigrated over here from Russia when I was little. Family life was... Goodish... Well, at least life with my mother and brothers was grand. My father made all our lives hell though. Out of the five of us, the twins had it the easiest since my father couldn't get away with too much shit over here in the states. Nikolai got it the hardest being the oldest, being groomed for the roll of Pakhan since he was born. I was second though, the contingency just in case something happened to Nikolai, and I was trained to be his protector and second in command." His body tensed with each hardening word while his breathing dragged out heavier and heavier.

"What happened to them? Your parents." He'd have to tell me at some point. Otherwise, this relationship wouldn't work. He knew things about my past, and I was more than open with him now about everything. So, it was only fair that I received the same from him.

"My brothers and I killed our father after he killed our mother for no other reason than he was done with her. Well, that and he hated the good influence she had on all of us. We locked him up in the basement and each took a turn at him for five days before Nikolai took the kill shot. Then we burned the house down to the ground with his body in it. Then we buried our mother with our sister in the gardens of the estate where Nikolai built the mansion." He wasn't torn up about the fact he tortured his father, no surprise there, but his voice did crack a little when he brought up his mother and sister.

Speaking of, "Wait, you have a sister?"

"Had. Had a sister. Natasha was born before the twins, best sibling of the bunch in my opinion, but the most tragic." Hesitancy chopped his wavering voice while his hands white-knuckled the steering wheel.

"What happened? If you don't mind." I had enough for now, so I didn't want to push him into some dark corner by forcing him to talk about the hurt in his life.

Stepan's eyes grew distant for a split second before his words came out almost scripted because of his restraint. "My father arranged her off into a marriage with another Pakhan to create an alliance. Needless to say, he was worse than alleyway trash. We all tried to stop the marriage, even went as far as hiding my sister, but they found her in the end and dragged her to the alter kicking and screaming. We never saw her again after the wedding, not even at the funeral because Nikolai demanded it be closed casket for our sakes, especially our mother's. Nikolai was the one who went over to Russia to identify her remains when she was found months later, and he was the one to retrieve the body back to the states, but he refuses even to this day to tell us a single detail about the state she was in when she was found. I don't know about the others, but I was stubborn and got my hands on the coroner's report. I've never had an urge to kill so bad until I read the thing."

"Did you get him in the end? Make him pay?" If he didn't, then I would love to have a go at the guy.

"Yeah, we wiped out the whole bratva in one bloody night." I'm not sure if the twisted grin on his face was intentional, but it almost seemed too giddy to be a controlled one.

"Is your sister the reason why you and your brothers hate arranged marriages and go against them?" Angel had told me about how their bratva had a ban of sorts on such relationships, and it made sense now if his sister was the reason.

His chest rose and fell in a steady movement before his head nodded in response to me. "Yeah. We didn't want any chance of that happening to any of us ever again or our children."

"Speaking of children—"

Then, we were off. The road, I meant.

We were—literally—on the road one second, then we were off the next.

Just as I was about to tell him the good news.

Chapter 48

Stepan

"Stepan, stop! You have—"

"No! Don't you dare fucking tell me to calm down!" Did I feel a little guilty about snapping at my pregnant sister-in-law? Yes, after the fact.

"Hey! Cool it." Nikolai warned me with a calm voice filled with silent anger. "You're not going to do any good with your mind frazzled."

As if I didn't know that. "I can't. They fucking took her!"

"And we will get her back. They fucked with the wrong family. You need to breathe, just take a second to recollect yourself before you do something stupid." Alexei told me, shoving me back into my seat at my dining table.

Turning my gaze outside the window, I gripped my hair and rubbed the back of my neck while taking heavy, erratic breaths. "Evenly, you're going to hyperventilate if you keep that up." Alexei sighed heavily.

"Stepan, she'll be okay out there until we get to her, she can handle herself just fine. If it's Lilian who took her then she'll be alive when we find her. If Lilian wanted her dead, then she would be." Angel tried to assure me with a worried smile.

"She's injured out there. They ran us off the road with a damn cargo truck. She was bleeding last I remembered before they dragged her dazed body out of the car window. They hit her 'cause she fought back, they hit her until she stopped moving." The accident came in like a tidal wave, flaring my emotional turmoil again.

"They shouldn't have gotten away. They shouldn't have. If only I'd been faster." Shooting down five men should've been child's play to me, done and gone in the blink of an eye.

Yet, I stumbled. I only got two of the five and clipped another. My body fought me; my fingers trembled and refused to pull the trigger faster. My eyes refused to focus. I couldn't land a clean headshot at such a short distance. I was useless, fucking useless. And Hanna has to suffer because of it all.

"Stepan, you were lucky to even be conscious enough to move let alone shoot. You're only human Stepan, and you're still not completely recovered from your ordeal before." Great, as if I needed a reminder about the fact my body was still in the shit hole from my brush with death. I knew Angel meant well, but I was being a piss poor asshole.

With an angry exhale, I ran a hand down my face and held my jaw. "Did you guys get anything off the two I shot down? And anything on my trackers on Hanna?"

As much as I wanted to charge out there like an angry bull, I'd have no idea which way to even go. I needed to get my head straight, whether I liked it or not. Going out back to shoot wasn't an option either because my body suffered from the impact earlier; I wouldn't be able to handle the recoil of a rifle right now. Plus, I'd just be straining myself and getting a lecture from both Angel and Alexei, so no thanks.

"Still pulling information as we speak. Mercs from what I know so far, but seems like they've worked with Lilian before quite frequently. Trackers on Hanna still aren't live yet, but almost." Bao replied from the couch, his head peeping up from his laptop for a moment. "There's also someone else besides Lilian who's been making huge deposits into these accounts, but Nicole's working on that along with tracing the call log."

"We'll get her back Stepan." Bao's sister, Nicole, assured me with a confident and bright smile. "You've got the two best hackers and techies in the world in your damn living room right now, so chill."

"What does she even want with Hanna?" Okay, that was a loaded question. We'd been royally screwing over her operations by taking out her business fronts and clientele; after the first few brothels burnt down, and word got out about specific clients being hunted down got around, many were more than eager to keep a low profile or dip town altogether.

"Beats me, they're more estranged than me and Lady Qing," Angel replied with a shrug of her shoulders before going back to wrapping up my beat-up arm that Alexei picked at for the past half an hour to get all the glass shards out.

The next hour dragged on forever, my anxiety weighing my heart down with each ticking second. My heart nearly went into shock when Nicole shrieked and jumped up from her spot like she'd won the lottery. "I got her location!"

Bolting over, I snatched the tablet out of her hand and searched the screen with frantic eyes. "Stepan, breathe." I hadn't realized my chest was puffed out with my bated breath, nor the dizziness that settled in my fogged-up head.

I didn't breathe until my eyes settled on the blinking red dot on the screen. Much to my surprise, the location wasn't somewhere remote; it was damn smack center of the city, or at least pretty damn close to the center. Not to my surprise, it was in a part of triad territory, the small part we didn't acquire with the takedown and merge because Lady Qing separated it in time. The territory was up for grabs, but Lilian had kept her footing thus far.

Well, it won't be hers for much longer.

"Give me aerial and live feed," I demanded after giving the tablet back to Nicole.

"Stepan, you're not going anywhere in your state." Nikolai objected, putting a hand against my chest to stop me from walking away.

"Like hell am I going to sit here while my wife is out there in danger. I'm going, and you can't stop me." My eyes scanned everyone in the room, "None of you can stop me. If you try, then you better be prepared to deal with the consequences. I can stand, I can walk, I can see, so I can damn well shoot."

Unless they all wanted to dogpile me so Alexei could sedate me, I wouldn't let any of them get in my way. I won't stop until Lilian Wu took a bullet through her head—my bullet from my gun. She was warned not to mess with me or Hanna, so she deserved all that was coming to her.

"Kolyenka." Angel grabbed Nikolai's wrist and pried him away from me. "If it were me then you'd charge in there even if you were half dead. Best we can do now is have his back, and mitigate."

No one budged an inch as I moved to the arsenal room to pack and prep in a hurry. I didn't care about my body screaming at me to stop and drop; it could do that after I had Hanna safe and sound in my arms. However, one look at my trusty rifle, and I could feel my arms shake and ache with my shoulders.

What if I couldn't pull the pin fast or efficiently enough? What if I couldn't steady myself enough to line a perfect shot? What if I shot Hanna by accident because of a last-minute twitch? Could I handle the blowback enough to keep shooting after two rounds?

The doubts gripped my mind as tightly as my hands did my rifle, and I began to wonder if it'd break. I hadn't even shot it yet I already felt my body react poorly. Ideally, it'd be best to wait, but I wasn't risking that when it came to Hanna. I'd be able to recover physically; I'd be alive at the end of it all. Hanna, who knows what would happen to her if I waited. I wanted her warm body next to me in bed, not hold her cold one in my arms.

Shoving my inhibitions away, I stuff my rifle into the duffle bag after putting it back in its case. I needed to remain strong for both Hanna and myself.

It's do or die, no doubts.

I won't miss.

I <u>can't</u> miss.

Once I'd packed everything, I quickly changed into a set of tactical gear and strapped my handguns and knives to their proper places before returning to the living room with my duffle.

"So, what's the plan?" Arseny asked as he inspected his blade in hand.

"I'm going to find a vantage point and set up, then I want you all to smoke them out of the place into the open. Kill whoever you want, make it damn bloody to send a message, but leave Lilian to me." I might be passive, but by no means was I a saint.

I kept myself tamed for everyone's sake. One kill was all I needed to set myself off. One single drop of blood was all I needed to taste. The snap of the trigger when I'd pull it with the lovely, smokey scent of gunpowder filling the air; the jump to my heart when my bullet would meet its mark. The fucking rush.

I was a killer through and through—we all were.

"Stepan, we can handle a rescue mission, are you sure—"

I interrupted my older brother with a snap, "Yes. It's *my* fucking wife out there. *My Hanna*. You'd damn well do the same if it were Angel, so don't try to stop me again."

"Alright, fine, but I am pulling you out the second I see you waver." Nikolai's hard tone meant no arguments. "You do not need to be put out of commission indefinitely because you pushed yourself too damn hard."

"You gotta live long enough to give us a mini Stepan." Arseny snickered with a cheeky grin.

God, me with kids? I never even thought that far yet. Did I even want that stress? I mean, a child or two with Hanna would be nice, no? But fuck, that was so much stress. Nikolai's kids weren't even born yet he already grew white hair. Were kids even for me? Could I even be a good father? What if I fucked up my own kids? Or worst, my own kid ends up dead because of this lifestyle? Children don't mix with mafia life, so why would I willingly subject my own blood to such?

But what about Hanna? We've never sat down and had *that* talk yet. I had no idea what her stance on children were. The two of us seemed more than content with what we had going on now with just the two of us. Maybe we both liked the child-free life.

The thought of our child being left with one—or maybe no—parent because something happened to us on the field stabbed at my heart like a blunt knife.

My recent accident had been the worst I've suffered since childhood, but what's to say it would be the last? What if someone made a grab at my child's life to get to me or Hanna? We were too prominent; not everyone could remain oblivious to our reputation and names.

I don't know how or why Nikolai would do it with his children, how he would protect them growing up. The Pakhan and his bride, the former heiress of the Qing Triad, and his children would be the first on the hit list for our enemies; mine would follow closely, being his second in command. Not as if my slate was clean either. I have made more than my fair share of enemies through bratva business and legal business with the company.

Taking a deep breath, I shove it all into the back of my mind, swallowing the anxious ball of nausea back down. I couldn't worry about that right now.

Forcing a half smile on my face, I lightly punched Arseny in the shoulder. "Man, go knock up your own girlfriend." I retorted with a roll of my eyes.

"How do you know I haven't already?" It was hard to determine whether he was fucking around or not with the lighthearted tone.

Alexei scoffed with a sneer and smacked his twin upside the head. "Because Mia won't let you between her legs, now shut up and let's move."

Alexei was impatient, which surprised me because he was the most level-headed of all of us besides me. However, one look in his eyes was all I needed; he wanted blood as much as me, but not for the same sane reason. No, Alexei wanted to spill blood for the hell of it to sate his lust.

I wanted to spill blood for Hanna's sake, and for my own madness.

They won't know what hit them; I'll show them all why I coined the name Silent Volk, and they won't know until it's too late.

I will rain bullets on them and fill the streets with their bodies and blood.

Chapter 49

Hanna

Strangled screams of pain filled the decrypted place, along with the sounds of electricity sparking.

"You. Stupid. Fucking. Bitch." Every word was punctuated with a jab from the cattle prod, causing me to scream out in agony. "You had one fucking job." My aunt's evil face floated like a ghost inches from the muzzle they'd put on me because I bit one of the guards and tore a chunk out of him.

"Funny, last I checked I didn't work for you." I snarked with a sneer, earning another jab to my aching body from the prod. "I'm gonna piss and dance on your fucking grave." If I even made it out of this alive.

"With how your new husband is going to lock you in the dungeons, I don't think so. Unless you convince the Volkovs to go into business with me, you better get used to being an obedient bitch again. Your new husband isn't so kind as the Russian." Gripping the top of my head, she wrenched my head over to a slob of a businessman who sat in the corner, leering at me with unsavory eyes. "Don't think your stupid boy will save you either, you'll be on a plane to China before the end of the day. He'll never find you there."

Growling, I mustered up as much strength as possible and threw my head forward at Lilian, catching her by the end of the metal muzzle, causing her to curse in Mandarin and reel back. No surprise, another shock came, this one longer than the others so far.

"The only place I'm going to is Hell with you." I sneered with a hateful scowl. "But I wouldn't count that blessing yet because I'm going to tear you limb from limb once I get you in The Catacombs."

Pooling a mouthful of saliva and blood—I bit my cheek when I convulsed from being tased—in my mouth, I waited until she got up in my face again and spat it out at her, earning a nice punch—yes, punch, not slap—to the face from the guard next to me. "You should have killed me all those years ago." Over a decade of budding revulsion and loathing, all the anger in my life, it'll all be taken out on her and my pathetic mother, who sat like a snake next to the vile man with beady eyes.

I never thought I'd get the urge to act on my hatred like this because I suppressed everything and actively ignored it all—out of sight, out of mind kind of shit. If I didn't bother her, then she'd pay me no attention.

Ever since Stepan made me face the music, something flipped in me. I wanted them all dead, anyone who touched me in this damn place—and I had the perfect weapon. All I had to do was point, and Stepan pulled the trigger. If I couldn't do it but wanted it done, then he'd step up and handle it for me. He had me covered until I was ready.

Honestly, I didn't expect to be so fine with him taking out the targets of our list as he did because they were my kill to make. Yet, I found myself eagerly waiting for his return every night he went out hunting. The excitement I felt when he'd walk through the door and hand me the bloodied bullet always brought a sense of satisfaction and peace to me as if every bullet to the collection was a piece of my burden being taken away. I enjoyed him taking care of my problems—I blamed that on my daddy issues.

"If those men could shoot for shit then you would be dead. You think you were supposed to survive? They were supposed to shoot both you and your father. Damn idiots couldn't even shoot a kid." Lilian spat in my face, her anger dripping out of her like a drooling dog.

Rage instantly rose to a high, burying the shock to nothing. "The fuck are you hissing about you snake?" My raspy voice seethed with acidic rage.

"You think it was a coincidence that your father got caught in a drive-by?" The unhinged grin on her face with the twisted glint in her eyes told me enough.

"YOU BITCH! I'M GONNA FUCKING KILL YOU!" The pain of my restraints digging into me, along with the warmth of my blood dripping down my bare skin, didn't come close to registering in my mind as I thrashed and struggled vehemently in the chair they kept me bound to.

In a split second, my sharp eyes snapped to my smug mother. "He was your fucking husband! He loved you! He gave you everything!" My father was the one who got her out of the gutters; she got lucky and married rich. Unlike many others I've seen, my father was a caring man who loved his wife. He treated her so right and doted on me like the most precious thing in the world.

I shouldn't be taken aback by how callous my mother was; she was never the warmest person or a decent mother, but still, maybe a part of me just hoped for something. "He wouldn't give me more. He could have been so much more, he could have been the Dragon Head, but no. No, he couldn't do that to his friend, his longtime buddy. He wanted to give up the triad life for the simple life, all that money and luxury, gone. At least his life was worth something dead."

"I'm going to drown you in your own blood after I put some holes in you." I seethed with a harsh tug of my arms, wincing when I felt the stretch in my shoulders.

"The hell you shipping me off to China for with this fat pig?" Not like he'd get some alliance with them, and no offense to myself, but there were many better girls out there.

"He paid for you, simple as that. He wants a dog, so I'm giving him one." My aunt shrugged her shoulders with an unbothered smile. "You'll break eventually, and he'll have a good warm body to use whenever he pleases along with a good weapon against his enemies. The Beast's reputation is far beyond California, and he wants that power and fear."

My eyes shifted over to him when he shifted and moved toward me with a sick smile on his face. "I swear, if you dare lay a single breath on me, I'll fucking gut you with my bare hands and feed you your innards and choke you with your own intestines." A bit much? Maybe, but pigs like him deserved it.

His hand shot out and grabbed at my collar, twisting it in his grubby hand until my oxygen cut off. "You wear a collar like a bitch, so you will be one." Cold metal sheers slipped between my neck and the leather collar.

"Don't you fucking dare." I seethed through gritted teeth, glaring at him with as much threat as possible.

Snip!

The pressure against my windpipe absolved in an instant, but my neck became naked for a split second before a clunky shock collar constricted it. "Fuck you! Give that ba—ah!" My scream of pain choked out from the shock of the collar.

"You'll get a pretty collar again once you learn to behave, and once you are broken as you should be." The man grinned in my face as he gripped it in his sweaty hand.

"Now, who's your master?" His grip tightened to where I could feel it in my bones—no doubt I'd have bruises.

"Stepa—ah!" Another shock cut me off. "I'd rather obey a turd than you." I spat with narrowed eyes.

"Why you little—"

Splatter!

A disgusted scowl crossed my face when the man's headless body slumped over onto me after his brains—surprised he had any—exploded all over me. "I'm gonna hurl." I bit out with flat sarcasm.

"Hold a gun to her head." Lilian ushered the guard next to me who obeyed without hesitation.

Before he could draw his gun, his head ceased to exist with a head-shot. Then not even a hair of a second later, the other guard next to me dropped—headless—as well.

A hopeful smile widened on my lips as I looked out the shattered window ahead of me. "Daddy!" The sight of Stepan's dirty blonde hair had me jumping in my seat.

Stepan always hated his hair, but I loved it for all the reasons he despised it. I loved how he stood out against the others—and how easily it was to spot him—with the shaded difference; he hated it because he didn't look like his brothers, which brought on his father's wrath because he was convinced for the longest time that their mother had an affair, hence Stepan's difference—their mother had blonde hair.

Honestly, his father sounded like a real piece of work who I would've loved to get my hands on. Besides fucking up all his children majorly, he killed his own wife and basically sentenced his own daughter to death with an arranged marriage to a lunatic. I had no idea why Stepan and his brother had such an aversion to arranged marriages until he told me the story about his little sister; she got carted off to some bratva boss in Russia and never returned alive.

Well, it was good to know our own children will never suffer such a fate if we ever have any. I never thought I wanted children in my life, given my upbringing—also, the world was just a shitty ass place. I didn't know how to be a mother, and not like I watched home videos growing up or observed good mothering. Yet, whenever I thought about the future with Stepan, somehow, children always popped in, whether I wanted them or not. It was beyond bizarre at first since neither of us touched on the subject matter at all.

Maybe it was some stupid biological need, I don't know. All I knew was that I wanted children with Stepan. Okay, maybe now *right now*, now, but in a year-ish...? I also banked on the idea of seeing how Angel's kids were before making a firm decision. As much as I wanted to spread my legs and beg Stepan to knock me up, maybe after interacting with Angel's babies once they were here would quickly change that idea.

Oh well, I could think about cute, blonde babies later when I wasn't—

"FUCK!"

She fucking stabbed me!

Son of a bitch of a fucking mother fucking stabbed me!

"I brought you into this world, so I'm damn well taking you out of it. You were nothing but a burden to me ever since I conceived you. You damn parasite." Her words sounded muffled to my pounding ears.

"Then why even have me in the first place?" I gasped through the pain of the knife in my gut.

"Your dad was too honorable of a man to leave me if I got pregnant. I tried to get rid of you after the shotgun wedding, but you survived like a damn cockroach in a nuclear bombing." Okay, that stung, no lie. I knew my mother never wanted me, but to hear about her attempted abortion on me struck a new blow to me. "If your damn father wasn't so doting then I would have smothered you the first day in the hospital. Damn fool hovered over you like a hawk."

"Hanna!"

I couldn't tear my raging eyes away from my mother to look at Lev when I heard his voice from the doorway. The only reason why I pulled my attention away was because of the gunshot a little ways from me.

Out of the corners of my eyes, I could see my aunt holding a gun in the door's direction, and more men started to crowd around. "No one move, or she'll get eviscerated," Lilian warned.

"You're not gonna walk out of here, so might as well surrender." Arseny—or maybe Alexei—spoke up.

"That's where you're wrong. If I die, then she," Lilian jabs a finger in my direction, "Dies too. If you do not let me and Gia leave the area unharmed then I'll have Hanna gutted on the spot."

"What if we just shoot you dead right now? We outgun you, and we can shoot Gia faster than she could inch that knife in Hanna." Lev challenged with a sneer—damn idiot.

"Shoot me or Gia dead and the whole building goes up in flames." Lilian's devilish smirk meant she'd won. "You see this?" Holding her free wrist up, she showed off an expensive-looking watch. "Specially designed by a good friend that detects vitals. I had them rig it to bombs in the area, so if my heart ceases to beat then the bombs go off. A good city block will go up in chaos."

Biting my tongue, I held my challenge of her bluff back. Half of me doubted her because she was too honorary of a person to kill herself like that—even if she did go out with a bang, literally. The other half very much believed her because she was a woman with nothing to lose at this point.

She had the means and connections to make such a thing happen, so I didn't doubt her there. If she had rigged the area, none of us would be safe. The last thing I wanted was to make Angel a widow with two kids—I caught a glimpse of Nikolai next to Stepan on the roof of the building. Being responsible for the end of the Volkov Bratva was not what I wanted to be known for in death.

Locking my shaky eyes with Lev, I gave him an apologetic look. "L-lower your weapons." I gasped out reluctantly. "Let them go."

Lev's eyes widened initially in response. "What? Is the blood loss getting to your brain? They ran you and Stepan off the road, kidnapped you, tortured you, sold you off to a pig of a man, oh and don't forget your own damn mother has a knife buried in you right now." Trust me, I didn't want to believe the words that came out of my own mouth either.

"I can't be responsible for your deaths, so let them go," I begged the Volkov brothers with a sad smile before turning my attention to Lilian, who zoned in on me with a smug expression. "Leave, just leave. You have more than enough money to live the rest of your life in luxury, so leave. You and I have no business together, so just accept that and leave."

"Or I can have them go into business with me now while I have everyone on the line." Lilian's lips curled into a dark grin.

"I'm going to tell you now, the longer you try to get your way, the less your chances of escape will be. No doubt Stepan and or Nikolai heard everything just now through their communications systems. It won't be long until they have Bao or Nicole dispatch an emp or their little bomb sniffers to disable everything before you even know it." It was a plausible bluff, and I only hoped they were stupid enough to buy it.

By some miracle, they did. "Fine, but if any of you pursue us then I will end you." With a nod at one of the live guards in the room, they came over and swapped places with Gia. "They will be on the phone with me until Gia and I are safe, if they give me any indication that something funny is happening, then I set the bombs off. Got it?"

With no other option currently, as if I could think of any with half of my blood on the floor, I agreed and gave the order to the others to stand down. God, I hope this won't blow up in my face, literally.

My aunt and mother ran away like rats in a matter of seconds. If only my torment lasted seconds; it felt like hours before my aunt's voice came on the other line, informing the guard of her safety. Poor guard thought that meant they were safe too, but they got played like a sacrificial pawn.

Fresh blood painted my face following a gunshot the moment news about my aunt's safety came over the speakers of the phone, and the guard's headless body joined at my feet with the others before him.

"Get this knife out of me," I demanded in a fading voice as the fog of unconsciousness further clouded my mind.

"No, do *not* move that knife," Alexei spoke up while shoving himself to the front. "Release her, then Lev, I'm gonna need you to carry her *very carefully* to the car. And I repeat, *do not* remove the knife."

Okay, general rule of thumb: do not remove an object from a body because that object is the only thing keeping the bleeding at bay. I knew the rule; everyone here in the room probably knew it, but fuck it. They weren't the one with the knife in them! I wanted the damn thing out! Now!

The pressure from the muzzle fell away from my face. "Hanna, I need you to stay with us, stay awake, talk and say anything you want, even if it's completely stupid, I just need you to stay awake." Alexei's face was right there, yet he sounded miles away underwater.

"Tired... Want Daddy." I intended to say a full sentence, but only some words came out coherently.

A wave of comfort washed over me when the familiar scent of spices and gunpowder drowned me, along with a pair of arms. "I am here, *malenkaya*, I'm here. Stay awake for me, can you do that? Stay awake for me like a good girl?"

"Want to... Can't... Sleep." Did God push the slo-mo button on his remote? Or was this a bad trip?

"Hanna!"

Good night.

Chapter 50
Hanna

BEEP... BEEP... BEEP

Oh my God, someone shut it up!

I barely made out the annoying machine next to my bedside through my half-opened eyes. "I'm alive, so shut it up." I groaned through my scratchy throat.

"Oh, Hanna!" Pressure tightened around my body. "Don't fucking scare me like that again." Angel's familiar voice sobbed against my chest.

"Heavy, off," I demanded with a weak smack to Angel's arm.

Angel scrambled off before adjusting the bed so I was slightly upright, then she shoved a straw into my mouth and made me sip at some fluids. "Both you and Stepan need to be locked away in your house, I swear." She fretted over me.

Giving out a weak, raspy chuckle, I reached over and took her hand in mine. "Shouldn't you be the one in bed resting? Or are you being a bad patient yourself and disobeying doctor's orders?" She was about ready to pop, or at least ready to be popped.

"You know what they say, nurses make the worst patients." She joked after cracking a smile.

I joked back with a raised eyebrow. "Nikolai let you out?" Her husband worried about her pregnancy more than her. If anything, she was the one who complained about the father of her children being insufferable.

"I don't need permission from him to do jack shit," Angel remarked with a tilt of her chin.

"Oh, really now?" Nikolai's amused voice made Angel's face drop.

"*Anh*, honey," Angel giggled sheepishly with a nervous grin.

"Bedroom, now." He growled in response, darkening his gaze at her.

Angel immediately hung her head regretfully, giving me a quick apologetic look before returning to Nikolai. "Yes, sir." She meekly shuffled her feet out of the medical suite, leaving me alone briefly before Alexei showed up.

"How are you feeling?" Calm and professional like always.

"Like I got stabbed." I quipped back with a sarcastic smile, earning a flat look from him. "I don't know, okay? Still feel weak and groggy, but other than that okay ish? I guess? I wasn't out for long, was I?"

"You were only out for a day, which isn't too bad considering the surgery and amount of blood you lost. I'm going to keep you here for a few days though to monitor you to make sure you're fine before releasing you into Stepan's care. Stepan will be by soon, we made him leave to go wash up and eat before he needed a bed himself for passing out. Judging by the look on your face though, you have another question?" Alexei stopped his exam to look at me with a flat expression.

"Nothing got too damaged, right? Getting stabbed in the stomach like this won't affect my ability to have kids, will it?" I couldn't hold back the wariness in my voice as I placed my hands over my stomach.

"It shouldn't, no, but if you do get pregnant then you'd just have to be closely monitored," Alexei assured me with his typical distanced smile that did little to damper the immense relief I felt from the news.

Once he was done with his assessment, he left me to my own empty thoughts until Stepan showed up minutes later with the brightest smile I'd seen in a while. Stepan was careful with his hug, not wanting to pop my stitches. *"Malen'kaya tigritsa,* fuck you had me so worried. We lost her, we tracked her to the docks, but then she went off the map after that."

"It's okay, she's bound to rear her ugly head sooner or later, and we'll catch her then. Let's not talk about her or any of that right now, I just want to enjoy this moment." I spoke into his neck before taking in deep breaths of him into my system.

As much as I hated her being in the wind, I didn't want to worry about Lilian or anything related to her. It's not like we could do much in our states anyway. Nikolai and Angel had to give the bulk of their attention and forces into maintaining the peace with the newly acquired territories to spare much help to us, and Stepan and I were far from tiptop shape after the recent shit we've been put through. It was going to be a few months before I could be fully functional again because of this stupid wound, and Stepan still had quite a bit of healing to do himself.

"Well, guess we're going to be stuck at home for another long while." Stepan chuckled, attempting to lighten up the mood.

The thought of being housebound with Stepan for the next few months had me groaning in complaint. Again, don't get me wrong, I love Stepan, but by God he was an insufferable man after so long without a break in between. I might work for him, but at least during our office hours, I was physically away from him. Granted, I could move my home office out of his and into a different room, but I doubt he'd fly by with that idea.

Also, I'm sure Stepan was just as sick of me but didn't make it known. "Don't worry, you'll have your peace with me away from the house. I'm gonna head back into the office part-time in a few weeks, then full-time again when you don't need much assistance." He assured me with a sly smirk.

"Thank fucking God." I groaned under my breath before looking at him with tired but happy eyes. "I love you, hon, but you're exhausting to be around twenty-four-seven with no breaks."

"The feeling is mutual, no offense. I love you, but seeing you all irritated and snappy gets me in a mood." At least we agreed on that, and surprisingly, I wasn't *too* offended by him.

With him next to me on the bed, I leaned into him as he kept his arms around me protectively. It might not be the wisest thing to bring up right now, but I needed to get it off my chest. "Hey Styosha? I know we never really talked about it, and I mean, I tried to bring it up that day in the car before we got so rudely interrupted, but I think I'm ready to try and have kids with you, if you want any. And, well, it doesn't have to be now, now, and obviously that's not going to happen given our current situation, but maybe in a few years we could have maybe one or two?" Yes, that was the good news I wanted to break to him before the crash.

I knew my heart was in rhythm because of the stupid monitor, but it felt like it took long pauses as tension squeezed at my chest. I couldn't pick apart Stepan's expression much after his initial surprise because it turned into something pensive in nature.

The only thing stopping us would be personal preference, and maybe our choice in profession. Other than that, we had a nice house to raise the children in, guards to protect them, and a huge line of uncles who'd scare off anyone who even looked their way; financially, we were more than stable and able, and Stepan and I were happy with our relationship.

Humming softly, Stepan leaned over and kissed my temple. "After we fully recover, we'll see. I want things with the bratva and Lilian to be completely settled before we try. The last thing I want is for Lilian or your mother to go after our child to get at us, nor do I want to bring our child while the bratva is trying to sort out the turmoil with the territories right now." It wasn't a no, so I'll take it as a win.

"Plus, I'm gonna need the time to read parenting books or at the very least need the time to watch Kolya and his kids to even see how to parent in the first place." Stepan's lighthearted comment made me giggle softly with a wince when I felt the tug in my stomach.

Tilting my head up, I smile at him warmly and lovingly. "You'll be a great father. I mean, you already take care of me perfectly fine, now just add more." I could picture it perfectly: Stepan cooking our meals, feeding the kids, playing in the yard with them, or even maybe teaching them to shoot, then he'd probably read them bedtime stories and tuck them in.

At the very least, he had a good idea from watching his siblings and helping his mother while growing up; he also had a good idea of what not to do from his father.

"I love you, Stepan, so much. *YA lyublyu tebya papochka.*"

His lips ghosted against mine in a chaste kiss, his words whispering against my lips, "I love you too, Hanna. *YA lyublyu tebya malen'kaya.*" Finally, he kissed me like I deserved it.

My heart leaped out of my chest as our lips became in sync with each other, the passion overloading my fragile body, causing my head to spin with pleasure.

"Fuck the next few weeks are going to be torture." Stepan groaned against my lips with a soft scowl.

"Poor Daddy can't get his dick wet, boo hoo." I teased with a snicker, sticking my tongue out at him.

"Don't think you can get away with being a brat just because you're injured and recovering. The counter doesn't stop." He warned me with a low growl, sending shivers down my spine. "*Ty sobirayesh'sya byt' khoroshey devochkoy?*"

"*Da papochka.*"

Epilogue 1
Stepan

~7 years later~

THE FACT THE SOUND of the door closing echoed through the house meant she was hiding. As much as I didn't want to entertain her, I couldn't say no—even if I was exhausted after a long day at the office.

Well, at least she made it easy. I could see the tips of her sparkly, purple shoes peeking out from under the curtains. As quiet as a mouse, I made my way over after tossing my jacket onto the kitchen counter.

Unable to help it, I let my lips curve in a playful smirk as I pooled the curtains in my hand. "Gotch—huh? Gah!" A heavy weight landing on my back threw off my balance.

"Get him!" My precious wife squealed with a laugh as she tightened her arms around my neck and shoulders and her legs around my waist.

"Gotchu daddy!" And there was our little spitfire, pelting me with Nerf darts from her latest Nerf gun—courtesy of Lev, her favorite uncle.

Joining in on their laughter, I hooked my arms under Hanna's knees to help hold her up as I ducked my head away to avoid a bullet to the eye—toys or not, those things could still blind an eye. "Alright, alright, you got me, I yield!" No, I wasn't fake laughing, it was genuine.

Everything was always genuine regarding my family, especially my wife and our daughter, Julia. "Told you it work mommy." She gave both of us a toothy grin as she bounced in her spot, causing her little blonde pigtails to bounce.

Julia was a cute little mixture of Hanna and I. She had my hair color with her mother's volume. Her eyes were primarily brown like Hanna's but the outer edges were blueish like my eye color, so almost a hazel brown-blue. Then, she had Hanna's little button nose and roundish face, which I hope she never grows out of.

"And I didn't doubt you, I just suggested you use different shoes to make it more believable." Hanna retorted with a roll of her eyes. "Now, go put your toys away and go get ready, aunt Angel and uncle Nikolai will be here soon with your cousins."

And the little head of blonde sped past us down the hallway, filling the house with her ear-piercing screech. "YAY! NATASHA!" No matter how much my ears pounded, I couldn't bring myself to damper her excitement about her cousin.

"God, those two are going to be terrors when they grow up." I commented out loud with a chuckle and shake of my head before craning my head back to kiss Hanna's cheek.

"The future bratva queens as they like to call themselves." Hanna's playful comment settled heavily in my chest.

I didn't want my precious little princess to become a bratva queen—or anything bratva. Even if things were different now with how we ran things, I didn't want Julia to live such a tumultuous life; I wanted her to finish college, get some boring degree, marry a boring guy, and live a normal and boring life. I didn't want to be sitting at home worrying about whether my only child would be coming home alive or not or if the next time my phone went off would be to come identify her body or come recover her. I couldn't handle it.

Julia was already showing a liking to violence and the mafia life, and we entertained it at first because it was cute, and we thought it was a phase that would pass. Two years later, and it still hadn't, and she was five now.

I wanted to nip it in the bud, but Hanna refused to let me control our child to such an extent. Hanna saw no problem with all of it, given how protected she would be and how we were her parents.

In theory, if I let Julia partake in the bratva life, she'd be a deadly force to be reckoned with. She'd be a top sniper and gunman—err, gunwoman—with training from me, and she'd have her bases with fighting forms covered by Hanna. But no way would I teach my kid how to shoot like that; the furthest I'd go is handgun training for the use of self-defense.

"Styosha, hon, you have that look on your face again." Hanna chided, jabbing at my cheek with her finger. "They are children, just let them have their fun. Now, wipe that sour look off your face, it's the eve of our anniversary."

Seven wonderful years I've been with this woman, and not a day has gone by where I've taken her for granted or regretted anything when it came to Hanna. Not a day goes by where I don't shower her with all the love and affection possible from me, from kisses to hugs to orgasms for hours.

"Did you pack like I told you?" I asked with a devious smirk after setting her down and turning around to wrap my arms around her.

"Yes, Daddy, I did." She muttered with flushed cheeks, shifting her legs a bit before reaching back and rubbing her ass.

There was no holding back the sly smile from my face as I looked down at her. Memories of last night flooded my mind of how I had Hanna tied to the spanking bench and flogged her bubbly cheeks raw.

"And you packed exactly what I told you?" Her sweet bottom would be displayed for me all weekend long if she listened. I couldn't wait to see her marked-up cheeks and add more to them.

"Yes, Daddy." The tail end of her response pitched up from my hand, groping her sore butt. "No more tonight, right? I was good all day, and I listened to you."

"No punishments, no. Just some light impact play if you're up for it, if not then we're going to see if we can break your last record of orgasms in a night." I whispered deeply into her ear as I molded her body into mine fully. "I wouldn't be *that* mean to you on our anniversary trip."

Reluctantly, I pulled away and gave her ass a quick spank—I couldn't help it—before urging her to the front door when the bell went off.

"NATASHA!" For a small girl, her footsteps thundered when she beat her mother to the front door and nearly threw it off its hinges.

"JULIA!" The two girls screamed and squealed while hugging each other tightly.

"*Malysh*, you just saw her the other day." Nikolai chuckled with a groan while rubbing his ear.

"Too long." Natasha, Nikolai and Angel's only daughter, huffed with crossed arms.

"Hi Anton, hi Anatoli, hi Misha!" Julia greeted the rest of Nikolai's children with a wave of her hands and a big grin. "Hi Uncle Kolya, hi Aunty Angel!"

After their first set, Nikolai and Angel ended up with another set of twins; Anton and Anatoli were two years older than Natasha and Mikhail, whom we all called Misha. Naturally, Julia and Natasha took an instant liking to each other and were practically joined at the hip ever since we could remember.

"Those two are gonna break so many hearts one day." Angel sighed playfully with a chuckle and shake of her head as she watched the kids run off to the living area.

"Excuse you? She's not going to have a heart to break in the first place, no boy or man is going near my *malysh*." Nikolai argued with a gruff huff. "And you aren't letting one near your little princess, right Stepan?" His desperate eyes searched mine for aid.

"Of course, not while I'm alive." The look Hanna gave me told me she doubted my words. "It's true, Julia doesn't need no man in her life, ever. As if anyone is worthy of her."

"I swear, you men and your daughters." Angel scoffed with a roll of her eyes before shoving Hanna and me towards the door. "You two have a trip to take, so no more idling. Everything will be fine, don't worry."

"Styosha, are you going to tell me why you dragged me out into the middle of the ocean? You know I hate the open water." Hanna whined with a pout as we lay in bed, cuddling.

Looking down at my watch and then out the window, I pat her bare ass playfully, "In a bit, not quite time yet." Also, I wanted to hold my wife for a little longer.

A soft silence filled the room again as I inched my eyes down her bare body along with my fingers. I couldn't help but linger at her stomach, tracing the scar that ran across her lower abdomen; it was a constant reminder of the best and worst day of my life.

"I'm sorry." Hanna's whisper broke the silence, making my eyes lock up into hers.

"Hm? What for?" She hadn't done anything yet.

"That I can't give you more kids." Her sad eyes averted from mine.

"Little tigress." I started, holding her face and kissing her passionately. "Don't be. I told you before, and I'll tell you whenever you need to hear it, but I don't care about that. We have a wonderful daughter who is perfect, and I still have my wife as well, and that's all I want and can ask for. You're not some baby-making factory, I don't care that we only have one child as long as I have my Hanna with me still, that's all I care about."

Julia's pregnancy and birth had been particularly hard on Hanna, and a complication nearly led Hanna to bleed out on the operating table the day she gave birth. I almost lost both Hanna and Julia that day because of a crap load of complications, and not a day went by where I wasn't thankful for both of them being here still.

Glancing down at my watch, I smiled at Hanna before pulling her into another deep kiss and patting her bottom to get up. "Get dressed, we should be within range now."

We pulled our clothes on in a hurry and made our way up to the deck, where I had my rifle set up on its pod at the end of the ship. "Hon, if you brought me all the way out here to make me watch you shoot at fish, I will throw you overboard right now." Hanna deadpanned with an unamused frown.

Rolling my eyes, I chuckled as I waved her towards me, handing her a pair of binoculars once she was close enough. "Take a look at that ship ahead and tell me what you see."

The sounds of calm water brushing against the boat splashed the air as we stood in silence, and slowly, a smile broke on Hanna's face. "Oh my God, is that?" Hanna stared at me in disbelief after lowering the viewing item.

"Seven long years, and I've finally tracked them down. They'd been living their lives out at sea this whole time, which made them very hard to pinpoint, but one of my sources caught them this recent time they docked to restock." I confirmed with a nod and smile.

Reaching into my pocket, I pull out two bullets and hold it out to Hanna. "Would you like to do the honors?"

A giggle of glee squealed from her jittery body as she snatched the two carved bullets from the palm of my hands. "Not yet, I don't want them shot yet. I want to watch the horror on their face as everyone around them drops dead one by one, then I want you to put holes in their boat and make it sink, make them float in the water."

Hanna paused for a second with a wide grin on her face that would put The Joker to shame. "Please tell me we have chum or stuff to make it, please, please, please."

"Somehow I thought we might need it, so I had the crew pack some buckets of it." I planned to shoot their heads off and let the sharks devour their body; I had no idea why Hanna wanted it.

"I want to chum the water with them in it, alive, then put the bullet through their stomachs to let them bleed out to tempt the sharks more." Should I be worried about how Hanna practically jumped for joy in her spot? Maybe, but I wasn't sane enough to care or do anything about it.

"As you wish, tigress." Anything to make the wife happy; happy wife, happy life.

The thundering boom of gunshots filled the vast ocean air after I got into position and took aim. Our ship was too far away for them to shoot back with their handguns, and I snipped down every sniper before they even got a chance to raise their rifle.

Lilian and Gia hunkered down in the haul when the shooting started, but they were forced back up to the deck when the ship began to sink from the holes I put into it. As their ship sank, I signaled the captain to get closer as we'd been nearly a mile away from them.

It was amusing to see Lilian and Gia's faces light up with hope when our ship approached, only to be utterly crestfallen at the sight of Hanna and me, who stood at the deck's railing. "Guess the number seven isn't so lucky for the two of you." I joked with a dark smirk.

My nerves would finally be at peace—somewhat—after seven years. The worry of Lilian striking back had dangled in the back of my mind ever since she made her escape, and my anxiety heightened to new levels when Julia came into the world; not only did I worry about Hanna, but I fretted over Julia nonstop on top of that. Hanna could potentially handle herself fine, but Julia was just a kid.

Lilian and Gia's death was for all our sakes and sanity.

As their boat disappeared into the dark waters, Hanna and I took our sweet time chumming the water to lure the sharks—who didn't take long to appear. The turbulent waters became violent in no time with the thrashing of their feeding frenzy.

While the sharks continued to work themselves up with the two panicking women inches away from being their next meal, I picked up the other rifle I'd set up and held it out to Hanna to load the bullets. Once she was done, the weapon was back in my hands.

Unfortunately, for me, it wouldn't be a kill shot.

Bang! Bang!

The two women screamed in pain while they held their bleeding thighs just moments before they slipped into the dangerous waters.

"Goodbye aunt Lilian. Goodbye, mother. Say hi to the devil for me when you meet him." Hanna watched her two estranged family members get torn apart and devoured by the beasts of the ocean.

Then, she started crying out of nowhere, which freaked me out. "*Malenkaya*, what's wrong?" Instantly, she was in my comforting arms.

"They're gone. Actually gone. They're finally gone from this world. I don't ever have to worry about them anymore, ever." Okay, tears of happiness, not despair or sorrow—good.

Looking up at me, Hanna grabbed my face and brought me down into a heated kiss full of passion and gratitude.

"Thank you, thank you so much."

And the list was finally completed.

Epilogue 2
Hana

~13 years later~

"*Malenkaya*, do you—"

Crack!

Both of us ducked to the floor out of instinct, remaining for a good while to see if any more bullets would make an appearance.

Cautiously, we got up after no more bullets sprayed through the window of Stepan's office. "Well, that answers my question." Stepan narrowed his eyes at the single bullet hole through his bulletproof window.

When Stepan's body moved for the door, I instantly placed myself in his path with spread arms. "Hon, wait, she—"

"Is supposed to be studying, not outside with my rifle." Stepan quickly finished my sentence on his own.

My shoulders fell with my long sigh. "Styosha." Stepping up to him, I placed my hands on his chest and drew lazy circles on it. "She just wants to practice to impress you."

"She can impress me by doing what she should be doing, not by going behind my back and playing with guns when she shouldn't." Stepan bit back with a tense face.

Shoving my hands off, he moved me aside and made his way outside to the backyard with me hot on his trail, spewing excuse after excuse to try and lessen his irritation towards our daughter—of course, he ignored it all.

"Julia!" Stepan's voice boomed across the backyard, making our daughter wince as she turned around and looked at him in shame with a hung head.

"Papa, I'm sorry, the bullet ricocheted, I didn't mean to." Julia was quick to apologize with genuine remorse.

"There shouldn't even be a ricocheting bullet in the first place because you shouldn't even be out here shooting. You're supposed to be inside studying for your finals, not out here trying to take off a wooden head. Hell, you're not even supposed to be out here alone with any kind of firearm period, let alone with my rifle." Stepan continued to dig into our daughter, who shrunk back at his words with teary eyes. "What the hell were you even thinking?"

"I already studied a lot today, I wanted to get more practice in, I need to practice otherwise I can't get fast enough," Julia argued back with a slight crack to her voice.

"You don't need to get fast enough for anything." Stepan retorted, crossing his arms as he stood before our daughter.

Steeling herself, Julia braved her face and looked up at Stepan with her hands clenched at her sides. "I need to get fast enough to shoot fast like you so you can get off my ass about taking over the bratva with Natasha when the time comes. I need to be able to shoot fast and efficiently enough to cover her back like you do Uncle Kolya."

"No, you fucking don't. I told you, it's never going to happen. You are never going to be bratva, ever, not while I'm still breathing on this earth." Stepan's frustration pooled at his rising shoulders as he narrowed his eyes sternly at Julia.

Of course, just like any teenager, she became defiant in response. It also didn't help that she had my attitude. "And you also told me that if I could pull off four shots in a second with the bolt action then you'd shut up about it, which is exactly what I am trying to do. But also, you can't ban me from taking part of the bratva, you're not in charge of my life, what I do is ultimately up to me and you can't do anything about it. When will you get your head out of your ass and see that I'm not your little princess anymore, that I'm grown up and have my own life to make and live! Ugh!"

"If that's how you think then you've got a lot of growing up to do still. I have the final say in everything. If I don't want you in the bratva then all I have to do is say the damn word and your uncle would never let it happen. If I want you locked at home then I will damn well do so, one word to the college and they'd take back your acceptance in a heartbeat." Okay, now that crossed the line.

"Stepan! That's enough!" I snapped, shoving myself between him and Julia with a hand on his chest. "You need to go cool off. You're her father, not her dictator. I understand that you love her and cherish her and want to protect her, but she is her own person at the end of the day. You have no right to control her life like that. Just because you can doesn't mean you should or could."

I knew Stepan would never cross that line; his words were said in anger. Still, he needed a verbal reminder sometimes. "Don't be like your father." It was a low blow, but he needed it. The wince I got in response meant I got through.

"Why are you even so against me joining the bratva? Both you and mom are bratva, and you're both alive and fine. Things have changed too, it's not like the 1900s where it's all violence and drugs and guns and death." Julia had a good point. Most of the bratva's business was underground now and clean.

Compared to what Stepan and I lived through, it was very much tamed and stable now for the Volkov children if they desired to take over.

"Just because it's not like that now doesn't mean it doesn't happen. I don't want to be living every day worrying with your mother as to whether or not you'll live through the day and the next, or if the next phone call we get about you is to inform us of your exit from this life. I don't want you living that dangerous life, clean or not, that shit still happens." Stepan rebutted with a deflated chest.

"I don't want to have to pull the plug on your life support or bury your casket. You and your mother are everything to me, and losing any of you would break me." Stepan admitted with a pained frown and vulnerability in his voice. "You're my only child, my precious daughter. I know I can't protect you forever, but I'll damn well try and do what I can while I still can. I know you're tough like your mother and I, that you can more than handle yourself because we taught you to, but still, you're my daughter and it's my job as your father to make sure you are safe and protected."

"Papa, you can't protect me forever. I'm grown up. I have my own life to live, and if you try to stop me from living my life to the fullest how I want it then I will hate you." Stepan winced at the last part as if Julia stabbed him in the chest with a knife. "I love you, but you're so overbearing."

"I know, and I'm sorry, I can't help it." Stepan sighed heavily before reaching out and pulling Julia into a tight hug. "You'll always be my precious little princess, no matter how much you grow. I'm sorry for snapping at you and raising my voice. We'll put this off for some other time, for now, I just want you to finish college first, then we can talk about this subject afterwards. Your uncle gave Natasha the same deal, so I guess it's only fair I give you the same. Finish college first, then if you really want to be bratva still then we can talk about it then, alright?"

Julia's face scrunched slightly with a pouting frown, but she didn't argue. "Okay, fine. I'm sorry for snapping back at you and cussing at you."

Chuckling, Stepan kissed her forehead before letting her go. "Go wash up for dinner."

Soon, the two of us were out back as Stepan packed up the rifle. "I swear, she's going to make me go gray sooner than later." He joked with a chuckle.

Leaning down, since he was squatting down, I hugged him around his shoulder and neck. "She's our daughter after all." Pretty sure I gave Stepan half his gray hairs with my antics. "But, you handled that well towards the end, good job."

"I'm still not happy about it, I'm just hoping college will change her." Hopeful of him, I'm sure he doubted his own words because we both knew how Julia was after raising her into a strong and intelligent woman.

"Oh, wait until she comes back from break with a boyfriend." I teased with a hearty laugh.

"Excuse me the fuck what? I don't think so, not if I can help it."

Glossary

- **Anh:** Vietnamese term of endearment towards male gender.

- **Blyat':** Fuck.

- **Bratik:** Brother.

- **Bratan (Bratan):** Brother/bro.

- **Bratok:** Brother/bro.

- **Chert, vot i vse, khoroshaya devochka:** Damn, that's it, good girl.

- **Chertov ad. YA rad, chto zastavil tebya vzyat' menya s soboy:** Fucking hell. I'm glad I made you take me with you.

- **Da papochka:** Yes daddy.

- **Dorogaya, vernis' ko mne. Ochnites' ot svoyego koshmara. Tvoya mechta zdes', derzhit tebya. Prosypaysya ko mne:** Darling, come back to me. Wake up from your nightmare. Your dream is here, holding you. Wake up to me.

- **Gospodi, blyad', Gospodi:** Lord, fuck, Lord.

- **Khorosho, khorosho, khorosho:** Okay, okay, okay.

- **Lisichka:** Little fox.

- **Malysh:** Baby

- **Malenkaya:** Little/small.

- **Malen'kaya tigritsa:** Little tigress.

- **Mne ochen' zhal' za to, chto ya sobirayus' sdelat', no eto dlya tvoyego zhe blaga. YA tebya lyublyu:** I'm really sorry for what I'm about to do, but it's for your own good. I love you.

- **Moya malen'kaya tigritsa, vse v poryadke. YA zdes', ya tebya poymal. Ty v bezopasnosti. Oni bol'she ne smogut prichinit' tebe vreda, tak chto vernis' ko mne. YA zdes' radi tebya, ya tebya poymal:** My little tigress, everything is fine. I'm here, I got you. You're safe. They can't hurt you anymore, so come back to me. I'm here for you, I got you.

- **Ne govorya uzhe o tom, chto ty malen'kiy der'mo:** Not to mention you're a little shit.

- **Pozhaluysta, papochka:** Please daddy.

- **Poshel ty, papochka:** Fuck you, daddy.

- **Yeshche pozhaluysta:** More please.

- **Takaya khoroshaya devochka dlya papy. YA tak toboy gorzhus':** Such a good girl for daddy. I'm so proud of you.

- **Tigritsa:** Tigress.

- **Ty, razdrazhayushcheye malen'koye der'mo:** You annoying little shit.

- **Ty sdelal potryasayushche, malenkaya. Vernis' ko mne. U menya yest' ty. Ty v bezopasnosti. Vernis' ko mne,**

malen'kaya tigritsa: You did amazing, little one. Come back to me. I have you. You're safe. Come back to me little tigress.

- **Ty sobirayesh'sya byt' khoroshey devochkoy:** You're going to be a good girl.

- **YA lyublyu tebya malen'kaya:** I love you little.

- **YA lyublyu tebya papochka:** I love you daddy.

- **YA tebya lyublyu:** I love you.

- **YA tut, u menya ty malen'kaya:** I'm here, I got you little.

Afterword

If you enjoyed the story then please leave a review!

Thank you so much for reading The Bratva's Beast, the second installment in my interconnected standalone Volkov Bratva Series. I hope you enjoyed Stepan and Hanna's story and are prepared for Lev's story where he meets his crazy match in Nicole who makes him jump through hoops of fire and bullets. If you're curious about Stepan's older brother, Nikolai, then you can catch his and Angel's story in The Bratva's Bride where Angel makes vows not only to her arranged husband but herself as well. And if you're into dark romcoms, then keep an eye out for my upcoming release, Killer in the Sheets, which is a story about a serial killer MMC and a sweet/sunshine CSI FMC.

If you like sneak peaks or want to follow my author journey then feel free to follow me on my social media!

tiktok.com/@rose.chase.author

instagram.com/rose.chase.author/

facebook.com/rose.chase.author

amazon.com/author/rose.chase

About the Author

ROSE CHASE, A DEDICATED nurse and loving mother to two boys, discovered her passion for storytelling in middle school on online forums and Wattpad. Despite her busy life, she delves into the captivating realm of contemporary romance, with a particular fascination for dark romance and morally gray characters. Through her skillful storytelling, Rose navigates the intricate dance between love, desire, and the shadows of human nature. When not saving lives or caring for her family, she immerses herself in the world of fiction, inviting readers to explore the depths of love and passion while confronting the complexities of the human heart.